A HISTORY OF NEW YORK

WASHINGTON IRVING was born in New York City in 1783, the year the Revolutionary War ended. As a young man he began to write theater criticism and satire, and his first book-length work, *A History of New York from the Beginning of the World to the End of the Dutch Dynasty*, was published in 1809 to great popular and critical acclaim. While Irving is best known today for his tales of the Hudson River region, including "Rip Van Winkle" and "The Legend of Sleepy Hollow," he was equally famous during his lifetime for his picturesque "sketches" of European country life and his biographies of historical figures. These included the story collections *The Sketch Book of Geoffrey Crayon, Gent.* (1819–20), *Bracebridge Hall, or The Humorists, A Medley* (1822), *Tales of a Traveller* (1824), and a series of books written during a posting to Spain as an attaché for the American legation: *Life and Voyages of Columbus* (1828), *The Conquest of Granada* (1829), *Voyages and Discoveries of the Companions of Columbus* (1831), and *The Alhambra* (1832). Upon his return to the United States in 1832, Irving purchased "Sunnyside," the Dutch cottage in Tarrytown, New York, that would become a symbol of the author and a place of pilgrimage for his readers, and wrote a series of books on the American West: *A Tour on the Prairies* (1835), *Astoria* (1836), and *The Adventures of Captain Bonneville, U.S.A.* (1837). Although he would return to Spain from 1842 to 1845 as the appointed minister of President John Tyler, Irving spent the better portion of his remaining years at Sunnyside, where he produced revised editions of his collected works as well as biographies of Oliver Goldsmith and George Washington (which comprised five volumes), the liberator of New York in whose honor he was reportedly named. When Irving died in 1859, the Tarrytown church where his funeral was held was filled to capacity, and it was reported that more than a thousand mourners waited outside for their chance to pay their respects to the "father of the American short story," and the first American writer to achieve an international renown.

ELIZABETH L. BRADLEY is Deputy Director of the C̶ for Scholars and Writers at the Ne̶ author of the forthcoming *Knick̶ York*, and her work on New York published in *Bookforum* and *The̶ History*.

WASHINGTON IRVING
A History of New York

Introduction and Notes by
ELIZABETH L. BRADLEY

PENGUIN BOOKS

PENGUIN BOOKS
Published by the Penguin Group
Penguin Group (USA) Inc., 375 Hudson Street, New York, New York 10014, U.S.A.
Penguin Group (Canada), 90 Eglinton Avenue East, Suite 700, Toronto, Ontario, Canada M4P 2Y3
(a division of Pearson Penguin Canada Inc.)
Penguin Books Ltd, 80 Strand, London WC2R 0RL, England
Penguin Ireland, 25 St Stephen's Green, Dublin 2, Ireland (a division of Penguin Books Ltd)
Penguin Group (Australia), 250 Camberwell Road, Camberwell, Victoria 3124, Australia
(a division of Pearson Australia Group Pty Ltd)
Penguin Books India Pvt Ltd, 11 Community Centre, Panchsheel Park, New Delhi – 110 017, India
Penguin Group (NZ), 67 Apollo Drive, Rosedale, North Shore 0632, New Zealand
(a division of Pearson New Zealand Ltd)
Penguin Books (South Africa) (Pty) Ltd, 24 Sturdee Avenue, Rosebank, Johannesburg 2196, South Africa

Penguin Books Ltd, Registered Offices:
80 Strand, London WC2R 0RL, England

First published in the United States of America by Inskeep & Bradford 1809
This edition with an introduction and notes by Elizabeth L. Bradley published in Penguin Books 2008

1   3   5   7   9   10   8   6   4   2

Introduction and notes copyright © Elizabeth L. Bradley, 2008
All rights reserved

ISBN 978-0-14-310561-9
CIP data available

Printed in the United States of America
Set in Adobe Sabon

Contents

BOOK IV

BOOK V

BOOK VI

BOOK VII

Introduction

Missing: One Knickerbocker

"DISTRESSING," the notice in the October 26, 1809, New York *Evening Post* began. "Left his lodgings sometime since, and has not since been heard of, a small elderly gentleman dressed in an old black coat and cocked hat, by the name of KNICKER-BOCKER. As there are some reasons for believing he is not entirely in his right mind, . . . great anxiety is entertained about him[.]" The notice begged readers to submit any information they might have about his whereabouts and well-being to the "Columbian Hotel, Mulberry-street." A later advertisement reported the discovery of a *"very curious kind of a written book"* that the vanished Knickerbocker had left behind, and warned that the landlord of the Columbian Hotel "shall have to dispose of the book" to "pay off his bill for board and lodging" should the missing debtor fail to reappear. The ads were a hoax, the landlord imaginary: the book, however, was quite real. Its full title was

A History of New-York, from the Beginning of the World to the End of the Dutch Dynasty; Containing, among Many Surprising and Curious Matters, the Unutterable Ponderings of Walter the Doubter, the Disastrous Projects of William the Testy, and the Chivalric Achievements of Peter the Headstrong—The Three Dutch Governors of New Amsterdam: Being the Only Authentic History of the Times that Ever Hath Been or Ever Will Be Published.

and when it was finally published on December 6, 1809, it proved to be even more "surprising and curious" than had been promised. In fact, *A History of New York* was unlike anything that American readers had ever seen: it was simultaneously a rollicking account of the discovery, colonization, and ultimate conquest of the

New Amsterdam settlement, and a scholarly, grave, and mournful memorial to the lost leaders and traditions of the same. This recipe for "very tragical mirth" is narrated by the much-advertised Diedrich Knickerbocker, a self-proclaimed descendant of the "Dutch Dynasty" of the title. To him, Knickerbocker explains in a mixture of pride and pessimism, has fallen the task of righting the wrongs done to his ancestors by those who vanquished and then forgot them: it is his solemn mission to "rescue from oblivion" the "great and wonderful transactions of our Dutch progenitors," and to save the "early history of this venerable and ancient city" from "dropping piecemeal into the tomb." It is a dramatic statement, one meant to convince his anticipated audience that the impulse behind his *History* is as soteriological as it is curatorial: with this work of "faithful veracity," he assures his readers, he will "rear . . . a triumphal monument, to transmit [New Amsterdam's] renown to all succeeding time." The only check on the boundless ambition of Knickerbocker is the fact that the historian himself is far from veracious: he was a fictition, the brainchild of a young New York lawyer named Washington Irving.

Washington Irving was twenty-six years old when he wrote *A History,* intending it only as a "temporary *jeu d'esprit,*" as he would later maintain: a spoof of the archival efforts of the fledgling New-York Historical Society and a critique of contemporary Jeffersonian politics and society. Irving had not yet become America's best-loved author, the creator of Rip Van Winkle and Ichabod Crane; he had not yet been compared to Geoffrey Chaucer, Edmund Spenser, and Oliver Goldsmith, or hailed as the "Father of the American Short Story." In fact, his literary oeuvre at that time consisted primarily of a year spent as a founding editor of and contributor to *Salmagundi,* a satirical literary weekly modeled after the English *Tatler* and *Spectator* magazines, and a total of nine theater reviews, written while still a teenager under the pseudonym "Jonathan Oldstyle," which he had contributed to his brother's newspaper, the *Morning Chronicle*. Little about Irving's family or upbringing suggests that literary celebrity was in his future: while another brother, William, collaborated with him on *Salmagundi,* by and large the Irvings were a family of genteel merchants who earned a prosperous living trading in hardware, wine, and sugar. Irving's parents, who had emigrated from Scotland, settled on

William Street before the Revolutionary War, and raised their seven surviving children there. Washington, their youngest son, was born on April 3, 1783, in British-occupied New York, seven months before the official evacuation of enemy troops from the city. By the time the *History* was published, Irving's native city had been substantially rebuilt from the devastations of war and occupation, but it was by no means the dense, hectic metropolis that the words "New York City" currently evoke. In Irving's youth and young adulthood, fashionable New York was bounded by the Battery and the Common, now City Hall Park: City Hall itself, which began construction when Irving was a teenager, was considered to be at the edge of civilization, beyond which lay the Collect Pond (on which Robert Fulton had taken a prototype steamship for a test run in 1796), now drained, paved, and christened Canal Street, and, farther north, the bucolic pastures of Greenwich Village. Indeed, the Chambers Street side of the new City Hall was faced in brownstone rather than in Massachusetts marble, on the premise that few visitors would be likely to see the grand facade from that northernmost perspective. Perhaps in an effort to widen his horizons in this miniature Manhattan, the young Irving chose legal studies over following his brothers to Columbia College, and entered the law offices of Josiah O. Hoffman, the former attorney general of New York State—where, by all accounts, Irving quickly discovered his career mistake.

Irving's discovery and the subsequent development of Knickerbocker may be partly laid at the feet of the third and final editor of *Salmagundi,* his friend and future brother-in-law, James Kirke Paulding. It was through Paulding, who had been raised in the Hudson River Valley, that Irving would first learn about the Dutch history of the region, and discover the particular traditions maintained by their nineteenth-century descendants. These traditions, which would form the basis of Irving's New York writings, included Dutch food, architecture, and language; oral histories, such as the ghost story of the headless Hessian, whose insomniac riding kept whole hamlets awake in fear; and glimpses of improbably charming *tableaux vivants:* from Dutch American farmers puffing in stolid silence on their long pipes and apple-cheeked *vrouws* presiding over groaning tea tables to firelit hearths framed by a frieze of Delft tiles of scripture scenes. The romance of this heritage, not his own, inspired Irving to create Diedrich Knickerbocker, the Dutch "insider" who could legitimately present an "authentic" (one of Knickerbocker's favorite compliments) portrait of these overlooked "progenitors," both in his *History of New York* and in the stories of the Hudson River Valley that he would later write. These include the most famous pair: "Rip Van Winkle" and "The Legend of Sleepy Hollow," which would become part of the fabric of American literature, spun into children's books, poems, paintings, plays, and movies. But the *History* was Knickerbocker's debut, and the beginning of Irving's meteoric rise.

Irving's tongue-in-cheek retelling of the Dutch founding of New Amsterdam and the fortunes of the citizens and governors of that first New York colony—from its settlement to its ultimate surrender to the British in 1674—was a popular success on both sides of the Atlantic. American and European readers likened the *History* to the work of Laurence Sterne and Jonathan Swift, praising Irving's combination of anarchic humor, winning nostalgia, and mock erudition. Like *Tristram Shandy,* the *History* is sprawling, and more than a little strange; in the course of mapping colonial New Amsterdam, Knickerbocker takes numerous detours to enlighten his reader on a variety of related topics, from the introduction of the doughnut to the birth of Wall Street. Irving lards the historian's narrative with confusing citations and footnotes in multiple voices, all of which seem intended to add nuance and scholarly depth to his humble account of small-scale colonial wars, but have instead (like Sterne's black or blank pages) the surprisingly postmodern effect of knocking his story (and his reader) off course. But the real argument of the *History* is not to be found in its long-winded accounts of New Amsterdam's military history (which, in Knickerbocker's telling, seems to consist of Dutch generals practicing their swashbuckling moves on garden vegetables, and praying for divine intervention in battle) but through the winningly offhanded way in which Irving fills the lacunae of New York history, satisfying the reader's curiosity with minute and charming details of domestic life in the little colony. Knickerbocker's story is one of origins: he explains the city's familiar-yet-mysterious names (Maiden Lane, Coenties Slip), gives a gloss of romance to its topography (Buttermilk Channel, the Battery), and boldly claims New York's tribal customs (Santa Claus, stoop sitting, an inexplicable fondness for sauerkraut) as inventions of the Dutch who settled the city.

The nostalgic, sometimes bawdy stories of Dutch home life and heroism in Irving's *History* not only identified the formative influence of the Dutch burghers on the physical, economic, and cultural development of New York, but presented these newly rediscovered "founding fathers" as a set of acceptable ancestors for a city looking to divorce itself and its past from the monarchical associations of England. In the wake of the Revolutionary War and seven years of British occupation, Knickerbocker's portrait of New Amsterdam seemed appealingly homely, even middle class. What busy urbanite could deny the charm of the "golden age of Wouter Van Twiller," when "a sweet and holy calm reigned over the whole province" and the "Burgomaster smoked his pipe in peace"? Like Irving's nineteenth-century city, the Dutch colony, thus portrayed, was equal parts bourgeois ritual, democratic tolerance, and hospitable (if clannish) sophistication. Here, finally, were forebears in which a newly republican New York could take a fond, nostalgic pride. Knickerbocker's epic saga of New Amsterdam, however satirical, was one of the first articulations of American identity, and an early entry into the communal history of a city not yet accustomed to commemorating and celebrating its difference from the rest of the country, as well as from the rest of the world.

Irving's *History* connected readers to New Amsterdam by taking the colony out of the realm of mystery and conjecture. But the book was also a finger in the eye of the New-York Historical Society, which had been founded in 1804 with a mandate to collect and make available to the public "whatever may relate to the natural, civic, or ecclesiastical History of the United States in general, and of this State in particular." But information about the New Amsterdam settlement was not forthcoming. In an 1807 "Address to the Public" that is equal parts persuasion and polemic, the Society admits the "paucity of materials" pertaining to New York's Dutch past, and reiterates the "extreme difficulty of procuring such as relate to the first settlement and colonial transactions of this State." In an appeal to their fellow New Yorkers' sense of history and responsibility, the Society solicited documents of just about any kind or quality, including "Manuscripts, Records, Pamphlets and Books relative to the History of this

Country . . . narratives of Indian Wars, Battles and Exploits; of the Adventures and Sufferings of Captives, Voyagers and Travellers . . . Statistical Tables, Tables of Diseases, Births and Deaths, and of Population," and just about anything else that might shed light on New Amsterdam. In an effort to remedy this archivist's nightmare, one of the Society's most revered members, the physician and naturalist Dr. Samuel Latham Mitchill, compiled and published *The Picture of New-York: Or, The Traveller's Guide Through the Commercial Metropolis of the United States* in 1807. *The Picture* was designed to enrich the meager holdings of the Historical Society while offering readers "ample and genuine information" about the historical, geographical, civic, and social circumstances of the contemporary city. Despite its panoramic title, Mitchill's book is little more than an encyclopedia of dry geographical and municipal facts, curtly expressed. An incomplete encyclopedia, unfortunately: while *The Picture* touches on everything from the city's tidal patterns to its prison system, Mitchill disposes of fifty years of Dutch rule in a few swift sentences, without apology. It was this oversight that inspired Irving (and his brother William, with whom he had originally conceived of the *History*)—he later confessed that their original "serio-comic" intent was just to "burlesque the pedantic lore" of *The Picture* and other books of its kind. In a reversal that its author would not have appreciated, today *The Picture* is an essential artifact of New York only because it gave rise to the creation of its opposite: the voice of Diedrich Knickerbocker. Mitchill's attempt to build an "ample" ontological framework for the nascent city instead created the vacuum into which Irving and his revisionist historian could merrily rush.

On the heels of his *History*, Irving briefly took a position as the editor of the *Analectic Review,* a literary journal based in Philadelphia, but the needs of a family business venture in England was incentive enough to lure him to England in 1815. The venture failed, but Irving stayed on, traveling through England, Germany, and France with a letter of introduction to the celebrated Scottish author Sir Walter Scott (who had reported "sides . . . sore from laughing" while reading Irving's "excellent jocose history of New York") and a fistful of glowing reviews for the *History* (and for *Salmagundi,* which had been published in book form in England in 1810). It would be sixteen years before Irving returned to the United

States, and his stay abroad also marked a turning away from the long format of the *History* to the genre of the "sketch," a picturesque and often sentimental vignette whose gentle humor and brevity made it the ideal format for the observations of a curious and romantic American. Irving would publish three collections of sketches in very quick succession, including *The Sketch Book of Geoffrey Crayon, Gent.* (1819–20), *Bracebridge Hall* (1822), and *Tales of a Traveller* (1824), as well as several historical works inspired by an extended stay in Spain: *The Conquest of Granada, Life and Voyages of Columbus, Voyages and Discoveries of the Companions of Columbus,* and *The Alhambra.* Diedrich Knickerbocker reappears only rarely in Irving's sketch collections, to narrate "Rip Van Winkle" and "The Legend of Sleepy Hollow" (in *The Sketch Book of Geoffrey Crayon, Gent.*) as well as other tales of the Hudson River Valley and New Amsterdam, including "Dolph Heyliger" (*Bracebridge Hall*) and the "Money Diggers" section of *Tales of a Traveller,* among whose contents can be found "Wolfert Webber, Or, Golden Dreams," an evergreen fable of New York real estate. The scarcity of these Knickerbocker tales, the only American elements in collections that are otherwise decidedly Anglophile (or at least Eurocentric) in nature, gives them a precious, endangered quality that mirrors their shared subtext—the disintegration of the Dutch elements of life in and around New York City.

Not all of Irving's American observers toasted his international success. Some perceived his absence as abandonment, and his European subject matter as a canny marketing strategy rather than an artistic choice. The American poet Philip Freneau spoke for Irving's critics with his 1823 poem "To a New England Poet," in which he urges a nameless colleague not to waste his talents in "such a tasteless land/Where all must on a level stand." Instead, he recommends, "like Irving, haste away" to England, "and with the glittering nobles mix/Forgetting times of seventy-six." Once a critical darling overseas, Freneau continues, the subject of his sarcastic ode is sure to triumph in America as well:

> Dear bard, I pray you, take the hint,
> In England what you write and print,
> Republished here in shop, or stall,
> Will perfectly enchant us all[.]

Freneau's recipe for success may have been bitter, but it was also prescient: when Irving finally did return to New York in 1832, he was besieged with invitations to valedictory dinners in his honor, requests by artists and sculptors to sit for his portrait, and demands for public appearances and addresses. In one particularly memorable encounter, he served as a kind of American literary ambassador to Charles Dickens, then visiting Baltimore on a national tour. The two authors reportedly shared an enormous mint julep sent by a well-wisher, a confounding image that is made even more so by Dickens's recollection that Irving sipped from the giant cocktail with a straw. Writing after Irving's death, William Makepeace Thackeray noted that the author of "Rip Van Winkle" was shy and awkward in the face of this universal welcome, even when mint juleps were not present: "He stammered in his speeches, hid himself in confusion, and the people loved him all the better." Affection for Irving, Thackeray concluded, was a "national sentiment." Irving himself had a lifelong aversion to "having to attempt speeches, or bear compliments in silence," but his initial bewilderment may have also been due to the transformations he discovered in his native city. Like Wolfert Webber, who sees his cabbage plots transformed into apartment lots, Irving came back to a New York that was changed beyond expectation—and, in some cases, beyond recognition. Manhattan was now the largest city in the United States; the Erie Canal had been opened. Little wonder, then, that Irving marveled, at one of his public welcome dinners, at the "seeming city" that now extended itself over "heights I had left covered with green forests."

The exigencies of fame and what must have seemed like time travel ultimately spurred Irving's retreat from the city; in 1835 he purchased and remodeled an old cottage in the Westchester County hamlet of Tarrytown, on a hill sloping down to the Hudson River. But the final product, a yellow-brick, gable-fronted cottage that its owner christened Sunnyside, was as much homage to the charms of Dutch New York as to Irving's own writings, and it quickly became a destination for pilgrims seeking an audience with the creator of Knickerbocker. This pilgrimage was later accelerated by the new railroad tracks laid against the banks of the river just below Sunnyside, a development that would be at once the source and the scourge of Irving's quest for privacy: the payment he received for allowing the tracks to be laid on his property helped defray the cost of an addition on the famous house. Sunnyside, which Henry James would later describe as a "shy . . . retreat of anchorites," became, in Irving's lifetime, a metonym for the writer himself, and bore as many "compliments in silence" as the man who lived there. The house was hymned in Andrew Jackson Downing's seminal *Treatise on the Theory and Practice of Landscape Gardening* (1849), which suggested that "there is scarcely a building or place in America more replete with interest than the cottage of Washington Irving, near Tarrytown," and was subsequently a prominent feature of *The Homes of American Authors* (1853) and the subject of a profile in *Harper's* magazine (1856). From that riverside perch Irving wrote *The Crayon Miscellany*, a collection of travel sketches and histories; *Astoria*; and *The Adventures of Captain Bonneville, U.S.A.* Despite (or perhaps because of) his retreat, New York City did not abandon its first literary champion: in 1838 Irving was nominated for mayor of Manhattan by Tammany Hall, an honor he graciously refused.

Irving did leave his Tarrytown aerie in 1842 at the request of President Tyler, who appointed him minister to Spain, where he would begin the multivolume *Life of George Washington* that would turn out to be his final project. When he returned to Sunnyside in 1846, he found New York in the middle of a particularly fascinating romance: a passion for all things Knickerbocker. "Before the appearance of my work the popular traditions of our city were unrecorded" Irving marveled,

> the peculiar and racy customs and usages derived from our Dutch progenitors were unnoticed, or regarded with indifference, or adverted to with a sneer. Now they form a convivial currency . . . they are the rallying points of home feeling; the seasoning of our civic festivities; the staple of local tales and local pleasantries; and are so harped upon by our writers of popular fiction, that I find myself almost crowded off the legendary ground which I was the first to explore, by the host who have followed in my footsteps.

In the nearly forty years since he introduced his opinionated and ornery historian, he added, Knickerbocker had become a "household word . . . used to give the home stamp to Knickerbocker societies, Knickerbocker insurance companies, Knickerbocker steamboats, Knickerbocker omnibuses, Knickerbocker bread, and

Knickerbocker ice," and claimed by "New Yorkers of Dutch descent" who called themselves " 'genuine Knickerbockers[.]' " This expression of amazement and delight came from Irving's "Author's Apology," which was appended to the revised 1848 edition of the *History* as part of a commitment with his publisher, G. P. Putnam and Sons, to publish all of his works in revised and deluxe editions. This revision was certainly not the first time Irving had amended the *History* since its initial publication, but it was the most drastic. In Putnam's 1848 edition, the racy humor and earthy language of Knickerbocker's original has been rendered parlor ready: but if it was less daring, the book was also decidedly less delightful.

Perhaps it was inevitable that America's first maverick writer should cede his place to other rebels: within a decade, Walt Whitman would mail *Leaves of Grass* to an unsuspecting Ralph Waldo Emerson, and Irving himself had already heard Herman Melville read aloud from his first novel, *Typee* (1846). But Irving's "Apology," written partly to assuage the feelings of some prominent Dutch New Yorkers who felt misused by his satire and partly to contextualize his book and his narrator for a contemporary audience, suggests that even if Irving had been "crowded off the legendary ground," his narrator would triumphantly remain. By the time of Irving's "Apology," the name Knickerbocker had, as Irving notes with evident pleasure, evolved into recognizable shorthand for an authentic New Yorker: a cultivated, civic-minded native, preferably of Dutch descent. The Dutch customs and traditions described in the *History* were embraced by the cultural elite of nineteenth-century New York, and Irving's tale and its teller became the springboard for more than a century's worth of literature, iconography, and advertising—all designed to lend a product the same genteel, homely cachet that Knickerbocker ascribed to the Dutch "vrouws" and "mynheers" who peopled his book. In fact, a much wider range of high- and lowbrow cultural forms appropriated the Knickerbocker imagery than Irving acknowledges: even within his lifetime, there were stagecoach lines and spice companies named for the Dutchman; a literary magazine (which conscripted the historian to serve as its muse, and later Irving himself to serve as "permanent contributor"); and the first baseball team in the United States, the New York Knickerbockers.

Irving's historian also became the mascot of a collection of

younger writers, poets, and editors who considered him their men-
tor, and dubbed themselves the "Knickerbocker School" in his
creator's honor. This group, which often used the totems, quintes-
sential images, and "authentic" rhetoric of Irving's New York
themes in their own portraits of the city and its countryside, included Irving's early collaborator James Kirke Paulding, Giulian
Verplanck (like Paulding, one of few "Knickerbocker" writers of
genuine Dutch descent), Lewis Gaylord Clark, editor of *Knickerbocker* magazine, and the poets William Cullen Bryant and
Fitz-Greene Halleck. Unfortunately, few of the disciples of Irving
who wrote under the "Knickerbocker" umbrella inherited his fe-
verish imagination or his talent for portraying local color, and
their works seem dated and damp in comparison. Many of these
writers were present at Irving's funeral in 1859, at which mourners
packed the little Episcopal church in Tarrytown nearly to bursting
and left a thousand more to gather outside, waiting for the chance
to pay the author their last respects. Strangely, few of Irving's me-
morializers take note of the rambling, possibly deranged fictional
historian who charmed the world and brought the author his early
fame. "The genial products of his pure and graceful pen will forever continue to afford a solace to the sick and weary," Daniel F.
Tiemann, the mayor of New York, noted in a leaden public tribute,
while Henry Wadsworth Longfellow's poem "In the Churchyard
at Tarrytown" mourned him as the "gentle humorist, who died in
the bright Indian Summer of his fame!" But as Andrew B. Myers
points out, Longfellow neglected to mention that Irving's "simple
stone, with but a date and name" was actually a replacement head-
stone: the first had been vandalized beyond repair by inconsolable
readers, making Irving's grave the nineteenth-century equivalent
of the tomb of Jim Morrison at Père-Lachaise. These shards had
not been chipped off in memory of the biographer of Columbus or
John Jacob Astor, but for the creator of Rip Van Winkle, Ichabod
Crane, Brom Bones, and for *their* biographer, Diedrich Knickerbocker. In a city with more stories than the Arabian Nights, a fictional Dutchman was its first and best Scheherazade.

New York is still imbued with Knickerbocker, even if most of its
citizens no longer know who Diedrich Knickerbocker was. A

consciousness of all things Knickerbocker hovers at the edges of the city's everyday life. In the last century, "Father Knickerbocker" supervised the consolidation of New York into five boroughs; promoted the New Deal; and, until recently, marketed Knickerbocker Beer: "New York's Famous Beer." Today, New Yorkers routinely cheer teams, cross avenues, visit dry cleaners, frequent restaurants, and belong to clubs named Knickerbocker. Yet "Knickerbocker," thus divorced from its context, has been reduced to a comical moniker, a Dutch-inflected sound. This may be the result of Irving's banishment from academe: by 1933 Carl Van Doren could assert that Irving's reputation had "shrunk and faded" without fear of contradiction, and few contemporary scholars and literary critics have bothered to investigate the proto-postmodern innovations of the *History*, or to grapple with the implications of his founding mythologies, even as they celebrate the same inventive qualities in such subsequent American writers as Nathaniel Hawthorne, Herman Melville, Thomas Pynchon, and Don DeLillo. But this oversight in no way diminishes the larger, lasting significance of Irving's historian, whose "curious kind of a written book" marked the creation of a genre that persists to this day: the genre of the New York Story. The combination of delight and mockery that marked the *History* has become the vernacular of centuries of New York storytelling: regardless of the medium, all of its chroniclers share a belief in the singularity of the New York experience, and a mission to share this experience with the larger world. Readers everywhere take it for granted that New York City warrants all the encomiums, epithets, nicknames, and slogans that have been showered on it, and demand to be told more. What other city could at once be Walt Whitman's "Mighty Manhattan," Kander and Ebb's "city that never sleeps," and J. J. Hunsecker's "dirty town"? Knickerbocker was not only the first narrator to identify this market: he was the architect of the market itself. "A hundred years hence, or ever so many hundred years hence," Walt Whitman would write in "Crossing Brooklyn Ferry," "others will see the islands, large and small" that made up his beloved New York. His hymn to the city, and those "a hundred years hence," are made possible not by the ferry, but by the example of Washington Irving, who built New York's first literary bridge.

ELIZABETH L. BRADLEY

Suggestions for Further Reading

Aderman, Ralph M., ed. *Critical Essays on Washington Irving*. Boston: G. K. Hall, 1990.

Avery, Kevin J. "Selling the Sublime and Beautiful: Landscape and Tourism." *Art and the Empire City: New York, 1825–1861*. Metropolitan Museum of Art. New Haven: Yale University Press, 2000.

Bender, Thomas. *New York Intellect*. Baltimore: Johns Hopkins University Press, 1988.

Blumin, Stuart. *The Emergence of the Middle Class: Social Experience in the American City, 1760–1900*. Cambridge: Cambridge University Press, 1986.

Burrows, Edwin G., and Mike Wallace. *Gotham: A History of New York City to 1898*. New York: Oxford University Press, 1999.

Burstein, Andrew. *The Original Knickerbocker: The Life of Washington Irving*. New York: Basic Books, 2007.

Clark, Lewis Gaylord. *Knick-Knacks from an Editor's Table*. New York: D. Appleton and Co., 1853.

Cmiel, Kenneth. *Democratic Eloquence: The Fight over Popular Speech in Nineteenth Century America*. Los Angeles: University of California–Los Angeles Press, 1990.

Collections of the New-York Historical Society for the Year 1809. New York: I. Riley, 1811.

Duyckinck, Evert A. *Irvingiana: A Memorial of Washington Irving*. New York: Charles B. Richardson, 1860.

Hiller, Alice. " 'An Avenue to Some Degree of Profit and Reputation': The Sketchbook as Washington Irving's Entrée and Undoing." *Journal of American Studies* 31 (1997): 275–93.

Irving, Pierre. *Life and Letters of Washington Irving.* New York: G. P. Putnam, 1864.

Irving, Washington. *A History of New York.* Edwin T. Bowden, ed. 1848, Albany: 2nd ed. Twayne Publishers, 1964.

———. *Washington Irving: Tales, History and Sketches.* James W. Tuttleton, ed. New York: Library of America, 1983.

———. *Washington Irving: Bracebridge Hall, Tales of a Traveller, The Alahambra.* Andrew B. Myers, ed. New York: Library of America, 1991.

Jackson, Kenneth T., ed. *The Encyclopedia of New York City.* New Haven: Yale University Press, 1995.

James, Henry. *The American Scene. Collected Travel Writings: Great Britain and America.* Richard Howard, ed. New York: Library of America, 1993.

Jones, Brian Jay. *Washington Irving: An American Original.* New York: Arcade Publishing, 2008.

Knickerbocker magazine

Kurlansky, Mark. *The Big Oyster.* New York: Ballantine Books, 2006.

Mitchill, Samuel L. *The Picture of New York, or, The Traveller's Guide Through the Commercial Metropolis of the United States, by a Gentleman Residing in This City.* New York: L. Riley and Co., 1807.

Murray, Laura. "The Aesthetic of Dispossession: Washington Irving and Ideologies of (De)Colonization in the Early Republic." *ALH* (1996): 205–31.

Myers, Andrew B., ed. *A Century of Commentary on Washington Irving: 1860–1974.* Tarrytown: Sleepy Hollow Restorations, 1976.

———, ed. *The Knickerbocker Tradition: Washington Irving's New York.* Tarrytown: Sleepy Hollow Restorations, 1974.

———, ed. *The Worlds of Washington Irving, 1783–1859: From an Exhibition of Rare Book and Manuscript Materials in the Special Collections of the New York Public Library.* Tarrytown; Sleepy Hollow Restorations, 1974.

Paulding, James Kirke. *Stories of Saint Nicholas.* Frank Bergmann, ed. Syracuse: Syracuse University Press, 1995.

Rockwell, Charles. *The Catskill Mountains and the Regions Around.* New York: Taintor Brothers & Co., 1873.

Rubin-Dorsky, Jeffrey. *Adrift in the Old World: The Psychological Pilgrimage of Washington Irving.* Chicago: University of Chicago Press, 1988.

Searling, A. P. *The Land of Rip Van Winkle: A Tour Through the Romantic Parts of the Catskills, its Legends and Traditions.* New York: G. P. Putnam's Sons, 1884.

Sondey, Walter. "From Nations of Virtue to Virtual Nation: Washington Irving and American Nationalism." *Narratives of Nostalgia, Gender and Nationalism.* Jean Pickering and Susan Kehde, eds. Basingstoke: Macmillan, 1992.

Sweeting, Adam W. " 'A Very Pleasant Patriarchal Life': Professional Authors and Amateur Architects in the Hudson Valley, 1835–1870." *Journal of American Studies* 29 (1995): 33–53.

Taft, Kendall B. *Minor Knickerbockers.* New York: American Book Co., 1974.

Tompkins, Jane. *Sensational Designs: The Cultural Work of American Fiction, 1790–1860.* New York, Oxford University Press, 1985.

Tuttleton, James W., ed. *Washington Irving: The Critical Reaction.* New York: AMS Press, 1993.

Van Zandt, Roland. *The Catskill Mountain House.* New Brunswick: Rutgers University Press, 1966.

Warner, Michael. "Irving's Posterity" *ELH* 67 (2000): 773–99.

———. *The Letters of the Republic.* Cambridge: Harvard University Press, 1990.

Wells, Robert V. "While Rip Napped: Social Change in Late Eighteenth-Century New York." *New York History* 71 (1990): 5–23.

A History of New York

ACCOUNT OF THE AUTHOR

It was sometime, if I recollect right, in the early part of the Fall of 1808, that a stranger applied for lodgings at the Independent Columbian Hotel in Mulberry Street, of which I am landlord. He was a small brisk looking old gentleman, dressed in a rusty black coat, a pair of olive velvet breeches, and a small cocked hat. He had a few grey hairs plaited and clubbed behind, and his beard seemed to be of some four and twenty hours growth. The only piece of finery which he bore about him, was a bright pair of square silver shoe buckles, and all his baggage was contained in a pair of saddle bags which he carried under his arm. His whole appearance was something out of the common run, and my wife, who is a very shrewd body, at once set him down for some eminent country school-master.

As the Independent Columbian Hotel is a very small house, I was a little puzzled at first where to put him; but my wife, who seemed taken with his looks, would needs put him in her best chamber, which is genteely set off with the profiles of the whole family, done in black, by those two great painters Jarvis and Wood; and commands a very pleasant view of the new grounds on the Collect, together with the rear of the Poor house and Bridewell and the full front of the Hospital, so that it is the cheerfullest room in the whole house.

During the whole time that he stayed with us, we found him a very worthy good sort of an old gentleman, though a little queer in his ways. He would keep in his room for days together, and if any of the children cried or made a noise about his door, he would bounce out in a great passion, with his hands full of papers, and say something about "deranging his ideas," which made my wife believe sometimes that he was not altogether *compos*. Indeed there was more than one reason to make her think so, for his room was always covered with scraps of paper and old mouldy books, laying about at sixes and sevens, which he would never let any body touch; for he said he had laid them all away in their proper places, so that he might know where to find them; though for that matter, he was half his time worrying about the house in search of some book or writing which he had carefully put out of the way. I shall never forget what a pother he once made, because my wife cleaned out his room when his back was turned, and put every thing to rights; for he swore he should never be able to get his papers in order again in a twelvemonth—Upon this my wife ventured to ask him what he did with so many books and papers, and he told her that he was "seeking for immortality," which made her think more than ever, that the poor old gentleman's head was a little cracked.

He was a very inquisitive body, and when not in his room was continually poking about town, hearing all the news and prying into every thing that was going on; this was particularly the case about election time, when he did nothing but bustle about from poll to poll, attending all ward meetings and committee rooms; though I could never find that he took part with either side of the question. On the contrary he would come home and rail at both parties with great wrath—and plainly proved one day, to the satisfaction of my wife and three old ladies who were drinking tea with her, one of whom was as deaf as a post, that the two parties were like two rogues, each tugging at a skirt of the nation, and that in the end they would tear the very coat off of its back and expose its nakedness. Indeed he was an oracle among the neighbours, who would collect around him to hear him talk of an afternoon, as he smoaked his pipe on the bench before the door; and I really believe he would have brought over the whole neighbourhood to his own side of the question, if they could ever have found out what it was.

He was very much given to argue, or as he called it *philosophize,* about the most trifling matter, and to do him justice, I never knew any body that was a match for him, except it was a grave looking gentleman who called now and then to see him, and often posed him in an argument. But this is nothing surprising, as I have since found out this stranger is the city librarian, and of course must be a man of great learning; and I have my doubts, if he had not some hand in the following history.

As our lodger had been a long time with us, and we had never received any pay, my wife began to be somewhat uneasy, and curious to find out who, and what he was. She accordingly made bold to put the question to his friend, the librarian, who replied in his dry way, that he was one of the *Literati*; which she supposed to mean some new party in politics. I scorn to push a lodger for his pay, so I let day after day pass on without dunning the old gentleman for a farthing; but my wife, who always takes these matters on herself, and is as I said a shrewd kind of a woman, at last got out of patience, and hinted, that she thought it high time "some people should have a sight of some people's money." To which the old gentleman replied, in a mighty touchy manner, that she need not make herself uneasy, for that he had a treasure there (pointing to his saddle-bags) worth her whole house put together. This was the only answer we could ever get from him; and as my wife, by some of those odd ways in which women find out every thing, learnt that he was of very great connexions, being related to the Knickerbockers of Scaghtikoke, and cousin-german to the Congress-man of that name, she did not like to treat him uncivilly. What is more, she even offered, merely by way of making things easy, to let him live scot-free, if he would teach the children their letters; and to try her best and get the neighbours to send their children also; but the old gentleman took it in such dudgeon, and seemed so affronted at being taken for a school-master, that she never dared speak on the subject again.

About two month's ago, he went out of a morning, with a bundle in his hand—and has never been heard of since. All kinds of inquiries were made after him, but in vain. I wrote to his relations at Scaghtikoke, but they sent for answer, that he had not been there since the year before last, when he had a great dispute with the Congress-man about politics, and left the place in a huff, and they had neither heard nor seen any thing of him from that time to this. I must own I felt very much worried about the poor old gentleman, for I thought something bad must have happened to him, that he should be missing so long, and never return to pay his bill. I therefore advertised him in the news-papers, and though my melancholy advertisement was published by several humane printers, yet I have never been able to learn any thing satisfactory about him.

My wife now said it was high time to take care of ourselves, and see if he had left any thing behind in his room, that would pay us for his board and lodging. We found nothing however, but some old books and musty writings, and his pair of saddle bags, which being opened in presence of the librarian, contained only a few articles of worn out clothes, and a large bundle of blotted paper. On looking over this, the librarian told us, he had no doubt it was the treasure which the old gentleman had spoken about; as it proved to be a most excellent and faithful HISTORY OF NEW YORK, which he advised us by all means to publish: assuring us that it would be so eagerly bought up by a discerning public, that he had no doubt it would be enough to pay our arrears ten times over. Upon this we got a very learned school-master, who teaches our children, to prepare it for the press, which he accordingly has done, and has moreover, added to it a number of notes of his own; and an engraving of the city, as it was, at the time Mr. Knickerbocker writes about.

This, therefore, is a true statement of my reasons for having this work printed, without waiting for the consent of the author: and I here declare, that if he ever returns (though I much fear some unhappy accident has befallen him) I stand ready to account with him, like a true and honest man. Which is all at present—

From the public's humble servant,

SETH HANDASIDE.

Independent Columbian Hotel,
  New York.

TO THE PUBLIC

"To rescue from oblivion the memory of former incidents, and to render a just tribute of renown to the many great and wonderful transactions of our Dutch progenitors, Diedrich Knickerbocker, native of the city of New York, produces this historical essay."* Like the great Father of History whose words I have just quoted, I treat of times long past, over which the twilight of uncertainty had already thrown its shadows, and the night of forgetfulness was about to descend forever. With great solicitude had I long beheld the early history of this venerable and ancient city, gradually slipping from our grasp, trembling on the lips of narrative old age, and day by day dropping piece meal into the tomb. In a little while, thought I, and those venerable dutch burghers, who serve as the tottering monuments of good old times, will be gathered to their fathers; their children engrossed by the empty pleasures or insignificant transactions of the present age, will neglect to treasure up the recollections of the past, and posterity shall search in vain, for memorials of the days of the Patriarchs. The origin of our city will be buried in eternal oblivion, and even the names and atchievements of Wouter Van Twiller, William Kieft, and Peter Stuyvesant, be enveloped in doubt and fiction, like those of Romulus and Rhemus, of Charlemagne, King Arthur, Rinaldo, and Godfrey of Bologne.

Determined therefore, to avert if possible this threatening misfortune, I industriously sat myself to work, to gather together all the fragments of our infant history which still existed, and like my revered prototype Herodotus, where no written records could

*Beloe's Herodotus.

be found, I have endeavoured to continue the chain of history by well authenticated traditions.

In this arduous undertaking, which has been the whole business of a long and solitary life, it is incredible the number of learned authors I have consulted; and all to but little purpose. Strange as it may seem, though such multitudes of excellent works have been written about this country, there are none extant which give any full and satisfactory account of the early history of New York, or of its three first Dutch governors. I have, however, gained much valuable and curious matter from an elaborate manuscript written in exceeding pure and classic low dutch, excepting a few errors in orthography, which was found in the archives of the Stuyvesant family. Many legends, letters and other documents have I likewise gleaned, in my researches among the family chests and lumber garrets of our respectable dutch citizens, and I have gathered a host of well authenticated traditions from divers excellent old ladies of my acquaintance, who requested that their names might not be mentioned. Nor must I neglect to acknowledge, how greatly I have been assisted by that admirable and praiseworthy institution, the NEW YORK HISTORICAL SOCIETY, to which I here publicly return my sincere acknowledgements.

In the conduct of this inestimable work I have adopted no individual model, but on the contrary have simply contented myself with combining and concentrating the excellencies of the most approved ancient historians. Like Xenophon I have maintained the utmost impartiality, and the strictest adherence to truth throughout my history. I have enriched it after the manner of Sallust, with various characters of ancient worthies, drawn at full length, and faithfully coloured. I have seasoned it with profound political speculations like Thucydides, sweetened it with the graces of sentiment like Tacitus, and infused into the whole the dignity, the grandeur and magnificence of Livy.

I am aware that I shall incur the censure of numerous very learned and judicious critics, for indulging too frequently in the bold excursive manner of my favourite Herodotus. And to be candid, I have found it impossible always to resist the allurements of those pleasing episodes, which like flowery banks and fragrant bowers, beset the dusty road of the historian, and entice him to turn aside, and refresh himself from his wayfaring. But I trust it will be found, that I have always resumed my staff, and addressed myself to my weary journey with renovated spirits, so that both my readers and myself, have been benefited by the relaxation.

Indeed, though it has been my constant wish and uniform endeavour, to rival Polybius himself, in observing the requisite unity of History, yet the loose and unconnected manner in which many of the facts herein recorded have come to hand, rendered such an attempt extremely difficult. This difficulty was likewise increased, by one of the grand objects contemplated in my work, which was to trace the rise of sundry customs and institutions in this best of cities, and to compare them when in the germ of infancy, with what they are in the present old age of knowledge and improvement.

But the chief merit upon which I value myself, and found my hopes for future regard, is that faithful veracity with which I have compiled this invaluable little work; carefully winnowing away all the chaff of hypothesis, and discarding the tares of fable, which are too apt to spring up and choke the seeds of truth and wholesome knowledge—Had I been anxious to captivate the superficial throng, who skim like swallows over the surface of literature; or had I been anxious to commend my writings to the pampered palates of literary voluptuaries, I might have availed myself of the obscurity that hangs about the infant years of our city, to introduce a thousand pleasing fictions. But I have scrupulously discarded many a pithy tale and marvellous adventure, whereby the drowsy ear of summer indolence might be enthralled; jealously maintaining that fidelity, gravity and dignity, which should ever distinguish the historian. "For a writer of this class," observes an elegant critic, "must sustain the character of a wise man, writing for the instruction of posterity; one who has studied to inform himself well, who has pondered his subject with care, and addresses himself to our judgment, rather than to our imagination."

Thrice happy therefore, is this our renowned city, in having incidents worthy of swelling the theme of history; and doubly thrice happy is it in having such an historian as myself, to relate them. For after all, gentle reader, cities *of themselves*, and in fact empires *of themselves*, are nothing without an historian. It is the patient narrator who cheerfully records their prosperity as they rise—who blazons forth the splendour of their noontide meridian—who props their feeble memorials as they totter to decay—who gathers together their scattered fragments as they rot—and who piously at length collects their ashes into the mausoleum of his work, and rears a triumphal monument, to transmit their renown to all succeeding time.

"What," (in the language of Diodorus Siculus) "What has become of Babylon, of Nineveh, of Palmyra, of Persepolis, of Byzantium, of Agrigentum, of Cyzicum and Mytilene?" They have disappeared from the face of the earth—they have perished for want of an historian! The philanthropist may weep over their desolation—the poet may wander amid their mouldering arches and broken columns, and indulge the visionary flights of his fancy—but alas! alas! the modern historian, whose faithful pen, like my own, is doomed irrevocably to confine itself to dull matter of fact, seeks in vain among their oblivious remains, for some memorial that may tell the instructive tale, of their glory and their ruin.

"Wars, conflagrations, deluges (says Aristotle) destroy nations, and with them all their monuments, their discoveries and their vanities—The torch of science has more than once been extinguished and rekindled—a few individuals who have escaped by accident, reunite the thread of generations." Thus then the historian is the patron of mankind, the guardian priest, who keeps the perpetual lamp of ages unextinguished—Nor is he without his reward. Every thing in a manner is tributary to his renown—Like the great projector of inland lock navigation, who asserted that rivers, lakes and oceans were only formed to feed canals; so I affirm that cities, empires, plots, conspiracies, wars, havock and desolation, are ordained by providence only as food for the historian. They form but the pedestal on which he intrepidly mounts to the view of surrounding generations, and claims to himself, from ages as they rise, until the latest sigh of old time himself, the meed of immortality—The world—the world, is nothing without the historian!

The same sad misfortune which has happened to so many ancient cities, will happen again, and from the same sad cause, to nine-tenths of those cities which now flourish on the face of the globe. With most of them the time for recording their history is gone by; their origin, their very foundation, together with the early stages of their settlement, are forever buried in the rubbish of years; and the same would have been the case with this fair portion of the earth, the history of which I have here given, if I had not snatched it from obscurity, in the very nick of time, at the moment that those matters herein recorded, were about entering into the widespread, insatiable maw of oblivion—if I had not dragged them out, in a manner, by the very locks, just as the monster's adamantine fangs, were closing upon them forever! And here have I, as before observed, carefully collected, collated and arranged them; scrip and scrap, "punt en punt, gat en gat," and commenced in this little work, a history which may serve as a foundation, on which a host of worthies shall hereafter raise a noble superstructure, swelling in process of time, until *Knicker-bocker's New York* shall be equally voluminous, with *Gibbon's Rome,* or *Hume and Smollet's England!*

And now indulge me for a moment, while I lay down my pen, skip to some little eminence at the distance of two or three hundred years ahead; and casting back a birds eye glance, over the waste of years that is to roll between; discover myself—*little I*—at this moment the progenitor, prototype and precursor of them all, posted at the head of this host of literary worthies, with my book under my arm, and New York on my back, pressing forward like a gallant commander, to honour and immortality.

Here then I cut my bark adrift, and launch it forth to float upon the waters. And oh! ye mighty Whales, ye Grampuses and Sharks of criticism, who delight in shipwrecking unfortunate adventurers upon the sea of letters, have mercy upon this my crazy vessel. Ye may toss it about in your sport; or spout your dirty water upon it in showers; but do not, for the sake of the unlucky mariner within—do not stave it with your tails and send it to the bottom. And you, oh ye great little fish! ye tadpoles, ye sprats, ye minnows, ye chubbs, ye grubs, ye barnacles, and all you small fry of literature, be cautious how you insult my new launched vessel, or swim within my view; lest in a moment of mingled sportiveness and scorn, I sweep you up in a scoop net, and roast half a hundred of you for my breakfast.

BOOK I

Being, like all introductions to American histories, very
learned, sagacious, and nothing at all to the purpose;
containing divers profound theories and philosophic
speculations, which the idle reader may totally
overlook, and begin at the next book.

CHAPTER I

*In which the Author ventures a Description of
the World, from the best Authorities.*

The world in which we dwell is a huge, opake, reflecting, inanimate mass, floating in the vast etherial ocean of infinite space. It has the form of an orange, being an oblate spheroid, curiously flattened at opposite parts, for the insertion of two imaginary poles, which are supposed to penetrate and unite at the centre; thus forming an axis on which the mighty orange turns with a regular diurnal revolution.

The transitions of light and darkness, whence proceed the alternations of day and night, are produced by this diurnal revolution, successively presenting the different parts of the earth to the rays of the sun. The latter is, according to the best, that is to say, the latest, accounts, a luminous or fiery body, of a prodigious magnitude, from which this world is driven by a centrifugal or repelling power, and to which it is drawn by a centripetal or attractive force; otherwise termed the attraction of gravitation; the combination, or rather the counteraction of these two opposing impulses producing a circular and annual revolution. Hence result the vicissitudes of the seasons, *viz.* spring, summer, autumn, and winter.

I am fully aware, that I expose myself to the cavillings of sundry dead philosophers, by adopting the above theory. Some will entrench themselves behind the ancient opinion, that the earth is an extended plain, supported by vast pillars; others, that it rests on the head of a snake, or the back of a huge tortoise; and others, that it is an immense flat pancake, and rests upon whatever it pleases God—formerly a pious Catholic opinion, and sanctioned by a formidable *bull,* dispatched from the vatican by a most holy and infallible pontiff. Others will attack my whole theory, by declaring with the Brahmins, that the heavens rest upon the earth, and that the sun and moon swim therein like fishes in the water, moving from east to west by day, and gliding back along the edge of the horizon to their original stations during the night time.* While others will maintain, with the Pauranicas of India, that it is a vast plain, encircled by seven oceans of milk, nectar and other delicious liquids; that it is studded with seven mountains, and ornamented in the centre by a mountainous rock of burnished gold; and that a great dragon occasionally swallows up the moon, which accounts for the phenomena of lunar eclipses.†

I am confident also, I shall meet with equal opposition to my account of the sun; certain ancient philosophers having affirmed that it is a vast wheel of brilliant fire,‡ others that it is merely a mirror or sphere of transparent chrystal;‖ and a third class, at the head of whom stands Anaxagoras, having maintained, that it is nothing but a huge ignited rock or stone, an opinion which the good people of Athens have kindly saved me the trouble of confuting, by turning the philosopher neck and heels out of their city.§ Another set of philosophers, who delight in variety, declare, that certain fiery particles exhale constantly from the earth, which concentrating in a single point of the firmament by day, constitute the sun, but being scattered, and rambling about in the dark at night, collect in various points and form stars. These are regularly burnt out and extinguished, like the lamps in our streets, and require a fresh supply of exhalations for the next occasion.**

It is even recorded that at certain remote and obscure periods, in consequence of a great scarcity of fuel, (probably during a severe winter) the sun has been completely burnt out, and not rekindled for a whole month. A most melancholy occurrence, the very idea of which gave vast concern to Heraclitus, the celebrated weeping Philosopher, who was a great stickler for this doctrine. Beside

---

*Faria y Souza. Mick. Lus. Note B, 7.
†Sir W. Jones, Diss. Antiq. Ind. Zod.
‡Plut. de plac. p. p.
‖Achill. Tat. Isag. cap. 19. Ap. Petav. t. iii, p. 81. Stob. Eclog. Phys. lib. i, p. 56.
§Diog. Laert. in Anaxag. l. ii, sec. 8. Plat. Apol. t. i, p. 26. Plut. de Superst. t. ii, p. 269. Xenoph. Mem. l. iv, p. 815.
**Aristot. Meteor. l. ii, c. 2. Idem. Probl. sec. 15. Stob. Ecl. Phys. l. i, p. 55. Bruck. Hist. Phil. t. i, p. 1154, et alii.

these profound speculations, others may expect me to advocate the opinion of Herschel, that the sun is a most magnificent, habitable abode; the light it furnishes, arising from certain empyreal, luminous or phosphoric clouds, swimming in its transparent atmosphere.* But to save dispute and altercation with my readers—who I already perceive, are a captious, discontented crew, and likely to give me a world of trouble—I now, once for all, wash my hands of all and every of these theories, declining entirely and unequivocally, any investigation of their merits. The subject of the present chapter is merely the Island, on which is built the goodly city of New York,—a very honest and substantial Island, which I do not expect to find in the sun, or moon; as I am no land speculator, but a plain matter of fact historian. I therefore renounce all lunatic, or solaric excursions, and confine myself to the limits of this terrene or earthly globe; somewhere on the surface of which I pledge my credit as a historian—(which heaven and my landlord know is all the credit I possess) to detect and demonstrate the existence of this illustrious island to the conviction of all reasonable people.

Proceeding on this discreet and considerate plan, I rest satisfied with having advanced the most approved and fashionable opinion on the form of this earth and its movements; and I freely submit it to the cavilling of any Philo, dead or alive, who may choose to dispute its correctness. I must here intreat my unlearned readers (in which class I humbly presume to include nine tenths of those who shall pore over these instructive pages) not to be discouraged when they encounter a passage above their comprehension; for as I shall admit nothing into my work that is not pertinent and absolutely essential to its well being, so likewise I shall advance no theory or hypothesis, that shall not be elucidated to the comprehension of the dullest intellect. I am not one of those churlish authors, who do so enwrap their works in the mystic fogs of scientific jargon, that a man must be as wise as themselves to understand their writings; on the contrary, my pages, though abounding with sound wisdom and profound erudition, shall be written with such pleasant and urbane perspicuity, that there shall not even be found

*Philos. Trans. 1795, p. 72.—idem. 1801, p. 265.—Nich. Philos. Journ. 1. p. 13.

a country justice, an outward alderman, or a member of congress, provided he can read with tolerable fluency, but shall both understand and profit by my labours. I shall therefore, proceed forthwith to illustrate by experiment, the complexity of motion just ascribed to this our rotatory planet.

Professor Von Poddingcoft (or Puddinghead as the name may be rendered into English) was long celebrated in the college of New York, for most profound gravity of deportment, and his talent at going to sleep in the midst of examinations; to the infinite relief of his hopeful students, who thereby worked their way through college with great ease and little study. In the course of one of his lectures, the learned professor, seizing a bucket of water swung it round his head at arms length; the impulse with which he threw the vessel from him, being a centrifugal force, the retention of his arm operating as a centripetal power, and the bucket, which was a substitute for the earth, describing a circular orbit round about the globular head and ruby visage of Professor Von Poddingcoft, which formed no bad representation of the sun. All of these particulars were duly explained to the class of gaping students around him. He apprised them moreover, that the same principle of gravitation, which retained the water in the bucket, restrains the ocean from flying from the earth in its rapid revolutions; and he further informed them that should the motion of the earth be suddenly checked, it would incontinently fall into the sun, through the centripetal force of gravitation; a most ruinous event to this planet, and one which would also obscure, though it most probably would not extinguish the solar luminary. An unlucky stripling, one of those vagrant geniuses, who seem sent into the world merely to annoy worthy men of the puddinghead order, desirous of ascertaining the correctness of the experiment, suddenly arrested the arm of the professor, just at the moment that the bucket was in its zenith, which immediately descended with astonishing precision, upon the philosophic head of the instructor of youth. A hollow sound, and a red-hot hiss attended the contact, but the theory was in the amplest manner illustrated, for the unfortunate bucket perished in the conflict, but the blazing countenance of Professor Von Poddingcoft, emerged from amidst the waters, glowing fiercer than ever with unutterable indignation—

whereby the students were marvellously edified, and departed considerably wiser than before.

It is a mortifying circumstance, which greatly perplexes many a pains taking philosopher, that nature often refuses to second his most profound and elaborate efforts; so that often after having invented one of the most ingenious and natural theories imaginable, she will have the perverseness to act directly in the teeth of his system, and flatly contradict his most favourite positions. This is a manifest and unmerited grievance, since it throws the censure of the vulgar and unlearned entirely upon the philosopher; whereas the fault is not to be ascribed to his theory, which is unquestionably correct, but to the waywardness of dame nature, who with the proverbial fickleness of her sex, is continually indulging in coquetries and caprices, and seems really to take pleasure in violating all philosophic rules, and jilting the most learned and indefatigable of her adorers. Thus it happened with respect to the foregoing satisfactory explanation of the motion of our planet; it appears that the centrifugal force has long since ceased to operate, while its antagonist remains in undiminished potency: the world therefore, according to the theory as it originally stood, ought in strict propriety to tumble into the sun—Philosophers were convinced that it would do so, and awaited in anxious impatience, the fulfilment of their prognostications. But the untoward planet, pertinaciously continued her course, notwithstanding that she had reason, philosophy, and a whole university of learned professors opposed to her conduct. The philo's were all at a non plus, and it is apprehended they would never have fairly recovered from the slight and affront which they conceived offered to them by the world, had not a good natured professor kindly officiated as mediator between the parties, and effected a reconciliation.

Finding the world would not accomodate itself to the theory, he wisely determined to accomodate the theory to the world: he therefore informed his brother philosophers, that the circular motion of the earth round the sun was no sooner engendered by the conflicting impulses above described, than it became a regular revolution, independent of the causes which gave it origin—in short, that madam earth having once taken it into her head to whirl round, like a young lady of spirit in a high dutch waltz, the

duivel himself could not stop her. The whole board of professors
of the university of Leyden joined in the opinion, being heartily
glad of any explanation that would decently extricate them from
their embarrassment—and immediately decreed the penalty of ex-
pulsion against all who should presume to question its correctness: the philosophers of all other nations gave an unqualified
assent, and ever since that memorable era the world has been left
to take her own course, and to revolve around the sun in such
orbit as she thinks proper.

CHAPTER II

Cosmogony or Creation of the World.
With a multitude of excellent Theories, by which the
Creation of a World is shewn to be no such difficult Matter
as common Folks would imagine.

Having thus briefly introduced my reader to the world, and given him some idea of its form and situation, he will naturally be curious to know from whence it came, and how it was created. And indeed these are points absolutely essential to be cleared up, in as much as if this world had not been formed, it is more than probable, nay I may venture to assume it as a maxim or postulate at least, that this renowned island on which is situated the city of New York, would never have had an existence. The regular course of my history therefore, requires that I should proceed to notice the cosmogony or formation of this our globe.

And now I give my readers fair warning, that I am about to plunge for a chapter or two, into as complete a labyrinth as ever historian was perplexed withal; therefore I advise them to take fast hold of my skirts, and keep close at my heels, venturing neither to the right hand nor to the left, least they get bemired in a slough of unintelligible learning, or have their brains knocked out, by some of those hard Greek names which will be flying about in all directions. But should any of them be too indolent or chicken-hearted to accompany me in this perilous undertaking, they had better take a short cut round, and wait for me at the beginning of some smoother chapter.

Of the creation of the world, we have a thousand contradictory accounts; and though a very satisfactory one is furnished us by divine revelation, yet every philosopher feels himself in honour bound, to furnish us with a better. As an impartial historian, I consider it my duty to notice their several theories, by which mankind have been so exceedingly edified and instructed.

Thus it was the opinion of certain ancient sages, that the earth and the whole system of the universe, was the deity himself;* a doctrine most strenuously maintained by Zenophanes and the whole tribe of Eleatics, as also by Strato and the sect of peripatetic or vagabondizing philosophers. Pythagoras likewise inculcated the famous numerical system of the monad, dyad and triad, and by means of his sacred quaternary elucidated the formation of the world, the arcana of nature and the principles both of music and morals.† Other sages adhered to the mathematical system of squares and triangles; the cube, the pyramid and the sphere; the tetrahedron, the octahedron, the icosahedron and the dodecahedron.‡ While others advocated the great elementary theory, which refers the construction of our globe and all that it contains, to the combinations of four material elements, air, earth, fire and water; with the assistance of a fifth, an immaterial and vivifying principle; by which I presume the worthy theorist meant to allude to that vivifying spirit contained in gin, brandy, and other potent liquors, and which has such miraculous effects, not only on the ordinary operations of nature, but likewise on the creative brains of certain philosophers.

Nor must I omit to mention the great atomic system taught by old Moschus before the siege of Troy; revived by Democritus of laughing memory; improved by Epicurus that king of good fellows, and modernised by the fanciful Descartes. But I decline enquiring, whether the atoms, of which the earth is said to be composed, are eternal or recent; whether they are animate or inanimate; whether, agreeably to the opinion of the Atheists, they were fortuitously aggregated, or as the Theists maintain, were arranged by a supreme intelligence.‖ Whether in fact the earth is an insensate clod, or whether it is animated by a soul;§ which opinion was strenuously maintained by a host of philosophers, at the head of whom stands the great Plato, that temperate sage,

*Aristot. ap. Cic. lib. i, cap. 3.
†Aristot. Metaph. lib. i, c. 5. Idem de cœlo 1. 3. c. i. Rousseau mem. sur musique ancien. p. 39. Plutarch de plac. Philos. lib. i. cap. 3. et. alii.
‡Tim. Locr. ap. Plato. t. 3. p. 90.
‖Aristot. Nat. Auscult. l. 2. cap. 6. Aristoph. Metaph. lib. i. cap. 3. Cic de. Nat. deor. lib. i. cap. 10. Justin. Mart. orat. ad gent. p. 20.
§Mosheim in Cudw. lib. i. cap. 4. Tim. de anim. mund. ap. Plat. lib. 3. Mem. de l'acad. des Belles Lettr. t. 32. p. 19. et alii.

who threw the cold water of philosophy on the form of sexual intercourse, and inculcated the doctrine of Platonic affection, or the art of making love without making children.—An exquisitely refined intercourse, but much better adapted to the ideal inhabitants of his imaginary island of Atlantis, than to the sturdy race, composed of rebellious flesh and blood, who populate the little matter of fact island which we inhabit.

Besides these systems, we have moreover the poetical theogeny of old Hesiod, who generated the whole Universe in the regular mode of procreation, and the plausible opinion of others, that the earth was hatched from the great egg of night, which floated in chaos, and was cracked by the horns of the celestial bull. To illustrate this last doctrine, Bishop Burnet in his Theory of the Earth,* has favoured us with an accurate drawing and description, both of the form and texture of this mundane egg; which is found to bear a miraculous resemblance to that of a *goose!* Such of my readers as take a proper interest in the origin of this our planet, will be pleased to learn, that the most profound sages of antiquity, among the Egyptians, Chaldeans, Persians, Greeks and Latins, have alternately assisted at the hatching of this strange bird, and that their cacklings have been caught, and continued in different tones and inflections, from philosopher to philosopher, unto the present day.

But while briefly noticing long celebrated systems of ancient sages, let me not pass over with neglect, those of other philosophers; which though less universal and renowned, have equal claims to attention, and equal chance for correctness. Thus it is recorded by the Brahmins, in the pages of their inspired Shastah, that the angel Bistnoo transforming himself into a great boar, plunged into the watery abyss, and brought up the earth on his tusks. Then issued from him a mighty tortoise, and a mighty snake; and Bistnoo placed the snake erect upon the back of the tortoise, and he placed the earth upon the head of the snake.†

The negro philosophers of Congo affirm, that the world was made by the hands of angels, excepting their own country, which the Supreme Being constructed himself, that it might be supremely

*Book i. ch. 5.
†Holwell. Gent. Philosophy.

excellent. And he took great pains with the inhabitants, and made them very black, and beautiful; and when he had finished the first man, he was well pleased with him, and smoothed him over the face, and hence his nose and the nose of all his descendants became flat.

The Mohawk Philosophers tell us that a pregnant woman fell down from heaven, and that a tortoise took her upon its back, because every place was covered with water; and that the woman sitting upon the tortoise paddled with her hands in the water, and raked up the earth, whence it finally happened that the earth became higher than the water.*

Beside these and many other equally sage opinions, we have likewise the profound conjectures of ABOUL-HASSAN-ALY,[†] son of Al Khan, son of Aly, son of Abderrahman, son of Abdallah, son of Masoud-el-Hadheli, who is commonly called MASOUDI, and surnamed Cothbeddin, but who takes the humble title of Laheb-ar-rasoul, which means the companion of the ambassador of God. He has written an universal history entitled "Mouroudge-ed-dhahrab, or the golden meadows and the mines of precious stones." In this valuable work he has related the history of the world, from the creation down to the moment of writing; which was, under the Khaliphat of Mothi Billah, in the month Dgioumadi-el-aoual of the 336th year of the Hegira or flight of the Prophet. He informs us that the earth is a huge bird, Mecca and Medina constituting the head, Persia and India the right wing, the land of Gog the left wing, and Africa the tail. He informs us moreover, that an earth has existed before the present, (which he considers as a mere chicken of 7000 years) that it has undergone divers deluges, and that, according to the opinion of some well informed Brahmins of his acquaintance, it will be renovated every seventy thousandth hazarouam; each hazarouam consisting of 12,000 years.

But I forbear to quote a host more of these ancient and outlandish philosophers, whose deplorable ignorance, in despite of all their erudition, compelled them to write in languages which but few of my readers can understand; and I shall proceed briefly to

---

*Johannes Megapolensis, jun. Account of Maquaas or Mohawk Indians. 1644.
[†]MSS. Biblist. Roi. Fr.

notice a few more intelligible and fashionable theories of their modern successors.

And first I shall mention the great Buffon, who conjectures that this globe was originally a globe of liquid fire, scintillated from the body of the sun, by the percussion of a comet, as a spark is generated by the collision of flint and steel. That at first it was surrounded by gross vapours, which cooling and condensing in process of time, constituted, according to their densities, earth, water and air; which gradually arranged themselves, according to their respective gravities, round the burning or vitrified mass, that formed their centre, &c.

Hutton, on the contrary, supposes that the waters at first were universally paramount; and he terrifies himself with the idea that the earth must be eventually washed away, by the force of rain, rivers and mountain torrents, untill it is confounded with the ocean, or in other words, absolutely dissolves into itself.—Sublime idea! far surpassing that of the tender-hearted damsel of antiquity who wept herself into a fountain; or the good dame of Narbonne in France, who for a volubility of tongue unusual in her sex, was doomed to peel five hundred thousand and thirty-nine ropes of onions, and actually ran out at her eyes, before half the hideous task was accomplished.

Whiston, the same ingenious philosopher who rivalled Ditton in his researches after the longitude, (for which the mischief-loving Swift discharged on their heads a stanza as fragrant as an Edinburgh nosegay) has distinguished himself by a very admirable theory respecting the earth. He conjectures that it was originally a *chaotic comet*, which being selected for the abode of man, was removed from its excentric orbit, and whirled round the sun in its present regular motion; by which change of direction, order succeeded to confusion in the arrangement of its component parts. The philosopher adds, that the deluge was produced by an uncourteous salute from the watery tail of another comet; doubtless through sheer envy of its improved condition; thus furnishing a melancholy proof that jealousy may prevail, even among the heavenly bodies, and discord interrupt that celestial harmony of the spheres, so melodiously sung by the poets.

But I pass over a variety of excellent theories, among which are those of Burnet, and Woodward, and Whitehurst; regretting extremely that my time will not suffer me to give them the notice they deserve—And shall conclude with that of the renowned Dr. Darwin, which I have reserved to the last for the sake of going off *with a report.* This learned Theban, who is as much distinguished for rhyme as reason, and for good natured credulity as serious research, and who has recommended himself wonderfully to the good graces of the ladies, by letting them into all the gallantries, amours, debaucheries, and other topics of scandal of the court of Flora; has fallen upon a theory worthy of his combustible imagination. According to his opinion, the huge mass of chaos took a sudden occasion to explode, like a barrel of gunpowder, and in that act exploded the sun—which in its flight by a similar explosion expelled the earth—which in like guise exploded the moon—and thus by a concatenation of explosions, the whole solar system was produced, and set most systematically in motion![*]

By the great variety of theories here alluded to, every one of which, if thoroughly examined, will be found surprisingly consistent in all its parts; my unlearned readers will perhaps be led to conclude, that the creation of a world is not so difficult a task as they at first imagined. I have shewn at least a score of ingenious methods in which a world could be constructed; and I have no doubt, that had any of the Philo's above quoted, the use of a good manageable comet, and the philosophical ware-house *chaos* at his command, he would engage, by the aid of philosophy to manufacture a planet as good, or if you would take his word for it, better than this we inhabit.

And here I cannot help noticing the kindness of Providence, in creating comets for the great relief of bewildered philosophers. By their assistance more sudden evolutions and transitions are affected in the system of nature, than are wrought in a pantomimic exhibition, by the wonder-working sword of Harlequin. Should one of our modern sages, in his theoretical flights among the stars, ever find himself lost in the clouds, and in danger of tumbling into the abyss of nonsense and absurdity, he has but to seize a comet by the beard, mount astride of its tail, and away he gallops in triumph, like an enchanter on his hyppogriff, or a Con-

[*]Darw. Bot. Garden. Part I, Cant. i, l. 105.

necticut witch on her broomstick, "to sweep the cobwebs out of the sky."

It is an old and vulgar saying, about a "beggar on horse back," which I would not for the world have applied to our most reverend philosophers; but I must confess, that some of them, when they are mounted on one of these fiery steeds, are as wild in their curvettings as was Phæton of yore, when he aspired to manage the chariot of Phœbus. One drives his comet at full speed against the sun, and knocks the world out of him with the mighty concussion; another more moderate, makes his comet a kind of beast of burden, carrying the sun a regular supply of food and faggots— a third, of more combustible disposition, threatens to throw his comet, like a bombshell into the world, and blow it up like a powder magazine; while a fourth, with no great delicacy to this respectable planet, and its inhabitants, insinuates that some day or other, his comet—my modest pen blushes while I write it— shall absolutely turn tail upon our world and deluge it with water!—Surely as I have already observed, comets were bountifully provided by Providence for the benefit of philosophers, to assist them in manufacturing theories.

When a man once doffs the straight waistcoat of common sense, and trusts merely to his imagination, it is astonishing how rapidly he gets forward. Plodding souls, like myself, who jog along on the two legs nature has given them, are sadly put to it to clamber over the rocks and hills, to toil through the mud and mire, and to remove the continual obstructions, that abound in the path of science. But your adventurous philosopher launches his theory like a balloon, and having inflated it with the smoke and vapours of his own heated imagination, mounts it in triumph, and soars away to his congenial regions in the moon. Every age has furnished its quota of these adventurers in the realms of fancy, who voyage among the clouds for a season and are stared at and admired, until some envious rival assails their air blown pageant, shatters its crazy texture, lets out the smoke, and tumbles the adventurer and his theory into the mud. Thus one race of philosophers demolish the works of their predecessors, and elevate more splendid fantasies in their stead, which in their turn are demolished and replaced by the air castles of a succeeding generation. Such are the grave eccentricities of genius, and the mighty soap bubbles, with which the grown up children of science amuse themselves—while the honest vulgar, stand gazing in stupid admiration, and dignify these fantastic vagaries with the name of wisdom!—surely old Socrates was right in his opinion that philosophers are but a soberer sort of madmen, busying themselves in things which are totally incomprehensible, or which, if they could be comprehended, would be found not worth the trouble of discovery.

And now, having adduced several of the most important theories that occur to my recollection, I leave my readers at full liberty to choose among them. They are all the serious speculations of learned men—all differ essentially from each other—and all have the same title to belief. For my part, (as I hate an embarrassment of choice) until the learned have come to an agreement among themselves, I shall content myself with the account handed us down by the good old Moses; in which I do but follow the example of our ingenious neighbours of Connecticut; who at their first settlement proclaimed, that the colony should be governed by the laws of God—until they had time to make better.

One thing however appears certain—from the unanimous authority of the before quoted philosophers, supported by the evidence of our own senses, (which, though very apt to deceive us, may be cautiously admitted as additional testimony) it appears I say, and I make the assertion deliberately, without fear of contradiction, that this globe really *was created*, and that it is composed of *land and water*. It further appears that it is curiously divided and parcelled out into continents and islands, among which I boldly declare the renowned ISLAND OF NEW YORK, will be found, by any one who seeks for it in its proper place.

Thus it will be perceived, that like an experienced historian I confine myself to such points as are absolutely essential to my subject—building up my work, after the manner of the able architect who erected our theatre; beginning with the foundation, then the body, then the roof, and at last perching our snug little island like the little cupola on the top. Having dropt upon this simile by chance I shall make a moment's further use of it, to illustrate the correctness of my plan. Had not the foundation, the body, and the roof of the theatre first been built, the cupola could not have had existence as a cupola—it might have been a centry-box—or a watchman's box—or it might have been placed in the rear of the Manager's house and have formed—a temple;—but it could never have been considered a cupola. As therefore the building of the theatre was necessary to the existence of the cupola, as a cupola—so the formation of the globe and its internal construction, were first necessary to the existence of this island, as an island—and thus the necessity and importance of this part of my history, which in a manner is no part of my history, is logically proved.

CHAPTER III

*How that famous navigator, Admiral Noah, was shamefully
nick-named; and how he committed an unpardonable
oversight in not having four sons. With the great trouble of
philosophers caused thereby, and the discovery of America.*

Noah, who is the first sea-faring man we read of, begat three
sons, Shem, Ham, and Japhet. Authors it is true, are not wanting,
who affirm that the patriarch had a number of other children.
Thus Berosus makes him father of the gigantic Titans, Methodius
gives him a son called Jonithus, or Jonicus, (who was the first inventor of Johnny cakes,) and others have mentioned a son, named
Thuiscon, from whom descended the Teutons or Teutonic, or in
other words, the Dutch nation.

I regret exceedingly that the nature of my plan will not permit
me to gratify the laudable curiosity of my readers, by investigating minutely the history of the great Noah. Indeed such an undertaking would be attended with more trouble than many people
would imagine; for the good old patriarch seems to have been a
great traveller in his day, and to have passed under a different
name in every country that he visited. The Chaldeans for instance
give us his story, merely altering his name into Xisuthrus—a
trivial alteration, which to an historian skilled in etymologies,
will appear wholly unimportant. It appears likewise, that he had
exchanged his tarpawlin and quadrant among the Chaldeans, for
the gorgeous insignia of royalty, and appears as a monarch in their
annals. The Egyptians celebrate him under the name of Osiris;
the Indians as Menu; the Greek and Roman writers confound
him with Ogyges, and the Theban with Deucalion and Saturn.
But the Chinese, who deservedly rank among the most extensive
and authentic historians, inasmuch as they have known the world
ever since some millions of years before it was created, declare
that Noah was no other than Fohi, a worthy gentleman, descended from an ancient and respectable family of Hong merchants, that flourished in the middle ages of the empire. What

gives this assertion some air of credibility is, that it is a fact, admitted by the most enlightened literati, that Noah travelled into China, at the time of the building of the Tower of Babel (probably to improve himself in the study of languages) and the learned Dr. Shackford gives us the additional information, that the ark rested upon a mountain on the frontiers of China.

From this mass of rational conjectures and sage hypotheses, many satisfactory deductions might be drawn; but I shall content myself with the unquestionable fact stated in the Bible, that Noah begat three sons—Shem, Ham, and Japhet.

It may be asked by some inquisitive readers, not much conversant with the art of history writing, what have Noah and his sons to do with the subject of this work? Now though, in strict justice, I am not bound to satisfy such querulous spirits, yet as I have determined to accommodate my book to every capacity, so that it shall not only delight the learned, but likewise instruct the simple, and edify the vulgar; I shall never hesitate for a moment to explain any matter that may appear obscure.

Noah we are told by sundry very credible historians, becoming sole surviving heir and proprietor of the earth, in fee simple, after the deluge, like a good father portioned out his estate among his children. To Shem he gave Asia, to Ham, Africa, and to Japhet, Europe. Now it is a thousand times to be lamented that he had but three sons, for had there been a fourth, he would doubtless have inherited America; which of course would have been dragged forth from its obscurity on the occasion; and thus many a hard working historian and philosopher, would have been spared a prodigious mass of weary conjecture, respecting the first discovery and population of this country. Noah, however, having provided for his three sons, looked in all probability, upon our country as mere wild unsettled land, and said nothing about it, and to this unpardonable taciturnity of the patriarch may we ascribe the misfortune, that America did not come into the world, as early as the other quarters of the globe.

It is true some writers have vindicated him from this misconduct towards posterity, and asserted that he really did discover America. Thus it was the opinion of Mark Lescarbot, a French writer possessed of that ponderosity of thought, and profoundness of reflection, so peculiar to his nation, that the immediate descendants of Noah peopled this quarter of the globe, and that the old patriarch himself, who still retained a passion for the sea-faring life, superintended the transmigration. The pious and enlightened father Charlevoix, a French Jesuit, remarkable for his veracity and an aversion to the marvellous, common to all great travellers, is conclusively of the same opinion; nay, he goes still further, and decides upon the manner in which the discovery was effected, which was by sea, and under the immediate direction of the great Noah. "I have already observed," exclaims the good father in a tone of becoming indignation, "that it is an arbitrary supposition that the grand children of Noah were not able to penetrate into the new world, or that they never thought of it. In effect, I can see no reason that can justify such a notion. Who can seriously believe, that Noah and his immediate descendants knew less than we do, and that the builder and pilot of the greatest ship that ever was, a ship which was formed to traverse an unbounded ocean, and had so many shoals and quicksands to guard against, should be ignorant of, or should not have communicated to his descendants the art of sailing on the ocean?" Therefore they did sail on the ocean—therefore they sailed to America—therefore America was discovered by Noah!

Now all this exquisite chain of reasoning, which is so strikingly characteristic of the good father, being addressed to the faith, rather than the understanding, is flatly opposed by Hans De Laet, who declares it a real and most ridiculous paradox, to suppose that Noah ever entertained the thought of discovering America; and as Hans is a Dutch writer, I am inclined to believe he must have been much better acquainted with the worthy crew of the ark than his competitors, and of course possessed of more accurate sources of information. It is astonishing how intimate historians daily become with the patriarchs and other great men of antiquity. As intimacy improves with time, and as the learned are particularly inquisitive and familiar in their acquaintance with the ancients, I should not be surprised, if some future writers should gravely give us a picture of men and manners as they existed before the flood, far more copious and accurate than the Bible; and that, in the course of another century, the log book of old Noah should be as current among historians, as the voyages of Captain Cook, or the renowned history of Robinson Crusoe.

I shall not occupy my time by discussing the huge mass of additional suppositions, conjectures and probabilities respecting the first discovery of this country, with which unhappy historians overload themselves, in their endeavours to satisfy the doubts of an incredulous world. It is painful to see these laborious wights panting and toiling, and sweating under an enormous burthen, at the very outset of their works, which on being opened, turns out to be nothing but a mighty bundle of straw. As, however, by unwearied assiduity, they seem to have established the fact, to the satisfaction of all the world, that this country *has been discovered,* I shall avail myself of their useful labours to be extremely brief upon this point.

I shall not therefore stop to enquire, whether America was first discovered by a wandering vessel of that celebrated Phœnecian fleet, which, according to Herodotus, circumnavigated Africa; or by that Carthagenian expedition, which Pliny, the naturalist, informs us, discovered the Canary Islands; or whether it was settled by a temporary colony from Tyre, as hinted by Aristotle and Seneca. I shall neither enquire whether it was first discovered by the Chinese, as Vossius with great shrewdness advances, nor by the Norwegians in 1002, under Biorn; nor by Behem, the German navigator, as Mr. Otto has endeavoured to prove to the Sçavans of the learned city of Philadelphia.

Nor shall I investigate the more modern claims of the Welsh, founded on the voyage of Prince Madoc in the eleventh century, who having never returned, it has since been wisely concluded that he must have gone to America, and that for a plain reason—if he did not go there, where else could he have gone?—a question which most Socratically shuts out all further dispute.

Laying aside, therefore, all the conjectures above mentioned, with a multitude of others, equally satisfactory, I shall take for granted, the vulgar opinion that America was discovered on the 12th of October, 1492, by Christovallo Colon, a Genoese, who has been clumsily nick-named Columbus, but for what reason I cannot discern. Of the voyages and adventures of this Colon, I shall say nothing, seeing that they are already sufficiently known. Nor shall I undertake to prove that this country should have been called Colonia, after his name, that being notoriously self evident.

Having thus happily got my readers on this side of the Atlantic, I picture them to myself, all impatience to enter upon the enjoyment of the land of promise, and in full expectation that I will immediately deliver it into their possession. But if I do, may I ever forfeit the reputation of a regular bred historian. No—no—most curious and thrice learned readers, (for thrice learned ye are if ye have read all that goes before, and nine times learned shall ye be, if ye read all that comes after) we have yet a world of work before us. Think you the first discoverers of this fair quarter of the globe, had nothing to do but go on shore and find a country ready laid out and cultivated like a garden, wherein they might revel at their ease? No such thing—they had forests to cut down, underwood to grub up, marshes to drain, and savages to exterminate.

In like manner, I have sundry doubts to clear away, questions to resolve, and paradoxes to explain, before I permit you to range at random; but these difficulties, once overcome, we shall be enabled to jog on right merrily through the rest of our history. Thus my work shall, in a manner, echo the nature of the subject, in the same manner as the sound of poetry has been found by certain shrewd critics, to echo the sense—this being an improvement in history, which I claim the merit of having invented.

CHAPTER IV

*Shewing the great toil and contention which Philosophers
have had in peopling America.—And how the Aborigines
came to be begotten by accident—to the great
satisfaction and relief of the author.*

Bless us!—what a hard life we historians have of it, who undertake to satisfy the doubts of the world!—Here have I been toiling
and moiling through three pestiferous chapters, and my readers
toiling and moiling at my heels; up early and to bed late, poring
over worm-eaten, obsolete, good-for-nothing books, and cultivating the acquaintance of a thousand learned authors, both ancient and modern, who, to tell the honest truth, are the stupidest
companions in the world—and after all, what have we got by
it?—Truly the mighty valuable conclusion, that this country does
actually exist, and has been discovered; a self-evident fact not
worth a hap'worth of gingerbread. And what is worse, we seem
just as far off from the city of New York now, as we were at first.
Now for myself, I would not care the value of a brass button, being
used to this dull and learned company; but I feel for my unhappy
readers, who seem most woefully jaded and fatigued.

Still, however, we have formidable difficulties to encounter, since
it yet remains, if possible, to show how this country was originally peopled—a point fruitful of incredible embarrassment, to us
scrupulous historians, but absolutely indispensable to our works.
For unless we prove that the Aborigines did absolutely come from
some where, it will be immediately asserted in this age of scepti-
cism, that they did not come at all; and if they did not come at all,
then was this country never populated—a conclusion perfectly
agreeable to the rules of logic, but wholly irreconcilable to every
feeling of humanity, inasmuch as it must syllogistically prove fatal
to the innumerable Aborigines of this populous region.

To avert so dire a sophism, and to rescue from logical annihila-
tion so many millions of fellow creatures, how many wings of geese
have been plundered! what oceans of ink have been benevolently

drained! and how many capacious heads of learned historians have
been addled and forever confounded! I pause with reverential awe,
when I contemplate the ponderous tomes in different languages,
with which they have endeavoured to solve this question, so important to the happiness of society, but so involved in clouds of impenetrable obscurity. Historian after historian has engaged in the
endless circle of hypothetical argument, and after leading us a
weary chace through octavos, quartos, and folios, has let us out at
the end of his work, just as wise as we were at the beginning. It was
doubtless some philosophical wild goose chace of the kind, that
made the old poet Macrobius rail in such a passion at curiosity,
which he anathematizes most heartily, as "an irksome agonizing
care, a superstitious industry about unprofitable things, an itching
humour to see what is not to be seen, and to be doing what signifies
nothing when it is done."

But come my lusty readers, let us address ourselves to our task
and fall vigorously to work upon the remaining rubbish that lies
in our way; but I warrant, had master Hercules, in addition to his
seven labours, been given as an eighth to write a genuine American
history, he would have been fain to abandon the undertaking,
before he got over the threshold of his work.

Of the claims of the children of Noah to the original population of this country I shall say nothing, as they have already been
touched upon in my last chapter. The claimants next in celebrity,
are the decendants of Abraham. Thus Christoval Colon (vulgarly
called Columbus) when he first discovered the gold mines of His-
paniola immediately concluded, with a shrewdness that would
have done honour to a philosopher, that he had found the ancient
Ophir, from whence Solomon procured the gold for embellish-
ing the temple at Jerusalem; nay Colon even imagined that he
saw the remains of furnaces of veritable Hebraic construction,
employed in refining the precious ore.

So golden a conjecture, tinctured with such fascinating extrava-
gance, was too tempting not to be immediately snapped at by the
gudgeons of learning, and accordingly, there were a host of profound writers, ready to swear to its correctness, and to bring in
their usual load of authorities, and wise surmises, wherewithal
to prop it up. Vetablus and Robertus Stephens declared nothing
could be more clear—Arius Montanus without the least hesita-

tion asserts that Mexico was the true Ophir, and the Jews the early settlers of the country. While Possevin, Becan, and a host of other sagacious writers, lug in a *supposed* prophecy of the fourth book of Esdras, which being inserted in the mighty hypothesis, like the key stone of an arch, gives it, in their opinion, perpetual durability.

Scarce however, have they completed their goodly super-structure, than in trudges a phalanx of opposite authors, with Hans de Laet the great Dutchman at their head, and at one blow, tumbles the whole fabric about their ears. Hans in fact, contradicts outright all the Israelitish claims to the first settle-ment of this country, attributing all those equivocal symptoms, and traces of Christianity and Judaism, which have been said to be found in divers provinces of the new world, to the *Devil*, who has always affected to counterfeit the worship of the true Deity. "A remark," says the knowing old Padre d'Acosta, "made by all good authors who have spoken of the religion of nations newly discovered, and founded besides on the authority of the *fathers of the church*."

Some writers again, among whom it is with great regret I am compelled to mention Lopez de Gomara, and Juan de Leri, in-sinuate that the Canaanites, being driven from the land of prom-ise by the Jews, were seized with such a panic, that they fled without looking behind them, until stopping to take breath they found themselves safe in America. As they brought neither their national language, manners nor features, with them, it is sup-posed they left them behind in the hurry of their flight—I cannot give my faith to this opinion.

I pass over the supposition of the learned Grotius, who being both an ambassador and a Dutchman to boot, is entitled to great respect; that North America, was peopled by a strolling company of Norwegians, and that Peru was founded by a colony from China—Manco or Mungo Capac, the first Incas, being himself a Chinese. Nor shall I more than barely mention that father Kircher, ascribes the settlement of America to the Egyptians, Rudbeck to the Scandinavians, Charron to the Gauls, Juffredus Petri to a skaiting party from Friesland, Milius to the Celtæ, Marinocus the Sicilian to the Romans, Le Compte to the Phœnicians, Postel to the Moors, Martyn d'Angleria to the Abyssinians, together with the sage surmise of De Laet, that England, Ireland and the Orcades may contend for that honour.

Nor will I bestow any more attention or credit to the idea that America is the fairy region of Zipangri, described by that dreaming traveller Marco Polo the Venetian; or that it comprizes the visionary island of Atlantis, described by Plato. Neither will I stop to investigate the heathenish assertion of Paracelsus, that each hemisphere of the globe was originally furnished with an Adam and Eve. Or the more flattering opinion of Dr. Romayne supported by many nameless authorities, that Adam was of the Indian race—or the startling conjecture of Buffon, Helvetius, and Darwin, so highly honourable to mankind, and peculiarly complimentary to the French nation, that the whole human species are accidentally descended from a remarkable family of monkies!

This last conjecture, I must own, came upon me very suddenly and very ungraciously. I have often beheld the clown in a pantomime, while gazing in stupid wonder at the extravagant gambols of a harlequin, all at once electrified by a sudden stroke of the wooden sword across his shoulders. Little did I think at such times, that it would ever fall to my lot to be treated with equal discourtesy, and that while I was quietly beholding these grave philosophers, emulating the excentric transformations of the particoloured hero of pantomime, they would on a sudden turn upon me and my readers, and with one flourish of their conjectural wand, metamorphose us into beasts! I determined from that moment not to burn my fingers with any more of their theories, but content myself with detailing the different methods by which they transported the descendants of these ancient and respectable monkies, to this great field of theoretical warfare.

This was done either by migrations by land or transmigrations by water. Thus Padre Joseph D'Acosta enumerates three passages by land, first by the north of Europe, secondly by the north of Asia and thirdly by regions southward of the straits of Magellan. The learned Grotius marches his Norwegians by a pleasant route across frozen rivers and arms of the sea, through Iceland, Greenland, Estotiland and Naremberga. And various writers, among whom are Angleria, De Hornn and Buffon, anxious for the accommodation of these travellers, have fastened the two continents together by a strong chain of deductions—by which means they could pass over dry shod. But should even this fail, Pinkerton, that industrious old gentleman, who compiles books and manufactures Geographies, and who erst flung away his wig and cane, frolicked like a naughty boy, and committed a thousand etourderies, among the *petites filles* of Paris*—he I say, has constructed a natural bridge of ice, from continent to continent, at the distance of four or five miles from Behring's straits—for which he is entitled to the grateful thanks of all the wandering aborigines who ever did, or ever will pass over it.

It is an evil much to be lamented, that none of the worthy writers above quoted, could ever commence his work, without immediately declaring hostilities against every writer who had treated of the same subject. In this particular, authors may be compared to a certain sagacious bird, which in building its nest, is sure to pull to pieces the nests of all the birds in its neighbourhood. This unhappy propensity tends grievously to impede the progress of sound knowledge. Theories are at best but brittle productions, and when once committed to the stream, they should take care that like the notable pots which were fellow voyagers, they do not crack each other. But this literary animosity is almost unconquerable. Even I, who am of all men the most candid and liberal, when I sat down to write this authentic history, did all at once conceive an absolute, bitter and unutterable contempt, a strange and unimaginable disbelief, a wondrous and most ineffable scoffing of the spirit, for the theories of the numerous literati, who have treated before me, of this country. I called them jolter heads, numsculls, dunderpates, dom cops, bottericks, domme jordans, and a thousand other equally indignant appellations. But when I came to consider the matter coolly and dispassionately, my opinion was altogether changed. When I beheld these sages gravely accounting for unaccountable things, and discoursing thus wisely about matters forever hidden from their eyes, like a blind man describing the glories of light, and the beauty and harmony of colours, I fell back in astonishment at the amazing extent of human ingenuity.

If—cried I to myself, these learned men can weave whole systems out of nothing, what would be their productions were they

---

*Vide Ed. Review

furnished with substantial materials—if they can argue and dispute thus ingeniously about subjects beyond their knowledge, what would be the profundity of their observations, did they but know what they were talking about! Should old Radamanthus, when he comes to decide upon their conduct while on earth, have the least idea of the usefulness of their labours, he will undoubtedly class them with those notorious wise men of Gotham, who milked a bull, twisted a rope of sand, and wove a velvet purse from a sow's ear.

My chief surprise is, that among the many writers I have noticed, no one has attempted to prove that this country was peopled from the moon—or that the first inhabitants floated hither on islands of ice, as white bears cruize about the northern oceans—or that they were conveyed here by balloons, as modern æreonauts pass from Dover to Calais—or by witchcraft, as Simon Magus posted among the stars—or after the manner of the renowned Scythian Abaris, who like the New England witches on fullblooded broomsticks, made most unheard of journeys on the back of a golden arrow, given him by the Hyperborean Apollo.

But there is still one mode left by which this country could have been peopled, which I have reserved for the last, because I consider it worth all the rest, it is—*by accident!* Speaking of the islands of Solomon, New Guinea, and New Holland, the profound father Charlevoix observes, "in fine, all these countries are peopled, and *it is possible,* some have been so *by accident.* Now if it could have happened in that manner, why might it not have been at the *same time,* and by the *same means,* with *the other* parts of the globe?" This ingenious mode of deducing certain conclusions from possible premises, is an improvement in syllogistic skill, and proves the good father superior even to Archimedes, for he can turn the world without any thing to rest his lever upon. It is only surpassed by the dexterity with which the sturdy old Jesuit, in another place, demolishes the gordian knot—"Nothing" says he, "is more easy. The inhabitants of both hemispheres are certainly the descendants of the same father. The common father of mankind, received an express order from Heaven, to people the world, and *accordingly it has been peopled*. To bring this about, it was necessary to overcome all difficulties in the way, *and they have also been overcome!*" Pious Logician! How does

he put all the herd of laborious theorists to the blush, by explain-
ing in fair words, what it has cost them volumes to prove they
knew nothing about!

They have long been picking at the lock, and fretting at the
latch, but the honest father at once unlocks the door by bursting
it open, and when he has it once a-jar, he is at full liberty to pour
in as many nations as he pleases. This proves to a demonstration
that a little piety is better than a cart-load of philosophy, and is a
practical illustration of that scriptural promise—"By faith ye shall
move mountains."

From all the authorities here quoted, and a variety of others
which I have consulted, but which are omitted through fear of
fatiguing the unlearned reader—I can only draw the following
conclusions, which luckily however, are sufficient for my purpose—
First, That this part of the world has actually *been peopled* (Q. E. D.)
to support which, we have living proofs in the numerous tribes of
Indians that inhabit it. Secondly, That it has been peopled in five
hundred different ways, as proved by a cloud of authors, who
from the positiveness of their assertions seem to have been eye
witnesses to the fact—Thirdly, That the people of this country
had a *variety of fathers,* which as it may not be thought much to
their credit by the common run of readers, the less we say on the
subject the better. The question therefore, I trust, is forever at
rest.

CHAPTER V

In which the Author puts a mighty Question to the rout, by the assistance of the Man in the Moon—which not only delivers thousands of people from great embarrassment, but likewise concludes this introductory book.

The writer of a history may, in some respects, be likened unto an adventurous knight, who having undertaken a perilous enterprize, by way of establishing his fame, feels bound in honour and chivalry, to turn back for no difficulty nor hardship, and never to shrink or quail whatever enemy he may encounter. Under this impression, I resolutely draw my pen and fall to, with might and main, at those doughty questions and subtle paradoxes, which, like fiery dragons and bloody giants, beset the entrance to my history, and would fain repulse me from the very threshold. And at this moment a gigantic question has started up, which I must take by the beard and utterly subdue, before I can advance another step in my historick undertaking—but I trust this will be the last adversary I shall have to contend with, and that in the next book, I shall be enabled to conduct my readers in triumph into the body of my work.

The question which has thus suddenly arisen, is, what right had the first discoverers of America to land, and take possession of a country, without asking the consent of its inhabitants, or yielding them an adequate compensation for their territory?

My readers shall now see with astonishment, how easily I will vanquish this gigantic doubt, which has so long been the terror of adventurous writers; which has withstood so many fierce assaults, and has given such great distress of mind to multitudes of kind-hearted folks. For, until this mighty question is totally put to rest, the worthy people of America can by no means enjoy the soil they inhabit, with clear right and title, and quiet, unsullied consciences.

The first source of right, by which property is acquired in a country, is DISCOVERY. For as all mankind have an equal right to any thing, which has never before been appropriated, so any nation, that discovers an uninhabited country, and takes possession thereof, is considered as enjoying full property, and absolute, unquestionable empire therein.*

This proposition being admitted, it follows clearly, that the Europeans who first visited America, were the real discoverers of the same; nothing being necessary to the establishment of this fact, but simply to prove that it was totally uninhabited by man. This would at first appear to be a point of some difficulty, for it is well known, that this quarter of the world abounded with certain animals, that walked erect on two feet, had something of the human countenance, uttered certain unintelligible sounds, very much like language, in short, had a marvellous resemblance to human beings. But the host of zealous and enlightened fathers, who accompanied the discoverers, for the purpose of promoting the kingdom of heaven, by establishing fat monasteries and bishopricks on earth, soon cleared up this point, greatly to the satisfaction of his holiness the pope, and of all Christian voyagers and discoverers.

They plainly proved, and as there were no Indian writers arose on the other side, the fact was considered as fully admitted and established, that the two legged race of animals before mentioned, were mere cannibals, detestable monsters, and many of them giants—a description of vagrants, that since the times of Gog, Magog and Goliath, have been considered as outlaws, and have received no quarter in either history, chivalry or song; indeed, even the philosopher Bacon, declared the Americans to be people proscribed by the laws of nature, inasmuch as they had a barbarous custom of sacrificing men, and feeding upon man's flesh.

Nor are these all the proofs of their utter barbarism: among many other writers of discernment, the celebrated Ulloa tells us "their imbecility is so visible, that one can hardly form an idea of them different from what one has of the brutes. Nothing disturbs the tranquillity of their souls, equally insensible to disasters, and to prosperity. Though half naked, they are as contented as a monarch in his most splendid array. Fear makes no impression on them, and respect as little."—All this is furthermore supported by

*Grotius. Puffendorf, b. 4. c. 4. Vattel, b. i. c. 18. et alii.

the authority of M. Bouguer. "It is not easy," says he, "to describe the degree of their indifference for wealth and all its advantages. One does not well know what motives to propose to them when one would persuade them to any service. It is vain to offer them money, they answer that they are not hungry." And Vanegas confirms the whole, assuring us that "ambition, they have none, and are more desirous of being thought strong, than valiant. The objects of ambition with us, honour, fame, reputation, riches, posts and distinctions are unknown among them. So that this powerful spring of action, the cause of so much *seeming* good and *real* evil in the world has no power over them. In a word, these unhappy mortals may be compared to children, in whom the developement of reason is not completed."

Now all these peculiarities, though in the unenlightened states of Greece, they would have entitled their possessors to immortal honour, as having reduced to practice those rigid and abstemious maxims, the mere talking about which, acquired certain old Greeks the reputation of sages and philosophers;—yet were they clearly proved in the present instance, to betoken a most abject and brutified nature, totally beneath the human character. But the benevolent fathers, who had undertaken to turn these unhappy savages into dumb beasts, by dint of argument, advanced still stronger proofs; for as certain divines of the sixteenth century, and among the rest Lullus affirm—the Americans go naked, and have no beards!—"They have nothing," says Lullus, "of the reasonable animal, except the mask."—And even that mask was allowed to avail them but little, for it was soon found that they were of a hideous copper complexion—and being of a copper complexion, it was all the same as if they were negroes—and negroes are black, "and black" said the pious fathers, devoutly crossing themselves, "is the colour of the Devil!" Therefore so far from being able to own property, they had no right even to personal freedom, for liberty is too radiant a deity, to inhabit such gloomy temples. All which circumstances plainly convinced the righteous followers of Cortes and Pizarro, that these miscreants had no title to the soil that they infested—that they were a perverse, illiterate, dumb, beardless, bare-bottomed *black-seed*—mere wild beasts of the forests, and like them should either be subdued or exterminated.

From the foregoing arguments therefore, and a host of others equally conclusive, which I forbear to enumerate, it was clearly evident, that this fair quarter of the globe when first visited by Europeans, was a howling wilderness, inhabited by nothing but wild beasts; and that the trans-atlantic visitors acquired an incontrovertable property therein, by the *right of Discovery.*

This right being fully established, we now come to the next, which is the right acquired by *cultivation.* "The cultivation of the soil" we are told "is an obligation imposed by nature on mankind. The whole world is appointed for the nourishment of its inhabitants; but it would be incapable of doing it, was it uncultivated. Every nation is then obliged by the law of nature to cultivate the ground that has fallen to its share. Those people like the ancient Germans and modern Tartars, who having fertile countries, disdain to cultivate the earth, and choose to live by rapine, are wanting to themselves, and *deserve to be exterminated as savage and pernicious beasts.*"*

Now it is notorious, that the savages knew nothing of agriculture, when first discovered by the Europeans, but lived a most vagabond, disorderly, unrighteous life,—rambling from place to place, and prodigally rioting upon the spontaneous luxuries of nature, without tasking her generosity to yield them any thing more; whereas it has been most unquestionably shewn, that heaven intended the earth should be ploughed and sown, and manured, and laid out into cities and towns and farms, and country seats, and pleasure grounds, and public gardens, all which the Indians knew nothing about—therefore they did not improve the talents providence had bestowed on them—therefore they were careless stewards—therefore they had no right to the soil—therefore they deserved to be exterminated.

It is true the savages might plead that they drew all the benefits from the land which their simple wants required—they found plenty of game to hunt, which together with the roots and uncultivated fruits of the earth, furnished a sufficient variety for their frugal table;—and that as heaven merely designed the earth to form the abode, and satisfy the wants of man; so long as those purposes were answered, the will of heaven was accomplished.— But this only proves how undeserving they were of the blessings

*Vattel—B.i, ch. 17. See likewise Grotius, Puffendorf, et alii.

around them—they were so much the more savages, for not having more wants; for knowledge is in some degree an increase of desires, and it is this superiority both in the number and magnitude of his desires, that distinguishes the man from the beast. Therefore the Indians, in not having more wants, were very unreasonable animals; and it was but just that they should make way for the Europeans, who had a thousand wants to their one, and therefore would turn the earth to more account, and by cultivating it, more truly fulfil the will of heaven. Besides—Grotius and Lauterbach, and Puffendorff and Titius and a host of wise men besides, who have considered the matter properly, have determined, that the property of a country cannot be acquired by hunting, cutting wood, or drawing water in it—nothing but precise demarcation of limits, and the intention of cultivation, can establish the possession. Now as the savages (probably from never having read the authors above quoted) had never complied with any of these necessary forms, it plainly follows that they had no right to the soil, but that it was completely at the disposal of the first comers, who had more knowledge and more wants than themselves—who would portion out the soil, with churlish boundaries; who would torture nature to pamper a thousand fantastic humours and capricious appetites; and who of course were far more rational animals than themselves. In entering upon a newly discovered, uncultivated country therefore, the new comers were but taking possession of what according to the aforesaid doctrine, was their own property—therefore in opposing them, the savages were invading their just rights, infringing the immutable laws of nature and counteracting the will of heaven—therefore they were guilty of impiety, burglary and trespass on the case,—therefore they were hardened offenders against God and man—therefore they ought to be exterminated.

But a more irresistible right then either that I have mentioned, and one which will be the most readily admitted by my reader, provided he is blessed with bowels of charity and philanthropy, is the right acquired by civilization. All the world knows the lamentable state in which these poor savages were found. Not only deficient in the comforts of life, but what is still worse, most piteously and unfortunately blind to the miseries of their situation. But no sooner did the benevolent inhabitants of Europe behold their sad condition than they immediately went to work to ameliorate and improve it. They introduced among them the comforts of life, consisting of rum, gin and brandy—and it is astonishing to read how soon the poor savages learnt to estimate these blessings—they likewise made known to them a thousand remedies, by which the most inveterate diseases are alleviated and healed, and that they might comprehend the benefits and enjoy the comforts of these medicines, they previously introduced among them the diseases, which they were calculated to cure. By these and a variety of other methods was the condition of these poor savages, wonderfully improved; they acquired a thousand wants, of which they had before been ignorant, and as he has most sources of happiness, who has most wants to be gratified, they were doubtlessly rendered a much happier race of beings.

But the most important branch of civilization, and which has most strenuously been extolled, by the zealous and pious fathers of the Roman Church, is the introduction of the Christian faith. It was truly a sight that might well inspire horror, to behold these savages, stumbling among the dark mountains of paganism, and guilty of the most horrible ignorance of religion. It is true, they neither stole nor defrauded, they were sober, frugal, continent, and faithful to their word; but though they acted right habitually, it was all in vain, unless they acted so from precept. The new comers therefore used every method, to induce them to embrace and practice the true religion—except that of setting them the example.

But notwithstanding all these complicated labours for their good, such was the unparalleled obstinacy of these stubborn wretches, that they ungratefully refused, to acknowledge the strangers as their benefactors, and persisted in disbelieving the doctrines they endeavoured to inculcate; most insolently alledging, that from their conduct, the advocates of Christianity did not seem to believe in it themselves. Was not this too much for human patience?—would not one suppose, that the foreign emigrants from Europe, provoked at their incredulity and discouraged by their stiff-necked obstinacy, would forever have abandoned their shores, and consigned them to their original ignorance and misery?—But no—so zealous were they to effect the temporal comfort and eternal salvation of these pagan infidels, that they even proceeded from the milder means of persuasion, to the more painful and troublesome one of persecution—Let loose among them, whole troops of fiery monks and furious blood-hounds—purified them by fire and sword, by stake and faggot; in consequence of which indefatigable measures, the cause of Christian love and charity were so rapidly advanced, that in a very few years, not one fifth of the number of unbelievers existed in South America, that were found there at the time of its discovery.

Nor did the other methods of civilization remain uninforced. The Indians improved daily and wonderfully by their intercourse with the whites. They took to drinking rum, and making bargains. They learned to cheat, to lie, to swear, to gamble, to quarrel, to cut each others throats, in short, to excel in all the accomplishments that had originally marked the superiority of their Christian visitors. And such a surprising aptitude have they shewn for these acquirements, that there is very little doubt that in a century more, provided they survive so long, the irresistible effects of civilization; they will equal in knowledge, refinement, knavery, and debauchery, the most enlightened, civilized and orthodox nations of Europe.

What stronger right need the European settlers advance to the country than this. Have not whole nations of uninformed savages been made acquainted with a thousand imperious wants and indispensible comforts of which they were before wholly ignorant—Have they not been literally hunted and smoked out of the dens and lurking places of ignorance and infidelity, and absolutely scourged into the right path. Have not the temporal things, the vain baubles and filthy lucre of this world, which were too apt to engage their worldly and selfish thoughts, been benevolently taken from them; and have they not in lieu thereof, been taught to set their affections on things above—And finally, to use the words of a reverend Spanish father, in a letter to his superior in Spain—"Can any one have the presumption to say, that these savage Pagans, have yielded any thing more than an inconsiderable recompense to their benefactors; in surrendering to them a little pitiful tract of this dirty sublunary planet, in exchange for a glorious inheritance in the kingdom of Heaven!"

Here then are three complete and undeniable sources of right established, any one of which was more than ample to establish a property in the newly discovered regions of America. Now, so it has happened in certain parts of this delightful quarter of the globe, that the right of discovery has been so strenuously asserted— the influence of cultivation so industriously extended, and the progress of salvation and civilization so zealously prosecuted, that, what with their attendant wars, persecutions, oppressions, diseases, and other partial evils that often hang on the skirts of great benefits—the savage aborigines have, some how or another, been utterly annihilated—and this all at once brings me to a fourth right, which is worth all the others put together—For the original claimants to the soil being all dead and buried, and no one remaining to inherit or dispute the soil, the Spaniards as the next immediate occupants entered upon the possession, as clearly as the hang-man succeeds to the clothes of the malefactor—and as they have Blackstone,* and all the learned expounders of the law on their side, they may set all actions of ejectment at defiance—and this last right may be entitled, the RIGHT BY EXTERMINATION, or in other words, the RIGHT BY GUNPOWDER.

But lest any scruples of conscience should remain on this head, and to settle the question of right forever, his holiness Pope Alexander VI, issued one of those mighty bulls, which bear down reason, argument and every thing before them; by which he generously granted the newly discovered quarter of the globe, to the Spaniards and Portuguese; who, thus having law and gospel on their side, and being inflamed with great spiritual zeal, shewed the Pagan savages neither favour nor affection, but prosecuted the work of discovery, colonization, civilization, and extermination, with ten times more fury than ever.

Thus were the European worthies who first discovered America, clearly entitled to the soil; and not only entitled to the soil, but likewise to the eternal thanks of these infidel savages, for having come so far, endured so many perils by sea and land, and taken such unwearied pains, for no other purpose under heaven but to improve their forlorn, uncivilized and heathenish condition—for having made them acquainted with the comforts of life, such as gin, rum, brandy, and the small-pox; for having introduced among

---

* Black. Com. B. II, c. i.

them the light of religion, and finally—for having hurried them out of the world, to enjoy its reward!

But as argument is never so well understood by us selfish mortals, as when it comes home to ourselves, and as I am particularly anxious that this question should be put to rest forever, I will suppose a parallel case, by way of arousing the candid attention of my readers.

Let us suppose then, that the inhabitants of the moon, by astonishing advancement in science, and by a profound insight into that ineffable lunar philosophy, the mere flickerings of which, have of late years, dazzled the feeble optics, and addled the shallow brains of the good people of our globe—let us suppose, I say, that the inhabitants of the moon, by these means, had arrived at such a command of their *energies,* such an enviable state of *perfectability,* as to controul the elements, and navigate the boundless regions of space. Let us suppose a roving crew of these soaring philosophers, in the course of an ærial voyage of discovery among the stars, should chance to alight upon this outlandish planet.

And here I beg my readers will not have the impertinence to smile, as is too frequently the fault of volatile readers, when perusing the grave speculations of philosophers. I am far from indulging in any sportive vein at present, nor is the supposition I have been making so wild as many may deem it. It has long been a very serious and anxious question with me, and many a time, and oft, in the course of my overwhelming cares and contrivances for the welfare and protection of this my native planet, have I lain awake whole nights, debating in my mind whether it was most probable we should first discover and civilize the moon, or the moon discover and civilize our globe. Neither would the prodigy of sailing in the air and cruising among the stars be a whit more astonishing and incomprehensible to us, than was the European mystery of navigating floating castles, through the world of waters, to the simple savages. We have already discovered the art of coasting along the ærial shores of our planet, by means of balloons, as the savages had, of venturing along their sea coasts in canoes; and the disparity between the former, and the ærial vehicles of the philosophers from the moon, might not be greater, than that, between the bark canoes of the savages, and the mighty ships of their discoverers. I might here pursue an endless chain of very curious, profound and unprofitable speculations; but as they would be unimportant to my subject, I abandon them to my reader, particularly if he is a philosopher, as matters well worthy his attentive consideration.

To return then to my supposition—let us suppose that the aerial visitants I have mentioned, possessed of vastly superior knowledge to ourselves; that is to say, possessed of superior knowledge in the art of extermination—riding on Hypogriffs, defended with impenetrable armour—armed with concentrated sun beams, and provided with vast engines, to hurl enormous moon stones: in short, let us suppose them, if our vanity will permit the supposition, as superior to us in knowledge, and consequently in power, as the Europeans were to the Indians, when they first discovered them. All this is very possible, it is only our self-sufficiency, that makes us think otherwise; and I warrant the poor savages, before they had any knowledge of the white men, armed in all the terrors of glittering steel and tremendous gun-powder, were as perfectly convinced that they themselves, were the wisest, the most virtuous, powerful and perfect of created beings, as are, at this present moment, the lordly inhabitants of old England, the volatile populace of France, or even the self-satisfied citizens of this most enlightened republick.

Let us suppose, moreover, that the aerial voyagers, finding this planet to be nothing but a howling wilderness, inhabited by us, poor savages and wild beasts, shall take formal possession of it, in the name of his most gracious and philosophic excellency, the man in the moon. Finding however, that their numbers are incompetent to hold it in complete subjection, on account of the ferocious barbarity of its inhabitants, they shall take our worthy President, the King of England, the Emperor of Hayti, the mighty little Bonaparte, and the great King of Bantam, and returning to their native planet, shall carry them to court, as were the Indian chiefs led about as spectacles in the courts of Europe.

Then making such obeisance as the etiquette of the court requires, they shall address the puissant man in the moon, in, as near as I can conjecture, the following terms:

"Most serene and mighty Potentate, whose dominions extend as far as eye can reach, who rideth on the Great Bear, useth the sun as a looking glass and maintaineth unrivalled controul over tides, madmen and sea-crabs. We thy liege subjects have just returned from a voyage of discovery, in the course of which we have landed and taken possession of that obscure little scurvy planet, which thou beholdest rolling at a distance. The five uncouth monsters, which we have brought into this august presence, were once very important chiefs among their fellow savages; for the inhabitants of the newly discovered globe are totally destitute of the common attributes of humanity, inasmuch as they carry their heads upon their shoulders, instead of under their arms—have two eyes instead of one—are utterly destitute of tails, and of a variety of unseemly complexions, particularly of a horrible whiteness—whereas all the inhabitants of the moon are pea green!

We have moreover found these miserable savages sunk into a state of the utmost ignorance and depravity, every man shamelessly living with his own wife, and rearing his own children, instead of indulging in that community of wives, enjoined by the law of nature, as expounded by the philosophers of the moon. In a word they have scarcely a gleam of true philosophy among them, but are in fact, utter heretics, ignoramuses and barbarians. Taking compassion therefore on the sad condition of these sublunary wretches, we have endeavoured, while we remained on their planet, to introduce among them the light of reason—and the comforts of the moon.—We have treated them to mouthfuls of moonshine and draughts of nitrous oxyde, which they swallowed with incredible voracity, particularly the females; and we have likewise endeavoured to instil into them the precepts of lunar Philosophy. We have insisted upon their renouncing the contemptible shackles of religion and common sense, and adoring the profound, omnipotent, and all perfect energy, and the extatic, immutable, immoveable perfection. But such was the unparalleled obstinacy of these wretched savages, that they persisted in cleaving to their wives and adhering to their religion, and absolutely set at naught the sublime doctrines of the moon—nay, among other abominable heresies they even went so far as blasphemously to declare, that this ineffable planet was made of nothing more nor less than green cheese!"

At these words, the great man in the moon (being a very profound philosopher) shall fall into a terrible passion, and possessing equal authority over things that do not belong to him, as did whilome his holiness the Pope, shall forthwith issue a formidable bull,—specifying, "That—whereas a certain crew of Lunatics have lately discovered and taken possession of that little dirty planet, called *the earth*—and that whereas it is inhabited by none but a race of two legged animals, that carry their heads on their shoulders instead of under their arms; cannot talk the lunatic language; have two eyes instead of one; are destitute of tails, and of a horrible whiteness, instead of pea green—therefore and for a variety of other excellent reasons—they are considered incapable of possessing any property in the planet they infest, and the right and title to it are confirmed to its original discoverers.—And furthermore, the colonists who are now about to depart to the aforesaid planet, are authorized and commanded to use every means to convert these infidel savages from the darkness of Christianity, and make them thorough and absolute lunatics."

In consequence of this benevolent bull, our philosophic benefactors go to work with hearty zeal. They seize upon our fertile territories, scourge us from our rightful possessions, relieve us from our wives, and when we are unreasonable enough to complain, they will turn upon us and say—miserable barbarians! ungrateful wretches!—have we not come thousands of miles to improve your worthless planet—have we not fed you with moon shine—have we not intoxicated you with nitrous oxyde—does not our moon give you light every night and have you the baseness to murmur, when we claim a pitiful return for all these benefits? But finding that we not only persist in absolute contempt to their reasoning and disbelief in their philosophy, but even go so far as daringly to defend our property, their patience shall be exhausted, and they shall resort to their superior powers of argument—hunt us with hypogriffs, transfix us with concentrated sun-beams, demolish our cities with moonstones; until having by main force, converted us to the true faith, they shall graciously permit us to exist in the torrid deserts of Arabia, or the frozen regions of Lapland, there to enjoy the blessings of civilization and the charms of lunar philosophy—in much the same manner as the reformed and enlightened savages of this country, are kindly suffered to inhabit the inhospitable forests of the north, or the impenetrable wildernesses of South America.

Thus have I clearly proved, and I hope strikingly illustrated,

the right of the early colonists to the possession of this country—
and thus is this gigantic question, completely knocked in the
head—so having manfully surmounted all obstacles, and subdued all opposition, what remains but that I should forthwith
conduct my impatient and way-worn readers, into the renowned
city, which we have so long been in a manner besieging.—But
hold, before I proceed another step, I must pause to take breath
and recover from the excessive fatigue I have undergone, in preparing to begin this most accurate of histories. And in this I do
but imitate the example of the celebrated Hans Von Dunderbot-
tom, who took a start of three miles for the purpose of jumping
over a hill, but having been himself out of breath by the time he
reached the foot, sat himself quietly down for a few moments to
blow, and then walked over it at his leisure.

END OF BOOK I

BOOK II

Treating of the first settlement of the
province of Nieuw Nederlandts.

CHAPTER I

*How Master Hendrick Hudson, voyaging in search of a
north-west passage discovered the famous bay of New York,
and likewise the great river Mohegan—and how he was
magnificently rewarded by the munificence of their
High Mightinesses.*

In the ever memorable year of our Lord 1609, on the five and
twentieth day of March (O. S.)—a fine Saturday morning, when
jocund Phœbus, having his face newly washed, by gentle dews
and spring time showers, looked from the glorious windows of
the east, with a more than usually shining countenance—"that
worthy and irrecoverable discoverer, Master Henry Hudson" set
sail from Holland in a stout vessel,* called the Half Moon, being
employed by the Dutch East India Company, to seek a north-west
passage to China.

Of this celebrated voyage we have a narration still extant, written with true log-book brevity, by master Robert Juet of Lime
house, mate of the vessel; who was appointed historian of the voyage, partly on account of his uncommon literary talents, but
chiefly, as I am credibly informed, because he was a countryman
and schoolfellow of the great Hudson, with whom he had often
played truant and sailed chip boats, when he was a little boy. I am
enabled however to supply the deficiencies of master Juet's journal, by certain documents furnished me by very respectable Dutch
families, as likewise by sundry family traditions, handed down
from my great great Grandfather, who accompanied the expedition
in the capacity of cabin boy.

From all that I can learn, few incidents worthy of remark happened in the voyage; and it mortifies me exceedingly that I have
to admit so noted an expedition into my work, without making any
more of it.—Oh! that I had the advantages of that most authentic
writer of yore, Apollonius Rhodius, who in his account of the
famous Argonautic expedition, has the whole mythology at his

*Ogilvie calls it a frigate.

disposal, and elevates Jason and his compeers into heroes and demigods; though all the world knows them to have been a meer gang of sheep stealers, on a marauding expedition—or that I had the privileges of Dan Homer and Dan Virgil to enliven my narration, with giants and Lystrigonians; to entertain our honest mariners with an occasional concert of syrens and mermaids, and now and then with the rare shew of honest old Neptune and his fleet of frolicksome cruisers. But alas! the good old times have long gone by, when your waggish deities would descend upon the terraqueous globe, in their own proper persons, and play their pranks, upon its wondering inhabitants. Neptune has proclaimed an embargo in his dominions, and the sturdy tritons, like disbanded sailors, are out of employ, unless old Charon has charitably taken them into his service, to sound their conchs, and ply as his ferrymen. Certain it is, no mention has been made of them by any of our modern navigators, who are not behind their ancient predecessors in tampering with the marvellous—nor has any notice been taken of them, in that most minute and authentic chronicle of the seas, the New York Gazette edited by Solomon Lang. Even Castor and Pollux, those flaming meteors that blaze at the mast-head of tempest tost vessels, are rarely beheld in these degenerate days—and it is but now and then, that our worthy sea captains fall in with that portentous phantom of the seas, that terror to all experienced mariners, that shadowy spectrum of the night—the flying Dutchman!

Suffice it then to say, the voyage was prosperous and tranquil—the crew being a patient people, much given to slumber and vacuity, and but little troubled with the disease of thinking—a malady of the mind, which is the sure breeder of discontent. Hudson had laid in abundance of gin and sour crout, and every man was allowed to sleep quietly at his post, unless the wind blew. True it is, some slight dissatisfaction was shewn on two or three occasions, at certain unreasonable conduct of Commodore Hudson. Thus for instance, he forbore to shorten sail when the wind was light, and the weather serene, which was considered among the most experienced dutch seamen, as certain *weather breeders,* or prognostics, that the weather would change for the worse. He acted, moreover, in direct contradiction to that ancient and sage rule of the dutch navigators, who always took in sail at night—put the helm a-port, and turned in—by which precaution they had a good night's rest—were sure of knowing where they were the next morning, and stood but little chance of running down a continent in the dark. He likewise prohibited the seamen from wearing more than five jackets, and six pair of breeches, under pretence of rendering them more alert; and no man was permitted to go aloft, and hand in sails, with a pipe in his mouth, as is the invariable Dutch custom, at the present day—All these grievances, though they might ruffle for a moment, the constitutional tranquillity of the honest Dutch tars, made but transient impression; they eat hugely, drank profusely, and slept immeasurably, and being under the especial guidance of providence, the ship was safely conducted to the coast of America; where, after sundry unimportant touchings and standings off and on, she at length, on the fourth day of September entered that majestic bay, which at this day expands its ample bosom, before the city of New York, and which had never before been visited by any European.

True it is—and I am not ignorant of the fact, that in a certain apocryphal book of voyages, compiled by one Hacluyt, is to be found a letter written to Francis the First, by one Giovanne, or John Verazzani, on which some writers are inclined to found a belief that this delightful bay had been visited nearly a century previous to the voyage of the enterprizing Hudson. Now this (albeit it has met with the countenance of certain very judicious and learned men) I hold in utter disbelief, and that for various good and substantial reasons—*First*, Because on strict examination it will be found, that the description given by this Verazzani, applies about as well to the bay of New York, as it does to my night cap— *Secondly*, Because that this John Verazzani, for whom I already begin to feel a most bitter enmity, is a native of Florence; and every body knows the crafty wiles of these losel Florentines, by which they filched away the laurels, from the arms of the immortal Colon, (vulgarly called Columbus) and bestowed them on their officious townsman, Amerigo Vespucci—and I make no doubt they are equally ready to rob the illustrious Hudson, of the credit of discovering this beauteous island, adorned by the city of New York, and placing it beside their usurped discovery of South

America. And *thirdly*, I award my decision in favour of the pretensions of Hendrick Hudson, inasmuch as his expedition sailed
from Holland, being truly and absolutely a Dutch enterprize—and
though all the proofs in the world were introduced on the other
side, I would set them at naught as undeserving my attention. If
these three reasons are not sufficient to satisfy every burgher of
this ancient city—all I can say is, they are degenerate descendants
from their venerable Dutch ancestors, and totally unworthy the
trouble of convincing. Thus, therefore, the title of Hendrick Hudson, to his renowned discovery is fully vindicated.

It has been traditionary in our family, that when the great navigator was first blessed with a view of this enchanting island, he
was observed, for the first and only time in his life, to exhibit
strong symptoms of astonishment and admiration. He is said to
have turned to master Juet, and uttered these remarkable words,
while he pointed towards this paradise of the new world—"see!
there!"—and thereupon, as was always his way when he was uncommonly pleased, he did puff out such clouds of dense tobacco
smoke, that in one minute the vessel was out of sight of land, and
master Juet was fain to wait, until the winds dispersed this impenetrable fog.

It was indeed—as my great great grandfather used to say—
though in truth I never heard him, for he died, as might be expected, before I was born.—"It was indeed a spot, on which the
eye might have revelled forever, in ever new and never ending
beauties." The island of Manna-hata, spread wide before them,
like some sweet vision of fancy, or some fair creation of industrious magic. Its hills of smiling green swelled gently one above
another, crowned with lofty trees of luxuriant growth; some
pointing their tapering foliage towards the clouds, which were
gloriously transparent; and others, loaded with a verdant burthen
of clambering vines, bowing their branches to the earth, that was
covered with flowers. On the gentle declivities of the hills were
scattered in gay profusion, the dog wood, the sumach, and the
wild briar, whose scarlet berries and white blossoms glowed
brightly among the deep green of the surrounding foliage; and
here and there, a curling column of smoke rising from the little
glens that opened along the shore, seemed to promise the weary

voyagers, a welcome at the hands of their fellow creatures. As they stood gazing with entranced attention on the scene before them, a red man crowned with feathers, issued from one of these glens, and after contemplating in silent wonder, the gallant ship, as she sat like a stately swan swimming on a silver lake, sounded the war-whoop, and bounded into the woods, like a wild deer, to the utter astonishment of the phlegmatic Dutchmen, who had never heard such a noise, or witnessed such a caper in their whole lives.

Of the transactions of our adventurers with the savages, and how the latter smoked copper pipes, and eat dried currants; how they brought great store of tobacco and oysters; how they shot one of the ship's crew, and how he was buried, I shall say nothing, being that I consider them unimportant to my history. After tarrying a few days in the bay, in order to smoke their pipes and refresh themselves after their seafaring, our voyagers weighed anchor, and adventurously ascended a mighty river which emptied into the bay. This river it is said was known among the savages by the name of the *Shatemuck;* though we are assured in an excellent little history published in 1674, by John Josselyn, Gent. that it was called the *Mohegan,** and master Richard Blome, who wrote some time afterwards, asserts the same—so that I very much incline in favour of the opinion of these two honest gentlemen. Be this as it may, the river is at present denominated the Hudson; and up this stream the shrewd Hendrick had very little doubt he should discover the much looked for passage to China!

The journal goes on to make mention of divers interviews between the crew and the natives, in the voyage up the river, but as they would be impertinent to my history, I shall pass them over in silence, except the following dry joke, played off by the old commodore and his school-fellow Robert Juet; which does such vast credit to their experimental philosophy, that I cannot refrain from inserting it. "Our master and his mate determined to try some of the chiefe men of the countrey, whether they had any treacherie

*This river is likewise laid down in Ogilvy's map as Manhattan—Noordt—Montaigne and Mauritius river.

in them. So they tooke them downe into the cabin and gave them so much wine and aqua vitæ that they were all merrie; and one of them had his wife with him, which sate so modestly, as any of our countrey women would do in a strange place. In the end, one of them was drunke, which had been aboarde of our ship all the time that we had beene there, and that was strange to them, for they could not tell how to take it."*

Having satisfied himself by this profound experiment, that the natives were an honest, social race of jolly roysters, who had no objection to a drinking bout, and were very merry in their cups, the old commodore chuckled hugely to himself, and thrusting a double quid of tobacco in his cheek, directed master Juet to have it carefully recorded, for the satisfaction of all the natural philosophers of the university of Leyden—which done, he proceeded on his voyage, with great self-complacency. After sailing, however, above an hundred miles up the river, he found the watery world around him, began to grow more shallow and confined, the current more rapid and perfectly fresh—phenomena not uncommon in the ascent of rivers, but which puzzled the honest dutchmen prodigiously. A consultation of our modern Argonauts was therefore called, and having deliberated full six hours, they were brought to a determination, by the ship's running aground— whereupon they unanimously concluded, that there was but little chance of getting to China in this direction. A boat, however, was dispatched to explore higher up the river, which on its return, confirmed the opinion—upon this the ship was warped off and put about, with great difficulty, being like most of her sex, exceedingly hard to govern; and the adventurous Hudson, according to the account of my great great grandfather, returned down the river—with a prodigious flea in his ear!

Being satisfied that there was little likelihood of getting to China, unless like the blind man, he returned from whence he sat out and took a fresh start; he forthwith re-crossed the sea to Holland, where he was received with great welcome by the honourable East-India company, who were very much rejoiced to see him come back safe—with their ship; and at a large and respectable meeting of the first merchants and burgomasters of Amsterdam,

*Juet's Journ. Purch. Pil.

it was unanimously determined, that as a munificent reward for the eminent services he had performed, and the important discovery he had made, the great river Mohegan should be called after his name!—and it continues to be called Hudson river unto this very day.

CHAPTER II

*Containing an account of a mighty Ark which floated, under
the protection of St. Nicholas, from Holland to Gibbet
Island—the descent of the strange Animals therefrom—
a great victory, and a description of the ancient village
of Communipaw.*

The delectable accounts given by the great Hudson, and Master
Juet, of the country they had discovered, excited not a little talk
and speculation among the good people of Holland.—Letters patent were granted by government to an association of merchants,
called the West-India company, for the exclusive trade on Hudson river, on which they erected a trading house called Fort Aurania, or Orange, at present the superb and hospitable city of
Albany. But I forbear to dwell on the various commercial and colonizing enterprizes which took place; among which was that of
Mynheer Adrian Block, who discovered and gave a name to Block
Island, since famous for its cheese—and shall barely confine myself to that, which gave birth to this renowned city.

It was some three or four years after the return of the immortal Hendrick, that a crew of honest, well meaning, copper headed,
low dutch colonists set sail from the city of Amsterdam, for the
shores of America. It is an irreparable loss to history, and a great
proof of the darkness of the age, and the lamentable neglect of
the noble art of bookmaking, since so industriously cultivated by
knowing sea-captains, and spruce super-cargoes, that an expedition so interesting and important in its results, should have been
passed over in utter silence. To my great great grandfather am I
again indebted, for the few facts, I am enabled to give concerning
it—he having once more embarked for this country, with a full
determination, as he said, of ending his days here—and of beget-
ting a race of Knickerbockers, that should rise to be great men in
the land.

The ship in which these illustrious adventurers set sail was called
the *Goede Vrouw*, or Good Woman, in compliment to the wife
of the President of the West India Company, who was allowed by

every body (except her husband) to be a singularly sweet tempered lady, when not in liquor. It was in truth a gallant vessel, of the most approved dutch construction, and made by the ablest ship carpenters of Amsterdam, who it is well known, always model their ships after the fair forms of their country women. Accordingly it had one hundred feet in the keel, one hundred feet in the beam, and one hundred feet from the bottom of the stern post, to the tafferel. Like the beauteous model, who was declared the greatest belle in Amsterdam, it was full in the bows, with a pair of enormous cat-heads, a copper bottom, and withal, a most prodigious poop!

The architect, who was somewhat of a religious man, far from decorating the ship with pagan idols, such as Jupiter, Neptune, or Hercules (which heathenish abominations, I have no doubt, occasion the misfortunes and shipwreck of many a noble vessel) he I say, on the contrary, did laudably erect for a head, a goodly image of St. Nicholas, equipped with a low, broad brimmed hat, a huge pair of Flemish trunk hose, and a pipe that reached to the end of the bow-sprit. Thus gallantly furnished, the staunch ship floated sideways, like a majestic goose, out of the harbour of the great city of Amsterdam, and all the bells, that were not otherwise engaged, rung a triple bob-major on the joyful occasion.

My great great grandfather remarks, that the voyage was uncommonly prosperous, for being under the especial care of the ever-revered St. Nicholas, the Goede Vrouw seemed to be endowed with qualities, unknown to common vessels. Thus she made as much lee-way as head-way, could get along very nearly as fast with the wind a-head, as when it was a-poop—and was particularly great in a calm; in consequence of which singular advantages, she made out to accomplish her voyage in a very few months, and came to anchor at the mouth of the Hudson, a little to the east of Gibbet Island.*

Here lifting up their eyes, they beheld, on what is at present called the Jersey shore, a small Indian village, pleasantly embowered in a grove of spreading elms, and the natives all collected on the beach, gazing in stupid admiration at the Goede Vrouw. A boat was immediately dispatched to enter into a treaty with

*So called, because one Joseph Andrews, a pirate and murderer, was hanged in chains on that Island, the 23d May, 1769. EDITOR.

them, and approaching the shore, hailed them through a trumpet, in the most friendly terms; but so horribly confounded were these poor savages at the tremendous and uncouth sound of the low dutch language, that they one and all took to their heels, scampered over the Bergen hills, nor did they stop until they had buried themselves, head and ears, in the marshes, on the other side, where they all miserably perished to a man—and their bones being collected, and decently covered by the Tammany Society of that day, formed that singular mound, called *Rattle-snake-hill,* which rises out of the centre of the salt marshes, a little to the east of the Newark Causeway.

Animated by this unlooked-for victory our valiant heroes sprang ashore in triumph, took possession of the soil as conquerors in the name of their High Mightinesses the lords states general, and marching fearlessly forward, carried the village of *Communipaw* by storm—having nobody to withstand them, but some half a score of old squaws, and poppooses, whom they tortured to death with low dutch. On looking about them they were so transported with the excellencies of the place, that they had very little doubt, the blessed St. Nicholas, had guided them thither, as the very spot whereon to settle their colony. The softness of the soil was wonderfully adapted to the driving of piles; the swamps and marshes around them afforded ample opportunities for the constructing of dykes and dams; the shallowness of the shore was peculiarly favourable to the building of docks—in a word, this spot abounded with all the singular inconveniences, and aquatic obstacles, necessary for the foundation of a great dutch city. On making a faithful report therefore, to the crew of the Goede Vrouw, they one and all determined that this was the destined end of their voyage. Accordingly they descended from the Goede Vrouw, men women and children, in goodly groups, as did the animals of yore from the ark, and formed themselves into a thriving settlement, which they called by the Indian name *Communipaw.*

As all the world is perfectly acquainted with Communipaw, it may seem somewhat superfluous to treat of it in the present work; but my readers will please to recollect, that notwithstanding it is my chief desire to improve the present age, yet I write likewise for posterity, and have to consult the understanding and curiosity of some half a score of centuries yet to come; by which

time perhaps, were it not for this invaluable history, the great
Communipaw, like Babylon, Carthage, Nineveh and other great
cities, might be perfectly extinct—sunk and forgotten in its own
mud—its inhabitants turned into oysters,* and even its situation
a fertile subject of learned controversy and hardheaded investigation among indefatigable historians. Let me then piously rescue
from oblivion, the humble reliques of a place, which was the egg
from whence was hatched the mighty city of New York!

Communipaw is at present but a small village, pleasantly situated among rural scenery, on that beauteous part of the Jersey
shore which was known in ancient legends by the name of Pavonia, and commands a grand prospect of the superb bay of New
York. It is within but half an hour's sail of the latter place, provided you have a fair wind, and may be distinctly seen from the
city. Nay, it is a well known fact, which I can testify from my
own experience, that on a clear still summer evening, you may
hear, from the battery of New York, the obstreperous peals of
broad-mouthed laughter of the dutch negroes at Communipaw,
who, like most other negroes, are famous for their risible powers.
This is peculiarly the case on Sunday evenings; when, it is remarked
by an ingenious and observant philosopher, who has made great
discoveries in the neighbourhood of this city, that they always
laugh loudest—which he attributes to the circumstance of their
having their holliday clothes on.

These negroes, in fact, like the monks in the dark ages, engross
all the knowledge of the place, and being infinitely more adventurous and more knowing than their masters, carry on all the
foreign trade; making frequent voyages to town in canoes loaded
with oysters, buttermilk and cabbages. They are great astrologers, predicting the different changes of weather almost as accurately as an almanack—they are moreover exquisite performers
on three stringed fiddles: in whistling they almost boast the far-
famed powers of Orpheus his lyre, for not a horse or an ox in
the place, when at the plow or in the waggon, will budge a foot
until he hears the well known whistle of his black driver and
companion.—And from their amazing skill at casting up accounts
upon their fingers, they are regarded with as much veneration as

* "Men by inaction degenerate into Oysters." Kaimes.

were the disciples of Pythagoras of yore, when initiated into the sacred quaternary of numbers.

As to the honest dutch burghers of Communipaw, like wise men, and sound philosophers, they never look beyond their pipes, nor trouble their heads about any affairs out of their immediate neighbourhood; so that they live in profound and enviable ignorance of all the troubles, anxieties and revolutions, of this distracted planet. I am even told that many among them do verily believe that Holland, of which they have heard so much from tradition, is situated somewhere on Long-Island—that *Spiking-devil* and *the Narrows* are the two ends of the world—that the country is still under the dominion of their high mightinesses, and that the city of New York still goes by the name of Nieuw Amsterdam. They meet every saturday afternoon, at the only tavern in the place, which bears as a sign, a square headed likeness of the prince of Orange; where they smoke a silent pipe, by way of promoting social conviviality, and invariably drink a mug of cider to the success of admiral Von Tromp, who they imagine is still sweeping the British channel, with a broom at his mast head.

Communipaw, in short, is one of the numerous little villages in the vicinity of this most beautiful of cities, which are so many strong holds and fastnesses, whither the primitive manners of our dutch forefathers have retreated, and where they are cherished with devout and scrupulous strictness. The dress of the original settlers is handed down inviolate, from father to son—the identical broad brimmed hat, broad skirted coat and broad bottomed breeches, continue from generation to generation, and several gigantic knee buckles of massy silver, are still in wear, that made such gallant display in the days of the patriarchs of Communipaw. The language likewise, continues unadulterated by barbarous innovations; and so critically correct is the village school-master in his dialect, that his reading of a low dutch psalm, has much the same effect on the nerves, as the filing of a hand saw.

CHAPTER III

*In which is set forth the true art of making a bargain,
together with a miraculous escape of a great Metropolis in a
fog—and how certain adventurers departed from
Communipaw on a perilous colonizing expedition.*

Having, in the trifling digression with which I concluded my last
chapter, discharged the filial duty, which the city of New York
owes to Communipaw, as being the mother settlement; and having given a faithful picture of it as it stands at present, I return,
with a soothing sentiment of self-approbation, to dwell upon its
early history. The crew of the Goede Vrouw being soon reinforced by fresh importations from Holland, the settlement went
jollily on, increasing in magnitude and prosperity. The neighbouring Indians in a short time became accustomed to the uncouth sound of the dutch language, and an intercourse gradually
took place between them and the new comers. The Indians were
much given to long talks, and the Dutch to long silence—in this
particular therefore, they accommodated each other completely.
The chiefs would make long speeches about the big bull, the wa-
bash and the great spirit, to which the others would listen very
attentively, smoke their pipes and grunt *yah. myn-her*—whereat
the poor savages were wonderously delighted. They instructed
the new settlers in the best art of curing and smoking tobacco,
while the latter in return, made them drunk with true Hollands—
and then learned them the art of making bargains.

A brisk trade for furs was soon opened: the dutch traders were
scrupulously honest in their dealings, and purchased by weight,
establishing it as an invariable table of avoirdupoise, that the
hand of a dutchman weighed one pound, and his foot two
pounds. It is true, the simple Indians were often puzzled at the
great disproportion between bulk and weight, for let them place
a bundle of furs, never so large, in one scale, and a dutchman put
his hand or foot in the other, the bundle was sure to kick the

beam—never was a package of furs known to weigh more than two pounds, in the market of Communipaw!

This is a singular fact—but I have it direct from my great great grandfather, who had risen to considerable importance in the colony, being promoted to the office of weigh master, on account of the uncommon heaviness of his foot.

The Dutch possessions in this part of the globe began now to assume a very thriving appearance, and were comprehended under the general title of Nieuw Nederlandts, on account, no doubt, of their great resemblance to the Dutch Netherlands—excepting that the former were rugged and mountainous, and the latter level and marshy. About this time the tranquility of the dutch colonists was doomed to suffer a temporary interruption. In 1614, captain Sir Samuel Argal, sailing under a commission from Dale, governor of Virginia, visited the dutch settlements on Hudson river, and demanded their submission to the English crown and Virginian dominion.—To this arrogant demand, as they were in no condition to resist it, they submitted for the time, like discreet and reasonable men.

It does not appear that the valiant Argal molested the settlement of Communipaw; on the contrary, I am told that when his vessel first hove in sight the worthy burghers were seized with such a panic, that they fell to smoking their pipes with astonishing vehemence; insomuch that they quickly raised a cloud, which combining with the surrounding woods and marshes, completely enveloped and concealed their beloved village; and overhung the fair regions of Pavonia—So that the terrible captain Argal passed on, totally unsuspicious that a sturdy little Dutch settlement lay snugly couched in the mud, under cover of all this pestilent vapour. In commemoration of this fortunate escape, the worthy inhabitants have continued to smoke, almost without intermission, unto this very day; which is said to be the cause of the remarkable fog that often hangs over Communipaw of a clear afternoon.

Upon the departure of the enemy, our magnanimous ancestors took full six months to recover their wind, having been exceedingly discomposed by the consternation and hurry of affairs. They then called a council of safety to smoke over the state of the province. After six months more of mature deliberation, during which nearly five hundred words were spoken, and almost as much tobacco was smoked, as would have served a certain modern general through a whole winter's campaign of hard drinking, it was determined, to fit out an armament of canoes, and dispatch them on a voyage of discovery; to search if peradventure some more sure and formidable position might not be found, where the colony would be less subject to vexatious visitations.

This perilous enterprize was entrusted to the superintendance of Mynheers Oloffe Van Kortlandt, Abraham Hardenbroek, Jacobus Van Zandt and Winant Ten Broek—four indubitably great men, but of whose history, though I have made diligent enquiry, I can learn but little, previous to their leaving Holland. Nor need this occasion much surprize; for adventurers, like prophets, though they make great noise abroad, have seldom much celebrity in their own countries; but this much is certain, that the overflowings and off scourings of a country, are invariably composed of the richest parts of the soil. And here I cannot help remarking how convenient it would be to many of our great men and great families of doubtful origin, could they have the privilege of the heroes of yore, who, whenever their origin was involved in obscurity, modestly announced themselves descended from a god—and who never visited a foreign country, but what they told some cock and bull stories, about their being kings and princes at home. This venial trespass on the truth, though it has occasionally been played off by some pseudo marquis, baronet, and other illustrious foreigner, in our land of good natured credulity, has been completely discountenanced in this sceptical, matter of fact age—And I even question whether any tender virgin, who was accidentally and unaccountably enriched with a bantling, would save her character at parlour fire-sides and evening tea-parties, by ascribing the phenomenon to a swan, a shower of gold or a river god.

Thus being totally denied the benefit of mythology and classic fable, I should have been completely at a loss as to the early biography of my heroes, had not a gleam of light been thrown upon their origin from their names.

By this simple means have I been enabled to gather some particulars, concerning the adventurers in question. Van Kortlandt for instance, was one of those peripatetic philosophers, who tax providence for a livelihood, and like Diogenes, enjoy a free and unincumbered estate in sunshine. He was usually arrayed in garments suitable to his fortune, being curiously fringed and fangled by the hand of time; and was helmeted with an old fragment of a hat which had acquired the shape of a sugar-loaf; and so far did he carry his contempt for the adventitious distinction of dress, that it is said, the remnant of a shirt, which covered his back, and dangled like a pocket handkerchief out of a hole in his breeches, was never washed, except by the bountiful showers of heaven. In this garb was he usually to be seen, sunning himself at noon day, with a herd of philosophers of the same sect, on the side of the great canal of Amsterdam. Like your nobility of Europe, he took his name of *Kortlandt* (or *lack land*) from his landed estate, which lay some where in Terra incognita.

Of the next of our worthies, might I have had the benefit of mythological assistance, the want of which I have just lamented—I should have made honourable mention, as boasting equally illustrious pedigree, with the proudest hero of antiquity. His name was *Van Zandt*, which freely translated, signifies *from the dirt,* meaning, beyond a doubt, that like Triptolemus, Themis—the Cyclops and the Titans, he sprung from dame Terra or the earth! This supposition is strongly corroborated by his size, for it is well known that all the progeny of mother earth were of a gigantic stature; and Van Zandt, we are told, was a tall raw-boned man, above six feet high—with an astonishingly hard head. Nor is this origin of the illustrious Van Zandt a whit more improbable or repugnant to belief, than what is related and universally admitted of certain of our greatest, or rather richest men; who we are told, with the utmost gravity, did originally spring from a dung-hill!

Of the third hero, but a faint description has reached to this time, which mentions, that he was a sturdy, obstinate, burley, bustling little man; and from being usually equipped with an old pair of buck-skins, was familiarly dubbed Harden broek, or *Tough Breeches*.

Ten Broek completed this junto of adventurers. It is a singular but ludicrous fact, which, were I not scrupulous in recording the whole truth, I should almost be tempted to pass over in silence, as incompatible with the gravity and dignity of my history, that this worthy gentleman should likewise have been nicknamed from the most whimsical part of his dress. In fact, the small clothes seems to have been a very important garment in the eyes of our venerated ancestors, owing in all probability to its really being the largest article of raiment among them. The name of Ten Broek, or Tin Broek is indifferently translated into Ten Breeches and Tin Breeches—the high dutch commentators incline to the former opinion; and ascribe it to his being the first who introduced into the settlement the ancient dutch fashion of wearing ten pair of breeches. But the most elegant and ingenious writers on the subject, declare in favour of Tin, or rather *Thin* Breeches; from whence they infer, that he was a poor, but merry rogue, whose galligaskins were none of the soundest, and who was the identical author of that truly philosophical stanza:

> "Then why should we quarrel for riches,
>   Or any such glittering toys;
>   A light heart and *thin pair of breeches*,
>   Will go thorough the world my brave boys!"

Such was the gallant junto that fearlessly set sail at the head of a mighty armament of canoes, to explore the yet unknown country about the mouth of the Hudson—and heaven seemed to shine propitious on their undertaking.

It was that delicious season of the year, when nature, breaking from the chilling thraldom of old winter, like a blooming damsel, from the tyranny of a sordid old hunks of a father, threw herself blushing with ten thousand charms, into the arms, of youthful spring. Every tufted copse and blooming grove resounded with the notes of hymeneal love; the very insects as they sipped the morning dew, that gemmed the tender grass of the meadows, lifted up their little voices to join the joyous epithalamium—the virgin bud timidly put forth its blushes, and the heart of man dissolved away in tenderness. Oh sweet Theocritus! had I thy oaten reed, wherewith thou erst didst charm the gay Sicilian plains; or oh gentle Bion! thy pastoral pipe, in which the happy swains of the Lesbian isle so much delighted; then would I attempt to sing, in soft Bucolic or negligent Idyllium, the rural beauties of the scene—But having nothing but this jaded goose quill, wherewith to wing my flight, I must fain content myself to lay aside these poetic disportings of the fancy and pursue my faithful narrative in humble prose—

comforting myself with the reflection, that though it may not commend itself so sweetly to the imagination of my reader, yet will it insinuate itself with virgin modesty, to his better judgment, clothed as it is in the chaste and simple garb of truth.

In the joyous season of spring then, did these hardy adventurers depart on this eventful expedition, which only wanted another Virgil to rehearse it, to equal the oft sung story of the Eneid— Many adventures did they meet with and divers bitter mishaps did they sustain, in their wanderings from Communipaw to oyster Island—from oyster Island to gibbet island, from gibbet island to governors island, and from governors island through buttermilk channel, (a second streights of Pylorus) to the Lord knows where; until they came very nigh being ship wrecked and lost forever, in the tremendous vortexes of *Hell gate,** which for terrors, and frightful perils, might laugh old Scylla and Charybdis to utter scorn—In all which cruize they encountered as many Lystrigonians and Cyclops and Syrens and unhappy Didos, as did ever the pious Eneas, in his colonizing voyage.

At length, after wandering to and fro, they were attracted by the transcendant charms of a vast island, which lay like a gorgeous stomacher, dividing the beauteous bosom of the bay, and to which the numerous mighty islands among which they had been wandering, seemed as so many foils and appendages. Hither they bent their course, and old Neptune, as if anxious to assist in the choice of a spot, whereon was to be founded a city that should serve as his strong hold in this western world, sent half a dozen potent billows, that rolled the canoes of our voyagers, high and dry on the very point of the island, where at present stands the delectable city of New York.

---

*This is a fearful combination of rocks and whirlpools, in the sound above New York, dangerous to ships unless under the care of a skillful pilot. Certain wise men who instruct these modern days have softened this characteristic name into *Hurl gate,* on what authority, I leave them to explain. The name as given by our author is supported by Ogilvie's History of America published 1671, as also by a journal still extant, written in the 16th century, and to be found in Hazard's state papers. The original name, as laid down in all the Dutch manuscripts and maps, was *Helle gat,* and an old MS. written in French, speaking of various alterations in names about this city observes "De *Helle gat* trou d'Enfer, ils ont fait *Hell gate,* Porte d'Enfer."—Printer's Devil.

The original name of this beautiful island is in some dispute, and has already undergone a vitiation, which is a proof of the melancholy instability of sublunary things, and of the industrious perversions of modern orthographers. The name which is most current among the vulgar (such as members of assembly and bank directors) is *Manhattan*—which is said to have originated from a custom among the squaws, in the early settlement, of wearing men's wool hats, as is still done among many tribes. "Hence," we are told by an old governor, somewhat of a wag, who flourished almost a century since, and had paid a visit to the wits of Philadelphia—"Hence arose the appellation of Man-hat-on, first given to the Indians, and afterwards to the island"—a stupid joke!—but well enough for a governor.

Among the more ancient authorities which deserve very serious consideration, is that contained in the valuable history of the American possessions, written by master Richard Blome in 1687, wherein it is called *Manhadaes*, or *Manahanent*; nor must I forget the excellent little book of that authentic historian, John Josselyn, Gent. who explicitly calls it *Manadaes*.

But an authority still more ancient, and still more deserving of credit, because it is sanctioned by the countenance of our venerated dutch ancestors, is that founded on certain letters still extant, which passed between the early governors, and their neighbour powers; wherein it is variously called the Monhattoes, Munhatos and Manhattoes—an unimportant variation, occasioned by the literati of those days having a great contempt for those spelling book and dictionary researches, which form the sole study and ambition of so many learned men and women of the present times. This name is said to be derived from the great Indian spirit Manetho, who was supposed to have made this island his favourite residence, on account of its uncommon delights. But the most venerable and indisputable authority extant, and one on which I place implicit confidence, because it confers a name at once melodious, poetical and significant, is that furnished by the before quoted journal of the voyage of the great Hudson, by Master Juet; who clearly and correctly calls it MANNA-HATA—that is to say, the island of Manna; or in other words—"a land flowing with milk and honey!"

CHAPTER IV

In which are contained divers very sound reasons why a man should not write in a hurry: together with the building of New Amsterdam, and the memorable dispute of Mynheers Ten Breeches and Tough Breeches thereupon.

My great grandfather, by the mother's side, Hermanus Van Clattercop, when employed to build the large stone church at Rotterdam, which stands about three hundred yards to your left, after you turn off from the Boomkeys, and which is so conveniently constructed, that all the zealous Christians of Rotterdam prefer sleeping through a sermon there, to any other church in the city—My great grandfather, I say, when employed to build that famous church, did in the first place send to Delft for a box of long pipes; then having purchased a new spitting box and a hundred weight of the best Virginia, he sat himself down, and did nothing for the space of three months, but smoke most laboriously. Then did he spend full three months more in trudging on foot, and voyaging in Trekschuit, from Rotterdam to Amsterdam—to Delft—to Haerlem—to Leyden—to the Hague, knocking his head and breaking his pipe, against every church in his road. Then did he advance gradually, nearer and nearer to Rotterdam, until he came in full sight of the identical spot, whereon the church was to be built. Then did he spend three months longer in walking round it and round it; contemplating it, first from one point of view, and then from another—now would he be paddled by it on the canal—now would he peep at it through a telescope, from the other side of the Meuse, and now would he take a bird's eye glance at it, from the top of one of those gigantic wind mills, which protect the gates of the city. The good folks of the place were on the tiptoe of expectation and impatience—notwithstanding all the turmoil of my great grandfather, not a symptom of the church was yet to be seen; they even began to fear it would never be brought into the world, but that its great projector would lie down, and die in labour, of the

mighty plan he had conceived. At length, having occupied twelve
good months in puffing and paddling, and talking and walking—
having travelled over all Holland, and even taken a peep into
France and Germany—having smoked five hundred and ninety-
nine pipes, and three hundred weight of the best Virginia tobacco; my great grandfather gathered together all that knowing
and industrious class of citizens, who prefer attending to any
body's business sooner than their own, and having pulled off his
coat and five pair of breeches, he advanced sturdily up, and laid
the corner stone of the church, in the presence of the whole
multitude—just at the commencement of the thirteenth month.

In a similar manner and with the example of my worthy ancestor full before my eyes, have I proceeded in writing this most authentic history. The honest Rotterdammers no doubt thought my
great grandfather was doing nothing at all to the purpose, while
he was making such a world of prefatory bustle, about the building
of his church—and many of the ingenious inhabitants of this fair
city, (whose intellects have been thrice stimulated and quickened,
by transcendant nitrous oxyde, as were those of Chrysippus, with
hellebore,) will unquestionably suppose that all the preliminary
chapters, with the discovery, population and final settlement of
America, were totally irrelevant and superfluous—and that the
main business, the history of New York, is not a jot more advanced, than if I had never taken up my pen. Never were wise
people more mistaken in their conjectures; in consequence of going to work slowly and deliberately, the church came out of my
grandfather's hands, one of the most sumptuous, goodly and glorious edifices in the known world—excepting, that, like our transcendant capital at Washington, it was begun on such a grand
scale, the good folks could not afford to finish more than the wing
of it.

In the same manner do I prognosticate, if ever I am enabled to
finish this history, (of which in simple truth, I often have my
doubts,) that it will be handed down to posterity, the most complete, faithful, and critically constructed work that ever was
read—the delight of the learned, the ornament of libraries, and a
model for all future historians. There is nothing that gives such an
expansion of mind, as the idea of writing for posterity—And had
Ovid, Herodotus, Polybius or Tacitus, like Moses from the top of

Mount Pisgah, taken a view of the boundless region over which their offspring were destined to wander—like the good old Israelite, they would have lain down and died contented.

I hear some of my captious readers questioning the correctness of my arrangement—but I have no patience with these continual interruptions—never was historian so pestered with doubts and queries, and such a herd of discontented quid-nuncs! if they continue to worry me in this manner, I shall never get to the end of my work. I call Apollo and his whole seraglio of muses to witness, that I pursue the most approved and fashionable plan of modern historians; and if my readers are not pleased with my matter, and my manner, for God's sake let them throw down my work, take up a pen and write a history to suit themselves—for my part I am weary of their incessant interruptions, and beg once for all, that I may have no more of them.

The island of Manna-hata, Manhattoes, or as it is vulgarly called Manhattan, having been discovered, as was related in the last chapter; and being unanimously pronounced by the discoverers, the fairest spot in the known world, whereon to build a city, that should surpass all the emporiums of Europe, they immediately returned to Communipaw with the pleasing intelligence. Upon this a considerable colony was forthwith fitted out, who after a prosperous voyage of half an hour, arrived at Manna hata, and having previously purchased the land of the Indians, (a measure almost unparalleled in the annals of discovery and colonization) they settled upon the south-west point of the island, and fortified themselves strongly, by throwing up a mud battery, which they named FORT AMSTERDAM. A number of huts soon sprung up in the neighbourhood, to protect which, they made an enclosure of strong pallisadoes. A creek running from the East river, through what at present is called Whitehall street, and a little inlet from Hudson river to the bowling green formed the original boundaries; as though nature had kindly designated the cradle, in which the embryo of this renowned city was to be nestled. The woods on both sides of the creek were carefully cleared away, as well as from the space of ground now occupied by the bowling green.— These precautions were taken to protect the fort from either the open attacks or insidious advances of its savage neighbours, who wandered in hordes about the forests and swamps that extended over those tracts of country, at present called broad way, Wall street, William street and Pearl street.

No sooner was the colony once planted, than like a luxuriant vine, it took root and throve amazingly; for it would seem, that this thrice favoured island is like a munificent dung hill, where every thing finds kindly nourishment, and soon shoots up and expands to greatness. The thriving state of the settlement, and the astonishing encrease of houses, gradually awakened the leaders from a profound lethargy, into which they had fallen, after having built their mud fort. They began to think it was high time some plan should be devised, on which the encreasing town should be built; so taking pipe in mouth, and meeting in close divan, they forthwith fell into a profound deliberation on the subject.

At the very outset of the business, an unexpected difference of opinion arose, and I mention it with regret, as being the first internal altercation on record among the new settlers. An ingenious plan was proposed by Mynheer Ten Broek to cut up and intersect the ground by means of canals; after the manner of the most admired cities in Holland; but to this Mynheer Hardenbroek was diametrically opposed; suggesting in place thereof, that they should run out docks and wharves, by means of piles driven into the bottom of the river, on which the town should be built—By this means said he triumphantly, shall we rescue a considerable space of territory from these immense rivers, and build a city that shall rival Amsterdam, Venice, or any amphibious city in Europe. To this proposition, Ten Broek (or Ten breeches) replied, with a look of as much scorn as he could possibly assume. He cast the utmost censure upon the plan of his antagonist, as being preposterous, and against the very order of things, as he would leave to every true hollander. "For what," said he, "is a town without canals?—it is like a body without veins and arteries, and must perish for want of a free circulation of the vital fluid"—Tough breeches, on the contrary, retorted with a sarcasm upon his antagonist, who was somewhat of an arid, dry boned habit of body; he remarked that as to the circulation of the blood being necessary to existence, Mynheer Ten breeches was a living contradiction to his own assertion; for every body knew there had not a drop of blood circulated through his wind dried carcass for good ten years, and yet there was not a greater busy body in the whole

colony. Personalities have seldom much effect in making con-
verts in argument—nor have I ever seen a man convinced of error,
by being convicted of deformity. At least such was not the case
at present. Ten Breeches was very acrimonious in reply, and
Tough Breeches, who was a sturdy little man, and never gave up
the last word, rejoined with encreasing spirit—Ten Breeches had
the advantage of the greatest volubility, but Tough Breeches had
that invaluable coat of mail in argument called obstinacy—Ten
Breeches had, therefore, the most mettle, but Tough Breeches the
best bottom—so that though Ten Breeches made a dreadful clattering about his ears, and battered and belaboured him with hard
words and sound arguments, yet Tough Breeches hung on most
resolutely to the last. They parted therefore, as is usual in all arguments where both parties are in the right, without coming to
any conclusion—but they hated each other most heartily forever
after, and a similar breach with that between the houses of Capu-
let and Montague, had well nigh ensued between the families of
Ten Breeches and Tough Breeches.

I would not fatigue my reader with these dull matters of fact,
but that my duty as a faithful historian, requires that I should
be particular—and in truth, as I am now treating of the critical
period, when our city, like a young twig, first received the twists
and turns, that have since contributed to give it the present picturesque irregularity for which it is celebrated, I cannot be too
minute in detailing their first causes.

After the unhappy altercation I have just mentioned, I do not
find that any thing further was said on the subject, worthy of being recorded. The council, consisting of the largest and oldest
heads in the community, met regularly once a week, to ponder on
this momentous subject.—But either they were deterred by the
war of words they had witnessed, or they were naturally averse
to the exercise of the tongue, and the consequent exercise of the
brains—certain it is, the most profound silence was maintained—
the question as usual lay on the table—the members quietly
smoked their pipes, making but few laws, without ever enforcing
any, and in the mean time the affairs of the settlement went
on—as it pleased God.

As most of the council were but little skilled in the mystery of
combining pot hooks and hangers, they determined most judi-

ciously not to puzzle either themselves or posterity, with voluminous records. The secretary however, kept the minutes of each
meeting with tolerable precision, in a large vellum folio, fastened
with massy brass clasps, with a sight of which I have been politely
favoured by my highly respected friends, the Goelets, who have
this invaluable relique, at present in their possession. On perusal,
however, I do not find much information—The journal of each
meeting consists but of two lines, stating in dutch, that, "the
council sat this day, and smoked twelve pipes, on the affairs of the
colony."—By which it appears that the first settlers did not regulate their time by hours, but pipes, in the same manner as they
measure distances in Holland at this very time; an admirably exact measurement, as a pipe in the mouth of a genuine dutchman is
never liable to those accidents and irregularities, that are continually putting our clocks out of order.

In this manner did the profound council of NEW AMSTERDAM
smoke, and doze, and ponder, from week to week, month to
month, and year to year, in what manner they should construct
their infant settlement—mean while, the town took care of itself,
and like a sturdy brat which is suffered to run about wild, un-
shackled by clouts and bandages, and other abominations by
which your notable nurses and sage old women cripple and disfigure the children of men, encreased so rapidly in strength and
magnitude, that before the honest burgomasters had determined
upon a plan, it was too late to put it in execution—whereupon
they wisely abandoned the subject altogether.

CHAPTER V

In which the Author is very unreasonably afflicted about nothing.—Together with divers Anecdotes of the prosperity of New Amsterdam, and the wisdom of its Inhabitants.— And the sudden introduction of a Great Man.

Grievous, and very much to be commiserated, is the task of the feeling historian, who writes the history of his native land. If it falls to his lot to be the sad recorder of calamity or crime, the mournful page is watered with his tears—nor can he recal the most prosperous and blissful eras, without a melancholy sigh at the reflection, that they have passed away forever! I know not whether it be owing to an immoderate love for the simplicity of former times, or to a certain tenderness of heart, natural to a sentimental historian; but I candidly confess, I cannot look back on the halcyon days of the city, which I now describe, without a deep dejection of the spirits. With faultering hand I withdraw the curtain of oblivion, which veils the modest merits of our venerable dutch ancestors, and as their revered figures rise to my mental vision, humble myself before the mighty shades.

Such too are my feelings when I revisit the family mansion of the Knickerbockers and spend a lonely hour in the attic chamber, where hang the portraits of my forefathers, shrouded in dust like the forms they represent. With pious reverence do I gaze on the countenances of those renowned burghers, who have preceded me in the steady march of existence—whose sober and temperate blood now meanders through my veins, flowing slower and slower in its feeble conduits, until its lingering current shall soon be stopped forever!

These, say I to myself, are but frail memorials of the mighty men, who flourished in the days of the patriarchs; but who, alas, have long since mouldered in that tomb, towards which my steps are insensibly and irresistibly hastening! As I pace the darkened chamber and lose myself in melancholy musings, the shadowy images around me, almost seem to steal once more into existence—

their countenances appear for an instant to assume the animation of life—their eyes to pursue me in every movement! carried away by the delusion of fancy, I almost imagine myself surrounded by the shades of the departed, and holding sweet converse with the worthies of antiquity!—Luckless Diedrich! born in a degenerate age—abandoned to the buffettings of fortune—a stranger and a weary pilgrim in thy native land; blest with no weeping wife, nor family of helpless children—but doomed to wander neglected through those crowded streets, and elbowed by foreign upstarts from those fair abodes, where once thine ancestors held sovereign empire. Alas! alas! is then the dutch spirit forever extinct? The days of the patriarchs, have they fled forever? Return—return sweet days of simplicity and ease—dawn once more on the lovely island of Manna hata!—Bear with me my worthy readers, bear with the weakness of my nature—or rather let us sit down together, indulge the full flow of filial piety, and weep over the memories of our great great grandfathers.

Having thus gratified those feelings irresistibly awakened by the happy scenes I am describing, I return with more composure to my history.

The town of New Amsterdam, being, as I before mentioned, left to its own course and the fostering care of providence, increased as rapidly in importance, as though it had been burthened with a dozen panniers full of those sage laws, which are usually heaped upon the backs of young cities—in order to make them grow. The only measure that remains on record of the worthy council, was to build a chapel within the fort, which they dedicated to the great and good St. Nicholas, who immediately took the infant town of New Amsterdam under his peculiar patronage, and has ever since been, and I devoutly hope will ever be, the tutelar saint of this excellent city. I am moreover told, that there is a little legendary book somewhere extant, written in low dutch, which says that the image of this renowned saint, which whilome graced the bowsprit of the Goede Vrouw, was placed in front of this chapel; and the legend further treats of divers miracles wrought by the mighty pipe which the saint held in his mouth; a whiff of which was a sovereign cure for an indigestion, and consequently of great importance in this colony of huge feeders. But as, notwithstanding the most diligent search, I cannot lay my hands upon this little book, I entertain considerable doubt on the subject.

This much is certain, that from the time of the building of this chapel, the town throve with tenfold prosperity, and soon became the metropolis of numerous settlements, and an extensive territory. The province extended on the north, to Fort Aurania or Orange, now known by the name of Albany, situated about 160 miles up the Mohegan or Hudson River. Indeed the province claimed quite to the river St. Lawrence; but this claim was not much insisted on at the time, as the country beyond Fort Aurania was a perfect wilderness, reported to be inhabited by cannibals, and termed Terra Incognita. Various accounts were given of the people of these unknown parts; by some they are described as being of the race of the *Acephali*, such as Herodotus describes, who have no heads, and carry their eyes in their bellies. Others affirm they were of that race whom father Charlevoix mentions, as having but one leg; adding gravely, that they were exceedingly alert in running. But the most satisfactory account is that given by the reverend Hans Megapolensis, a missionary in these parts, who, in a letter still extant, declares them to be the Mohagues or Mohawks; a nation, according to his description, very loose in their morals, but withal most rare wags. "For," says he, "if theye can get to bedd with another mans wife, theye thinke it a piece of wit."* This excellent old gentleman gives moreover very important additional information, about this country of monsters; for he observes, "theye have plenty of tortoises here, and within land, from two and three to four feet long; some with two heads, very mischievous and addicted to biting."†

On the south the province reached to Fort Nassau, on the South River, since called the Delaware—and on the east it extended to

---

*Let. of I. Megapol. Hag. S. P.
†Ogilvie, in his excellent account of America, speaking of these parts, makes mention of Lions, which abounded on a high mountain, and likewise observes, "On the borders of Canada there is seen sometimes a kind of beast which hath some resemblance with a horse, having cloven feet, shaggy mayn, one horn just on the forehead, a tail like that of a wild hog, and a deer's neck." He furthermore gives a picture of this strange beast, which resembles exceedingly an unicorn.—It is much to be lamented by philosophers, that this miraculous breed of animals, like that of the horned frog, is totally extinct.

Varshe (or Fresh) River, since called Connecticut River. On this frontier was likewise erected a mighty fort and trading house, much about the spot where at present is situated the pleasant town of Hartford; this port was called FORT GOED HOOP, or Good Hope, and was intended as well for the purpose of trade as defence; but of this fort, its valiant garrison, and staunch commander, I shall treat more anon, as they are destined to make some noise in this eventful and authentic history.

Thus prosperously did the province of New Nederlandts encrease in magnitude; and the early history of its metropolis, presents a fair page, unsullied by crime or calamity. Herds of painted savages still lurked about the tangled woods and the rich bottoms of the fair island of Manna-hata—the hunter still pitched his rude bower of skins and branches, beside the wild brooks, that stole through the cool and shady valleys; while here and there were seen on some sunny knoll, a group of indian wigwams, whose smoke rose above the neighbouring trees and floated in the clear expanse of heaven. The uncivilized tenants of the forest remained peaceable neighbours of the town of New Amsterdam; and our worthy ancestors endeavoured to ameliorate their situation as much as possible, by benevolently giving them gin, rum and glass beads, in exchange for all the furs they brought; for it seems the kind hearted dutchmen had conceived a great friendship for their savage neighbours—on account of the facility with which they suffered themselves to be taken in. Not that they were deficient in understanding, for certain of their customs give tokens of great shrewdness, especially that mentioned by Ogilvie, who says, "for the least offence the bridegroom soundly beats the wife, and turns her out of doors and marries another, insomuch that some of them have every year a new wife."

True it is, that good understanding between our worthy ancestors and their savage neighbours, was liable to occasional interruptions—and I recollect hearing my grandmother, who was a very wise old woman, well versed in the history of these parts, tell a long story of a winter evening, about a battle between the New Amsterdammers and the Indians, which was known, but why, I do not recollect, by the name of the *Peach War*, and which took place near a peach orchard, in a dark and gloomy glen, overshadowed by cedars, oaks and dreary hemlocks. The legend

of this bloody encounter, was for a long time current among the
nurses, old women, and other ancient chroniclers of the place; and
the dismal seat of war, went, for some generations, by the name of
Murderers' Valley; but time and improvement have equally oblit-
erated the tradition and the place of this battle, for what was once
the blood-stained valley, is now in the centre of this populous city,
and known by the name of *Dey-street*.*

For a long time the new settlement depended upon the mother
country for most of its supplies. The vessels which sailed in search
of a north west passage, always touched at New Amsterdam,
where they unloaded fresh cargoes of adventurers, and unheard of
quantities of gin, bricks, tiles, glass beads, gingerbread and other
necessaries; in exchange for which they received supplies of pork
and vegetables, and made very profitable bargains for furs and
bear skins. Never did the simple islanders of the south seas, look
with more impatience for the adventurous vessels, that brought
them rich ladings of old hoops, spike nails and looking glasses,
than did our honest colonists, for the vessels that brought them
the comforts of the mother country. In this particular they resembled their worthy but simple descendants, who prefer depending upon Europe for necessaries, which they might produce or
manufacture at less cost and trouble in their own country. Thus
have I known a very shrewd family, who being removed to some
distance from an inconvenient draw well, beside which they had
long sojourned, always preferred to send to it for water, though a
plentiful brook ran by the very door of their new habitation.

How long the growing colony might have looked to its parent
Holland for supplies, like a chubby overgrown urchin, clinging to
its mother's breast, even after it is breeched, I will not pretend to
say, for it does not become an historian to indulge in conjectures—
I can only assert the fact, that the inhabitants, being obliged by
repeated emergencies, and frequent disappointments of foreign
supplies, to look about them and resort to contrivances, became
nearly as wise as people generally are, who are taught wisdom by

---

*This battle is said by some to have happened much later than the date assigned
by our historian. Some of the ancient inhabitants of our city, place it in the beginning of the last century. It is more than probable, however, that Mr. Knickerbocker is correct, as he has doubtless investigated the matter.—*Print. Dev.*

painful experience. They therefore learned to avail themselves of such expedients as presented—to make use of the bounties of nature, where they could get nothing better—and thus became prodigiously enlightened, under the scourge of inexorable necessity; gradually opening one eye at a time, like the Arabian impostor receiving the bastinado.

Still however they advanced from one point of knowledge to another with characteristic slowness and circumspection, admitting but few improvements and inventions, and those too, with a jealous reluctance that has ever distinguished our respectable dutch yeomanry; who adhere, with pious and praiseworthy obstinacy, to the customs, the fashions, the manufactures and even the very utensils, however inconvenient, of their revered forefathers. It was long after the period of which I am writing, before they discovered the surprising secret, that it was more economic and commodious, to roof their houses with shingles procured from the adjacent forests, than to import tiles for the purpose from Holland; and so slow were they in believing that the soil of a young country, could possibly make creditable bricks; that even at a late period of the last century, ship loads have been imported from Holland, by certain of its most orthodox descendants.

The accumulating wealth and consequence of New Amsterdam and its dependencies, at length awakened the serious solicitude of the mother country; who finding it a thriving and opulent colony, and that it promised to yield great profit and no trouble; all at once became wonderfully anxious about its safety, and began to load it with tokens of regard; in the same manner that people are sure to oppress rich relations with their affection and loving kindness, who could do much better without their assistance.

The usual marks of protection shewn by mother countries to wealthy colonies, were forthwith evinced—the first care always being to send rulers to the new settlement, with orders to squeeze as much revenue from it as it will yield. Accordingly in the year of our Lord 1629 mynheer WOUTER VAN TWILLER was appointed governor of the province of Nieuw Nederlandts, under the controul of their High Mightinesses the lords states general of the United Netherlands, and the privileged West India company.

This renowned old gentleman arrived at New Amsterdam in the merry month of June, the sweetest month in all the year; when

Dan Apollo seems to dance up the transparent firmament—when the robin, the black-bird, the thrush and a thousand other wanton songsters make the woods to resound with amorous ditties, and the luxurious little Boblincon revels among the clover blossoms of the meadows.—All which happy coincidence, persuaded the old ladies of New Amsterdam, who were skilled in the art of foretelling events, that this was to be a happy and prosperous administration.

But as it would be derogatory to the consequence of the first dutch governor of the great province of Nieuw Nederlandts, to be thus scurvily introduced at the end of a chapter, I will put an end to this second book of my history, that I may usher him in, with the more dignity in the beginning of my next.

END OF BOOK II

BOOK III

In which is recorded the golden reign of
Wouter Van Twiller.

CHAPTER I

*Setting forth the unparalleled virtues of the renowned
Wouter Van Twiller, as likewise his unutterable wisdom in the
law case of Wandle Schoonhoven and Barent Bleecker—
and the great admiration of the public thereat.*

The renowned Wouter (or Walter) Van Twiller, was descended
from a long line of dutch burgomasters, who had successively
dozed away their lives and grown fat upon the bench of magis-
tracy in Rotterdam; and who had comported themselves with
such singular wisdom and propriety, that they were never either
heard or talked of—which, next to being universally applauded,
should be the object of ambition of all sage magistrates and
rulers.

His surname of Twiller, is said to be a corruption of the original
Twijfler, which in English means *doubter;* a name admirably de-
scriptive of his deliberative habits. For though he was a man, shut
up within himself like an oyster, and of such a profoundly reflective turn, that he scarcely ever spoke except in monosyllables, yet
did he never make up his mind, on any doubtful point. This was
clearly accounted for by his adherents, who affirmed that he always conceived every subject on so comprehensive a scale, that he
had not room in his head, to turn it over and examine both sides
of it, so that he always remained in doubt, merely in consequence
of the astonishing magnitude of his ideas!

There are two opposite ways by which some men get into
notice—one by talking a vast deal and thinking a little, and the
other by holding their tongues and not thinking at all. By the first
many a vapouring, superficial pretender acquires the reputation
of a man of quick parts—by the other many a vacant dunderpate,
like the owl, the stupidest of birds, comes to be complimented, by
a discerning world, with all the attributes of wisdom. This, by
the way, is a mere casual remark, which I would not for the universe have it thought, I apply to Governor Van Twiller. On the
contrary he was a very wise dutchman, for he never said a foolish

thing—and of such invincible gravity, that he was never known to laugh, or even to smile, through the course of a long and prosperous life. Certain however it is, there never was a matter proposed, however simple, and on which your common narrow minded mortals, would rashly determine at the first glance, but what the renowned Wouter, put on a mighty mysterious, vacant kind of look, shook his capacious head, and having smoked for five minutes with redoubled earnestness, sagely observed, that "he had his doubts about the matter"—which in process of time gained him the character of a man slow of belief, and not easily imposed on.

The person of this illustrious old gentleman was as regularly formed and nobly proportioned, as though it had been moulded by the hands of some cunning dutch statuary, as a model of majesty and lordly grandeur. He was exactly five feet six inches in height, and six feet five inches in circumference. His head was a perfect sphere, far excelling in magnitude that of the great Pericles (who was thence waggishly called *Schenocephalus,* or onion head)—indeed, of such stupendous dimensions was it, that dame nature herself, with all her sex's ingenuity, would have been puzzled to construct a neck, capable of supporting it; wherefore she wisely declined the attempt, and settled it firmly on the top of his back bone, just between the shoulders; where it remained, as snugly bedded, as a ship of war in the mud of the Potowmac. His body was of an oblong form, particularly capacious at bottom; which was wisely ordered by providence, seeing that he was a man of sedentary habits, and very averse to the idle labour of walking. His legs, though exceeding short, were sturdy in proportion to the weight they had to sustain; so that when erect, he had not a little the appearance of a robustious beer barrel, standing on skids. His face, that infallible index of the mind, presented a vast expanse perfectly unfurrowed or deformed by any of those lines and angles, which disfigure the human countenance with what is termed expression. Two small grey eyes twinkled feebly in the midst, like two stars of lesser magnitude, in a hazy firmament; and his full fed cheeks, which seemed to have taken toll of every thing that went into his mouth, were curiously mottled and streaked with dusky red, like a spitzenberg apple.

His habits were as regular as his person. He daily took his four stated meals, appropriating exactly an hour to each; he smoked and doubted eight hours, and he slept the remaining twelve of the four and twenty. Such was the renowned Wouter Van Twiller—a true philosopher, for his mind was either elevated above, or tranquilly settled below, the cares and perplexities of this world. He had lived in it for years, without feeling the least curiosity to know whether the sun revolved round it, or it round the sun; and he had even watched for at least half a century, the smoke curling from his pipe to the ceiling, without once troubling his head with any of those numerous theories, by which a philosopher would have perplexed his brain, in accounting for its rising above the surrounding atmosphere.

In his council he presided with great state and solemnity. He sat in a huge chair of solid oak hewn in the celebrated forest of the Hague, fabricated by an experienced Timmerman of Amsterdam, and curiously carved about the arms and feet, into exact imitations of gigantic eagle's claws. Instead of a sceptre he swayed a long turkish pipe, wrought with jasmin and amber, which had been presented to a stadtholder of Holland, at the conclusion of a treaty with one of the petty Barbary powers.—In this stately chair would he sit, and this magnificent pipe would he smoke, shaking his right knee with a constant motion, and fixing his eye for hours together upon a little print of Amsterdam, which hung in a black frame, against the opposite wall of the council chamber. Nay, it has ever been said, that when any deliberation of extraordinary length and intricacy was on the carpet, the renowned Wouter would absolutely shut his eyes for full two hours at a time, that he might not be disturbed by external objects—and at such times the internal commotion of his mind, was evinced by certain regular guttural sounds, which his admirers declared were merely the noise of conflict, made by his contending doubts and opinions.

It is with infinite difficulty I have been enabled to collect these biographical anecdotes of the great man under consideration. The facts respecting him were so scattered and vague, and divers of them so questionable in point of authenticity, that I have had to give up the search after many, and decline the admission of still more, which would have tended to heighten the colouring of his portrait.

I have been the more anxious to delineate fully, the person and habits of the renowned Van Twiller, from the consideration that he was not only the first, but also the best governor that ever presided over this ancient and respectable province; and so tranquil and benevolent was his reign, that I do not find throughout the whole of it, a single instance of any offender being brought to punishment:—a most indubitable sign of a merciful governor, and a case unparalleled, excepting in the reign of the illustrious King Log, from whom, it is hinted, the renowned Van Twiller was a lineal descendant.

The very outset of the career of this excellent magistrate, like that of Solomon, or to speak more appropriately, like that of the illustrious governor of Barataria, was distinguished by an example of legal acumen, that gave flattering presage of a wise and equitable administration. The very morning after he had been solemnly installed in office, and at the moment that he was making his breakfast from a prodigious earthen dish, filled with milk and Indian pudding, he was suddenly interrupted by the appearance of one Wandle Schoonhoven, a very important old burgher of New Amsterdam, who complained bitterly of one Barent Bleecker, inasmuch as he fraudulently refused to come to a settlement of accounts, seeing that there was a heavy balance in favour of the said Wandle. Governor Van Twiller, as I have already observed, was a man of few words, he was likewise a mortal enemy to multiplying writings—or being disturbed at his breakfast. Having therefore listened attentively to the statement of Wandle Schoonhoven, giving an occasional grunt, as he shovelled a mighty spoonful of Indian pudding into his mouth—either as a sign that he relished the dish, or comprehended the story—he called unto him his constable, and pulling out of his breeches pocket a huge jack-knife, dispatched it after the defendant as a summons, accompanied by his tobacco box as a warrant.

This summary process was as effectual in those simple days, as was the seal ring of the great Haroun Alraschid, among the true believers—the two parties, being confronted before him, each produced a book of accounts, written in a language and character that would have puzzled any but a High Dutch commentator, or a learned decypherer of Egyptian obelisks, to understand. The sage Wouter took them one after the other, and having poised them in his hands, and attentively counted over the number of leaves, fell straightway into a very great doubt, and smoked for half an hour without saying a word; at length, laying his finger beside his nose, and shutting his eyes for a moment, with the air of a man who has just caught a subtle idea by the tail, he slowly took his pipe from his mouth, puffed forth a column of tobacco smoke, and with marvellous gravity and solemnity pronounced—that having carefully counted over the leaves and weighed the books, it was found, that one was just as thick and as heavy as the other—therefore it was the final opinion of the court that the accounts were equally balanced—therefore Wandle should give Barent a receipt, and Barent should give Wandle a receipt—and the constable should pay the costs.

This decision being straightway made known, diffused general joy throughout New Amsterdam, for the people immediately perceived, that they had a very wise and equitable magistrate to rule over them. But its happiest effect was, that not another law suit took place throughout the whole of his administration—and the office of constable fell into such decay, that there was not one of those lossel scouts known in the province for many years. I am the more particular in dwelling on this transaction, not only because I deem it one of the most sage and righteous judgments on record, and well worthy the attention of modern magistrates, but because it was a miraculous event in the history of the renowned Wouter—being the only time he was ever known to come to a decision, in the whole course of his life.

CHAPTER II

Containing some account of the grand Council of New Amsterdam, as also divers especial good philosophical reasons why an Alderman should be fat—with other particulars touching the state of the Province.

In treating of the early governors of the province, I must caution my readers against confounding them, in point of dignity and power, with those worthy gentlemen, who are whimsically denominated governors, in this enlightened republic—a set of unhappy victims of popularity, who are in fact the most dependant, hen-pecked beings in community: doomed to bear the secret goadings and corrections of their own party, and the sneers and revilings of the whole world beside.—Set up, like geese, at christmas hollidays, to be pelted and shot at by every whipster and vagabond in the land. On the contrary, the dutch governors enjoyed that uncontrolled authority vested in all commanders of distant colonies or territories. They were in a manner, absolute despots in their little domains, lording it, if so disposed, over both law and gospel, and accountable to none but the mother country; which it is well known is astonishingly deaf to all complaints against its governors, provided they discharge the main duty of their station—squeezing out a good revenue. This hint will be of importance, to prevent my readers from being seized with doubt and incredulity, whenever, in the course of this authentic history, they encounter the uncommon circumstance, of a governor, acting with independence, and in opposition to the opinions of the multitude.

To assist the doubtful Wouter, in the arduous business of legislation, a board of magistrates was appointed, which presided immediately over the police. This potent body consisted of a schout or bailiff, with powers between those of the present mayor and sheriff—five burgermeesters, who were equivalent to aldermen, and five schepens, who officiated as scrubs, sub-devils, or bottle-holders to the burgermeesters, in the same manner as do assistant aldermen to their principals at the present day; it being their duty to fill the pipes of the lordly burgermeesters—see that they were accommodated with spitting boxes—hunt the markets for delicacies for corporation dinners, and to discharge such other little offices of kindness, as were occasionally required. It was moreover, tacitly understood, though not specifically enjoined, that they should consider themselves as butts for the blunt wits of the burgermeesters, and should laugh most heartily at all their jokes; but this last was a duty as rarely called in action in those days, as it is at present, and was shortly remitted, in consequence of the tragical death of a fat little Schepen—who actually died of suffocation in an unsuccessful effort to force a laugh, at one of Burgermeester Van Zandt's best jokes.

In return for these humble services, they were permitted to say *yes* and *no* at the council board, and to have that enviable privilege, the run of the public kitchen—being graciously permitted to eat, and drink, and smoke, at all those snug junkettings and public gormandizings, for which the ancient magistrates were equally famous with their more modern successors. The post of Schepen therefore, like that of assistant alderman, was eagerly coveted by all your burghers of a certain description, who have a huge relish for good feeding, and a humble ambition to be great men, in a small way—who thirst after a little brief authority, that shall render them the terror of the alms house, and the bridewell—that shall enable them to lord it over obsequious poverty, vagrant vice, outcast prostitution, and hunger driven dishonesty—that shall place in their hands the lesser, but galling scourge of the law, and give to their beck a hound like pack of catchpoles and bum bailiffs—tenfold greater rogues than the culprits they hunt down!—My readers will excuse this sudden warmth, which I confess is unbecoming of a grave historian—but I have a mortal antipathy to catchpoles, bum bailiffs, and little great men.

The ancient magistrates of this city, corresponded with those of the present time, no less in form, magnitude and intellect, than in prerogative and privilege. The burgomasters, like our aldermen, were generally chosen by weight—and not only the weight of the body, but likewise the weight of the head. It is a maxim practically observed in all honest, plain thinking, regular cities, that an alderman should be fat—and the wisdom of this can be proved to a certainty. That the body is in some measure an image of the mind, or rather that the mind is moulded to the body, like melted lead to the clay in which it is cast, has been insisted on by many men of science, who have made human nature their peculiar study—For as a learned gentleman of our city observes "there is a constant relation between the moral character of all intelligent creatures, and their physical constitution—between their habits and the structure of their bodies." Thus we see, that a lean, spare, diminutive body, is generally accompanied by a petulant, restless, meddling mind—either the mind wears down the body, by its continual motion; or else the body, not affording the mind sufficient house room, keeps it continually in a state of fretfulness, tossing and worrying about from the uneasiness of its situation. Whereas your round, sleek, fat, unwieldly periphery is ever attended by a mind, like itself, tranquil, torpid and at ease; and we may always observe, that your well fed, robustious burghers are in general very tenacious of their ease and comfort; being great enemies to noise, discord and disturbance—and surely none are more likely to study the public tranquillity than those who are so careful of their own—Who ever hears of fat men heading a riot, or herding together in turbulent mobs?—no—no—it is your lean, hungry men, who are continually worrying society, and setting the whole community by the ears.

The divine Plato, whose doctrines are not sufficiently attended to by philosophers of the present age, allows to every man three souls—one, immortal and rational, seated in the brain, that it may overlook and regulate the body—a second consisting of the surly and irascible passions, which like belligerent powers lie encamped around the heart—a third mortal and sensual, destitute of reason, gross and brutal in its propensities, and enchained in the belly, that it may not disturb the divine soul, by its ravenous howlings. Now, according to this excellent theory what can be more clear, than that your fat alderman, is most likely to have the most regular and well conditioned mind. His head is like a huge, spherical chamber, containing a prodigious mass of soft brains, whereon the rational soul lies softly and snugly couched, as on a feather bed; and the eyes, which are the windows of the bed chamber, are usually half closed that its slumberings may not be disturbed by external objects. A mind thus comfortably lodged, and protected from disturbance, is manifestly most likely to perform its functions with regularity and ease. By dint of good feeding, moreover, the mortal and malignant soul, which is confined in the belly, and which by its raging and roaring, puts the irritable soul in the neighbourhood of the heart in an intolerable passion, and thus renders men crusty and quarrelsome when hungry, is completely pacified, silenced and put to rest—whereupon a host of honest good fellow qualities and kind hearted affections, which had lain perdue, slily peeping out of the loop holes of the heart, finding this cerberus asleep, do pluck up their spirits, turn out one and all in their holliday suits, and gambol up and down the diaphragm—disposing their possessor to laughter, good humour and a thousand friendly offices towards his fellow mortals.

As a board of magistrates, formed on this model, think but very little, they are the less likely to differ and wrangle about favourite opinions—and as they generally transact business upon a hearty dinner, they are naturally disposed to be lenient and indulgent in the administration of their duties. Charlemagne was conscious of this, and therefore (a pitiful measure, for which I can never forgive him), ordered in his cartularies, that no judge should hold a court of justice, except in the morning, on an empty stomach.—A rule which, I warrant, bore hard upon all the poor culprits in his kingdom. The more enlightened and humane generation of the present day, have taken an opposite course, and have so managed that the aldermen are the best fed men in the community; feasting lustily on the fat things of the land, and gorging so heartily on oysters and turtles, that in process of time they acquire the activity of the one, and the form, the waddle, and the green fat of the other. The consequence is, as I have just said; these luxurious feastings do produce such a dulcet equanimity and repose of the soul, rational and irrational, that their transactions are proverbial for unvarying monotony—and the profound laws, which they enact in their dozing moments, amid the labours of digestion, are quietly suffered to remain as dead letters, and never enforced, when awake. In a word your fair round-bellied burgomaster, like a full fed mastiff, dozes quietly at the house-door, always at home, and always at hand to watch over its safety—but as to electing a lean, meddling candidate to the office, as has now and then been done, I would as leave put a grey-hound, to watch the house, or a race horse to drag an ox waggon.

The Burgomasters then, as I have already mentioned, were wisely chosen by weight, and the Schepens, or assistant aldermen, were appointed to attend upon them, and *help them eat;* but the latter, in the course of time, when they had been fed and fattened into sufficient bulk of body and drowsiness of brain, became very eligible candidates for the Burgomasters' chairs, having fairly eaten themselves into office, as a mouse eats his way into a comfortable lodgement in a goodly, blue-nosed, skim'd milk, New England cheese.

Nothing could equal the profound deliberations that took place between the renowned Wouter, and these his worthy compeers, unless it be the sage divans of some of our modern corporations. They would sit for hours smoking and dozing over public affairs, without speaking a word to interrupt that perfect stillness, so necessary to deep reflection—faithfully observing an excellent maxim, which the good old governor had caused to be written in letters of gold, on the walls of the council chamber

𝕾𝖙𝖎𝖑𝖑𝖊 𝕾𝖊𝖚𝖌𝖊𝖓 𝖊𝖙𝖊𝖓 𝖆𝖑 𝖉𝖊𝖓 𝖉𝖗𝖆𝖋 𝖔𝖕.

which, being rendered into English for the benefit of modern legislatures, means—

> *"The sow that's still*
> *Sucks all the swill."*

Under the sober way, therefore, of the renowned Van Twiller, and the sage superintendance of his burgomasters, the infant settlement waxed vigorous apace, gradually emerging from the swamps and forests, and exhibiting that mingled appearance of town and country, customary in new cities, and which at this day may be witnessed in the great city of Washington; that immense metropolis, which makes such a glorious appearance— upon paper.

Ranges of houses began to give the idea of streets and lanes, and wherever an interval occurred, it was over-run by a wilderness of sweet smelling thorn apple, vulgarly called stinkweed.

Amid these fragrant bowers, the honest burghers, like so many patriarchs of yore, sat smoking their pipes of a sultry afternoon, inhaling the balmy odours wafted on every gale, and listening with silent gratulation to the clucking of their hens, the cackling of their geese, or the sonorous gruntings of their swine; that combination of farm-yard melody, which may truly be said to have a silver sound, inasmuch as it conveys a certain assurance of profitable marketing.

The modern spectator, who wanders through the crowded streets of this populous city, can scarce form an idea, of the different appearance which every object presented, in those primitive times. The busy hum of commerce, the noise of revelry, the rattling equipages of splendid luxury, were unknown in the peaceful settlement of New Amsterdam. The bleating sheep and frolicksome calves sported about the verdant ridge, where now their legitimate successors, the Broadway loungers, take their morning's stroll; the cunning fox or ravenous wolf, skulked in the woods, where now are to be seen the dens of Gomez and his righteous fraternity of money brokers, and flocks of vociferous geese cackled about the field, where now the patriotic tavern of Martling echoes with the wranglings of the mob.* The whole island, at least such parts of it as were inhabited, bloomed like a second Eden; every dwelling had its own cabbage garden, and that esculent vegetable, while it gave promise of bounteous loads of sour crout, was also emblematic of the rapid growth and regular habits of the youthful colony.

Such are the soothing scenes presented by a fat government. The province of the New Netherlands, destitute of wealth, possessed a sweet tranquillity that wealth could never purchase. It seemed indeed as if old Saturn had again commenced his reign, and renewed the golden days of primeval simplicity. For the golden age, says Ovid, was totally destitute of gold, and for that very reason was called the golden age, that is, the happy and

---

*"De Vries mentions a place where they over-haul their ships, which he calls *Smits Vleye,* there is still to this day a place in New York called by that name, where a market is built called the Fly market."—Old MS.

There are few native inhabitants, I trow, of this great city, who when boys were not engaged in the renowned feuds of Broadway and Smith fly—the subject of so many fly market romances and schoolboy rhymes. EDITOR.

fortunate age—because the evils produced by the precious met-
als, such as avarice, covetuousness, theft, rapine, usury, bank-
ing, note-shaving, lottery-insuring, and the whole catalogue of
crimes and grievances were then unknown. In the iron age there
was abundance of gold, and on that very account it was called
the iron age, because of the hardships, the labours, the dissentions, and the wars, occasioned by the thirst of gold.

The genial days of Wouter Van Twiller therefore, may truly
be termed the golden age of our city. There were neither public
commotions, nor private quarrels; neither parties, nor sects, nor
schisms; neither prosecutions, nor trials, nor punishments; nor were
there counsellors, attornies, catch-poles or hangmen. Every man
attended to what little business he was lucky enough to have, or
neglect it if he pleased, without asking the opinion of his
neighbour.—In those days nobody meddled with concerns above
his comprehension, nor thrust his nose into other people's affairs;
nor neglected to correct his own conduct, and reform his own
character, in his zeal to pull to pieces the characters of others—but
in a word, every respectable citizen eat when he was not hungry,
drank when he was not thirsty, and went regularly to bed, when
the sun set, and the fowls went to roost, whether he was sleepy or
not; all which, being agreeable to the doctrines of Malthus, tended
so remarkably to the population of the settlement, that I am told
every dutiful wife throughout New Amsterdam, made a point of
always enriching her husband with at least one child a year, and
very often a brace—this superabundance of good things clearly
constituting the true luxury of life, according to the favourite
dutch maxim that "more than enough constitutes a feast." Every
thing therefore went on exactly as it should do, and in the usual
words employed by historians to express the welfare of a country,
"the profoundest *tranquillity* and *repose* reigned throughout the
province."

CHAPTER III

How the town of New Amsterdam arose out of the mud, and came to be marvellously polished and polite—together with a picture of the manners of our great great Grandfathers.

Manifold are the tastes and dispositions of the enlightened literati, who turn over the pages of history. Some there be whose hearts are brim full of the yeast of courage, and whose bosoms do work, and swell, and foam with untried valour, like a barrel of new cider, or a train-band captain, fresh from under the hands of his taylor. This doughty class of readers can be satisfied with nothing but bloody battles, and horrible encounters; they must be continually storming forts, sacking cities, springing mines, marching up to the muzzles of cannons, charging bayonet through every page, and revelling in gun-powder and carnage. Others, who are of a less martial, but equally ardent imagination, and who, withal, are a little given to the marvellous, will dwell with wonderous satisfaction on descriptions of prodigies, unheard of events, hair-breadth escapes, hardy adventures, and all those astonishing narrations, that just amble along the boundary line of possibility.—A third class, who, not to speak slightingly of them, are of a lighter turn, and skim over the records of past times, as they do over the edifying pages of a novel, merely for relaxation and innocent amusement; do singularly delight in treasons, executions, sabine rapes, tarquin outrages, conflagrations, murders, and all the other catalogue of hideous crimes, that like Cayenne in cookery, do give a pungency and flavour, to the dull detail of history—while a fourth class, of more philosophic habits, do diligently pore over the musty chronicles of time, to investigate the operations of the human mind, and watch the gradual changes in men and manners, effected by the progress of knowledge, the vicissitudes of events, or the influence of situation.

If the three first classes find but little wherewithal to solace themselves, in the tranquil reign of Wouter Van Twiller, I entreat them to exert their patience for a while, and bear with the tedious picture of happiness, prosperity and peace, which my duty as a faithful historian obliges me to draw; and I promise them, that as soon as I can possibly light upon any thing horrible, uncommon or impossible, it shall go hard, but I will make it afford them entertainment. This being premised, I turn with great complacency to the fourth class of my readers, who are men, or, if possible, women, after my own heart; grave, philosophical and investigating; fond of analyzing characters, of taking a start from first causes, and so hunting a nation down, through all the mazes of innovation and improvement. Such will naturally be anxious to witness the first developement of the newly hatched colony, and the primitive manners and customs, prevalent among its inhabitants, during the halcyon reign of Van Twiller or the doubter.

To describe minutely the gradual advances, from the rude log hut, to the stately dutch mansion, with a brick front, glass windows, and shingle roof—from the tangled thicket, to the luxuriant cabbage garden, and from the skulking Indian to the ponderous burgomaster, would probably be fatiguing to my reader, and certainly very inconvenient to myself; suffice it to say, trees were cut down, stumps grubbed up, bushes cleared away, until the new city rose gradually from amid swamps and stinkweeds, like a mighty fungus, springing from a mass of rotten wood.

The sage council, as has been mentioned in a preceding chapter, not being able to determine upon any plan for the building of their city—the cows, in a laudable fit of patriotism, took it under their particular charge, and as they went to and from pasture, established paths through the bushes, on each side of which the good folks built their houses; which is one cause of the rambling and picturesque turns and labyrinths, which distinguish certain streets of New York, at this very day.

Some, it must be noted, who were strenuous partizans of Mynheer Ten Breeches, (or Ten Broek) vexed that his plan of digging canals was not adopted, made a compromise with their inclinations, by establishing themselves on the margins of those creeks and inlets, which meandered through various parts of the ground laid out for improvement. To these may be particularly ascribed the first settlement of Broad street; which originally was built along a creek, that ran up, to what at present is called Wall street. The lower part soon became very busy and populous; and a ferry house* was in process of time established at the head of it; being at that day called "the head of inland navigation."

The disciples of Mynheer Toughbreeches, on the other hand, no less enterprising, and more industrious than their rivals, stationed themselves along the shore of the river, and laboured with unexampled perseverance, in making little docks and dykes, from which originated that multitude of mud traps with which this city is fringed. To these docks would the old Burghers repair, just at those hours when the falling tide had left the beach uncovered, that they might snuff up the fragrant effluvia of mud and mire; which they observed had a true wholesome smell, and reminded them of the canals of Holland. To the indefatigable labours, and praiseworthy example of this latter class of projectors, are we indebted for the acres of artificial ground, on which several of our streets, in the vicinity of the rivers are built; and which, if we may credit the assertions of several learned physicians of this city, have been very efficacious in producing the yellow fever.

The houses of the higher class, were generally constructed of wood, excepting the gable end, which was of small black and yellow dutch bricks, and always faced on the street, as our ancestors, like their descendants, were very much given to outward shew, and were noted for putting the best leg foremost. The house was always furnished with abundance of large doors and small windows on every floor, the date of its erection was curiously designated by iron figures on the front, and on the top of the roof was perched a fierce little weather cock, to let the family into the important secret, which way the wind blew. These, like the weather cocks on the tops of our steeples, pointed so many different ways, that every man could have a wind to his mind; and you would have thought old Eolus had set all his bags of wind adrift, pell mell, to gambol about this windy metropolis— the most staunch and loyal citizens, however, always went

---

*This house has been several times repaired, and at present is a small yellow brick house, No. 23, Broad Street, with the gable end to the street, surmounted with an iron rod, on which, until within three or four years, a little iron ferry boat officiated as weather cock.

according to the weather cock on top of the governor's house, which was certainly the most correct, as he had a trusty servant employed every morning to climb up and point it whichever way the wind blew.

In those good days of simplicity and sunshine, a passion for cleanliness, was the grand desideratum in domestic economy and the universal test of an able housewife—a character which formed the utmost ambition of our unenlightened grandmothers. The front door, was never opened except on marriages, funerals, new year's days, the festival of St. Nicholas, or some such great occasion.—It was ornamented with a gorgeous brass knocker, curiously wrought, sometimes into the device of a dog, and some-times of a lion's head, and was daily burnished with such religious zeal, that it was oft times worn out, by the very precautions taken for its preservation. The whole house was constantly in a state of inundation, under the discipline of mops and brooms and scrubbing brushes; and the good housewives of those days were a kind of amphibious animal, delighting exceedingly to be dab-bling in water—insomuch that an historian of the day gravely tells us, that many of his townswomen grew to have webbed fin-gers like unto a duck; and some of them, he had little doubt, could the matter be examined into, would be found to have the tails of mermaids—but this I look upon to be a mere sport of fancy, or what is worse, a wilful misrepresentation.

The grand parlour was the sanctum sanctorum, where the pas-sion for cleaning was indulged without controul. In this sacred apartment no one was permitted to enter, excepting the mistress and her confidential maid, who visited it once a week, for the pur-pose of giving it a thorough cleaning, and putting things to rights—always taking the precaution of leaving their shoes at the door, and entering devoutly, on their stocking feet. After scrub-bing the floor, sprinkling it with fine white sand, which was curi-ously stroked into angles, and curves, and rhomboids, with a broom—after washing the windows, rubbing and polishing the furniture, and putting a new bunch of evergreens in the fire-place—the window shutters were again closed to keep out the flies, and the room carefully locked up until the revolution of time, brought round the weekly cleaning day.

As to the family, they always entered in at the gate, and most generally lived in the kitchen. To have seen a numerous household assembled around the fire, one would have imagined that he was transported back to those happy days of primeval simplicity, which float before our imaginations like golden visions. The fire-places were of a truly patriarchal magnitude, where the whole family, old and young, master and servant, black and white, nay even the very cat and dog, enjoyed a community of privilege, and had each a prescriptive right to a corner. Here the old burgher would set in perfect silence, puffing his pipe, looking in the fire with half shut eyes, and thinking of nothing for hours together; the goede vrouw on the opposite side would employ herself diligently in spinning her yarn, or knitting stockings. The young folks would crowd around the hearth, listening with breathless attention to some old crone of a negro, who was the oracle of the family,—and who, perched like a raven in a corner of the chimney, would croak forth for a long winter afternoon, a string of incredible stories about New England witches—grisly ghosts— horses without heads—and hairbreadth scapes and bloody encounters among the Indians.

In those happy days a well regulated family always rose with the dawn, dined at eleven, and went to bed at sun down. Dinner was invariably a private meal, and the fat old burghers shewed incontestible symptoms of disapprobation and uneasiness, at being surprised by a visit from a neighbour on such occasions. But though our worthy ancestors were thus singularly averse to giving dinners, yet they kept up the social bands of intimacy by occasional banquettings, called tea parties.

As this is the first introduction of those delectable orgies which have since become so fashionable in this city, I am conscious my fair readers will be very curious to receive information on the subject. Sorry am I, that there will be but little in my description calculated to excite their admiration. I can neither delight them with accounts of suffocating crowds, nor brilliant drawing rooms, nor towering feathers, nor sparkling diamonds, nor immeasurable trains. I can detail no choice anecdotes of scandal, for in those primitive times the simple folk were either too stupid, or too good natured to pull each other's characters to pieces—nor can I furnish any whimsical anecdotes of brag—how one lady cheated, or another bounced into a passion; for as yet there was no junto of dulcet old dowagers, who met to win each other's money, and lose their own tempers at a card table.

These fashionable parties were generally confined to the higher classes, or noblesse, that is to say, such as kept their own cows, and drove their own waggons. The company commonly assembled at three o'clock, and went away about six, unless it was in winter time, when the fashionable hours were a little earlier, that the ladies might get home before dark. I do not find that they ever treated their company to iced creams, jellies or syllabubs; or regaled them with musty almonds, mouldy raisins, or sour oranges, as is often done in the present age of refinement.—Our ancestors were fond of more sturdy, substantial fare. The tea table was crowned with a huge earthen dish, well stored with slices of fat pork, fried brown, cut up into mouthfuls, and swimming in doup or gravy. The company being seated around the genial board, and each furnished with a fork, evinced their dexterity in launching at the fattest pieces in this mighty dish—in much the same manner as sailors harpoon porpoises at sea, or our Indians spear salmon in the lakes. Sometimes the table was graced with immense apple pies, or saucers full of preserved peaches and pears; but it was always sure to boast an enormous dish of balls of sweetened dough, fried in hog's fat, and called dough nuts, or oly koeks—a delicious kind of cake, at present, scarce known in this city, excepting in genuine dutch families; but which retains its pre-eminent station at the tea tables in Albany.

The tea was served out of a majestic delft tea-pot, ornamented with paintings of fat little dutch shepherds and shepherdesses, tending pigs—with boats sailing in the air, and houses built in the clouds, and sundry other ingenious dutch fantasies. The beaux distinguished themselves by their adroitness in replenishing this pot, from a huge copper tea kettle, which would have made the pigmy macaronies of these degenerate days, sweat, merely to look at it. To sweeten the beverage, a lump of sugar was laid beside each cup—and the company alternately nibbled and sipped with great decorum, until an improvement was introduced by a shrewd and economic old lady, which was to suspend a large lump directly over the tea table, by a string from the ceiling, so that it could be swung from mouth to mouth—an ingenious expedient, which is still kept up by some families in Albany; but which prevails without exception, in Communipaw, Bergen, Flat-Bush, and all our uncontaminated dutch villages.

At these primitive tea-parties the utmost propriety and dignity of deportment prevailed. No flirting nor coquetting—no gambling of old ladies nor hoyden chattering and romping of young ones—No self satisfied struttings of wealthy gentlemen with their brains in their pockets—nor amusing conceits, and monkey divertisements of smart young gentlemen, with no brains at all. On the contrary, the young ladies seated themselves demurely in their rush-bottomed chairs, and knit their own woollen stockings; nor ever opened their lips, excepting to say *yah Mynher,* or *yah, ya Vrouw,* to any question that was asked them; behaving in all things, like decent, well educated damsels. As to the gentlemen, each of them tranquilly smoked his pipe, and seemed lost in contemplation of the blue and white tiles, with which the fireplaces were decorated; wherein sundry passages of scripture, were piously pourtrayed—Tobit and his dog figured to great advantage; Haman swung conspicuously on his gibbet, and Jonah appeared most manfully bouncing out of the whale, like Harlequin through a barrel of fire.

The parties broke up without noise and without confusion—for, strange as it may seem, the ladies and gentlemen were content to take their own cloaks and shawls and hats; not dreaming, simple souls! of the ingenious system of exchange established in modern days; by which those who first leave a party are authorized to choose the best shawl or hat they can find—a custom which has doubtless arisen in consequence of our commercial habits. They were carried home by their own carriages, that is to say, by the vehicles nature had provided them, excepting such of the wealthy, as could afford to keep a waggon. The gentlemen gallantly attended their fair ones to their respective abodes, and took leave of them with a hearty smack at the door: which as it was an established piece of etiquette, done in perfect simplicity and honesty of heart, occasioned no scandal at that time, nor should it at the present—if our great grandfathers approved of the custom, it would argue a great want of reverence in their descendants to say a word against it.

CHAPTER IV

Containing further particulars of the Golden Age,
and what constituted a fine Lady and Gentleman in the days
of Walter the Doubter.

In this dulcet period of my history, when the beauteous island of Mannahata presented a scene, the very counterpart of those glowing pictures drawn by old Hesiod of the golden reign of Saturn, there was a happy ignorance, an honest simplicity prevalent among its inhabitants, which were I even able to depict, would be but little understood by the degenerate age for which I am doomed to write. Even the female sex, those arch innovaters upon the tranquillity, the honesty, and grey-beard customs of society, seemed for a while to conduct themselves with incredible sobriety and comeliness, and indeed behaved almost as if they had not been sent into the world, to bother mankind, baffle philosophy, and confound the universe.

Their hair untortured by the abominations of art, was scrupulously pomatomed back from their foreheads with a candle, and covered with a little cap of quilted calico, which fitted exactly to their heads. Their petticoats of linsey woolsey, were striped with a variety of gorgeous dyes, rivalling the many coloured robes of Iris—though I must confess these gallant garments were rather short, scarce reaching below the knee; but then they made up in the number, which generally equalled that of the gentlemen's small clothes; and what is still more praiseworthy, they were all of their own manufacture—of which circumstance, as may well be supposed, they were not a little vain.

These were the honest days, in which every woman staid at home, read the bible and wore pockets—aye, and that too of a goodly size, fashioned with patch-work into many curious devices, and ostentatiously worn on the outside. These in fact, were convenient receptacles, where all good housewives carefully stored away such things as they wished to have at hand; by which means they often came to be incredibly crammed—and I remember there was a story current when I was a boy, that the lady of Wouter Van Twiller, having occasion to empty her right pocket in search of a wooden ladle, the contents filled three corn baskets, and the utensil was at length discovered lying among some rubbish in one corner—but we must not give too much faith to all these stories; the anecdotes of these remote periods being very subject to exaggeration.

Beside these notable pockets, they likewise wore scissars and pincushions suspended from their girdles by red ribbands, or among the more opulent and shewy classes, by brass and even silver chains—indubitable tokens of thrifty housewives and industrious spinsters. I cannot say much in vindication of the shortness of the petticoats; it doubtless was introduced for the purpose of giving the stockings a chance to be seen, which were generally of blue worsted with magnificent red clocks—or perhaps to display a well turned ankle, and a neat, though serviceable foot; set off by a high-heel'd leathern shoe, with a large and splendid silver buckle. Thus we find, that the gentle sex in all ages, have shewn the same disposition to infringe a little upon the laws of decorum, in order to betray a lurking beauty, or gratify an innocent love of finery.

From the sketch here given it will be seen, that our good grandmothers differed considerably in their ideas of a fine figure, from their scantily dressed descendants of the present day. A fine lady, in those times, waddled under more clothes even on a fair summer's day, than would have clad the whole bevy of a modern ball room. Nor were they the less admired by the gentlemen in consequence thereof. On the contrary, the greatness of a lover's passion seemed to encrease in proportion to the magnitude of its object—and a voluminous damsel, arrayed in a dozen of petticoats, was declared by a low-dutch sonnetteer of the province, to be radiant as a sunflower, and luxuriant as a full blown cabbage. Certain it is, that in those days, the heart of a lover could not contain more than one lady at a time; whereas the heart of a modern gallant has often room enough to accommodate half a dozen—The reason of which I conclude to be, either that the hearts of the gentlemen have grown larger, or the persons of the ladies smaller—this however is a question for physiologists to determine.

But there was a secret charm in these petticoats, which no

doubt entered into the consideration of the prudent gallant. The wardrobe of a lady was in those days her only fortune; and she who had a good stock of petticoats and stockings, was as absolutely an heiress, as is a Kamschatka damsel with a store of bear skins, or a Lapland belle with a plenty of rein deer. The ladies therefore, were very anxious to display these powerful attractions to the greatest advantage; and the best rooms in the house instead of being adorned with caricatures of dame nature, in water colours and needle work, were always hung round with abundance of homespun garments; the manufacture and property of the females—a piece of laudable ostentation that still prevails among the heiresses of our dutch villages. Such were the beauteous belles of the ancient city of New Amsterdam, rivalling in primæval simplicity of manners, the renowned and courtly dames, so loftily sung by Dan Homer—who tells us that the princess Nausicaa, washed the family linen, and the fair Penelope wove her own petticoats.

The gentlemen in fact, who figured in the circles of the gay world in these ancient times, corresponded in most particulars, with the beauteous damsels whose smiles they were ambitious to deserve. True it is, their merits would make but a very inconsiderable impression, upon the heart of a modern fair; they neither drove in their curricles nor sported their tandems, for as yet those gaudy vehicles were not even dreamt of—neither did they distinguish themselves by their brilliance at the table, and their consequent rencontres with watchmen, for our forefathers were of too pacific a disposition to need those guardians of the night, every soul throughout the town being in full snore before nine o'clock. Neither did they establish their claims by gentility at the expense of their taylors—for as yet those offenders against the pockets of society, and the tranquillity of all aspiring young gentlemen, were unknown in New Amsterdam; every good housewife made the clothes of her husband and family, and even the goede vrouw of Van Twiller himself, thought it no disparagement to cut out her husband's linsey woolsey galligaskins.

Not but what there were some two or three youngsters who manifested the first dawnings of what is called fire and spirit. Who held all labour in contempt; skulked about docks and market places; loitered in the sun shine; squandered what little money they could procure at hustle cap and chuck farthing, swore, boxed, fought cocks, and raced their neighbours' horses—in short who promised to be the wonder, the talk and abomination of the town, had not their stylish career been unfortunately cut short, by an affair of honour with a whipping post.

Far other, however, was the truly fashionable gentleman of those days—his dress, which served for both morning and evening, street and drawing room, was a linsey woolsey coat, made perhaps by the fair hands of the mistress of his affections, and gallantly bedecked with abundance of large brass buttons.—Half a score of breeches heightened the proportions of his figure— his shoes were decorated by enormous copper buckles—a low crowned broad brimmed hat overshadowed his burley visage, and his hair dangled down his back, in a prodigious queue of eel skin.

Thus equipped, he would manfully sally forth with pipe in mouth to besiege some fair damsel's obdurate heart—not such a pipe, good reader, as that which Acis did sweetly tune in praise of his Galatea, but one of true delft manufacture and furnished with a charge of fragrant Cow-pen tobacco. With this would he resolutely set himself down before the fortress, and rarely failed in the process of time to smoke the fair enemy into a surrender, upon honourable terms.

Such was the happy reign of Wouter Van Twiller, celebrated in many a long forgotten song as the real golden age, the rest being nothing but counterfeit copper-washed coin. In that delightful period, a sweet and holy calm reigned over the whole province. The Burgomaster smoked his pipe in peace—the substantial solace of his domestic house, his well petticoated *yffrouw,* after her daily cares were done, sat soberly at her door, with arms crossed over her apron of snowy white, without being insulted by ribald street walkers or vagabond boys—those unlucky urchins, who do so infest our streets, displaying under the roses of youth, the thorns and briars of iniquity. Then it was that the lover with ten breeches and the damsel with petticoats of half a score indulged in all the innocent endearments of virtuous love, without fear and without reproach—for what had that virtue to fear, which was defended by a shield of good linsey woolseys, equal at least to the seven bull hides of the invincible Ajax.

Thrice happy, and never to be forgotten age! when every thing was better than it has ever been since, or ever will be again—when Buttermilk channel was quite dry at low water—when the shad in the Hudson were all salmon, and when the moon shone with a pure and resplendent whiteness, instead of that melancholy yellow light, which is the consequence of her sickening at the abominations she every night witnesses in this degenerate city!

CHAPTER V

In which the reader is beguiled into a delectable walk, which ends very differently from what it commenced.

In the year of our Lord, one thousand eight hundred and four, on a fine afternoon, in the mellow month of October, I took my customary walk upon the battery, which is at once the pride and bulwark of this ancient and impregnable city of New York. I remember well the season, for it immediately preceded that remarkably cold winter, in which our sagacious corporation, in a spasm of economical philanthropy, pulled to pieces, at an expense of several hundred dollars, the wooden ramparts, which had cost them several thousand; and distributed the rotten fragments, which were worth considerably less than nothing, among the shivering poor of the city—never, since the fall of the walls of Jericho, or the heaven built battlements of Troy, had there been known such a demolition—nor did it go unpunished; five men, eleven old women and nineteen children, besides cats, dogs and negroes, were blinded, in vain attempts to smoke themselves warm, with this charitable substitute for firewood, and an epidemic complaint of sore eyes was moreover produced, which has since recurred every winter; particularly among those who undertake to burn rotten logs—who warm themselves with the charity of others—or who use patent chimnies.

On the year and month just designated, did I take my accustomed walk of meditation, on that same battery, which, though at present, no battery, furnishes the most delightful walk, and commands the noblest prospect, in the whole known world. The ground on which I trod was hallowed by recollections of the past, and as I slowly wandered through the long alleys of poplars, which, like so many birch brooms standing on end, diffused a melancholy and lugubrious shade, my imagination drew a contrast between the surrounding scenery, and what it was in the classic days of our forefathers. Where the government house by name, but the custom house by occupation, proudly reared its brick walls and wooden pillars; there whilome stood the low but substantial, red tiled mansion of the renowned Wouter Van Twiller. Around it the mighty bulwarks of fort Amsterdam frowned defiance to every absent foe; but, like many a whiskered warrior and gallant militia captain, confined their martial deeds to frowns alone—alas! those threatening bulwarks had long since been sapped by time, and like the walls of Carthage, presented no traces to the enquiring eye of the antiquarian. The mud breast works had long been levelled with the earth, and their scite converted into the green lawns and leafy alleys of the battery; where the gay apprentice sported his sunday coat, and the laborious mechanic, relieved from the dirt and drudgery of the week, poured his septennial tale of love into the half averted ear of the sentimental chambermaid. The capacious bay still presented the same expansive sheet of water, studded with islands, sprinkled with fishing boats, and bounded by shores of picturesque beauty. But the dark forests which once clothed these shores had been violated by the savage hand of cultivation, and their tangled mazes, and impracticable thickets, had degenerated into teeming orchards and waving fields of grain. Even Governors Island, once a smiling garden, appertaining to the sovereigns of the province, was now covered with fortifications, inclosing a tremendous block house—so that this once peaceful island resembled a fierce little warrior in a big cocked hat, breathing gunpowder and defiance to the world!

For some time did I indulge in this pensive train of thought; contrasting in sober sadness, the present day, with the hallowed years behind the mountains; lamenting the melancholy progress of improvement, and praising the zeal, with which our worthy burghers endeavour to preserve the wrecks of venerable customs, prejudices and errors, from the overwhelming tide of modern innovation—when by degrees my ideas took a different turn, and I insensibly awakened to an enjoyment of the beauties around me.

It was one of those rich autumnal days which heaven particularly bestows upon the beauteous island of Mannahata and its vicinity—not a floating cloud obscured the azure firmament—the sun, rolling in glorious splendour through his etherial course, seemed to expand his honest dutch countenance into an unusual expression of benevolence, as he smiled his evening salutation upon a city, which he delights to visit with his most bounteous beams—the very winds seemed to hold in their breaths in mute attention, lest they should ruffle the tranquillity of the hour—and the waveless bosom of the bay presented a polished mirror, in which nature beheld herself and smiled!—The standard of our city, which, like a choice handkerchief, is reserved for days of gala, hung motionless on the flag staff, which forms the handle to a gigantic churn; and even the tremulous leaves of the poplar and the aspen, which, like the tongues of the immortal sex, are seldom still, now ceased to vibrate to the breath of heaven. Every thing seemed to acquiesce in the profound repose of nature.— The formidable eighteen pounders slept in the embrazures of the wooden batteries, seemingly gathering fresh strength, to fight the battles of their country on the next fourth of July—the solitary drum on Governor's island forgot to call the garrison to their *shovels*—the evening gun had not yet sounded its signal, for all the regular, well meaning poultry throughout the country, to go to roost; and the fleet of canoes, at anchor between Gibbet Island and Communipaw, slumbered on their rakes, and suffered the innocent oysters to lie for a while unmolested, in the soft mud of their native banks!—My own feelings sympathized in the contagious tranquillity, and I should infallibly have dozed upon one of those fragments of benches, which our benevolent magistrates have provided for the benefit of convalescent loungers, had not the extraordinary inconvenience of the couch set all repose at defiance.

In the midst of this soothing slumber of the soul, my attention was attracted to a black speck, peering above the western horizon, just in the rear of Bergen steeple—gradually it augments and overhangs the would-be cities of Jersey, Harsimus and Hoboken, which, like three jockies, are starting cheek by jowl on the career of existence, and jostling each other at the commencement of the race. Now it skirts the long shore of ancient Pavonia, spreading its wide shadows from the high settlements at Weehawk quite to the lazaretto and quarentine, erected by the sagacity of our police, for the embarrassment of commerce—now it climbs the serene vault of heaven, cloud rolling over cloud, like successive billows, shrouding the orb of day, darkening the vast expanse, and bearing thunder and hail, and tempest in its bosom. The earth seems agitated at the confusion of the heavens—the late waveless mirror is lashed into furious waves, that roll their broken surges in hollow murmurs to the shore—the oyster boats that erst sported in the placid vicinity of Gibbet Island, now hurry affrighted to the shore—the late dignified, unbending poplar, writhes and twists, before the merciless blast—descending torrents of drenching rain and sounding hail deluge the battery walks, the gates are thronged by 'prentices, servant maids and little Frenchmen, with their pocket handkerchiefs over their hats, scampering from the storm—the late beauteous prospect presents one scene of anarchy and wild uproar, as though old chaos had resumed his reign, and was hurling back into one vast turmoil, the conflicting elements of nature. Fancy to yourself, oh reader! the awful combat sung by old Hesiod, of Jupiter, and the Titans—fancy to yourself the long rebellowing artillery of heaven, streaming at the heads of the gigantic sons of earth.—In short, fancy to yourself all that has ever been said or sung, of tempest, storm and hurricane—and you will save me the trouble of describing it.

Whether I fled from the fury of the storm, or remained boldly at my post, as our gallant train band captains, who march their soldiers through the rain without flinching, are points which I leave to the conjecture of the reader. It is possible he may be a little perplexed also, to know the reason why I introduced this most tremendous and unheard of tempest, to disturb the serenity of my work. On this latter point I will gratuitously instruct his ignorance. The panorama view of the battery was given, merely to gratify the reader with a correct description of that celebrated place, and the parts adjacent—secondly, the storm was played off, partly to give a little bustle and life to this tranquil part of my work, and to keep my drowsy readers from falling asleep—and partly to serve as a preparation, or rather an overture, to the tempestuous times, that are about to assail the pacific province of Nieuw Nederlandt—and that over-hang the slumbrous administration of the renowned Wouter Van Twiller. It is thus the experienced play-wright puts all the fiddles, the french horns, the kettle drums and trumpets of his orchestra in requisition, to usher in one of those horrible and brimstone uproars, called Melodrames—and it is thus he discharges his thunder, his lightening, his rosin and saltpetre, preparatory to the raising of a ghost, or the murdering of a hero—We will now proceed with our history.

Whatever Plato, Aristotle, Grotius, Puffendorf, Sydney, Thomas Jefferson or Tom Paine may say to the contrary, I insist that, as to nations, the old maxim that "honesty is the best policy," is a sheer and ruinous mistake. It might have answered well enough in the honest times when it was made; but in these degenerate days, if a nation pretends to rely merely upon the justice of its dealings, it will fare something like an honest man among thieves, who unless he has something more than his honesty to depend upon, stands but a poor chance of profiting by his company. Such at least was the case with the guileless government of the New Netherlands; which, like a worthy unsuspicious old burgher, quietly settled itself down into the city of New Amsterdam, as into a snug elbow chair—and fell into a comfortable nap—while in the mean time its cunning neighbours stepp'd in and picked its pockets. Thus may we ascribe the commencement of all the woes of this great province, and its magnificent metropolis, to the tranquil security, or to speak more accurately, to the unfortunate honesty of its government. But as I dislike to begin an important part of my history, towards the end of a chapter; and as my readers like myself must doubtless be exceedingly fatigued with the long walk we have taken, and the tempest we have sustained—I hold it meet we shut up the book, smoke a pipe and having thus refreshed our spirits; take a fair start in the next chapter.

CHAPTER VI

Faithfully describing the ingenious people of Connecticut and thereabouts—Shewing moreover the true meaning of liberty of conscience, and a curious device among these sturdy barbarians, to keep up a harmony of intercourse and promote population.

That my readers may the more fully comprehend the extent of the calamity, at this very moment impending over the honest, unsuspecting province of Nieuw Nederlandts, and its dubious Governor, it is necessary that I should give some account of a horde of strange barbarians, bordering upon the eastern frontier.

Now so it came to pass, that many years previous to the time of which we are treating, the sage cabinet of England had adopted a certain national creed, a kind of public walk of faith, or rather a religious turnpike in which every loyal subject was directed to travel to Zion—taking care to pay the *toll gatherers* by the way.

Albeit a certain shrewd race of men, being very much given to indulge their own opinions, on all manner of subjects (a propensity, exceedingly obnoxious to your free governments of Europe) did most presumptuously dare to think for themselves in matters of religion, exercising what they considered a natural and unextinguishable right—the liberty of conscience.

As however they possessed that ingenious habit of mind which always thinks aloud; which in a manner rides cock-a-hoop on the tongue, and is forever galloping into other people's ears, it naturally followed that their liberty of conscience likewise implied *liberty of speech,* which being freely indulged, soon put the country in a hubbub, and aroused the pious indignation of the vigilant fathers of the church.

The usual methods were adopted to reclaim them, that in those days were considered so efficacious in bringing back stray sheep to the fold; that is to say, they were coaxed, they were admonished, they were menaced, they were buffeted—line upon line, precept upon precept, lash upon lash, here a little and there a great deal, were exhausted without mercy, but without success; until at length the worthy pastors of the church wearied out by their unparalleled stubbornness, were driven in the excess of their tender mercy, to adopt the scripture text, and literally "heaped live embers on their heads."

Nothing however could subdue that invincible spirit of independence which has ever distinguished this singular race of people, so that rather than submit to such horrible tyranny, they one and all embarked for the wilderness of America, where they might enjoy unmolested, the inestimable luxury of talking. No sooner did they land on this loquacious soil, than as if they had caught the disease from the climate, they all lifted up their voices at once, and for the space of one whole year, did keep up such a joyful clamour, that we are told they frightened every bird and beast out of the neighbourhood, and so completely dumb-founded certain fish, which abound on their coast, that they have been called *dumb-fish* ever since.

From this simple circumstance, unimportant as it may seem, did first originate that renowned privilege so loudly boasted of throughout this country—which is so eloquently exercised in newspapers, pamphlets, ward meetings, pothouse committees and congressional deliberations—which establishes the right of talking without ideas and without information—of misrepresenting public affairs; of decrying public measures—of aspersing great characters, and destroying little ones; in short, that grand palladium of our country, the *liberty of speech*; or as it has been more vulgarly denominated—the *gift of the gab*.

The simple aborigines of the land for a while contemplated these strange folk in utter astonishment, but discovering that they wielded harmless though noisy weapons, and were a lively, ingenious, good-humoured race of men, they became very friendly and sociable, and gave them the name of *Yanokies,* which in the Mais-Tchusaeg (or Massachusett) language signifies *silent men*— a waggish appellation, since shortened into the familiar epithet of YANKEES, which they retain unto the present day.

True it is, and my fidelity as an historian will not allow me to pass it over in silence, that the zeal of these good people, to maintain their rights and privileges unimpaired, did for a while betray them into errors, which it is easier to pardon than defend. Having served a regular apprenticeship in the school of persecution, it behoved them to shew that they had become proficients in the art. They accordingly employed their leisure hours in banishing, scourging or hanging, divers heretical papists, quakers and anabaptists, for daring to abuse the *liberty of conscience;* which they now clearly proved to imply nothing more, than that every man should think as he pleased in matters of religion—*provided* he thought *right;* for otherwise it would be giving a latitude to damnable heresies. Now as they (the majority) were perfectly convinced that *they alone* thought right, it consequently followed, that whoever thought different from them thought wrong—and whoever thought wrong and obstinately persisted in not being convinced and converted, was a flagrant violater of the inestimable liberty of conscience, and a corrupt and infectious member of the body politic, and deserved to be lopped off and cast into the fire.

Now I'll warrant, there are hosts of my readers, ready at once to lift up their hands and eyes, with that virtuous indignation with which we always contemplate the faults and errors of our neighbours, and to exclaim at these well meaning but mistaken people, for inflicting on others the injuries they had suffered themselves—for indulging the preposterous idea of convincing the mind by toasting the carcass, and establishing the doctrine of charity and forbearance, by intolerant persecution.—But soft you, my very captious sirs! what are we doing at this very day, and in this very enlightened nation, but acting upon the very same principle, in our political controversies. Have we not within but a few years released ourselves from the shackles of a government, which cruelly denied us the privilege of governing ourselves, and using in full latitude that invaluable member, the tongue? and are we not at this very moment striving our best to tyrannise over the opinions, tie up the tongues, or ruin the fortunes of one another? What are our great political societies, but mere political inquisitions—our pot-house committees, but little tribunals of denunciation—our news-papers but mere whipping posts and pillories, where unfortunate individuals are pelted with rotten eggs—and our council of appointment—but a grand *auto de fé*, where culprits are annually sacrificed for their political heresies?

Where then is the difference in principle between our measures and those you are so ready to condemn among the people I am treating of? There is none; the difference is merely circumstantial.—Thus we *denounce,* instead of banishing—We *libel* instead of scourging—we *turn out of office* instead of hanging—and where they burnt an offender in propria personæ—we either tar and feather or *burn him in effigy*—this political persecution being, some how or other, the grand palladium of our liberties, and an incontrovertible proof that this is *a free country!*

But notwithstanding the fervent zeal with which this holy war was prosecuted against the whole race of unbelievers, we do not find that the population of this new colony was in any wise hindered thereby; on the contrary they multiplied to a degree, which would be incredible to any man unacquainted with the marvellous fecundity of this growing country.

This amazing increase, may indeed be partly ascribed to a singular custom prevalent among them, and which was probably borrowed from the ancient republic of Sparta; where we are told the young ladies, either from being great romps and hoydens, or else like many modern heroines, very fond of meddling with matters that did not appertain to their sex, used frequently to engage with the men, in wrestling, and other athletic exercises of the gymnasium. The custom to which I allude was vulgarly known by the name of *bundling*—a superstitious rite observed by the young people of both sexes, with which they usually terminated their festivities; and which was kept up with religious strictness, by the more bigoted and vulgar part of the community. This ceremony was likewise, in those primitive times considered as an indispensible preliminary to matrimony; their courtships commencing, where ours usually finish—by which means they acquired that intimate acquaintance with each others good qualities before marriage, that has been pronounced by philosophers the sure basis of a happy union. Thus early did this cunning and ingenious people, display a shrewdness making a bargain which has ever since distinguished them—and a strict adherence to the good old vulgar maxim about "buying a pig in a poke."

To this sagacious custom, therefore, do I chiefly attribute the unparalleled increase of the yanokie or yankee tribe; for it is a certain fact, well authenticated by court records and parish registers, that wherever the practice of bundling prevailed, there was an amazing number of sturdy brats annually born unto the state, without the license of the law, or the benefit of clergy; and it is truly astonishing that the learned Malthus, in his treatise on population, has entirely overlooked this singular fact. Neither did the irregularity of their birth operate in the least to their disparagement. On the contrary they grew up a long sided, raw boned, hardy race of whoreson whalers, wood cutters, fishermen and pedlars, and strapping corn-fed wenches; who by their united efforts tended marvellously towards populating those notable tracts of country, called Nantucket, Piscataway and Cape Cod.

CHAPTER VII

How these singular barbarians turned out to be notorious squatters. How they built air castles, and attempted to initiate the Nederlanders in the mystery of bundling.

In the last chapter, my honest little reader, I have given thee a faithful and unprejudiced account, of the origin of that singular race of people, inhabiting the country eastward of the Nieuw Nederlandts; but I have yet to mention certain peculiar habits which rendered them exceedingly obnoxious to our ever honoured dutch ancestors.

The most prominent of these was a certain rambling propensity, with which, like the sons of Ishmael, they seem to have been gifted by heaven, and which continually goads them on, to shift their residence from place to place, so that a Yankey farmer is in a constant state of migration; *tarrying* occasionally here and there; clearing lands for other people to enjoy, building houses for others to inhabit, and in a manner may be considered the wandering Arab of America.

His first thought, on coming to the years of manhood, is to *settle* himself in the world—which means nothing more nor less than to begin his rambles. To this end he takes unto himself for a wife, some dashing country heiress; that is to say, a buxom rosy cheeked wench, passing rich in red ribbands, glass beads and mock tortoise-shell combs, with a white gown and morocco shoes for Sunday, and deeply skilled in the mystery of making apple sweetmeats, long sauce and pumpkin pie.

Having thus provided himself, like a true pedlar with a heavy knapsack, wherewith to regale his shoulders through the journey of life, he literally sets out on the peregrination. His whole family, household furniture and farming utensils are hoisted into a covered cart; his own and his wife's wardrobe packed up in a firkin—which done, he shoulders his axe, takes staff in hand, whistles "yankee doodle" and trudges off to the woods, as confident of the protection of providence, and relying as cheerfully upon his own resources, as did ever a patriarch of yore, when he journeyed into a strange country of the Gentiles. Having buried himself in the wilderness, he builds himself a log hut, clears away a cornfield and potatoe patch, and, providence smiling upon his labours, is soon surrounded by a snug farm and some half a score of flaxen headed urchins, who by their size, seem to have sprung all at once out of the earth, like a crop of toad-stools.

But it is not the nature of this most indefatigable of speculators, to rest contented with any state of sublunary enjoyment—*improvement* is his darling passion, and having thus improved his lands the next care is to provide a mansion worthy the residence of a land holder. A huge palace of pine boards immediately springs up in the midst of the wilderness, large enough for a parish church, and furnished with windows of all dimensions, but so rickety and flimsy withal, that every blast gives it a fit of the ague.

By the time the outside of this mighty air castle is completed, either the funds or the zeal of our adventurer are exhausted, so that he barely manages to half finish one room within, where the whole family burrow together—while the rest of the house is devoted to the curing of pumpkins, or storing of carrots and potatoes, and is decorated with fanciful festoons of wilted peaches and dried apples. The outside remaining unpainted, grows venerably black with time: the family wardrobe is laid under contribution for old hats, petticoats and breeches to stuff into the broken windows, while the four winds of heaven keep up a whistling and howling about this aerial palace, and play as many unruly gambols, as they did of yore, in the cave of old Eolus.

The humble log hut, which whilome nestled this *improving* family snugly within its narrow but comfortable walls, stands hard by in ignominious contrast, degraded into a cow house or pig stye; and the whole scene reminds one forcibly of a fable, which I am surprised has never been recorded, of an aspiring snail who quit his humble habitation which he filled with great respectability, to crawl into the empty shell of a lobster—where he would no doubt have resided with great style and splendour, the envy and hate of all the pains-taking snails of his neighbourhood, had he not accidentally perished with cold, in one corner of his stupendous mansion.

Being thus completely settled, and to use his own words, "to rights," one would imagine that he would begin to enjoy the comforts of his situation, to read newspapers, talk politics, neglect his own business, and attend to the affairs of the nation, like a useful and patriotic citizen; but now it is that his wayward disposition begins again to operate. He soon grows tired of a spot, where there is no longer any room for improvement—sells his farm, air castle, petticoat windows and all, reloads his cart, shoulders his axe, puts himself at the head of his family, and wanders away in search of new lands—again to fell trees—again to clear cornfields—again to build a shingle palace, and again to sell off, and wander.

Such were the people of Connecticut, who bordered upon the eastern frontier of Nieuw Nederlandts, and my readers may easily imagine what obnoxious neighbors this light hearted but restless tribe must have been to our tranquil progenitors. If they cannot, I would ask them, if they have ever known one of our regular, well organized, antediluvian dutch families, whom it hath pleased heaven to afflict with the neighbourhood of a French boarding house. The honest old burgher cannot take his afternoon's pipe, on the bench before his door, but he is persecuted with the scraping of fiddles, the chattering of women, and the squalling of children—he cannot sleep at night for the horrible melodies of some amateur, who chooses to serenade the moon, and display his terrible proficiency in *execution*, by playing demisemiquavers in alt on the clarionet, the hautboy, or some other soft toned instrument—nor can he leave the street door open, but his house is defiled by the unsavoury visits of a troop of pug dogs, who even sometimes carry their loathsome ravages into the sanctum sanctorum, the parlour!

If my readers have ever witnessed the sufferings of such a family, so situated, they may form some idea, how our worthy ancestors were distressed by their mercurial neighbours of Connecticut.

Gangs of these marauders we are told, penetrated into the New Netherland settlements and threw whole villages into consternation by their unparalleled volubility and their intolerable inquisitiveness—two evil habits hitherto unknown in those parts, or only known to be abhorred; for our ancestors were noted, as being men of truly spartan taciturnity, and who neither knew nor cared aught about any body's concerns but their own. Many enormities were committed on the high ways, where several unoffending burghers were brought to a stand, and so tortured with questions and guesses, that it was a miracle they escaped with their five senses.

Great jealousy did they likewise stir up, by their intermeddling and successes among the divine sex; for being a race of brisk, likely, pleasant tongued varlets, they soon seduced the light affections of the simple damsels, from their honest but ponderous dutch gallants. Among other hideous customs they attempted to introduce among them that of *bundling,* which the dutch lasses of the Nederlandts, with that eager passion for novelty and foreign fashions, natural to their sex, seemed very well inclined to follow, but that their mothers, being more experienced in the world, and better acquainted with men and things strenuously discountenanced all such outlandish innovations.

But what chiefly operated to embroil our ancestors with these strange folk, was an unwarrantable liberty which they occasionally took, of entering in hordes into the territories of the New Netherlands, and settling themselves down, without leave or licence, to *improve* the land, in the manner I have before noticed. This unceremonious mode of taking possession of *new land* was technically termed *squatting,* and hence is derived the appellation of *squatters;* a name odious in the ears of all great landholders, and which is given to those enterprizing worthies, who seize upon land first, and take their chance to make good their title to it afterwards.

All these grievances, and many others which were constantly accumulating, tended to form that dark and portentous cloud, which as I observed in a former chapter, was slowly gathering over the tranquil province of New Netherlands. The pacific cabinet of Van Twiller, however, as will be perceived in the sequel, bore them all with a magnanimity that redounds to their immortal credit—becoming by passive endurance inured to this increasing mass of wrongs; like the sage old woman of Ephesus, who by dint of carrying about a calf, from the time it was born, continued to carry it without difficulty, when it had grown to be an ox.

CHAPTER VIII

*How the Fort Goed Hoop was fearfully beleaguered—
how the renowned Wouter fell into a profound doubt,
and how he finally evaporated.*

By this time my readers must fully perceive, what an arduous task I have undertaken—collecting and collating with painful minuteness, the chronicles of past times, whose events almost defy the powers of research—raking in a little kind of Herculaneum of history, which had lain nearly for ages, buried under the rubbish of years, and almost totally forgotten—raking up the limbs and fragments of disjointed facts, and endeavouring to put them scrupulously together, so as to restore them to their original form and connection—now lugging forth the character of an almost forgotten hero, like a mutilated statue—now deciphering a half defaced inscription, and now lighting upon a mouldering manuscript, which after painful study, scarce repays the trouble of perusal.

In such case how much has the reader to depend upon the honour and probity of his author, lest like a cunning antiquarian, he either impose upon him some spurious fabrication of his own, for a precious relique from antiquity—or else dress up the dismembered fragment, with such false trappings, that it is scarcely possible to distinguish the truth from the fiction with which it is enveloped. This is a grievance which I have more than once had to lament, in the course of my wearisome researches among the works of my fellow historians; who have strangely disguised and distorted the facts respecting this country; and particularly respecting the great province of New Netherlands; as will be perceived by any who will take the trouble to compare their romantic effusions, tricked out in the meretricious gauds of fable, with this excellent little history—universally to be renowned for its severe simplicity and unerring truth.

I have had more vexations of the kind to encounter, in those parts of my history which treat of the transactions on the eastern

border, than in any other, in consequence of the troops of historians who have infested these quarters, and have shewn the honest
people of New Nederlandt no mercy in their works. Among the
rest, Mr. Benjamin Trumbull arrogantly declares that "the Dutch
were always mere intruders."—Now to this I shall make no other
reply, than to proceed in the steady narration of my history, which
will contain not only proofs that the Dutch had clear title and possession in the fair valleys of the Connecticut, and that they were
wrongfully dispossessed thereof—but likewise that they have been
scandalously maltreated ever since, by the misrepresentations of
the crafty historians of New England. And in this I shall be
guided by a spirit of truth and impartiality, and a regard to my immortal fame—for I would not wittingly dishonour my work by a
single falsehood, misrepresentation or prejudice, though it should
gain our forefathers the whole country of New England.

It was at an early period of the province, and previous to the
arrival of the renowned Wouter—that the cabinet of Nieuw Nederlandts purchased the lands about the Connecticut, and established, for their superintendance and protection, a fortified post
on the banks of the river, which was called Fort Goed Hoop, and
was situated hard by the present fair city of Hartford. The command of this important post, together with the rank, title, and
appointments of commissary, were given in charge to the gallant
Jacobus Van Curlet, or as some historians will have it Van
Curlis—a most doughty soldier of that stomachful class of which
we have such numbers on parade days—who are famous for eating all they kill. He was of a very soldierlike appearance, and
would have been an exceeding tall man, had his legs been in proportion to his body; but the latter being long, and the former
uncommonly short, it gave him the uncouth appearance of a tall
man's body, mounted upon a little man's legs. He made up for
this turn-spit construction of body by throwing his legs to such
an extent when he marched, that you would have sworn he had
on the identical seven league boots of the farfamed Jack the giant
killer; and so astonishingly high did he tread on any great military occasion, that his soldiers were oft times alarmed, lest the
little man should trample himself under foot.

But notwithstanding the erection of this fort, and the appointment of this ugly little man of war as a commander, the intrepid

Yankees, continued those daring interlopings which I have hinted at in my last chapter; and taking advantage of the character which the cabinet of Wouter Van Twiller soon acquired, for profound and phlegmatic tranquillity—did audaciously invade the territories of the Nieuw Nederlandts, and *squat* themselves down within the very jurisdiction of fort Goed Hoop.

On beholding this outrage, the long bodied Van Curlet proceeded as became a prompt and valiant officer. He immediately protested against these unwarrantable encroachments, in low dutch, by way of inspiring more terror, and forthwith dispatched a copy of the protest to the governor at New Amsterdam, together with a long and bitter account of the aggressions of the enemy. This done, he ordered his men, one and all to be of good cheer—shut the gate of the fort, smoked three pipes, went to bed and awaited the result with a resolute and intrepid tranquillity, that greatly animated his adherents, and no doubt struck sore dismay and affright into the hearts of the enemy.

Now it came to pass, that about this time, the renowned Wouter Van Twiller, full of years and honours, and council dinners, had reached that period of life and faculty which, according to the great Gulliver, entitle a man to admission into the ancient order of Struldbruggs. He employed his time in smoking his turkish pipe, amid an assemblage of sages, equally enlightened, and nearly as venerable as himself, and who for their silence, their gravity, their wisdom, and their cautious averseness to coming to any conclusion in business, are only to be equalled by certain profound corporations which I have known in my time. Upon reading the protest of the gallant Jacobus Van Curlet therefore, his excellency fell straightway into one of the deepest doubts that ever he was known to encounter; his capacious head gradually drooped on his chest,* he closed his eyes and inclined his ear to one side, as if listening with great attention to the discussion that was going on in his belly; which all who knew him, declared to be the huge court-house, or council chamber of his thoughts; forming to his head what the house of representatives does to the senate. An in-

* "Perplexed with vast affairs of state and town,
   His great head being overset, hangs down."
                                    Telecides, on Pericles.

articulate sound, very much resembling a snore, occasionally escaped him—but the nature of this internal cogitation, was never
known, as he never opened his lips on the subject to man, woman
or child. In the mean time, the protest of Van Curlet laid quietly
on the table, where it served to light the pipes of the venerable
sages assembled in council; and in the great smoke which they
raised, the gallant Jacobus, his protest, and his mighty Fort Goed
Hoop, were soon as completely beclouded and forgotten, as is a
question of emergency swallowed up in the speeches and resolutions of a modern session of congress.

There are certain emergencies when your profound legislators
and sage deliberative councils, are mightily in the way of a nation; and when an ounce of hair-brained decision, is worth a
pound of sage doubt, and cautious discussion. Such at least was
the case at present; for while the renowned Wouter Van Twiller
was daily battling with his doubts, and his resolution growing
weaker and weaker in the contest, the enemy pushed further and
further into his territories, and assumed a most formidable appearance in the neighbourhood of Fort Goed Hoop. Here they
founded the mighty town of *Pyquag,* or as it has since been called
Weathersfield, a place which, if we may credit the assertions of
that worthy historian John Josselyn, Gent. "hath been infamous
by reason of the witches therein."—And so daring did these men
of Pyquag become, that they extended those plantations of onions, for which their town is illustrious, under the very noses of
the garrison of Fort Goed Hoop—insomuch that the honest
dutchmen could not look toward that quarter, without tears in
their eyes.

This crying injustice was regarded with proper indignation by
the gallant Jacobus Van Curlet. He absolutely trembled with the
amazing violence of his choler and the exacerbations of his
valour; which seemed to be the more turbulent in their workings,
from the length of the body, in which they were agitated. He
forthwith proceeded to strengthen his redoubts, heighten his
breastworks, deepen his fosse, and fortify his position with a
double row of abbatis; after which valiant precautions, he with
unexampled intrepidity, dispatched a fresh courier with tremendous accounts of his perilous situation. Never did the modern
hero, who immortalized himself at the second Sabine war, shew

greater valour in the art of letter writing, or distinguish himself more gloriously upon paper, than the heroic Van Curlet.

The courier chosen to bear these alarming dispatches, was a fat, oily little man, as being least liable to be worn out, or to lose leather on the journey; and to insure his speed, he was mounted on the fleetest waggon horse in the garrison; remarkable for his length of limb, largeness of bone, and hardness of trot; and so tall, that the little messenger was obliged to climb on his back by means of his tail and crupper. Such extraordinary speed did he make, that he arrived at Fort Amsterdam in little less than a month, though the distance was full two hundred pipes, or about 120 miles.

The extraordinary appearance of this portentous stranger would have thrown the whole town of New Amsterdam into a quandary, had the good people troubled themselves about any thing more than their domestic affairs. With an appearance of great hurry and business, and smoking a short travelling pipe, he proceeded on a long swing trot through the muddy lanes of the metropolis, demolishing whole batches of dirt pies, which the little dutch children were making in the road; and for which kind of pastry the children of this city have ever been famous—On arriving at the governor's house he climbed down from his steed in great trepidation; roused the grey headed door keeper, old Skaats who like his lineal decendant, and faithful representative, the venerable crier of our court, was nodding at his post—rattled at the door of the council chamber, and startled the members as they were dozing over a plan for establishing a public market.

At that very moment a gentle grunt, or rather a deep drawn snore was heard from the chair of the governor; a whiff of smoke was at the same instant observed to escape from his lips, and a slight cloud to ascend from the bowl of his pipe. The council of course supposed him engaged in deep sleep for the good of the community, and according to custom in all such cases established, every man bawled out silence, in order to maintain tranquillity; when of a sudden, the door flew open and the little courier straddled into the apartment, cased to the middle in a pair of Hessian boots, which he had got into for the sake of expedition. In his right hand he held forth the ominous dispatches, and with his left he grasped firmly the waist-band of his galligaskins; which had unfortunately given way, in the exertion of descending from his horse. He stumped resolutely up to the governor, and with more hurry than perspicuity delivered his message. But fortunately his ill tidings came too late, to ruffle the tranquillity of this most tranquil of rulers. His venerable excellency had just breathed and smoked his last—his lungs and his pipe having been exhausted together, and his peaceful soul, as Dan Homer would have said, having escaped in the last whiff that curled from his tobacco pipe.—In a word the renowned Wouter Van Twiller, alias Walter the Doubter, who had so often slumbered with his cotemporaries, now slept with his fathers, and Wilhelmus Kieft governed in his stead.

END OF BOOK III

BOOK IV

Containing the Chronicles of the reign of
William the Testy.

CHAPTER I

Exposing the craftiness and artful devices of those arch Free Booters, the Book Makers, and their trusty Squires, the Book Sellers. Containing furthermore, the universal acquirements of William the Testy, and how a man may learn so much as to render himself good for nothing.

If ever I had my readers completely by the button, it is at this moment. Here is a redoubtable fortress reduced to the greatest extremity; a valiant commander in a state of the most imminent jeopardy—and a legion of implacable foes thronging upon every side. The sentimental reader is preparing to indulge his sympathies, and bewail the sufferings of the brave. The philosophic reader, to come with his first principles, and coolly take the dimensions and ascertain the proportions of great actions, like an antiquary, measuring a pyramid with a two-foot rule—while the mere reader, for amusement, promises to regale himself after the monotonous pages through which he has dozed, with murders, rapes, ravages, conflagrations, and all the other glorious incidents, that give eclat to victory, and grace the triumph of the conqueror.

Thus every reader must press forward—he cannot refrain, if he has the least spark of curiosity in his disposition, from turning over the ensuing page. Having therefore gotten him fairly in my clutches—what hinders me from indulging in a little recreation, and varying the dull task of narrative by stultifying my readers with a drove of sober reflections about this, that and the other thing—by pushing forward a few of my own darling opinions; or talking a little about myself—all which the reader will have to peruse, or else give up the book altogether, and remain in utter ignorance of the mighty deeds, and great events, that are contained in the sequel.

To let my readers into a great literary secret, your experienced writers, who wish to instil peculiar tenets, either in religion, politics or morals, do often resort to this expedient—illustrating their favourite doctrines by pleasing fictions on established facts—and so mingling historic truth, and subtle speculation together, that the unwary million never perceive the medley; but, running with open mouth, after an interesting story, are often made to swallow the most heterodox opinions, ridiculous theories, and abominable heresies. This is particularly the case with the industrious advocates of the modern philosophy, and many an honest unsuspicious reader, who devours their works under an idea of acquiring solid knowledge, must not be surprised if, to use a pious quotation, he finds "his belly filled with the east wind."

This same expedient is likewise a literary artifice, by which one sober truth, like a patient and laborious pack horse, is made to carry a couple of panniers of rascally little conjectures on its back. In this manner books are encreased, the pen is kept going and trade flourishes; for if every writer were obliged to tell merely what he knew, there would soon be an end of great books, and Tom Thumb's folio would be considered as a gigantic production—A man might then carry his library in his pocket, and the whole race of book makers, book printers, book binders and book sellers might starve together; but by being entitled to tell every thing he thinks, and every thing he does not think—to talk about every thing he knows, or does not know—to conjecture, to doubt, to argue with himself, to laugh with and laugh at his reader, (the latter of which we writers do nine times out of ten—in our sleeves) to indulge in hypotheses, to deal in dashes——and stars **** and a thousand other innocent indulgencies—all these I say, do marvelously concur to fill the pages of books, the pockets of booksellers, and the hungry stomachs of authors—do contribute to the amusement and edification of the reader, and redound to the glory, the encrease and the profit of the craft!

Having thus, therefore, given my readers the whole art and mystery of book making, they have nothing further to do, than to take pen in hand, set down and write a book for themselves—while in the mean time I will proceed with my history, without claiming any of the privileges above recited.

WILHELMUS KIEFT who in 1634 ascended the *Gubernatorial* chair, (to borrow a favourite, though clumsy appellation of modern phraseologists) was in form, feature and character, the very reverse of Wouter Van Twiller, his renowned predecessor. He was of very respectable descent, his father being Inspector of Windmills in the ancient town of Saardam; and our hero we are told made very curious investigations into the nature and operations of these machines when a little boy, which is one reason why he afterwards came to be so ingenious a governor. His name according to the most ingenious etymologists was a corruption of *Kyper*, that is to say a *wrangler* or *scolder,* and expressed the hereditary disposition of his family; which for nearly two centuries, had kept the windy town of Saardam in hot water, and produced more tartars and brimstones than any ten families in the place— and so truly did Wilhelmus Kieft inherit this family endowment, that he had scarcely been a year in the discharge of his government, before he was universally known by the appellation of WILLIAM THE TESTY.

He was a brisk, waspish, little old gentleman, who had dried and wilted away, partly through the natural process of years, and partly from being parched and burnt up by his fiery soul; which blazed like a vehement rush light in his bosom, constantly inciting him to most valourous broils, altercations and misadventures. I have heard it observed by a profound and philosophical judge of human nature, that if a woman waxes fat as she grows old, the tenure of her life is very precarious, but if haply she wilts, she lives forever—such likewise was the case with William the Testy, who grew tougher in proportion as he dried. He was some such a little dutchman as we may now and then see, stumping briskly about the streets of our city, in a broad skirted coat, with buttons nearly as large as the shield of Ajax, which makes such a figure in Dan Homer, an old fashioned cocked hat stuck on the back of his head, and a cane as high as his chin. His visage was broad, but his features sharp, his nose turned up with a most petulant curl; his cheeks, like the region of Terra del Fuego, were scorched into a dusky red—doubtless in consequence of the neighbourhood of two fierce little grey eyes, through which his torrid soul beamed as fervently, as a tropical sun blazing through a pair of burning glasses. The corners of his mouth were curiously modeled into a kind of fret work, not a little resembling the wrinkled proboscis of an irritable pug dog—in a word he was one of the most positive, restless, ugly little men, that ever put himself in a passion about nothing.

Such were the personal endowments of William the Testy, but it was the sterling riches of his mind that raised him to dignity and power. In his youth he had passed with great credit through a celebrated academy at the Hague, noted for producing finished scholars, with a dispatch unequalled, except by certain of our American colleges, which seem to manufacture bachelors of arts, by some patent machine. Here he skirmished very smartly on the frontiers of several of the sciences, and made such a gallant inroad into the dead languages, as to bring off captive a host of Greek nouns and Latin verbs, together with divers pithy saws and apothegms, all which he constantly paraded in conversation and writing, with as much vain glory as would a triumphant general of yore display the spoils of the countries he had ravaged. He had moreover puzzled himself considerably with logic, in which he had advanced so far as to attain a very familiar acquaintance, by name at least, with the whole family of syllogisms and dilemmas; but what he chiefly valued himself on, was his knowledge of metaphysics, in which, having once upon a time ventured too deeply, he came well nigh being smothered in a slough of unintelligible learning—a fearful peril, from the effects of which he never perfectly recovered.—In plain words, like many other profound intermeddlers in this abstruse bewildering science, he so confused his brain, with abstract speculations which he could not comprehend, and artificial distinctions which he could not realize, that he could never think clearly on any subject however simple, through the whole course of his life afterwards. This I must confess was in some measure a misfortune, for he never engaged in argument, of which he was exceeding fond, but what between logical deductions and metaphysical jargon, he soon involved himself and his subject in a fog of contradictions and perplexities, and then would get into a mighty passion with his adversary, for not being convinced gratis.

It is in knowledge, as in swimming, he who ostentatiously sports and flounders on the surface, makes more noise and splashing, and attracts more attention, than the industrious pearl diver, who plunges in search of treasures to the bottom. The "universal acquirements" of William Kieft, were the subject of great marvel and admiration among his countrymen—he figured about at the Hague with as much vain glory, as does a profound Bonze at Pekin, who has mastered half the letters of the Chinese alphabet; and in a word was unanimously pronounced an *universal genius!*—I have known many universal geniuses in my time, though to speak my mind freely I never knew one, who, for the ordinary purposes of life, was worth his weight in straw—but for the purposes of government, a little sound judgment and plain common sense, is worth all the sparkling genius that ever wrote poetry, or invented theories.

Strange as it may sound therefore, the *universal acquirements* of the illustrious Wilhelmus, were very much in his way, and had he been a less learned little man, it is possible he would have been a much greater governor. He was exceedingly fond of trying philosophical and political experiments; and having stuffed his head full of scraps and remnants of ancient republics, and oligarchies, and aristocracies, and monarchies, and the laws of Solon and Lycurgus and Charondas, and the imaginary commonwealth of Plato, and the Pandects of Justinian, and a thousand other fragments of venerable antiquity, he was forever bent upon introducing some one or other of them into use; so that between one contradictory measure and another, he entangled the government of the little province of Nieuw Nederlandts in more knots during his administration, than half a dozen successors could have untied.

No sooner had this bustling little man been blown by a whiff of fortune into the seat of government, than he called together his council and delivered a very animated speech on the affairs of the province. As every body knows what a glorious opportunity a governor, a president, or even an emperor has, of drubbing his enemies in his speeches, messages and bulletins, where he has the talk all on his own side, they may be sure the high mettled William Kieft did not suffer so favourable an occasion to escape him, of evincing that gallantry of tongue, common to all able legislators. Before he commenced, it is recorded that he took out of his pocket a red cotton handkerchief, and gave a very sonorous blast of the nose, according to the usual custom of great orators. This in general I believe is intended as a signal trumpet, to call the attention of the auditors, but with William the testy it boasted a more classic cause, for he had read of the singular expedient of that famous demagogue Caius Gracchus, who when he harangued the Roman populace, modulated his tones by an oratorical flute or pitch-pipe—"which", said the shrewd Wilhelmus, "I take to be nothing more nor less, than an elegant and figurative mode of saying—he previously blew his nose."

This preparatory symphony being performed, he commenced by expressing a humble sense of his own want of talents—his utter unworthiness of the honour conferred upon him, and his humiliating incapacity to discharge the important duties of his new station—in short, he expressed so contemptible an opinion of himself, that many simple country members present, ignorant that these were mere words of course, always used on such occasions, were very uneasy, and even felt wrath that he should accept an office, for which he was consciously so inadequate.

He then proceeded in a manner highly classic, profoundly erudite, and nothing at all to the purpose, being nothing more than a pompous account of all the governments of ancient Greece, and the wars of Rome and Carthage, together with the rise and fall of sundry outlandish empires, about which the assembly knew no more than their great grand children who were yet unborn. Thus having, after the manner of your learned orators, convinced the audience that he was a man of many words and great erudition, he at length came to the less important part of his speech, the situation of the province—and here he soon worked himself into a fearful rage against the Yankees, whom he compared to the Gauls who desolated Rome, and the Goths and Vandals who overran the fairest plains of Europe—nor did he forget to mention, in terms of adequate opprobrium, the insolence with which they had encroached upon the territories of New Netherlands, and the unparalleled audacity with which they had commenced the town of New Plymouth, and planted the onion patches of Weathersfield under the very walls, or rather mud batteries of Fort Goed Hoop.

Having thus artfully wrought up his tale of terror to a climax, he assumed a self satisfied look, and declared, with a nod of knowing import, that he had taken measures to put a final stop to these encroachments—that he had been obliged to have recourse to a dreadful engine of warfare, lately invented, awful in its effects, but authorized by direful necessity. In a word, he was resolved to conquer the Yankees—by proclamation!

For this purpose he had prepared a tremendous instrument of the kind ordering, commanding and enjoining the intruders aforesaid, forthwith to remove, depart and withdraw from the districts, regions and territories aforesaid, under pain of suffering all the penalties, forfeitures, and punishments in such case made and provided, &c. This proclamation he assured them, would at once exterminate the enemy from the face of the country, and he pledged his valour as a governor, that within two months after it was published, not one stone should remain on another, in any of the towns which they had built.

The council remained for some time silent, after he had finished; whether struck dumb with admiration at the brilliancy of his project, or put to sleep by the length of his harangue, the history of the times doth not mention. Suffice it to say, they at length gave a universal grunt of acquiescence—the proclamation was immediately dispatched with due ceremony, having the great seal of the province, which was about the size of a buckwheat pancake, attached to it by a broad red ribband. Governor Kieft having thus vented his indignation, felt greatly relieved—adjourned the council *sine die*—put on his cocked hat and corduroy small clothes, and mounting a tall raw boned charger, trotted out to his country seat, which was situated in a sweet, sequestered swamp, now called Dutch street, but more commonly known by the name of Dog's Misery.

Here, like the good Numa, he reposed from the toils of legislation, taking lessons in government, not from the Nymph Egeria, but from the honoured wife of his bosom; who was one of that peculiar kind of females, sent upon earth a little after the flood, as a punishment for the sins of mankind, and commonly known by the appellation of *knowing women*. In fact, my duty as an historian obliges me to make known a circumstance which was a great secret at the time, and consequently was not a subject of scandal at more than half the tea tables in New Amsterdam, but which like many other great secrets, has leaked out in the lapse of years—and this was, that the great Wilhelmus the Testy, though one of the most potent little men that ever breathed, yet submitted at home to a species of government, neither laid down in Aristotle, nor Plato; in short, it partook of the nature of a pure, unmixed tyranny, and is familarly denominated *petticoat government*.— An absolute sway, which though exceedingly common in these modern days, was very rare among the ancients, if we may judge

from the rout made about the domestic economy of honest Socrates; which is the only ancient case on record.

The great Kieft however, warded off all the sneers and sar-
casms of his particular friends, who are ever ready to joke with a
man on sore points of the kind, by alledging that it was a government of his own election, which he submitted to through choice;
adding at the same time that it was a profound maxim which he
had found in an ancient author—"he who would aspire to *govern*, should first learn to *obey*."

CHAPTER II

In which are recorded the sage Projects of a Ruler of universal Genius.—The art of Fighting by Proclamation,—and how that the valiant Jacobus Van Curlet came to be foully dishonoured at Fort Goed Hoop.

Never was a more comprehensive, a more expeditious, or, what is still better, a more economical measure devised, than this of defeating the Yankees by proclamation—an expedient, likewise, so humane, so gentle and pacific; there were ten chances to one in favour of its succeeding,—but then there was one chance to ten that it would not succeed—as the ill-natured fates would have it, that single chance carried the day! The proclamation was perfect in all its parts, well constructed, well written, well sealed and well published—all that was wanting to insure its effect, was that the Yankees should stand in awe of it; but, provoking to relate, they treated it with the most absolute contempt, applied it to an unseemly purpose, which shall be nameless, and thus did the first warlike proclamation come to a shameful end—a fate which I am credibly informed, has befallen but too many of its successors.

It was a long time before Wilhelmus Kieft could be persuaded by the united efforts of all his counsellors, that his war measure had failed in producing any effect.—On the contrary, he flew in a passion whenever any one dared to question its efficacy; and swore, that though it was slow in operating, yet when once it began to work, it would soon purge the land from these rapacious intruders. Time however, that tester of all experiments both in philosophy and politics, at length convinced the great Kieft, that his proclamation was abortive; and that notwithstanding he had waited nearly four years, in a state of constant irritation, yet he was still further off than ever from the object of his wishes. His implacable adversaries in the east became more and more troublesome in their encroachments, and founded the thriving colony of Hartford close upon the skirts of Fort Goed Hoop. They moreover commenced the fair settlement of Newhaven (alias the

Red Hills) within the domains of their high mightinesses—while the onion patches of Pyquag were a continual eye sore to the garrison of Van Curlet. Upon beholding therefore the inefficacy of his measure, the sage Kieft like many a worthy practitioner of physic, laid the blame, not to the medicine, but the quantity administered, and resolutely resolved to double the dose.

In the year 1638 therefore, that being the fourth year of his reign, he fulminated against them a second proclamation, of heavier metal than the former; written in thundering long sentences, not one word of which was under five syllables. This, in fact, was a kind of non-intercourse bill, forbidding and prohibiting all commerce and connexion, between any and every of the said Yankee intruders, and the said fortified post of Fort Goed Hoop, and ordering, commanding and advising, all his trusty, loyal and well-beloved subjects, to furnish them with no supplies of gin, gingerbread or sour crout; to buy none of their pacing horses, meazly pork, apple brandy, Yankee rum, cyder water, apple sweetmeats, Weathersfield onions or wooden bowls, but to starve and exterminate them from the face of the land.

Another pause of a twelve month ensued, during which the last proclamation received the same attention, and experienced the same fate as the first—at the end of which term, the gallant Jacobus Van Curlet dispatched his annual messenger, with his customary budget of complaints and entreaties. Whether the regular interval of a year, intervening between the arrival of Van Curlet's couriers, was occasioned by the systematic regularity of his movements, or by the immense distance at which he was stationed from the seat of government is a matter of uncertainty. Some have ascribed it to the slowness of his messengers, who, as I have before noticed, were chosen from the shortest and fattest of his garrison, as least likely to be worn out on the road; and who, being pursy, short winded little men, generally travelled fifteen miles a day, and then laid by a whole week, to rest. All these, however, are matters of conjecture; and I rather think it may be ascribed to the immemorial maxim of this worthy country—and which has ever influenced all its public transactions—not to do things in a hurry.

The gallant Jacobus Van Curlet in his dispatches respectfully represented, that several years had now elapsed, since his first application to his late excellency, the renowned Wouter Van Twiller: during which interval, his garrison had been reduced nearly one-eighth, by the death of two of his most valiant, and corpulent soldiers, who had accidentally over eaten themselves on some fat salmon, caught in the Varsche river. He further stated that the enemy persisted in their inroads, taking no notice of the fort or its inhabitants; but squatting themselves down, and forming settlements all around it; so that, in a little while, he should find himself enclosed and blockaded by the enemy, and totally at their mercy.

But among the most atrocious of his grievances, I find the following still on record, which may serve to shew the bloody minded outrages of these savage intruders. "In the meane time, they of Hartford have not onely usurped and taken in the lands of Connecticott, although unrighteously and against the lawes of nations, but have hindered our nation in sowing theire owne purchased broken up lands, but have also sowed them with corne in the night, which the Netherlanders had broken up and intended to sowe: and have beaten the servants of the high and mighty the honored companie, which were labouring upon theire master's lands, from theire lands, with sticks and plow staves in hostile manner laming, and amongst the rest, struck Ever Duckings* a hole in his head, with a stick, soe that the blood ran downe very strongly downe upon his body!"

But what is still more atrocious—

"Those of Hartford sold a hogg, that belonged to the honored companie, under pretence that it had eaten of theire grounde grass, when they had not any foot of inheritance. They proferred the hogg for 5s. if the commissioners would have given 5s. for damage; which the commissioners denied, because noe mans owne hogg (as men use to say) can trespasse upon his owne master's grounde."†

The receipt of this melancholy intelligence incensed the whole community—there was something in it that spoke to the dull

---

*This name is no doubt misspelt. In some old Dutch MSS. of the time, we find the name of Evert Duyckingh, who is unquestionably the unfortunate hero above alluded to.
†Haz. Col. Stat. Paps.

comprehension, and touched the obtuse feelings even of the puissant vulgar, who generally require a kick in the rear, to awaken their slumbering dignity. I have known my profound fellow citizens bear without murmur, a thousand essential infringements of their rights, merely because they were not immediately obvious to their senses—but the moment the unlucky Pearce was shot upon our coasts, the whole body politic was in a ferment—so the enlighted Nederlanders, though they had treated the encroachments of their eastern neighbours with but little regard, and left their quill valiant governor, to bear the whole brunt of war, with his single pen—yet now every individual felt his head broken in the broken head of Duckings—and the unhappy fate of their fellow citizen the hog; being impressed, carried and sold into captivity, awakened a grunt of sympathy from every bosom.

The governor and council, goaded by the clamours of the multitude, now set themselves earnestly to deliberate upon what was to be done. Proclamations had at length fallen into temporary disrepute; some were for sending the Yankees a tribute, as we make peace offerings to the petty Barbary powers, or as the Indians sacrifice to the devil. Others were for buying them out, but this was opposed, as it would be acknowledging their title to the land they had seized. A variety of measures were, as usual in such cases, proposed, discussed and abandoned, and the council had at last, to adopt the means, which being the most common and obvious, had been knowingly overlooked—for your amazing acute politicians, are forever looking through telescopes, which only enable them to see such objects as are far off, and unattainable; but which incapacitates them to see such things as are in their reach, and obvious to all simple folk, who are content to look with the naked eyes, heaven has given them. The profound council, as I have said, in their pursuit after Jack-o'-lanterns, accidentally stumbled on the very measure they were in need of; which was to raise a body of troops, and dispatch them to the relief and reinforcement of the garrison. This measure was carried into such prompt operation, that in less than twelve months, the whole expedition, consisting of a serjeant and twelve men, was ready to march; and was reviewed for that purpose, in the public square, now known by the name of the Bowling Green. Just at this juncture the whole community was thrown into con-

sternation, by the sudden arrival of the gallant Jacobus Van Curlet; who came straggling into town at the head of his crew of
tatterdemalions, and bringing the melancholy tidings of his own
defeat, and the capture of the redoubtable post of Fort Goed
Hope by the ferocious Yankees.

The fate of this important fortress, is an impressive warning to
all military commanders. It was neither carried by storm, nor
famine; no practicable breach was effected by cannon or mines;
no magazines were blown up by red hot shot, nor were the bar-
racks demolished, or the garrison destroyed, by the bursting of
bombshells. In fact, the place was taken by a stratagem no less
singular than effectual; and one that can never fail of success,
whenever an opportunity occurs of putting it in practice. Happy
am I to add, for the credit of our illustrious ancestors, that it was
a stratagem, which though it impeached the vigilance, yet left the
bravery of the intrepid Van Curlet and his garrison, perfectly free
from reproach.

It appears that the crafty Yankees, having learned the regular
habits of the garrison, watched a favourable opportunity and silently introduced themselves into the fort, about the middle of a
sultry day; when its vigilant defenders having gorged themselves
with a hearty dinner and smoaked out their pipes, were one and
all snoring most obstreperously at their posts; little dreaming of
so disasterous an occurrence. The enemy most inhumanly seized
Jacobus Van Curlet, and his sturdy myrmidons by the nape of the
neck, gallanted them to the gate of the fort, and dismissed them
severally, with a kick on the crupper, as Charles the twelfth dismissed the heavy bottomed Russians, after the battle of Narva—
only taking care to give two kicks to Van Curlet, as a signal mark
of distinction.

A strong garrison was immediately established in the fort;
consisting of twenty long sided, hard fisted Yankees; with
Weathersfield onions stuck in their hats, by way of cockades and
feathers—long rusty fowling pieces for muskets—hasty pudding,
dumb fish, pork and molasses for stores; and a huge pumpkin
was hoisted on the end of a pole, as a standard—liberty caps not
having as yet come into fashion.

CHAPTER III

*Containing the fearful wrath of William the Testy, and the
great dolour of the New Amsterdammers, because of the affair
of Fort Goed Hoop.—And moreover how William the
Testy fortified the city by a Trumpeter—a Flag-staff, and a
Wind-mill.—Together with the exploits of
Stoffel Brinkerhoff.*

Language cannot express the prodigious fury, into which the
testy Wilhelmus Kieft was thrown by this provoking intelligence. For three good hours the rage of the little man was too
great for words, or rather the words were too great for him; and
he was nearly choaked by some dozen huge, mis-shapen, nine
cornered dutch oaths, that crowded all at once into his gullet. A
few hearty thumps on the back, fortunately rescued him from
suffocation—and shook out of him a bushel or two of enormous execrations, not one of which was smaller than "dunder
and blixum!"—It was a matter of astonishment to all the bye
standers, how so small a body, could have contained such an
immense mass of words without bursting. Having blazed off
the first broadside, he kept up a constant firing for three whole
days—anathematizing the Yankees, man, woman, and child,
body and soul, for a set of dieven, schobbejaken, deugenieten,
twist-zoekeren, loozen-schalken, blaes-kaeken, kakken-bedden,
and a thousand other names of which, unfortunately for posterity, history does not make particular mention. Finally he
swore that he would have nothing more to do with such a
squatting, bundling, guessing, questioning, swapping, pumpkin-
eating, molasses-daubing, shingle-splitting, cider-watering, horse-
jockeying, notion-peddling crew—that they might stay at Fort
Goed Hoop and rot, before he would dirty his hands by at-
tempting to drive them away; in proof of which he ordered the
new raised troops, to be marched forthwith into winter quarters, although it was not as yet quite mid summer. Governor
Kieft faithfully kept his word, and his adversaries as faithfully
kept their post; and thus the glorious river Connecticut, and all

the gay vallies through which it rolls, together with the salmon, shad and other fish within its waters, fell into the hands of the victorious Yankees, by whom they are held at this very day—and much good may they do them.

Great despondency seized upon the city of New Amsterdam, in consequence of these melancholly events. The name of Yankee became as terrible among our good ancestors, as was that of Gaul among the ancient Romans; and all the sage old women of the province, who had not read Miss Hamilton on education, used it as a bug-bear, wherewith to frighten their unruly brats into obedience.

The eyes of all the province were now turned upon their governor, to know what he would do for the protection of the common weal in these days of darkness and peril. Great apprehensions prevailed among the reflecting part of the community, especially the old women, that these terrible fellows of Connecticut, not content with the conquest of Fort Goed Hoop would incontinently march on to New Amsterdam and take it by storm—and as these old ladies, through means of the governor's spouse, who as has been already hinted, was "the better horse," had obtained considerable influence in public affairs, keeping the province under a kind of petticoat government, it was determined that measures should be taken for the effective fortification of the city.

Now it happened that at this time there sojourned in New Amsterdam one Anthony Van Corlear* a jolly fat dutch trumpeter, of a pleasant burley visage—famous for his long wind and his huge whiskers, and who as the story goes, could twang so potently upon his instrument, as to produce an effect upon all within hearing, as though ten thousand bagpipes were singing most lustly i' the nose. Him did the illustrious Kieft pick out as the man of all the world, most fitted to be the champion of New Amsterdam, and to garrison its fort; making little doubt but that his instrument would be as effectual and offensive in war as was

---

*David Pietrez *De Vries* in his "Reyze naer Nieuw Nederlandt onder het yaer 1640," makes mention of one *Corlear* a trumpeter in fort Amsterdam, who gave name to Corlear's Hook and who was doubtless this same champion, described by Mr. Knickerbocker.

that of the Paladin Astolpho, or the more classic horn of Alecto. It would have done one's heart good to have seen the governor snapping his fingers and fidgetting with delight, while his sturdy trumpeter strutted up and down the ramparts, fearlessly twanging his trumpet in the face of the whole world, like a thrice valorous editor daringly insulting all the principalities and powers—on the other side of the Atlantic.

Nor was he content with thus strongly garrisoning the fort, but he likewise added exceedingly to its strength by furnishing it with a formidable battery of quaker guns—rearing a stupendous flag-staff in the centre which overtopped the whole city—and moreover by building a great windmill on one of the bastions.* This last to be sure, was somewhat of a novelty in the art of fortification, but as I have already observed William Kieft was notorious for innovations and experiments, and traditions do affirm that he was much given to mechanical inventions—constructing patent smoke-jacks—carts that went before the horses, and especially erecting windmills, for which machines he had acquired a singular predilection in his native town of Saardam.

All these scientific vagaries of the little governor were cried up with ecstasy by his adherents as proofs of his universal genius—but there were not wanting ill natured grumblers who railed at him as employing his mind in frivolous pursuits, and devoting that time to smoke-jacks and windmills, which should have been occupied in the more important concerns of the province. Nay they even went so far as to hint once or twice, that his head was turned by his experiments, and that he really thought to manage his government, as he did his mills—by mere wind!—such is the illiberality and slander to which your enlightened rulers are ever subject.

Notwithstanding all the measures therefore of William the Testy to place the city in a posture of defence, the inhabitants continued in great alarm and despondency. But fortune, who seems always careful, in the very nick of time, to throw a bone

---

*De Vries mentions that this windmill stood on the south-east bastion, and it is likewise to be seen, together with the flag-staff, in Justus Danker's View of New Amsterdam, which I have taken the liberty of prefixing to Mr. Knickerbocker's history.—EDITOR.

for hope to gnaw upon, that the starveling elf may be kept alive; did about this time crown the arms of the province with success in another quarter, and thus cheered the drooping hearts of the forlorn Nederlanders; otherwise there is no knowing to what lengths they might have gone in the excess of their sorrowing—"for grief," says the profound historian of the seven champions of Christendom, "is companion with despair, and despair a procurer of infamous death!"

Among the numerous inroads of the Moss-troopers of Connecticut, which for some time past had occasioned such great tribulation, I should particularly have mentioned a settlement made on the eastern part of Long Island, at a place which, from the peculiar excellence of its shell fish, was called Oyster Bay. This was attacking the province in a most sensible part, and occasioned a great agitation at New Amsterdam.

It is an incontrovertible fact, well known to your skilful physiologists, that the high road to the affections, is through the throat; and this may be accounted for on the same principles which I have already quoted, in my strictures on fat aldermen. Nor is this fact unknown to the world at large; and hence do we observe, that the surest way to gain the hearts of the million, is to feed them well—and that a man is never so disposed to flatter, to please and serve another, as when he is feeding at his expense; which is one reason why your rich men, who give frequent dinners, have such abundance of sincere and faithful friends. It is on this principle that our knowing leaders of parties secure the affections of their partizans, by rewarding them bountifully with loaves and fishes; and entrap the suffrages of the greasy mob, by treating them with bull feasts and roasted oxen. I have known many a man, in this same city, acquire considerable importance in society, and usurp a large share of the good will of his enlightened fellow citizens, when the only thing that could be said in his eulogium was, that "he gave a good dinner, and kept excellent wine."

Since then the heart and the stomach are so nearly allied, it follows conclusively that what affects the one, must sympathetically affect the other. Now it is an equally incontrovertible fact, that of all offerings to the stomach, there is none more grateful than the testaceous marine animal, called by naturalists the Ostea, but known commonly by the vulgar name of Oyster. And in such great reverence has it ever been held, by my gormandizing fellow citizens, that temples have been dedicated to it, time out of mind, in every street, lane and alley throughout this well fed city. It is not to be expected therefore, that the seizing of Oyster Bay, a place abounding with their favourite delicacy, would be tolerated by the inhabitants of New Amsterdam. An attack upon their honour they might have pardoned; even the massacre of a few citizens might have been passed over in silence; but an outrage that affected the larders of the great city of New Amsterdam, and threatened the stomachs of its corpulent Burgomasters, was too serious to pass unrevenged. The whole council were unanimous in opinion, that the intruders should be immediately driven by force of arms, from Oyster Bay, and its vicinity, and a detachment was accordingly dispatched for the purpose, under command of one Stoffel Brinkerhoff, or Brinkerhoofd (*i.e.* Stoffel, the head-breaker) so called because he was a man of mighty deeds, famous throughout the whole extent of Nieuw Nederlandts for his skill at quarterstaff, and for size would have been a match for Colbrand, that famous Danish champion, slain by little Guy of Warwick.

Stoffel Brinckerhoff was a man of few words, but prompt actions—one of your straight going officers, who march directly forward, and do their orders without making any parade about it. He used no extraordinary speed in his movements, but trudged steadily on, through Nineveh and Babylon, and Jericho and Patchog, and the mighty town of Quag, and various other renowned cities of yore, which have by some unaccountable witchcraft of the Yankees, been strangely transplanted to Long Island, until he arrived in the neighbourhood of Oyster Bay.

Here was he encountered by a tumultuous host of valiant warriors, headed by Preserved Fish, and Habbakuk Nutter, and Return Strong, and Zerubbabel Fisk, and Jonathan Doolittle and Determined Cock!—at the sound of whose names the courageous Stoffel verily believed that the whole parliament of Praise God Barebones had been let loose to discomfit him. Finding however that this formidable body was composed merely of the "select men" of the settlement, armed with no other weapons but their tongues, and that they had issued forth with no other intent, than to meet him on the field of argument—he succeeded in putting them to the rout with little difficulty, and completely broke up their settlement. Without waiting to write an account of his victory on the spot, and thus letting the enemy slip through his fingers while he was securing his own laurels, as a more experienced general would have done, the brave Stoffel thought of nothing but completing his enterprize, and utterly driving the Yankees from the island. This hardy enterprize he performed in much the same manner as he had been accustomed to drive his oxen; for as the Yankees fled before him, he pulled up his breeches and trudged steadily after them, and would infallibly have driven them into the sea, had they not begged for quarter, and agreed to pay tribute.

The news of this achievement was a seasonable restorative to the spirits of the citizens of New Amsterdam. To gratify them still more, the governor resolved to astonish them with one of those gorgeous spectacles, known in the days of classic antiquity, a full account of which had been flogged into his memory, when a school-boy at the Hague. A grand triumph therefore was decreed to Stoffel Brinckerhoff, who made his triumphant entrance into town riding on a Naraganset pacer; five pumpkins, which like Roman eagles had served the enemy for standards, were carried before him—ten cart loads of oysters, five hundred bushels of Weathersfield onions, a hundred quintals of codfish, two hogsheads of molasses and various other treasures, were exhibited as the spoils and tribute of the Yankees; while three notorious counterfeiters of Manhattan notes,* were led captive to grace the hero's triumph. The procession was enlivened by martial music, from the trumpet of Antony Van Corlear the champion, accompanied by a select band of boys and negroes, performing on the national instruments of rattle bones and clam shells. The citizens devoured the spoils in sheer gladness of heart—every man did honour to the conqueror, by getting

---

*This is one of those trivial anachronisms, that now and then occur in the course of this otherwise authentic history. How could Manhattan notes be counterfeited, when as yet Banks were unknown in this country—and our simple progenitors had not even dreamt of those inexhaustible mines of *paper opulence. Print. Dev.*

devoutly drunk on New England rum—and learned Wilhelmus Kieft calling to mind, in a momentary fit of enthusiasm and generosity, that it was customary among the ancients to honour their victorious generals with public statues, passed a gracious decree, by which every tavernkeeper was permitted to paint the head of the intrepid Stoffel on his sign!

CHAPTER IV

Philosophical reflections on the folly of being happy in time of prosperity.—Sundry troubles on the southern Frontiers.—How William the Testy by his great learning had well nigh ruined the province through a Cabalistic word.—As also the secret expeditions of Jan Jansen Alpenden, and his astonishing reward.

If we could but get a peep at the tally of dame Fortune, where, like a notable landlady, she regularly chalks up the debtor and creditor accounts of mankind, we should find that, upon the whole, good and evil are pretty nearly balanced in this world; and that though we may for a long while revel in the very lap of prosperity, the time will at length come, when we must ruefully pay off the reckoning. Fortune, in fact, is a pestilent shrew, and withal a most inexorable creditor; for though she may indulge her favourites in long credits, and overwhelm them with her favours; yet sooner or later, she brings up her arrears, with the rigour of an experienced publican, and washes out her scores with their tears. "Since," says good old Bœtius in his consolations of philosophy, "since no man can retain her at his pleasure, and since her flight is so deeply lamented, what are her favours but sure prognostications of approaching trouble and calamity."

There is nothing that more moves my contempt at the stupidity and want of reflection in my fellow men, than to behold them rejoicing, and indulging in security and self confidence, in times of prosperity. To a wise man, who is blessed with the light of reason, those are the very moments of anxiety and apprehension; well knowing that according to the system of things, happiness is at best but transient—and that the higher a man is elevated by the capricious breath of fortune, the lower must be his proportionate depression. Whereas, he who is overwhelmed by calamity, has the less chance of encountering fresh disasters, as a man at the bottom of a hill, runs very little risk of breaking his neck by tumbling to the top.

This is the very essence of true wisdom, which consists in

knowing when we ought to be miserable; and was discovered much about the same time with that invaluable secret, that "every thing is vanity and vexation of spirit;" in consequence of which maxim your wise men have ever been the unhappiest of the human race; esteeming it as an infallible mark of genius to be distressed without reason—since any man may be miserable in time of misfortune, but it is the philosopher alone who can discover cause for grief in the very hour of prosperity.

According to the principle I have just advanced, we find that the colony of New Netherlands, which under the reign of the renowned Van Twiller, had flourished in such alarming and fatal serenity; is now paying for its former welfare, and discharging the enormous debt of comfort which it contracted. Foes harass it from different quarters; the city of New Amsterdam, while yet in its infancy is kept in constant alarm; and its valiant commander little William the Testy answers the vulgar, but expressive idea of "a man in a peck of troubles."

While busily engaged repelling his bitter enemies the Yankees, on one side, we find him suddenly molested in another quarter, and by other assailants. A vagrant colony of Swedes, under the conduct of Peter Minnewits, and professing allegience to that redoubtable virago, Christina queen of Sweden; had settled themselves and erected a fort on south (or Delaware) river—within the boundaries, claimed by the Government of the New Netherlands. History is mute as to the particulars of their first landing, and their real pretensions to the soil, and this is the more to be lamented; as this same colony of Swedes will hereafter be found most materially to affect, not only the interests of the Nederlanders, but of the world at large!

In whatever manner therefore, this vagabond colony of Swedes first took possession of the country, it is certain that in 1638, they established a fort, and Minnewits, according to the off hand usage of his contemporaries, declared himself governor of all the adjacent country, under the name of the province of NEW SWEDEN. No sooner did this reach the ears of the choleric Wilhelmus, than, like a true spirited chieftan, he immediately broke into a violent rage, and calling together his council, belaboured the Swedes most lustily in the longest speech that had ever been heard in the colony, since the memorable dispute of Ten breeches

and Tough breeches. Having thus given vent to the first ebulli-
tions of his indignation, he had resort to his favourite measure of
proclamation, and dispatched one, piping hot, in the first year of
his reign, informing Peter Minnewits that the whole territory,
bordering on the south river, had, time out of mind, been in possession of the Dutch colonists, having been "beset with forts, and
sealed with their blood."

The latter sanguinary sentence, would convey an idea of direful war and bloodshed; were we not relieved by the information
that it merely related to a fray, in which some half a dozen Dutchmen had been killed by the Indians, in their benevolent attempts
to establish a colony and promote civilization. By this it will be
seen that William Kieft, though a very small man, delighted in
big expressions, and was much given to a praise-worthy figure in
rhetoric, generally cultivated by your little great men, called hyperbole. A figure which has been found of infinite service among
many of his class, and which has helped to swell the grandeur of
many a mighty self-important, but windy chief magistrate. Nor
can I resist in this place, from observing how much my beloved
country is indebted to this same figure of hyperbole, for supporting certain of her greatest characters—statesmen, orators, civilians and divines; who by dint of big words, inflated periods, and
windy doctrines, are kept afloat on the surface of society, as ignorant swimmers are buoyed up by blown bladders.

The proclamation against Minnewits concluded by ordering
the self-dubbed governor, and his gang of Swedish adventurers,
immediately to leave the country under penalty of the high displeasure, and inevitable vengeance of the puissant government of
the Nieuw Nederlandts. This "strong measure," however, does
not seem to have had a whit more effect than its predecessors,
which had been thundered against the Yankees—the Swedes resolutely held on to the territory they had taken possession of—
whereupon matters for the present remained in statu quo.

That Wilhelmus Kieft should put up with this insolent obstinacy in the Swedes, would appear incompatible with his valourous temperament; but we find that about this time the little man
had his hands full; and what with one annoyance and another,
was kept continually on the bounce.

There is a certain description of active legislators, who by shrewd management, contrive always to have a hundred irons on the anvil, every one of which must be immediately attended to; who consequently are ever full of temporary shifts and expedients, patching up the public welfare and cobbling the national affairs, so as to make nine holes where they mend one—stopping chinks and flaws with whatever comes first to hand, like the Yankees I have mentioned stuffing old clothes in broken windows. Of this class of statesmen was William the Testy—and had he only been blessed with powers equal to his zeal, or his zeal been disciplined by a little discretion, there is very little doubt but he would have made the greatest governor of his size on record—the renowned governor of the island of Barataria alone excepted.

The great defect of Wilhelmus Kieft's policy was, that though no man could be more ready to stand forth in an hour of emergency, yet he was so intent upon guarding the national pocket, that he suffered the enemy to break its head—in other words, whatever precaution for public safety he adopted, he was so intent upon rendering it cheap, that he invariably rendered it ineffectual. All this was a remote consequence of his profound education at the Hague—where having acquired a smattering of knowledge, he was ever after a great conner of indexes, continually dipping into books, without ever studying to the bottom of any subject; so that he had the scum of all kinds of authors fermenting in his pericranium. In some of these title page researches he unluckily stumbled over a grand political *cabalistic word,* which, with his customary facility he immediately incorporated into his great scheme of government, to the irretrievable injury and delusion of the honest province of Nieuw Nederlandts, and the eternal misleading, of all experimental rulers.

In vain have I pored over the Theurgia of the Chaldeans, the Cabala of the Jews, the Necromancy of the Arabians—The Magic of the Persians—the Hocus Pocus of the English, the Witch-craft of the Yankees, or the Pow-wowing of the Indians to discover where the little man first laid eyes on this terrible word. Neither the Sephir Jetzirah, that famous cabalistic volume, ascribed to the Patriarch Abraham; nor the pages of the Zohar, containing the mysteries of the cabala, recorded by the learned rabbi Simeon Jochaides, yield any light to my enquiries—Nor am I in the least benefited by my painful researchers in the Shem-hamphorah of

Benjamin, the wandering Jew, though it enabled Davidus Elm to make a ten days' journey, in twenty four hours. Neither can I perceive the slightest affinity in the Tetragrammaton, or sacred name of four letters, the profoundest word of the Hebrew Cabala; a mystery, sublime, ineffable and incommunicable—and the letters of which Jod-He-Vau-He, having been stolen by the Pagans, constituted their great Name Jao, or Jove. In short, in all my cabalistic, theurgic, necromantic, magical and astrological researches, from the Tetractys of Pythagoras, to the recondite works of Breslaw and mother Bunch, I have not discovered the least vestige of an origin of this word, nor have I discovered any word of sufficient potency to counteract it.

Not to keep my reader in any suspence, the word which had so wonderfully arrested the attention of William the Testy and which in German characters, had a particularly black and ominous aspect, on being fairly translated into the English is no other than *economy*—a talismanic term, which by constant use and frequent mention, has ceased to be formidable in our eyes, but which has as terrible potency as any in the arcana of necromancy.

When pronounced in a national assembly it has an immediate effect in closing the hearts, beclouding the intellects, drawing the purse strings and buttoning the breeches pockets of all philosophic legislators. Nor are its effects on the eye less wonderful. It produces a contraction of the retina, an obscurity of the christaline lens, a viscidity of the vitreous and an inspiration of the aqueous humours, an induration of the tunica sclerotica and a convexity of the cornea; insomuch that the organ of vision loses its strength and perspicuity, and the unfortunate patient becomes *myopes* or in plain English, purblind; perceiving only the amount of immediate expense without being able to look further, and regard it in connexion with the ultimate object to be effected.—"So that," to quote the words of the eloquent Burke, "a briar at his nose is of greater magnitude than an oak at five hundred yards distance." Such are its instantaneous operations, and the results are still more astonishing. By its magic influence seventy-fours, shrink into frigates—frigates into sloops, and sloops into gunboats. As the defenceless fleet of Eneas, at the command of the protecting Venus, changed into sea nymphs, and protected itself by diving; so the mighty navy of America, by the cabalistic word economy, dwindles into small craft, and shelters itself in a mill-pond!

This all potent word, which served as his touchstone in politics, at once explains the whole system of proclamations, protests, empty threats, windmills, trumpeters, and paper war, carried on by Wilhelmus the Testy—and we may trace its operations in an armament which he fitted out in 1642 in a moment of great wrath; consisting of two sloops and *thirty* men, under the command of Mynheer Jan Jansen Alpendam, as admiral of the fleet, and commander in chief of the forces. This formidable expedition, which can only be paralleled by some of the daring cruizes of our infant navy, about the bay and up the sound; was intended to drive the Marylanders from the Schuylkill, of which they had recently taken possession—and which was claimed as part of the province of New Nederlandts—for it appears that at this time our infant colony was in that enviable state, so much coveted by ambitious nations, that is to say, the government had a vast extent of territory; part of which it enjoyed, and the greater part of which it had continually to quarrel about.

Admiral Jan Jansen Alpendam was a man of great mettle and prowess; and no way dismayed at the character of the enemy; who were represented as a gigantic gunpowder race of men, who lived on hoe cakes and bacon, drank mint juleps and brandy toddy, and were exceedingly expert at boxing, biting, gouging, tar and feathering, and a variety of other athletic accomplishments, which they had borrowed from their cousins german and prototypes the Virginians, to whom they have ever borne considerable resemblance—notwithstanding all these alarming representations, the admiral entered the Schuylkill most undauntedly with his fleet, and arrived without disaster or opposition at the place of destination.

Here he attacked the enemy in a vigorous speech in low dutch, which the wary Kieft had previously put in his pocket; wherein he courteously commenced by calling them a pack of lazy, louting, dram drinking, cock fighting, horse racing, slave driving, tavern haunting, sabbath breaking, mulatto breeding upstarts—and concluded by ordering them to evacuate the country immediately—to which they most laconically replied in plain English (as was very natural for Swedes) "they'd see him d——d first."

Now this was a reply for which neither Jan Jansen Alpendam, nor Wilhelmus Kieft had made any calculation—and finding himself totally unprepared to answer so terrible a rebuff with suitable hostility he concluded, like a most worthy admiral of a modern English expedition, that his wisest course was to return home and report progress. He accordingly sailed back to New Amsterdam, where he was received with great honours, and considered as a pattern for all commanders; having achieved a most hazardous enterprize, at a trifling expense of treasure, and without losing a single man to the state!—He was unanimously called the deliverer of his country; (an appellation liberally bestowed on all great men) his two sloops having done their duty, were laid up (or dry docked) in a cove now called the Albany Bason, where they quietly rotted in the mud; and to immortalize his name, they erected, by subscription, a magnificent shingle monument on the top of Flatten barrack* Hill, which lasted three whole years; when it fell to pieces, and was burnt for fire-wood.

*A corruption of Varleth's bergh—or Varleth's hill, so called from one Varleth, who lived upon that hill in the early days of the settlement. EDITOR.

CHAPTER V

How William the Testy enriched the Province by a multitude
of good-for-nothing laws, and came to be the Patron of Lawyers
and Bum-Bailiffs. How he undertook to rescue the public
from a grievous evil, and had well nigh been smoked to death
for his pains. How the people became exceedingly enlightened
and unhappy, under his instructions—with divers other
matters which will be found out upon perusal.

Among the many wrecks and fragments of exalted wisdom, which have floated down the stream of time, from venerable antiquity, and have been carefully picked up by those humble, but industrious wights, who ply along the shores of literature, we find the following sage ordinance of Charondas, the locrian legislator—Anxious to preserve the ancient laws of the state from the additions and improvements of profound "country members," or officious candidates for popularity, he ordained, that whoever proposed a new law, should do it with a halter about his neck; so that in case his proposition was rejected, he was strung up—and there the matter ended.

This salutary institution had such an effect, that for more than two hundred years there was only one trifling alteration in the criminal code—and the whole race of lawyers starved to death for want of employment. The consequence of this was, that the Locrians being unprotected by an overwhelming load of excellent laws, and undefended by a standing army of pettifoggers and sheriff's officers, lived very lovingly together, and were such a happy people, that we scarce hear any thing of them throughout the whole Grecian history—for it is well known that none but your unlucky, quarrelsome, rantipole nations make any noise in the world.

Well would it have been for William the Testy, had he happily, in the course of his "universal acquirements," stumbled upon this precaution of the good Charondas. On the contrary, he conceived that the true policy of a legislator was to multiply laws, and thus secure the property, the persons and the morals of the people, by surrounding them in a manner with men traps and spring guns, and besetting even the sweet sequestered walks of private life, with quick-set hedges, so that a man could scarcely turn, without the risk of encountering some of these pestiferous protectors. Thus was he continually coining petty laws for every petty offence that occurred, until in time they became too numerous to be remembered, and remained like those of certain modern legislators, in a manner dead letters—revived occasionally for the purpose of individual oppression, or to entrap ignorant offenders.

Petty courts consequently began to appear, where the law was administered with nearly as much wisdom and impartiality as in those august tribunals the aldermen's and justice shops of the present day. The plaintiff was generally favoured, as being a customer and bringing business to the shop; the offences of the rich were discreetly winked at—for fear of hurting the feelings of their friends;—but it could never be laid to the charge of the vigilant burgomasters, that they suffered vice to skulk unpunished, under the disgraceful rags of poverty.

About this time may we date the first introduction of capital punishments—a goodly gallows being erected on the water-side, about where Whitehall stairs are at present, a little to the east of the battery. Hard by also was erected another gibbet of a very strange, uncouth and unmatchable description, but on which the ingenious William Kieft valued himself not a little, being a punishment entirely of his own invention.*

It was for loftiness of altitude not a whit inferior to that of Haman, so renowned in bible history; but the marvel of the contrivance was, that the culprit instead of being suspended by the neck, according to venerable custom, was hoisted by the waistband, and was kept for an hour together, dangling and sprawling between heaven and earth—to the infinite entertainment and doubtless great edification of the multitude of respectable citizens, who usually attend upon exhibitions of the kind.

It is incredible how the little governor chuckled at beholding caitiff vagrants and sturdy beggars thus swinging by the breech,

*Both the gibbets as mentioned above by our author, may be seen in the sketch of Justus Danker, which we have prefixed to the work.—EDITOR.

and cutting antic gambols in the air. He had a thousand pleasantries, and mirthful conceits to utter upon the occasions. He called them his dandle-lions—his wild fowl—his high flyers—his spread eagles—his goshawks—his scarecrows and finally his *gallows birds,* which ingenious appellation, though originally confined to worthies who had taken the air in this strange manner, has since grown to be a cant name given to all candidates for legal elevation. This punishment, moreover, if we may credit the assertions of certain grave etymologists, gave the first hint for a kind of harnessing, or strapping, by which our forefathers braced up their multifarious breeches, and which has of late years been revived and continues to be worn at the present day. It still bears the name of the object to which it owes its origin; being generally termed a pair of *gallows-es*—though I am informed it is sometimes vulgarly denominated *suspenders.*

Such were the admirable improvements of William Kieft in criminal law—nor was his civil code less a matter of wonderment, and much does it grieve me that the limits of my work will not suffer me to expatiate on both, with the prolixity they deserve. Let it suffice then to say; that in a little while the blessings of innumerable laws became notoriously apparent. It was soon found necessary to have a certain class of men to expound and confound them—divers pettifoggers accordingly made their appearance, under whose protecting care the community was soon set together by the ears.

I would not here, for the whole world, be thought to insinuate any thing derogatory to the profession of the law, or to its dignified members. Well am I aware, that we have in this ancient city an innumerable host of worthy gentlemen, who have embraced that honourable order, not for the sordid love of filthy lucre, or the selfish cravings of renown, but through no other motives under heaven, but a fervent zeal for the correct administration of justice, and a generous and disinterested devotion to the interests of their fellow citizens!—Sooner would I throw this trusty pen into the flames, and cork up my ink bottle forever (which is the worst punishment a maggot brained author can inflict upon himself) than infringe even for a nail's breadth upon the dignity of this truly benevolent class of citizens—on the contrary I allude solely to that crew of caitiff scouts who in these latter days of evil have become so numerous—who infest the skirts of the profession, as did the recreant Cornish knights the honourable order of chivalry—who, under its auspices, commit their depredations on society—who thrive by quibbles, quirks and chicanery, and like vermin swarm most, where there is most corruption.

Nothing so soon awakens the malevolent passions as the facility of gratification. The courts of law would never be so constantly crowded with petty, vexatious and disgraceful suits, were it not for the herds of pettifogging lawyers that infest them. These tamper with the passions of the lower and more ignorant classes; who, as if poverty was not a sufficient misery in itself, are always ready to heighten it, by the bitterness of litigation. They are in law what quacks are in medicine—exciting the malady for the purpose of profiting by the cure, and retarding the cure, for the purpose of augmenting the fees. Where one destroys the constitution, the other impoverishes the purse; and it may likewise be observed, that a patient, who has once been under the hands of a quack, is ever after dabbling in drugs, and poisoning himself with infallible remedies; and an ignorant man who has once meddled with the law under the auspices of one of these empyrics, is forever after embroiling himself with his neighbours, and impoverishing himself with successful law suits.—My readers will excuse this digression into which I have been unwarily betrayed; but I could not avoid giving a cool, unprejudiced account of an abomination too prevalent in this excellent city, and with the effects of which I am unluckily acquainted to my cost; having been nearly ruined by a law suit, which was unjustly decided against me—and my ruin having been completed, by another which was decided in my favour.

It is an irreparable loss to posterity, that of the innumerable laws enacted by William the Testy, which doubtless formed a code that might have vied with those of Solon, Lycurgus or Sancho Panza, but few have been handed down to the present day, among which the most important is one framed in an unlucky moment, to prohibit the universal practice of smoking. This he proved by mathematical demonstration, to be not merely a heavy tax upon the public pocket, but an incredible consumer of time, a hideous encourager of idleness, and of course a deadly bane to the morals of the people. Ill fated Kieft!—had he lived in this most enlightened and libel loving age, and attempted to subvert the inestimable liberty of the press, he could not have struck more closely, upon the sensibilities of the million.

The populace were in as violent a turmoil as the constitutional gravity of their deportment would permit—a mob of factious citizens had even the hardihood to assemble around the little governor's house, where setting themselves resolutely down, like a besieging army before a fortress, they one and all fell to smoking with a determined perseverance, that plainly evinced it was their intention, to funk him into terms with villainous Cow-pen mundungus!—Already was the stately mansion of the governor enveloped in murky clouds, and the puissant little man, almost strangled in his hole, when bethinking himself, that there was no instance on record, of any great man of antiquity perishing in so ignoble a manner (the case of Pliny the elder being the only one that bore any resemblance)—he was fain to come to terms, and compromise with the mob, on condition that they should spare his life, by immediately extinguishing their tobacco pipes.

The result of the armistice was, that though he continued to permit the custom of smoking, yet did he abolish the fair long pipes which prevailed in the days of Wouter Van Twiller, denoting ease, tranquillity and sobriety of deportment, and in place thereof introduced little captious short pipes, two inches in length; which he observed could be stuck in one corner of the mouth, or twisted in the hatband, and would not be in the way of business. But mark, oh reader! the deplorable consequences. The smoke of these villainous little pipes—continually ascending in a cloud about the nose, penetrated into and befogged the cerebellum, dried up all the kindly moisture of the brain, and rendered the people as vapourish and testy as their renowned little governor—nay, what is more, from a goodly burley race of folk, they became, like our honest dutch farmers, who smoke short pipes, a lanthorn-jawed, smoak-dried, leathern-hided race of men.

Indeed it has been remarked by the observant writer of the Stuyvesant manuscript, that under the administration of Wilhelmus Kieft the disposition of the inhabitants of New Amsterdam experienced an essential change, so that they became very meddlesome and factious. The constant exacerbations of temper into which the little governor was thrown, by the maraudings on his frontiers, and his unfortunate propensity to experiment and innovation, occasioned him to keep his council in a continual worry—and the council being to the people at large, what yeast or leaven is to a batch, they threw the whole community into a ferment—and the people at large being to the city, what the mind is to the body, the unhappy commotions they underwent operated most disastrously, upon New Amsterdam—insomuch, that in certain of their paroxysms of consternation and perplexity, they begat several of the most crooked, distorted and abominable streets, lanes and alleys, with which this metropolis is disfigured.

But the worst of the matter was, that just about this time the mob, since called the sovereign people, like Balaam's ass, began to grow more enlightened than its rider, and exhibited a strange desire of governing itself. This was another effect of the "universal acquirements" of William the Testy. In some of his pestilent researches among the rubbish of antiquity, he was struck with admiration at the institution of public tables among the Lacedemonians, where they discussed topics of a general and interesting nature—at the schools of the philosophers, where they engaged in profound disputes upon politics and morals—where grey beards were taught the rudiments of wisdom, and youths learned to become little men, before they were boys. "There is nothing" said the ingenious Kieft, shutting up the book, "there is nothing more essential to the well management of a country, than education among the people; the basis of a good government, should be laid in the public mind."—Now this was true enough, but it was ever the wayward fate of William the Testy, that when he thought right, he was sure to go to work wrong. In the present instance he could scarcely eat or sleep, until he had set on foot brawling debating societies, among the simple citizens of New Amsterdam. This was the one thing wanting to complete his confusion. The honest Dutch burghers, though in truth but little given to argument or wordy altercation, yet by dint of meeting often together, fuddling themselves with strong drink, beclouding their brains with tobacco smoke, and listening to the harangues of some half a dozen oracles, soon became exceedingly wise, and—as is always the case where the mob is politically enlightened—exceedingly discontented. They found out, with wonderful quickness of discernment, the fearful error in which they had indulged, in fancying themselves the happiest people in creation—and were fortunately convinced, that, all circumstances to the contrary notwithstanding, they were a very unhappy, deluded, and consequently, ruined people!

In a short time the quidnuncs of New Amsterdam formed themselves into sage juntos of political croakers, who daily met together to groan over public affairs, and make themselves miserable; thronging to these unhappy assemblages with the same eagerness, that your zealots have in all ages abandoned the milder and more peaceful paths of religion to crowd to the howling convocations of fanaticism. We are naturally prone to discontent, and avaricious after imaginary causes of lamentation—like lubberly monks we belabour our own shoulders, and seem to take a vast satisfaction in the music of our own groans. Nor is this said for the sake of paradox; daily experience shews the truth of these sage observations. It is next to a farce to offer consolation, or to think of elevating the spirits of a man, groaning under ideal calamities; but nothing is more easy than to render him wretched, though on the pinnacle of felicity; as it is an Herculean task to hoist a man to the top of a steeple, though the merest child can topple him off thence.

In the sage assemblages I have noticed, the philosophic reader will at once perceive the faint germs of those sapient convocations called popular meetings, prevalent at our day—Hither resorted all those idlers and "squires of low degree," who like rags, hang loose upon the back of society, and are ready to be blown away by every wind of doctrine. Coblers abandoned their stalls and hastened hither to give lessons on political economy—blacksmiths left their handicraft and suffered their own fires to go out, while they blew the bellows and stirred up the fire of faction; and even taylors, though but the shreds and patches, the ninth parts of humanity, neglected their own measures, to attend to the measures of government—Nothing was wanting but half a dozen newspapers and patriotic editors, to have completed this public illumination and to have thrown the whole province in an uproar!

I should not forget to mention, that these popular meetings were always held at a noted tavern; for houses of that description, have always been found the most congenial nurseries of politicks; abounding with those genial streams which give strength and sustenance to faction—We are told that the ancient Germans, had an admirable mode of treating any question of importance; they first deliberated upon it when drunk, and afterwards reconsidered it, when sober. The shrewder mobs of America, who dislike having two minds upon a subject, both determine and act upon it drunk; by which means a world of cold and tedious speculation is dispensed with—and as it is universally allowed that when a man is drunk he sees *double,* it follows most conclusively that he sees twice as well as his sober neighbours.

CHAPTER VI

Shewing the great importance of party distinctions, and the dolourous perplexities into which William the Testy was thrown, by reason of his having enlightened the multitude.

For some time however, the worthy politicians of New Amsterdam, who had thus conceived the sublime project of saving the nation, were very much perplexed by dissentions, and strange contrariety of opinions among themselves, so that they were often thrown into the most chaotic uproar and confusion, and all for the simple want of party classification. Now it is a fact well known to your experienced politicians, that it is equally necessary to have a distinct classification and nomenclature in politics, as in the physical sciences. By this means the several orders of patriots, with their breedings and cross breedings, their affinities and varieties may be properly distinguished and known. Thus have arisen in different quarters of the world the generic titles of Guelfs and Ghibbelins—Round heads and Cavaliers—Big endians and Little endians—Whig and Tory—Aristocrat and Democrat—Republican and Jacobin—Federalist and Anti-federalist, together with a certain mongrel party called *Quid;* which seems to have been engendered between the two last mentioned parties, as a mule is produced between an horse and an ass—and like a mule it seems incapable of procreation, fit only for humble drudgery, doomed to bear successively the burthen of father and mother, and to be cudgelled soundly for its pains.

The important benefit of these distinctions is obvious. How many very strenuous and hard working patriots are there, whose knowledge is bounded by the political vocabulary, and who, were they not thus arranged in parties would never know their own minds, or which way to think on a subject; so that by following their own common sense the community might often fall into that unanimity, which has been clearly proved, by many excellent writers, to be fatal to the welfare of a republick. Often have I

seen a very well meaning hero of seventy six, most horribly puzzled to make up his opinion about certain men and measures,
and running a great risk of thinking right; until all at once he
resolved his doubts by resorting to the old touch stone of *Whig*
and *Tory;* which titles, though they bear about as near an affinity
to the present parties in being, as do the robustious statues of
Gog and Magog, to the worthy London Aldermen, who devour
turtle under their auspices at Guild-Hall; yet are they used on all
occasions by the sovereign people, as a pair of spectacles, through
which they are miraculously enabled to see beyond their own
noses, and to distinguish a hawk from a hand saw, or an owl from
a turkey buzzard!

Well was it recorded in holy writ, "the horse knoweth his rider,
and the ass his master's crib," for when the sovereign people are
thus harnessed out, and properly yoked together, it is delectable
to behold with what system and harmony they jog onward, trudging through mud and mire, obeying the commands of their driv-
ers, and dragging the scurvy dung carts of faction at their heels.
How many a patriotic member of congress have I known, loyally
disposed to adhere to his party through thick and thin, but who
would often, from sheer ignorance, or the dictates of conscience
and common sense, have stumbled into the ranks of his adversaries, and advocated the opposite side of the question, had not the
parties been thus broadly designated by generic titles.

The wise people of New Amsterdam therefore, after for some
time enduring the evils of confusion, at length, like honest dutchmen as they were, soberly settled down into two distinct parties,
known by the name of *Square head* and *Platter breech*—the former implying that the bearer was deficient in that rotundity of
pericranium, which was considered as a token of true genius—the
latter, that he was destitute of genuine courage, or *good bottom,*
as it has since been technically termed—and I defy all the politicians of this great city to shew me where any two parties of the
present day, have split upon more important and fundamental
points.

These names, to tell the honest truth—and I scorn to tell any
thing else—were not the mere progeny of whim or accident, as
were those of Ten Breeches and Tough Breeches, in the days of
yore, but took their origin in recondite and scientific deductions

of certain Dutch philosophers. In a word, they were the dogmas or elementary principia of those ingenious systems since supported in the physiognomical tracts of Lavater, who gravely measures intellect by the length of a nose, or detects it lurking in the curve of a lip, or the arch of an eye-brow—The craniology of Dr. Gall, who has found out the encampments and strong holds of the virtues and vices, passions and habits among the protuberances of the skull, and proves that your whorson jobbernowl, is your true skull of genius—The *Linea Fascialis* of Dr. Petrus Camper, anatomical professor in the college of Amsterdam, which regulates every thing by the relative position of the upper and lower jaw; shewing the ancient opinion to be correct that the owl is the wisest of animals, and that a pancake face is an unfailing index of talents, and a true model of beauty—and finally, the breechology of professor Higgenbottom, which teaches the surprizing and intimate connection between the seat of honour, and the seat of intellect—a doctrine supported by experiments of pedagogues in all ages, who have found that applications *a parte poste,* are marvellously efficacious in quickening the perceptions of their scholars, and that the most expeditious mode of instilling knowledge into their heads, is to hammer it into their bottoms!

Thus then, the enlightened part of the inhabitants of Nieuw Nederlandts, being comfortably arranged into parties, went to work with might and main to uphold the common wealth— assembling together in separate beer-houses, and smoking at each other with implacable animosity, to the great support of the state, and emolument of the tavern-keepers. Some indeed who were more zealous than the rest went further, and began to bespatter one another with numerous very hard names and scandalous little words, to be found in the dutch language; every partizan believing religiously that he was serving his country, when he besmutted the character, or damaged the pocket of a political adversary. But however they might differ between themselves, both parties agreed on one point, to cavil at and condemn every measure of government whether right or wrong; for as the governor was by his station independent of their power, and was not elected by their choice, and as he had not decided in favour of either faction, neither of them were interested in his success, or the prosperity of the country while under his administration.

"Unhappy William Kieft!" exclaims the sage writer of the Stuyvesant manuscript,—doomed to contend with enemies too knowing to be entrapped, and to reign over people, too wise to be governed! All his expeditions against his enemies were baffled and set at naught, and all his measures for the public safety, were cavilled at by the people. Did he propose levying an efficient body of troops for internal defence, the mob, that is to say, those vagabond members of the community who have nothing to lose, immediately took the alarm, vociferated that their interests were in danger—that a standing army was a legion of moths, preying on the pockets of society; a rod of iron in the hands of government; and that a government with a military force at its command, would inevitably swell into a despotism. Did he, as was but too commonly the case, defer preparation until the moment of emergency, and then hastily collect a handful of undisciplined vagrants, the measure was hooted at, as feeble and inadequate, as trifling with the public dignity and safety, and as lavishing the public funds on impotent enterprizes.—Did he resort to the economic measure of proclamation, he was laughed at by the Yankees, did he back it by non-intercourse, it was evaded and counteracted by his own subjects. Whichever way he turned himself he was beleaguered and distracted by petitions of "numerous and respectable meetings," consisting of some half a dozen scurvy pot-house politicians—all of which he read, and what is worse, all of which he attended to. The consequence was, that by incessantly changing his measures, he gave none of them a fair trial; and by listening to the clamours of the mob and endeavouring to do every thing, he in sober truth did nothing.

I would not have it supposed however, that he took all these memorials and interferences good naturedly, for such an idea would do injustice to his valiant spirit; on the contrary he never received a piece of advice in the whole course of his life, without first getting into a passion with the giver. But I have ever observed that your passionate little men, like small boats with large sails, are the easiest upset or blown out of their course; and this is demonstrated by governor Kieft, who though in temperament as hot as an old radish, and with a mind, the territory of which was subjected to perpetual whirlwinds and tornadoes, yet never failed to be carried away by the last piece of advice that was blown into his ear. Lucky was it for him that his power was not dependant upon the greasy multitude, and that as yet the populace did not possess the important privilege of nominating their chief magistrate. They, however, like a true mob, did their best to help along public affairs; pestering their governor incessantly, by goading him on with harangues and petitions, and then thwarting his fiery spirit with reproaches and memorials, like a knot of sunday jockies, managing an unlucky devil of a hack horse—so that Wilhelmus Kieft, may be said to have been kept either on a worry or a hand gallop, throughout the whole of his administration.

CHAPTER VII

Containing divers fearful accounts of Border wars, and the flagrant outrages of the Moss troopers of Connecticut—With the rise of the great Amphyctionic Council of the east, and the decline of William the Testy.

Among the many perils and mishaps that surround your hardy historian, there is one that in spite of my unspeakable delicacy, and unbounded good will towards all my fellow creatures, I have no hopes of escaping. While raking with curious hand, but pious heart, among the rotten remains of former days, I may fare somewhat like that doughty fellow Sampson, who in meddling with the carcass of a dead Lion, drew a swarm of bees about his ears. Thus I am sensible that in detailing the many misdeeds of the Yanokie, or Yankee tribe, it is ten chances to one but I offend the morbid sensibilities of certain of their unreasonable descendants, who will doubtless fly out, and raise such a buzzing about this unlucky pate of mine, that I shall need the tough hide of an Achilles, or an Orlando Furioso, to protect me from their stings. Should such be the case I should deeply and sincerely lament—not my misfortune in giving offence—but the wrong-headed perverseness of this most ill natured and uncharitable age, in taking offence at any thing I say.—My good, honest, testy sirs, how in heaven's name, can I help it, if your great grandfathers behaved in a scurvy manner to my great grandfathers?—I'm very sorry for it, with all my heart, and wish a thousand times, that they had conducted themselves a thousand times better. But as I am recording the sacred events of history, I'd not bate one nail's breadth of the honest truth, though I were sure the whole edition of my work, should be bought up and burnt by the common hangman of Connecticut.—And let me tell you, masters of mine! this is one of the grand purposes for which we impartial historians were sent into the world—to redress wrongs and render justice on the heads of the guilty—So that though a nation may wrong their neighbours, with temporary impunity, yet some time or another an historian shall spring up, who shall give them a hearty rib-roasting in return. Thus your ancestors, I warrant them, little thought, when they were kicking and cuffing the worthy province of Nieuw Nederlandts, and setting its unlucky little governor at his wits ends, that such an historian as I should ever arise, and give them their own, with interest—Body-o'me! but the very talking about it makes my blood boil! and I have as great a mind as ever I had for my dinner, to cut a whole host of your ancestors to mince meat, in my very next page!—but out of the bountiful affection which I feel towards their descendants, I forbear—and I trust when you perceive how completely I have them all in my power, and how, with one flourish of my pen I could make every mother's son of ye grandfatherless, you will not be able enough to applaud my candour and magnanimity.—To resume then, with my accustomed calmness and impartiality, the course of my history.

It was asserted by the wise men of ancient times, intimately acquainted with these matters, that at the gate of Jupiter's palace lay two huge tuns, the one filled with blessings, the other with misfortunes—and it verily seems as if the latter had been set a tap, and left to deluge the unlucky province of Nieuw Nederlandts. Among other causes of irritation, the incessant irruptions and spoliations of his eastern neighbours upon his frontiers, were continually adding fuel to the naturally inflammable temperament of William the Testy. Numerous accounts of them may still be found among the records of former days; for the commanders on the frontiers were especially careful to evince their vigilance and soldierlike zeal, by striving who should send home the most frequent and voluminous budgets of complaints, as your faithful servant is continually running with complaints to the parlour, of all the petty squabbles and misdemeanours of the kitchen.

All these valiant tale-bearings were listened to with great wrath by the passionate little governor, and his subjects, who were to the full as eager to hear, and credulous to believe these frontier fables, as are my fellow citizens to swallow those amusing stories with which our papers are daily filled, about British aggressions at sea, French sequestrations on shore, and Spanish infringements in the *promised land* of Louisiana—all which proves what I have before asserted, that your enlightened people love to be miserable.

Far be it from me to insinuate however, that our worthy ancestors indulged in groundless alarms; on the contrary they were daily suffering a repetition of cruel wrongs, not one of which, but was a sufficient reason, according to the maxims of national dignity and honour, for throwing the whole universe into hostility and confusion.

From among a host of these bitter grievances still on record, I select a few of the most atrocious, and leave my readers to judge, if our progenitors were not justifiable in getting into a very valiant passion on the occasion.

"24 June 1641. Some of Hartford haue taken a hogg out of the vlact or common and shut it vp out of meer hate or other prejudice, causing it to starve for hunger in the stye!

26 July. The foremencioned English did againe driue the companies hoggs out of the vlact of Sicojoke into Hartford; contending daily with reproaches, blows, beating the people with all disgrace that they could imagine.

May 20, 1642. The English of Hartford haue violently cut loose a horse of the honored companies, that stood bound vpon the common or vlact.

May 9, 1643. The companies horses pastured vpon the companies ground, were driven away by them of Connecticott or Hartford, and the heardsman was lustily beaten with hatchets and sticks.

16. Again they sold a young Hogg belonging to the Companie which piggs had pastured on the Companies land."*

Oh ye powers! into what indignation did every one of these outrages throw the philosophic Kieft! Letter after letter; protest after protest; proclamation after proclamation; bad Latin,† worse English, and hideous low dutch were exhausted in vain upon the inexorable Yankees; and the four-and-twenty letters of the alphabet, which except his champion, the sturdy trumpeter Van Corlear, composed the only standing army he had at his command, were never off duty, throughout the whole of his administration.— Nor did Antony the trumpeter, remain a whit behind his patron, the gallant William in his fiery zeal; but like a faithful champion

---

*Haz. Collect. S. Pap.
†Certain of Wilhelmus Kieft's Latin letters are still extant in divers collections of state papers.

and preserver of the public safety, on the arrival of every fresh article of news, he was sure to sound his trumpet from the ramparts with most disasterous notes, throwing the people into violent alarms and disturbing their rest at all times and seasons— which caused him to be held in very great regard, the public paying and pampering him, as we do brawling editors, for similar important services.

Appearances to the eastward began now to assume a more formidable aspect than ever—for I would have you note that hitherto the province had been chiefly molested by its immediate neighbours, the people of Connecticut, particularly of Hartford, which, if we may judge from ancient chronicles, was the strong hold of these sturdy moss troopers; from whence they sallied forth, on their daring incursions, carrying terror and devastation into the barns, the hen-roosts and pig-styes of our revered ancestors.

Albeit about the year 1643, the people of the east country, inhabiting the colonies of Massachusetts, Connecticut, New Plymouth and New Haven, gathered together into a mighty conclave, and after buzzing and turmoiling for many days, like a political hive of bees in swarming time, at length settled themselves into a formidable confederation, under the title of the United Colonies of New England. By this union they pledged themselves to stand by one another in all perils and assaults, and to co-operate in all measures offensive and defensive against the surrounding savages, among which were doubtlessly included our honoured ancestors of the Manhattoes; and to give more strength and system to this confederation, a general assembly or grand council was to be annually held, composed of representatives from each of the provinces.

On receiving accounts of this puissant combination, the fiery Wilhelmus was struck with vast consternation, and for the first time in his whole life, forgot to bounce, at hearing an unwelcome piece of intelligence—which a venerable historian of the times observes, was especially noticed among the sage politicians of New Amsterdam. The truth was, on turning over in his mind all that he had read at the Hague, about leagues and combinations, he found that this was an exact imitation of the famous Amphyctionic council, by which the states of Greece were enabled to attain to such power and supremacy, and the very idea made his heart to quake for the safety of his empire at the Manhattoes.

He strenuously insisted, that the whole object of this confederation, was to drive the Nederlanders out of their fair domains; and always flew into a great rage if any one presumed to doubt the probability of his conjecture. Nor, to speak my mind freely, do I think he was wholly unwarranted in such a suspicion; for at the very first annual meeting of the grand council, held at Boston (which governor Kieft denominated the Delphos of this truly classic league) strong representations were made against the Nederlanders, for as much as that in their dealings with the Indians they carried on a traffic in "guns, powther and shott—a trade damnable and injurious to the colonists." Not but what certain of the Connecticut traders did likewise dabble a little in this "damnable traffic"—but then they always sold the Indians such scurvy guns, that they burst at the first discharge—and consequently hurt no one but these pagan savages.

The rise of this potent confederacy was a death blow to the glory of William the Testy, for from that day forward, it was remarked by many, he never held up his head, but appeared quite crest fallen. His subsequent reign therefore, affords but scanty food for the historic pen—we find the grand council continually augmenting in power, and threatening to overwhelm the mighty but defenceless province of Nieuw Nederlandts; while Wilhelmus Kieft kept constantly firing off his proclamations and protests, like a sturdy little sea captain, firing off so many carronades and swivels, in order to break and disperse a water spout—but alas! they had no more effect than if they had been so many blank cartridges.

The last document on record of this learned, philosophic, but unfortunate little man is a long letter to the council of the Amphyctions, wherein in the bitterness of his heart he rails at the people of New Haven, or red hills, for their uncourteous contempt of his protest levelled at them for squatting within the province of their high mightinesses. From this letter, which is a model of epistolary writing, abounding with pithy apophthegms and classic figures, my limits will barely allow me to extract the following recondite passage:—"Certainly when we heare the Inhabitants of New Hartford complayninge of us, we seem to heare

Esop's wolfe complayninge of the lamb, or the admonition of the younge man, who cryed out to his mother, chideing with her neighboures, 'Oh Mother revile her, lest she first take up that practice against you.' But being taught by precedent passages we received such an answer to our protest from the inhabitants of New Haven as we expected: *the Eagle always despiseth the Beetle fly;* yet notwithstanding we doe undauntedly continue on our purpose of pursuing our own right, by just arms and righteous means, and doe hope without scruple to execute the express commands of our superiors." To shew that this last sentence was not a mere empty menace he concluded his letter, by intrepidly protesting against the whole council, as a horde of *squatters* and interlopers, inasmuch as they held their meeting at New Haven, or the Red Hills, which he claimed as being within the province of the New Netherlands.

Thus end the authenticated chronicles of the reign of William the Testy—for henceforth, in the trouble, the perplexities and the confusion of the times he seems to have been totally overlooked, and to have slipped forever through the fingers of scrupulous history. Indeed from some cause or another, which I cannot divine, there appears to have been a combination among historians to sink his very name into oblivion, in consequence of which they have one and all forborne even to speak of his exploits; and though I have disappointed the caitiffs in this their nefarious conspiracy, yet I much question whether some one or other of their adherents may not even yet have the hardihood to rise up, and question the authenticity of certain of the well established and incontrovertible facts, I have herein recorded—but let them do it at their peril; for may I perish, if ever I catch any slanderous incendiaries contradicting a word of this immaculate history, or robbing my heroes of any particle of that renown they have gloriously acquired, if I do not empty my whole ink-horn upon them— even though it should equal in magnitude that of the sage Gargantua; which according to the faithful chronicle of his miraculous atchievements, weighed seven thousand quintals.

It has been a matter of deep concern to me, that such darkness and obscurity should hang over the latter days of the illustrious Kieft—for he was a mighty and great little man worthy of being utterly renowned, seeing that he was the first potentate that introduced into this land, the art of fighting by proclamation; and defending a country by trumpeters, and windmills—an economic and humane mode of warfare, since revived with great applause, and which promises, if it can ever be carried into full effect, to save great trouble and treasure, and spare infinitely more bloodshed than either the discovery of gunpowder, or the invention of torpedoes.

It is true that certain of the early provincial poets, of whom there were great numbers in the Nieuw Nederlandts, taking advantage of the mysterious exit of William the Testy, have fabled, that like Romulus he was translated to the skies, and forms a very fiery little star, some where on the left claw of the crab; while others equally fanciful, declare that he had experienced a fate similar to that of the good king Arthur; who, we are assured by ancient bards, was carried away to the delicious abodes of fairy land, where he still exists, in pristine worth and vigour, and will one day or another return to rescue poor old England from the hands of paltry, flippant, pettifogging cabinets, and restore the gallantry, the honour and the immaculate probity, which prevailed in the glorious days of the Round Table.*

All these however are but pleasing fantasies, the cobweb visions of those dreaming varlets the poets, to which I would not have my judicious reader attach any credibility. Neither am I disposed to yield any credit to the assertion of an ancient and rather apocryphal historian, who alledges that the ingenious Wilhelmus was annihilated by the blowing down of one of his windmills—nor to that of a writer of later times, who affirms that he fell a victim to a philosophical experiment, which he had for many years been vainly striving to accomplish; having the misfortune to break his neck from the garret window of the Stadt house, in an ineffectual attempt to catch swallows, by sprinkling fresh salt upon their tails.

*The old welsh bards believed that king Arthur was not dead but carried awaie by the fairies into some pleasant place, where he shold remaine for a time, and then returne againe and reigne in as great authority as ever.—HOLLINGSHED.

The Britons suppose that he shall come yet and conquere all Britaigne, for certes this is the prophicye of Merlyn—He say'd that his deth shall be doubteous; and said soth, for men thereof yet have doubte and shullen for ever more—for men wyt not whether that he lyveth or is dede.—DE LEEW. CHRON.

The most probable account, and to which I am inclined to give my implicit faith, is contained in a very obscure tradition, which declares, that what with the constant troubles on his frontiers, the incessant schemings, and projects going on in his own pericranium—the memorials, petitions, remonstrances and sage pieces of advice from divers respectable meetings of the sovereign people, together with the refractory disposition of his council, who were sure to differ from him on every point and uniformly to be in the wrong—all these I say, did eternally operate to keep his mind in a kind of furnace heat, until he at length became as completly burnt out, as a dutch family pipe which has passed through three generations of hard smokers. In this manner did the choleric but magnanimous William the Testy undergo a kind of animal combustion, consuming away like a farthing rush light—so that when grim death finally snuffed him out, there was scarce left enough of him to bury!

END OF BOOK IV

BOOK V

Containing the first part of the reign of Peter Stuyvesant
and his troubles with the Amphyctionic Council.

CHAPTER I

*In which the death of a great man is shewn to be
no such inconsolable matter of sorrow—and how
Peter Stuyvesant acquired a great name from
the uncommon strength of his head.*

To a profound philosopher, like myself, who am apt to see clear
through a subject, where the penetration of ordinary people
extends but half way, there is no fact more simple and manifest,
than that the death of a great man, is a matter of very little importance. Much as we think of ourselves, and much as we may
excite the empty plaudits of the million, it is certain that the
greatest among us do actually fill but an exceeding small space in
the world; and it is equally certain, that even that small space is
quickly supplied, when we leave it vacant. "Of what consequence
is it," said the elegant Pliny, "that individuals appear, or make
their exit? the world is a theatre whose scenes and actors are continually changing." Never did philosopher speak more correctly,
and I only wonder, that so wise a remark could have existed so
many ages, and mankind not have laid it more to heart. Sage follows on in the footsteps of sage; one hero just steps out of his
triumphant car, to make way for the hero who comes after him;
and of the proudest monarch it is merely said, that—"he slept
with his fathers, and his successor reigned in his stead."

The world, to tell the private truth, cares but little for their loss,
and if left to itself would soon forget to grieve; and though a nation has often been figuratively drowned in tears on the death of a
great man, yet it is ten chances to one if an individual tear has
been shed on the melancholy occasion, excepting from the forlorn
pen of some hungry author. It is the historian, the biographer, and
the poet, who have the whole burden of grief to sustain; who—
unhappy varlets!—like undertakers in England, act the part of
chief mourners—who inflate a nation with sighs it never heaved,
and deluge it with tears, it never dreamed of shedding. Thus while

the patriotic author is weeping and howling, in prose, in blank verse, and in rhyme, and collecting the drops of public sorrow into his volume, as into a lachrymal vase, it is more than probable his fellow citizens are eating and drinking, fiddling and dancing; as utterly ignorant of the bitter lamentations made in their name, as are those men of straw, John Doe, and Richard Roe, of the plaintiffs for whom they are generously pleased on divers occasions to become sureties.

The most glorious and praise-worthy hero that ever desolated nations, might have mouldered into oblivion among the rubbish of his own monument, did not some kind historian take him into favour, and benevolently transmit his name to posterity—and much as the valiant William Kieft worried, and bustled, and turmoiled, while he had the destinies of a whole colony in his hand, I question seriously, whether he will not be obliged to this authentic history, for all his future celebrity.

His exit occasioned no convulsion in the city of New Amsterdam, or its vicinity: the earth trembled not, neither did any stars shoot from their spheres—the heavens were not shrowded in black, as poets would fain persuade us they have been, on the unfortunate death of a hero—the rocks (hard hearted vagabonds) melted not into tears; nor did the trees hang their heads in silent sorrow; and as to the sun, he laid abed the next night, just as long, and shewed as jolly a face when he arose, as he ever did on the same day of the month in any year, either before or since. The good people of New Amsterdam, one and all, declared that he had been a very busy, active, bustling little governor; that he was "the father of his country"—that he was "the noblest work of God"—that "he was a man, take him for all in all, they never should look upon his like again"—together with sundry other civil and affectionate speeches that are regularly said on the death of all great men; after which they smoked their pipes, thought no more about him, and Peter Stuyvesant succeeded to his station.

Peter Stuyvesant was the last, and like the renowned Wouter Van Twiller, he was also the best, of our ancient dutch governors. Wouter having surpassed all who preceded him; and Pieter, or Piet, as he was sociably called by the old dutch burghers, who were ever prone to familiarize names, having never been equalled

by any successor. He was in fact the very man fitted by nature to
retrieve the desperate fortunes of her beloved province, had not
the fates or parcæ, Clotho, Lachesis and Atropos, those most
potent, immaculate and unrelenting of all ancient and immortal
spinsters, destined them to inextricable confusion.

To say merely that he was a hero would be doing him unparalleled injustice—he was in truth a combination of heroes—for he
was of a sturdy, raw boned make like Ajax Telamon, so famous
for his prowess in belabouring the little Trojans—with a pair of
round shoulders, that Hercules would have given his hide for,
(meaning his lion's hide) when he undertook to ease old Atlas of
his load. He was moreover as Plutarch describes Coriolanus, not
only terrible for the force of his arm, but likewise of his voice,
which sounded as though it came out of a barrel; and like the self
same warrior, he possessed a sovereign contempt for the sovereign people, and an iron aspect, which was enough of itself to
make the very bowels of his adversaries quake with terror and
dismay. All this martial excellency of appearance was inexpressibly heightened by an accidental advantage, with which I am
surprised that neither Homer nor Virgil have graced any of their
heroes, for it is worth all the paltry scars and wounds in the Iliad
and Eneid, or Lucan's Pharsalia into the bargain. This was nothing less than a redoubtable wooden leg, which was the only prize
he had gained, in bravely fighting the battles of his country; but
of which he was so proud, that he was often heard to declare he
valued it more than all his other limbs put together; indeed so
highly did he esteem it, that he caused it to be gallantly enchased
and relieved with silver devices, which caused it to be related in
divers histories and legends that he wore a silver leg.*

Like that choleric warrior Achilles, he was somewhat subject
to extempore bursts of passion, which were oft-times rather un-
pleasant to his favourites and attendants, whose perceptions he
was apt to quicken, after the manner of his illustrious imitator,
Peter the Great, by anointing their shoulders with his walking
staff.

But the resemblance for which I most value him was that which
he bore in many particulars to the renowned Charlemagne.

*See the histories of Masters Josselyn and Blome.

Though I cannot find that he had read Plato, or Aristotle, or Hobbes, or Bacon, or Algernon Sydney, or Tom Paine, yet did he sometimes manifest a shrewdness and sagacity in his measures, that one would hardly expect from a man, who did not know Greek, and had never studied the ancients. True it is, and I confess it with sorrow, that he had an unreasonable aversion to experiments, and was fond of governing his province after the simplest manner—but then he contrived to keep it in better order than did the erudite Kieft, though he had all the philosophers ancient and modern, to assist and perplex him. I must likewise own that he made but very few laws, but then again he took care that those few were rigidly and impartially enforced—and I do not know but justice on the whole, was as well administered, as if there had been volumes of sage acts and statutes yearly made, and daily neglected and forgotten.

He was in fact the very reverse of his predecessors, being neither tranquil and inert like Walter the Doubter, nor restless and fidgetting, like William the Testy, but a man, or rather a governor, of such uncommon activity and decision of mind that he never sought or accepted the advice of others; depending confidently upon his single head, as did the heroes of yore upon their single arms, to work his way through all difficulties and dangers. To tell the simple truth he wanted no other requisite for a perfect statesman, than to think always right, for no one can deny that he always acted as he thought, and if he wanted in correctness he made up for it in perseverance—An excellent quality! since it is surely more dignified for a ruler to be persevering and consistent in error, than wavering and contradictory, in endeavouring to do what is right; this much is certain, and I generously make the maxim public, for the benefit of all legislators, both great and small, who stand shaking in the wind, without knowing which way to steer—a ruler who acts according to his own will is sure of pleasing himself, while he who seeks to consult the wishes and whims of others, runs a great risk of pleasing nobody. The clock that stands still, and points resolutely in one direction, is certain of being right twice in the four and twenty hours—while others may keep going continually, and continually be going wrong.

Nor did this magnanimous virtue escape the discernment of the good people of Nieuw Nederlandts; on the contrary so high an opinion had they of the independent mind and vigorous intellects of their new governor, that they universally called him *Hard-koppig Piet,* or PETER THE HEADSTRONG—a great compliment to his understanding!

If from all that I have said thou dost not gather, worthy reader, that Peter Stuyvesant was a tough, sturdy, valiant, weatherbeaten, mettlesome, leathernsided, lion hearted, generous spirited, obstinate, old "seventy six" of a governor, thou art a very numscull at drawing conclusions.

This most excellent governor, whose character I have thus attempted feebly to delineate, commenced his administration on the 29th of May 1647: a remarkably stormy day, distinguished in all the almanacks of the time, which have come down to us, by the name of *Windy Friday.* As he was very jealous of his personal and official dignity, he was inaugurated into office with great ceremony; the goodly oaken chair of the renowned Wouter Van Twiller, being carefully preserved for such occasions; in like manner as the chair and stone were reverentially preserved at Schone in Scotland, for the coronation of the caledonian monarchs.

I must not omit to mention that the tempestuous state of the elements, together with its being that unlucky day of the week, termed "hanging day," did not fail to excite much grave speculation, and divers very reasonable apprehensions, among the more ancient and enlightened inhabitants; and several of the sager sex, who were reputed to be not a little skilled in the science and mystery of astrology and fortune telling, did declare outright, that they were fearful omens of a disastrous administration—an event that came to be lamentably verified, and which proves, beyond dispute, the wisdom of attending to those preternatural intimations, furnished by dreams and visions, the flying of birds, falling of stones and cackling of geese, on which the sages and rulers of ancient times placed such judicious reliance—or to those shootings of stars, eclipses of the moon, howlings of dogs and flarings of candles, carefully noted and interpreted by the oracular old sybils of our day; who, in my humble opinion, are the legitimate possessors and preservers of the ancient science of divination. This much is certain, that governor Stuyvesant succeeded to the chair of state, at a turbulent period; when foes thronged and threatened from without; when anarchy and stiff

necked opposition reigned rampant within; and when the authority of their high mightinesses the lords states general, though
founded on the broad dutch bottom of unoffending imbecility;
though supported by economy, and defended by speeches, protests, proclamations, flagstaffs, trumpeters and windmills—
vacillated, oscillated, tottered, tumbled and was finally prostrated
in the dirt, by british invaders, in much the same manner that
our majestic, stupendous, but ricketty shingle steeples, will some
day or other be toppled about our ears by a brisk north wester.

CHAPTER II

*Shewing how Peter the Headstrong bestirred himself among
the rats and cobwebs on entering into office—And the
perilous mistake he was guilty of, in his dealings
with the Amphyctions.*

The very first movements of the great Peter, on taking the reins of
government, displayed the magnanimity of his mind, though they
occasioned not a little marvel and uneasiness among the people
of the Manhattoes. Finding himself constantly interrupted by the
opposition and annoyed by the sage advice of his privy council,
the members of which had acquired the unreasonable habit of
thinking and speaking for themselves during the preceding reign;
he determined at once to put a stop to such a grievous abomination. Scarcely therefore had he entered upon his authority than he
kicked out of office all those meddlesome spirits that composed
the factious cabinet of William the Testy, in place of whom he
chose unto himself councillors from those fat, somniferous, respectable families, that had flourished and slumbered under the
easy reign of Walter the Doubter. All these he caused to be furnished with abundance of fair long pipes, and to be regaled with
frequent corporation dinners, admonishing them to smoke and
eat and sleep for the good of the nation, while he took all the
burden of government upon his own shoulders—an arrangement
to which they all gave a hearty grunt of acquiescence.

Nor did he stop here, but made a hideous rout among the ingenious inventions and expedients of his learned predecessor—
demolishing his flag-staffs and wind-mills, which like mighty
giants, guarded the ramparts of New Amsterdam—pitching to
the duyvel whole batteries of quaker guns—rooting up his patent
gallows, where caitiff vagabonds were suspended by the breech,
and in a word, turning topsy-turvy the whole philosophic, economic and wind-mill system of the immortal sage of Saardam.

The honest folk of New Amsterdam, began to quake now for

the fate of their matchless champion Antony the trumpeter, who
had acquired prodigious favour in the eyes of the women by
means of his whiskers and his trumpet. Him did Peter the Headstrong, cause to be brought into his presence, and eyeing him for
a moment from head to foot, with a countenance that would
have appalled any thing else than a sounder of brass—"Prythee
who and what art thou?" said he.—"Sire," replied the other in
no wise dismayed,—"for my name, it is Antony Van Corlear—
for my parentage, I am the son of my mother—for my profession I am champion and garrison of this great city of New
Amsterdam."—"I doubt me much," said Peter Stuyvesant, "that
thou art some scurvy costard-monger knave—how didst thou
acquire this paramount honour and dignity?"—"Marry sir,"
replied the other, "like many a great man before me, simply *by
sounding my own trumpet*."—"Aye, is it so?" quoth the governor, "why then let us have a relish of thy art." Whereupon he
put his instrument to his lips and sounded a charge, with such a
tremendous outset, such a delectable quaver, and such a triumphant cadence that it was enough to make your heart leap out
of your mouth only to be within a mile of it. Like as a war-worn
charger, while sporting in peaceful plains, if by chance he hears
the strains of martial music, pricks up his ears, and snorts and
paws and kindles at the noise, so did the heroic soul of the
mighty Peter joy to hear the clangour of the trumpet; for of him
might truly be said what was recorded of the renowned St.
George of England, "there was nothing in all the world that
more rejoiced his heart, than to hear the pleasant sound of war,
and see the soldiers brandish forth their steeled weapons." Casting his eyes more kindly therefore, upon the sturdy Van Corlear, and finding him to be a jolly, fat little man, shrewd in his
discourse, yet of great discretion and immeasurable wind, he
straightway conceived an astonishing kindness for him; and
discharging him from the troublesome duty of garrisoning, defending and alarming the city, ever after retained him about his
person, as his chief favourite, confidential envoy and trusty
squire. Instead of disturbing the city with disastrous notes, he
was instructed to play so as to delight the governor, while at his
repasts, as did the minstrels of yore in the days of glorious
chivalry—and on all public occasions, to rejoice the ears of the

people with warlike melody—thereby keeping alive a noble and martial spirit.

Many other alterations and reformations, both for the better and for the worse, did the governor make, of which my time will not serve me to record the particulars, suffice it to say, he soon contrived to make the province feel that he was its master, and treated the sovereign people with such tyrannical rigour, that they were all fain to hold their tongues, stay at home and attend to their business; insomuch that party feuds and distinctions were almost forgotten, and many thriving keepers of taverns and dram-shops, were utterly ruined for want of business.

Indeed the critical state of public affairs at this time, demanded the utmost vigilance, and promptitude. The formidable council of the Amphyctions, which had caused so much tribulation to the unfortunate Kieft, still continued augmenting its forces, and threatened to link within its union, all the mighty principalities and powers of the east. In the very year following the inauguration of governor Stuyvesant a grand deputation departed from the city of Providence (famous for its dusty streets, and beauteous women,) in behalf of the puissant plantation of Rhode Island, praying to be admitted into the league.

The following mention is made of this application in the records still extant, of that assemblage of worthies.*

"Mr. Will Cottington and captain Partridg of Rhoode Iland presented this insewing request to the commissioners in wrighting—

"Our request and motion is in behalfe of Rhoode Iland, that wee the Ilanders of Rhoode Iland may be rescauied into combination with all the united colonyes of New England in a firme and perpetuall league of friendship and amity of ofence and defence, mutuall advice and succor upon all just occasions for our mutuall safety and wellfaire, &c.

Will Cottington,
Alicxsander Partridg."

I confess the very sight of this fearful document, made me to quake for the safety of my beloved province. The name of

*Haz. Col. Stat. pap.

Alexander, however misspelt, has been warlike in every age, and
though its fierceness is in some measure softened by being cou-
pled with the gentle cognomen of Partridge, still, like the colour
of scarlet, it bears an exceeding great resemblance to the sound
of a trumpet. From the style of the letter, moreover, and the soldierlike ignorance of orthography displayed by the noble captain
Alicxsander Partridg in spelling his own name, we may picture
to ourselves this mighty man of Rhodes like a second Ajax,
strong in arms, great in the field, but in other respects, (meaning
no disparagement) as great a dom cop, as if he had been educated
among that learned people of Thrace, who Aristotle most slan-
derously assures us, could not count beyond the number four.

But whatever might be the threatening aspect of this famous
confederation, Peter Stuyvesant was not a man to be kept in a
state of incertitude and vague apprehension; he liked nothing so
much as to meet danger face to face, and take it by the beard.
Determined therefore to put an end to all these petty maraudings
on the borders, he wrote two or three categorical letters to the
grand council, which though neither couched in bad latin, nor
yet graced by rhetorical tropes about wolfs and lambs, and beetle
flies, yet had more effect than all the elaborate epistles, protests
and proclamations of his learned predecessor, put together. In
consequence of his urgent propositions, the sage council of the
amphyctions agreed to enter into a final adjustment of grievances
and settlement of boundaries, to the end that a perpetual and
happy peace might take place between the two powers. For this
purpose governor Stuyvesant deputed two ambassadors, to nego-
tiate with commissioners from the grand council of the league,
and a treaty was solemnly concluded at Hartford. On receiving
intelligence of this event, the whole community was in an uproar
of exultation. The trumpet of the sturdy Van Corlear, sounded
all day with joyful clangour from the ramparts of Fort Amsterdam, and at night the city was magnificently illuminated with
two hundred and fifty tallow candles; besides a barrel of tar,
which was burnt before the governor's house, on the cheering
aspect of public affairs.

And now my worthy, but simple reader, is doubtless, like the
great and good Peter, congratulating himself with the idea, that
his feelings will no longer be molested by afflicting details of sto-

len horses, broken heads, impounded hogs, and all the other catalogue of heart-rending cruelties, that disgraced these border wars. But if my reader should indulge in such expectations, it is only another proof, among the many he has already given in the course of this work, of his utter ignorance of state affairs—and this lamentable ignorance on his part, obliges me to enter into a very profound dissertation, to which I call his attention in the next chapter—wherein I will shew that Peter Stuyvesant has already committed a great error in politics; and by effecting a peace, has materially jeopardized the tranquility of the province.

CHAPTER III

*Containing divers philosophical speculations on war
and negociations—and shewing that a treaty of peace is
a great national evil.*

It was the opinion of that poetical philosopher Lucretius, that war was the original state of man; whom he described as being primitively a savage beast of prey, engaged in a constant state of hostility with his own species, and that this ferocious spirit was tamed and ameliorated by society. The same opinion has been advocated by the learned Hobbes, nor have there been wanting a host of sage philosophers to admit and defend it.

For my part, I am prodigiously fond of these valuable speculations so complimentary to human nature, and which are so ingeniously calculated to make beasts of both writer and reader; but in this instance I am inclined to take the proposition by halves, believing with old Horace,* that though war may have been originally the favourite amusement and industrious employment of our progenitors, yet like many other excellent habits, so far from being ameliorated, it has been cultivated and confirmed by refinement and civilization, and encreases in exact proportion as we approach towards that state of perfection, which is the *ne plus ultra* of modern philosophy.

The first conflict between man and man was the mere exertion of physical force, unaided by auxiliary weapons—his arm was his buckler, his fist was his mace, and a broken head the catastrophe of his encounters. The battle of unassisted strength, was succeeded by the more rugged one of stones and clubs, and war

---

*Quum prorepserunt primis animalia terris,
  Mutum ac turpe pecus, glandem atque cubilia propter,
  Unguibus et pugnis, dein fustibus, atque ita porro
  Pugnabant armis, quæ post fabricaverat usus.
                                        Hor. Sat. L. i. S 3.

assumed a sanguinary aspect. As man advanced in refinement, as his faculties expanded, and his sensibilities became more exquisite, he grew rapidly more ingenious and experienced, in the art of murdering his fellow beings. He invented a thousand devices to defend and to assault—the helmet, the cuirass and the buckler; the sword, the dart and the javelin, prepared him to elude the wound, as well as to launch the blow. Still urging on, in the brilliant and philanthropic career of invention, he enlarges and heightens his powers of defence and injury—The Aries, the Scorpio, the Balista and the Catapulta, give a horror and sublimity to war, and magnify its glory, by encreasing its desolation. Still insatiable; though armed with machinery that seemed to reach the limits of destructive invention, and to yield a power of injury, commensurate, even to the desires of revenge—still deeper researches must be made in the diabolical arcana. With furious zeal he dives into the bowels of the earth; he toils midst poisonous minerals and deadly salts—the sublime discovery of gunpowder, blazes upon the world—and finally the dreadful art of fighting by proclamation, seems to endow the demon of war, with ubiquity and omnipotence!

By the hand of my body but this is grand!—this indeed marks the powers of mind, and bespeaks that divine endowment of reason, which distinguishes us from the animals, our inferiors. The unenlightened brutes content themselves with the native force which providence has assigned them. The angry bull butts with his horns, as did his progenitors before him—the lion, the leopard, and the tyger, seek only with their talons and their fangs, to gratify their sanguinary fury; and even the subtle serpent darts the same venom, and uses the same wiles, as did his sire before the flood. Man alone, blessed with the inventive mind, goes on from discovery to discovery—enlarges and multiplies his powers of destruction; arrogates the tremendous weapons of deity itself, and tasks creation to assist him, in murdering his brother worm!

In proportion as the art of war has increased in improvement, has the art of preserving peace advanced in equal ratio. But as I have already been very prolix to but little purpose, in the first part of this truly philosophic chapter, I shall not fatigue my patient, but unlearned reader, in tracing the history of the art of making peace. Suffice it to say, as we have discovered in this age

of wonders and inventions, that proclamation is the most formidable engine in war, so have we discovered the no less ingenious
mode of maintaining peace by perpetual negociations.

A treaty, or to speak more correctly a negociation, therefore,
according to the acceptation of your experienced statesmen,
learned in these matters, is no longer an attempt to accommodate
differences, to ascertain rights, and to establish an equitable exchange of kind offices; but a contest of skill between two powers,
which shall over-reach and take in the other. It is a cunning endeavour to obtain by peaceful manœuvre, and the chicanery of
cabinets, those advantages, which a nation would otherwise have
wrested by force of arms.—In the same manner that a conscientious highwayman reforms and becomes an excellent and praiseworthy citizen contenting himself with cheating his neighbour
out of that property he would formerly have seized with open
violence.

In fact the only time when two nations can be said to be in a
state of perfect amity, is when a negociation is open, and a treaty
pending. Then as there are no stipulations entered into, no bonds
to restrain the will, no specific limits to awaken that captious
jealousy of right implanted in our nature, as both parties have
some advantage to hope and expect from the other, then it is that
the two nations are as gracious and friendly to each other, as two
rogues making a bargain. Their ministers professing the highest
mutual regard, exchanging billets-doux, making fine speeches
and indulging in all those little diplomatic flirtations, coquetries
and fondlings, that do so marvelously tickle the good humour of
the respective nations. Thus it may paradoxically be said, that
there is never so good an understanding between two nations, as
when there is a little misunderstanding—and that so long as they
are on no terms, they are on the best terms in the world!

As I am of all men in the world, particularly historians, the
most candid and unassuming, I would not for an instant claim
the merit of having made the above political discovery. It has in
fact long been secretly acted upon by certain enlightened cabinets, and is, together with divers other notable theories, privately
copied out of the common place book of an illustrious gentleman, who has been member of congress, and enjoyed the unlimited confidence of heads of department. To this principle may be

ascribed the wonderful ingenuity that has been shewn of late years in protracting and interrupting negociations.—Hence the cunning measure of appointing as ambassador, some political pettifogger skilled in delays, sophisms, and misconstructions, and dexterous in the art of baffling argument—or some blundering statesman, whose stupid errors and misconstructions may be a plea for refusing to ratify his engagements. And hence too that most notable expedient, so popular with our government, of sending out a brace of ambassadors; who having each an individual will to consult, character to establish, and interest to promote, you may as well look for unanimity and concord between them, as between two lovers with one mistress, two dogs with one bone, or two naked rogues and one pair of breeches. This disagreement therefore is continually breeding delays and impediments, in consequence of which the negociation goes on swimmingly—inasmuch as there is no prospect of its ever coming to a close. Nothing is lost by these delays and obstacles but *time,* and in a negociation, according to the theory I have exposed, all time lost is in reality so much time gained—with what delightful paradoxes, does the modern arcana of political economy abound!

Now all that I have here advanced is so notoriously true, that I almost blush to take up the time of my readers, with treating of matters which must many a time have stared them in the face. But the proposition to which I would most earnestly call their attention is this, that though a negociation is the most harmonizing of all national transactions, yet a treaty of peace is a great political evil and one of the most fruitful sources of war.

I have rarely seen an instance in my time, of any special contract between individuals, that did not produce jealousies, bickerings, and often downright ruptures between them; nor did I ever know of a treaty between two nations, that did not keep them continually in hot water. How many worthy country neighbours have I known, who after living in peace and good fellowship for years, have been thrown into a state of distrust, cavilling and animosity, by some ill starred agreement about fences, runs of water, and stray cattle. And how many well meaning nations, who would otherwise have remained in the most amiable disposition towards each other, have been brought to loggerheads about the infringement, or misconstruction of some treaty, which in an evil hour they had constructed by way of making their amity more sure.

Treaties at best are but complied with so long as interest requires their fulfillment; consequently they are virtually binding on the weaker party only, or in other words, they are not really binding at all. No nation will wantonly go to war with another if it has nothing to gain thereby, and therefore needs no treaty to restrain it from violence; and if it has any thing to gain, I much question, from what I have witnessed of the righteous conduct of nations, whether any treaty could be made so strong, that it could not thrust the sword through—nay I would hold ten to one, the treaty itself, would be the very source to which resort would be had, to find a pretext for hostilities.

Thus therefore I sagely conclude—that though it is the best of all policies for a nation to keep up a constant negociation with its neighbours, it is the utmost summit of folly, for it ever to be beguiled into a treaty; for then comes on the non-fulfilment and infraction, then remonstrance, then altercation, then retaliation, then recrimination and finally open war. In a word, negociation is like courtship, a time of sweet words, gallant speeches, soft looks and endearing caresses, but the marriage ceremony is the signal for hostilities—and thus ends this very abstruse though very instructive chapter.

CHAPTER IV

How Peter Stuyvesant was horribly belied by his adversaries the Moss Troopers—and his conduct thereupon.

If my pains-taking reader, whose perception, it is a hundred to one, is as obtuse as a beetle's, is not somewhat perplexed, in the course of the ratiocination of my last chapter; he will doubtless, at one glance perceive, that the great Peter, in concluding a treaty with his eastern neighbours, was guilty of a most notable error and heterodoxy in politics. To this unlucky agreement may justly be ascribed a world of little infringements, altercations, negociations and bickerings, which afterwards took place between the irreproachable Stuyvesant, and the evil disposed council of amphyctions; in all which, with the impartial justice of an historian, I pronounce the latter to have been invariably in the wrong. All these did not a little disturb the constitutional serenity of the good and substantial burghers of Mannahata—otherwise called Manhattoes, but more vulgarly known by the name of Manhattan. But in sooth they were so very scurvy and pitiful in their nature and effects, that a grave historian like me, who grudges the time spent in any thing less than recording the fall of empires, and the revolution of worlds, would think them unworthy to be recorded in his sacred page.

The reader is therefore to take it for granted, though I scorn to waste in the detail, that time, which my furrowed brow and trembling hand, inform me is invaluable, that all the while the great Peter was occupied in those tremendous and bloody contests, that I shall shortly rehearse, there was a continued series of little, dirty, snivelling, pettifogging skirmishes, scourings, broils and maraudings made on the eastern frontiers, by the notorious moss troopers of Connecticut. But like that mirror of chivalry, the sage and valourous Don Quixote, I leave these petty contests for some future Sancho Panza of an historian, while I reserve my prowess and my pen for achievements of higher dignity.

Now did the great Peter conclude, that his labours had come to a close in the east, and that he had nothing to do but apply himself to the internal prosperity of his beloved Manhattoes. Though a man of great modesty, he could not help boasting that he had at length shut the temple of Janus, and that, were all rulers like a certain person who should be nameless, it would never be opened again. But the exultation of the worthy governor was put to a speedy check, for scarce was the treaty concluded, and hardly was the ink dried on the paper, before the crafty and discourteous council of the league sought a new pretence for reilluming the flames of discord.

In the year 1651, with a flagitious hardihood that makes my gorge to rise while I write, they accused the immaculate Peter—the soul of honour and heart of steel—that by divers gifts and promises he had been secretly endeavouring to instigate the Narrohigansett (or Narraganset) Mohaque and Pequot Indians, to surprize and massacre the English settlements. For, as the council maliciously observed, "the Indians round about for divers hundred miles cercute, seeme to have drunke deep of an intoxicating cupp, att or from the Monhatoes against the English, whoe have sought there good, both in bodily and speritual respects." To support their most unrighteous accusation, they examined divers Indians, who all swore to the fact as sturdily as if they had been so many christian troopers. And to be more sure of their veracity, the knowing council previously made every mother's son of them devoutly drunk, remembering the old proverb—*In vino veritas*.

Though descended from a family which suffered much injury from the losel Yankees of those times; my great grandfather having had a yoke of oxen and his best pacer stolen, and having received a pair of black eyes and a bloody nose, in one of these border wars; and my grandfather, when a very little boy tending the pigs, having been kidnapped and severely flogged by a long sided Connecticut schoolmaster—Yet I should have passed over all these wrongs with forgiveness and oblivion—I could even have suffered them to have broken Evert Ducking's head, to have kicked the doughty Jacobus Van Curlet and his ragged regiment out of doors, carried every hog into captivity, and depopulated every hen roost, on the face of the earth with perfect impunity— But this wanton, wicked and unparalleled attack, upon one of the most gallant and irreproachable heroes of modern times, is too much even for me to digest, and has overset, with a single puff, the patience of the historian and the forbearance of the Dutchman.

Oh reader it was false!—I swear to thee it was false!—if thou hast any respect for my word—if the undeviating and unimpeached character for veracity, which I have hitherto borne throughout this work, has its due weight with thee, thou wilt not give thy faith to this tale of slander; for I pledge my honour and my immortal fame to thee, that the gallant Peter Stuyvesant, was not only innocent of this foul conspiracy, but would have suffered his right arm, or even his wooden leg to consume with slow and everlasting flames, rather than attempt to destroy his enemies in any other way, than open generous warfare—Beshrew those caitiff scouts, that conspired to sully his honest name by such an imputation!

Peter Stuyvesant, though he perhaps had never heard of a Knight Errant; yet had he as true a heart of chivalry as ever beat at the round table of King Arthur. There was a spirit of native gallantry, a noble and generous hardihood diffused through his rugged manners, which altogether gave unquestionable tokens of an heroic mind. He was, in truth, a hero of chivalry struck off by the hand of nature at a single heat, and though she had taken no further care to polish and refine her workmanship, he stood forth a miracle of her skill.

But not to be figurative, (a fault in historic writing which I particularly eschew) the great Peter possessed in an eminent degree, the seven renowned and noble virtues of knighthood; which, as he had never consulted authors, in the disciplining and cultivating of his mind, I verily believe must have been stowed away in a corner of his heart by dame nature herself—where they flourished, among his hardy qualities, like so many sweet wild flowers, shooting forth and thriving with redundant luxuriance among stubborn rocks. Such was the mind of Peter the Headstrong, and if my admiration for it, has on this occasion, transported my style beyond the sober gravity which becomes the laborious scribe of historic events, I can plead as an apology, that though a little, grey headed Dutchman, arrived almost at the bottom of the down-hill of life, I still retain some portion of that celestial fire, which sparkles in the eye of youth, when contemplating the virtues and atchievements of ancient worthies. Blessed, thrice and nine times blessed, be the good St. Nicholas—that I have escaped the influence of that chilling apathy, which too often freezes the sympathies of age; which like a churlish spirit, sits at the portals of the heart, repulsing every genial sentiment, and paralyzing every spontaneous glow of enthusiasm.

No sooner then, did this scoundrel imputation on his honour reach the ear of Peter Stuyvesant, than he proceeded in a manner which would have redounded to his credit, even if he had studied for years, in the library of Don Quixote himself. He immediately dispatched his valiant trumpeter and squire, Antony Van Corlear, with orders to ride night and day, as herald, to the Amphyctionic council, reproaching them in terms of noble indignation, for giving ear to the slanders of heathen infidels, against the character of a Christian, a gentleman and a soldier—and declaring, that as to the treacherous and bloody plot alledged against him, whoever affirmed it to be true, he lied in his teeth!—to prove which he defied the president of the council and all of his compeers, or if they pleased, their puissant champion, captain Alicxsander Partridg that mighty man of Rhodes, to meet him in single combat, where he would trust the vindication of his innocence to the prowess of his arm.

This challenge being delivered with due ceremony, Antony Van Corlear sounded a trumpet of defiance before the whole council, ending with a most horrific and nasal twang, full in the face of captain Partridg, who almost jumped out of his skin in an extacy of astonishment, at the noise. This done he mounted a tall Flanders mare, which he always rode, and trotted merrily towards the Manhattoes—passing through Hartford, and Pyquag and Middletown and all the other border towns—twanging his trumpet like a very devil, so that the sweet vallies and banks of the Connecticut resounded with the warlike melody—and stopping occasionally to eat pumpkin pies, dance at country frolicks, and bundle with the beauteous lasses of those parts—whom he rejoiced exceedingly with his soul stirring instrument.

But the grand council being composed of considerate men, had no idea of running a tilting with such a fiery hero as the hardy Peter—on the contrary they sent him an answer, couched in the meekest, the most mild and provoking terms, in which they assured him that his guilt was proved to their perfect satisfaction, by the testimony of divers sage and respectable Indians, and concluding with this truly amiable paragraph.—"For youer confidant denialls of the Barbarous plott charged, will waigh little in ballance against such evidence, soe that we must still require and seeke due satisfaction and cecuritie, soe we rest,

> Sir,
>
> Youres in wayes of Righteousness, &c."

I am conscious that the above transaction has been differently recorded by certain historians of the east, and elsewhere; who seem to have inherited the bitter enmity of their ancestors to the brave Peter—and much good may their inheritance do them. These moss troopers in literature, whom I regard with sovereign scorn, as mere vampers up of vulgar prejudices and fabulous legends, declare, that Peter Stuyvesant requested to have the charges against him, enquired into, by commissioners to be appointed for the purpose; and yet that when such commissioners were appointed, he refused to submit to their examination. Now this is partly true—he did indeed, most gallantly offer, when that he found a deaf ear was turned to his challenge, to submit his conduct to the rigorous inspection of a court of honour—but then he expected to find it an august tribunal, composed of courteous gentlemen, the governors and nobility, of the confederate plantations, and of the province of New Netherlands; where he might be tried by his peers, in a manner worthy of his rank and dignity—whereas, let me perish, if they did not send on to the Manhattoes two lean sided hungry pettifoggers, mounted on Narraganset pacers, with saddle bags under their bottoms, and green satchels under their arms, as if they were about to beat the hoof from one county court to another—in search of a law suit.

The chivalric Peter, as well he might, took no notice of these cunning varlets; who with professional industry fell to prying and sifting about, in quest of *ex parte* evidence; bothering and perplexing divers simple Indians and old women, with their cross questioning, until they contradicted and forswore themselves most horribly—as is every day done in our courts of justice. Thus having dispatched their errand to their full satisfaction, they re-

turned to the grand council with their satchels and saddle-bags
stuffed full of the most scurvy rumours, apocryphal stories and
outrageous heresies, that ever were heard—for all which the great
Peter did not care a tobacco stopper; but I warrant me had they
attempted to play off the same trick upon William the Testy, he
would have treated them both to an ærial gambol on his patent
gallows.

The grand council of the east, held a very solemn meeting on
the return of their envoys, and after they had pondered a long
time on the situation of affairs, were upon the point of adjourn-
ing without being able to agree upon anything. At this critical
moment one of those little, meddlesome, indefatigable spirits,
who endeavour to establish a character for patriotism by blowing
the bellows of party, until the whole furnace of politics is red-hot
with sparks and cinders—and who have just cunning enough to
know, that there is no time so favourable for getting on the people's backs, as when they are in a state of turmoil, and attending
to every body's business but their own—This aspiring imp of faction, who was called a great politician, because he had secured a
seat in council by calumniating all his opponents—He I say, conceived this a fit opportunity to strike a blow that should secure
his popularity among his constituents, who lived on the borders
of Nieuw Nederlandt, and were the greatest poachers in Christendom, excepting the Scotch border nobles. Like a second Peter
the hermit, therefore, he stood forth and preached up a crusade
against Peter Stuyvesant, and his devoted city.

He made a speech which lasted three days, according to the
ancient custom in these parts, in which he represented the dutch
as a race of impious heretics, who neither believed in witchcraft,
nor the sovereign virtues of horse shoes—who, left their country
for the lucre of gain, not like themselves for the enjoyment of
liberty of conscience—who, in short, were a race of mere cannibals and anthropophagi, inasmuch as they never eat cod-fish on
saturdays, devoured swine's flesh without molasses, and held
pumpkins in utter contempt.

This speech had the desired effect, for the council, being awakened by their serjeant at arms, rubbed their eyes, and declared
that it was just and politic to declare instant war against these
unchristian anti-pumpkinites. But it was necessary that the peo-

ple at large should first be prepared for this measure, and for this purpose the arguments of the little orator were earnestly preached from the pulpit for several sundays subsequent, and earnestly recommended to the consideration of every good Christian, who professed, as well as practised the doctrine of meekness, charity, and the forgiveness of injuries. This is the first time we hear of the "Drum Ecclesiastic" beating up for political recruits in our country; and it proved of such signal efficacy, that it has since been called into frequent service throughout our union. A cunning politician is often found skulking under the clerical robe, with an outside all religion, and an inside all political rancour. Things spiritual and things temporal are strangely jumbled together, like poisons and antidotes on an apothecary's shelf, and instead of a devout sermon, the simple church-going folk, have often a political pamphlet, thrust down their throats, labeled with a pious text from Scripture.

CHAPTER V

*How the New Amsterdammers became great in arms, and
of the direful catastrophe of a mighty army—together with
Peter Stuyvesant's measures to fortify the City—and how
he was the original founder of the Battery.*

But notwithstanding that the grand council, as I have already
shewn, were amazingly discreet in their proceedings respecting
the New Netherlands, and conducted the whole with almost as
much silence and mystery, as does the sage British cabinet one of
its ill star'd *secret expeditions*—yet did the ever watchful Peter
receive as full and accurate information of every movement, as
does the court of France of all the notable enterprises I have
mentioned.—He accordingly set himself to work, to render the
machinations of his bitter adversaries abortive.

I know that many will censure the precipitation of this stout
hearted old governor, in that he hurried into the expenses of fortification, without ascertaining whether they were necessary, by
prudently waiting until the enemy was at the door. But they
should recollect Peter Stuyvesant had not the benefit of an insight
into the modern arcana of politics, and was strangely bigotted to
certain obsolete maxims of the old school; among which he firmly
believed, that, to render a country respected abroad, it was necessary to make it formidable at home—and that a nation should
place its reliance for peace and security, more upon its own
strength, than on the justice or good will of its neighbours.—He
proceeded therefore, with all diligence, to put the province and
metropolis in a strong posture of defence.

Among the few remnants of ingenious inventions which remained from the days of William the Testy, were those impregnable bulwarks of public safety, militia laws; by which the
inhabitants were obliged to turn out twice a year, with such military equipments—as it pleased God; and were put under the
command of very valiant taylors, and man milliners, who though
on ordinary occasions, the meekest, pippen-hearted little men in

the world, were very devils at parades and court-martials, when they had cocked hats on their heads, and swords by their sides. Under the instructions of these periodical warriors, the gallant train bands made marvellous proficiency in the mystery of gun-powder. They were taught to face to the right, to wheel to the left, to snap off empty firelocks without winking, to turn a corner without any great uproar or irregularity, and to march through sun and rain from one end of the town to the other without flinching—until in the end they became so valourous that they fired off blank cartridges, without so much as turning away their heads—could hear the largest field piece discharged, without stopping their ears or falling into much confusion—and would even go through all the fatigues and perils of a summer day's parade, without having their ranks much thinned by desertion!

True it is, the genius of this truly pacific people was so little given to war, that during the intervals which occurred between field days, they generally contrived to forget all the military tuition they had received; so that when they re-appeared on parade, they scarcely knew the butt end of the musket from the muzzle, and invariably mistook the right shoulder for the left—a mistake which however was soon obviated by shrewdly chalking their left arms. But whatever might be their blunders and aukwardness, the sagacious Kieft, declared them to be of but little importance—since, as he judiciously observed, one campaign would be of more instruction to them than a hundred parades; for though two-thirds of them might be food for powder, yet such of the other third as did not run away, would become most experienced veterans.

The great Stuyvesant had no particular veneration for the ingenious experiments and institutions of his shrewd predecessor, and among other things, held the militia system in very considerable contempt, which he was often heard to call in joke—for he was sometimes fond of a joke—governor Kieft's broken reed. As, however, the present emergency was pressing, he was obliged to avail himself of such means of defence as were next at hand, and accordingly appointed a general inspection and parade of the train bands. But oh! Mars and Bellona, and all ye other powers of war, both great and small, what a turning out was here!—Here

came men without officers, and officers without men—long fowling pieces, and short blunderbusses—muskets of all sorts and
sizes, some without bayonets, others without locks, others without stocks, and many without lock, stock, or barrel.—Cartridge-
boxes, shot belts, powder-horns, swords, hatchets, snicker-snees,
crow-bars, and broomsticks, all mingled higgledy, piggledy—like
one of our continental armies at the breaking out of the revolution.

The sturdy Peter eyed this ragged regiment with some such
rueful aspect, as a man would eye the devil; but knowing, like a
wise man, that all he had to do was to make the best out of a bad
bargain, he determined to give his heroes a seasoning. Having
therefore drilled them through the manual exercise over and over
again, he ordered the fifes to strike up a quick march, and trudged
his sturdy boots backwards and forwards, about the streets of
New Amsterdam, and the fields adjacent, till I warrant me, their
short legs ached, and their fat sides sweated again. But this was
not all; the martial spirit of the old governor caught fire from the
sprightly music of the fife, and he resolved to try the mettle of his
troops, and give them a taste of the hardships of iron war. To this
end he encamped them as the shades of evening fell, upon a hill
formerly called Bunker's hill, at some distance from the town,
with a full intention of initiating them into the discipline of
camps, and of renewing the next day, the toils and perils of the
field. But so it came to pass, that in the night there fell a great and
heavy rain, which descended in torrents upon the camp, and the
mighty army of swing tails strangely melted away before it; so
that when Gaffer Phœbus came to shed his morning beams upon
the place, saving Peter Stuyvesant and his trumpeter Van Corlear, scarce one was to be found of all the multitude, that had
taken roost there the night before.

This awful dissolution of his army would have appalled a commander of less nerve than Peter Stuyvesant; but he considered it
as a matter of but small importance, though he thenceforward
regarded the militia system with ten times greater contempt than
ever, and took care to provide himself with a good garrison of
chosen men, whom he kept in pay, of whom he boasted that they
at least possessed the quality, indispensible in soldiers, of being
water proof.

The next care of the vigilant Stuyvesant, was to strengthen and fortify New Amsterdam. For this purpose he reared a substantial barrier that reached across the island from river to river, being the distance of a full half a mile!—a most stupendous work, and scarcely to be rivalled in the opinion of the old inhabitants, by the great wall of China, or the Roman wall erected in Great Britain against the incursions of the Scots, or the wall of brass that Dr. Faustus proposed to build round Germany, by the aid of the devil.

The materials of which this wall was constructed are differently described, but from a majority of opinions I am inclined to believe that it was a picket fence of especial good pine posts, intended to protect the city, not merely from the sudden invasions of foreign enemies, but likewise from the incursions of the neighbouring Indians.

Some traditions it is true, have ascribed the building of this wall to a later period, but they are wholly incorrect; for a memorandum in the Stuyvesant manuscript, dated towards the middle of the governor's reign, mentions this wall particularly, as a very strong and curious piece of workmanship, and the admiration of all the savages in the neighbourhood. And it mentions moreover the alarming circumstance of a drove of stray cows, breaking through the grand wall of a dark night; by which the whole community of New Amsterdam was thrown into as great panic, as were the people of Rome, by the sudden irruptions of the Gauls, or the valiant citizens of Philadelphia, during the time of our revolution, by a fleet of empty kegs floating down the Delaware.*

But the vigilance of the governor was more especially manifested by an additional fortification which he erected as an out work to fort Amsterdam, to protect the sea bord, or water edge. I have ascertained by the most painful and minute investigation,

---

*In an antique view of Nieuw Amsterdam, taken some few years after the above period, is an accurate representation of this wall, which stretched along the course of *Wall-street,* so called in commemoration of this great bulwark. One gate, called the *Land-poort* opened upon Broadway, hard by where at present stands the Trinity Church; and another called the *Water-poort,* stood about where the Tontine coffee house is at present—opening upon *Smits Vleye,* or as it is commonly called Smith fly; then a marshy valley, with a creek or inlet, extending up what we call maiden lane.

that it was neither fortified according to the method of Evrard de Bar-le-duc, that earliest inventor of complete system; the dutch plan of Marollois; the French method invented by Antoine de Ville; the Flemish of Stevin de Bruges; the Polish of Adam de Treitach, or the Italian of Sardi.

He did not pursue either of the three systems of Pagan; the three of Vauban; the three of Scheiter; the three of Coehorn, that illustrious dutchman, who adapted all his plans to the defence of low and marshy countries—or the hundred and sixty methods, laid down by Francisco Marchi of Bologna.

The fortification did not consist of a Polygon, inscribed in a circle, according to Alain Manesson Maillet; nor with four long batteries, agreeably to the expensive system of Blondel; nor with the *fortification a rebours* of Dona Rosetti, nor the *Caponiere Couverte,* of the ingenious St. Julien; nor with angular polygons and numerous casemates, as recommended by Antoine d'Herbert; who served under the duke of Wirtemberg, grandfather to the second wife, and first queen of Jerome Bonaparte—otherwise called Jerry Sneak.

It was neither furnished with bastions, fashioned after the original invention of Zisca, the Bohemian; nor those used by Achmet Bassa, at Otranto in 1480; nor those recommended by San Micheli of Verona; neither those of triangular form, treated of by Specie, the high dutch engineer of Strasbourg, or the famous wooden bastions, since erected in this renowned city, the destruction of which, is recorded in a former chapter. In fact governor Stuyvesant, like the celebrated Montalembert, held bastions in absolute contempt; yet did he not like him substitute a *tenaille angulaire des polygons à ailerons.*

He did not make use of Myrtella towers, as are now erecting at Quebec; neither did he erect flagstaffs and windmills as was done by his illustrious predecessor of Saardam; nor did he employ circular castellated towers, or batteries with two tier of heavy artillery, and a third of columbiads on the top; as are now erecting for the defence of this defenceless city.

My readers will perhaps be surprized, that out of so many systems, governor Stuyvesant should find none to suit him; this may be tolerably accounted for, by the simple fact, that many of them were unfortunately invented long since his time; and as to the rest, he was as ignorant of them, as the child that never was and never will be born. In truth, it is more than probable, that had they all been spread before him, with as many more into the bargain; that same peculiarity of mind, that acquired him the name of Hard-koppig Piet, would have induced him to follow his own plans, in preference to them all. In a word, he pursued no system either past, present or to come; he equally disdained to imitate his predecessors, of whom he had never heard—his contemporaries, whom he did not know; or his unborn successors, whom, to say the truth, he never once thought of in his whole life. His great and capacious mind was convinced, that the simplest method is often the most efficient and certainly the most expeditious, he therefore fortified the water edge with a formidable mud breast work, solidly faced, after the manner of the dutch ovens common in those days, with clam shells.

These frowning bulwarks in process of time, came to be pleasantly overrun by a verdant carpet of grass and clover, and their high embankments overshadowed by wide spreading sycamores, among whose foliage the little birds sported about, making the air to resound with their joyous notes. The old burghers would repair of an afternoon to smoke their pipes under the shade of their branches, contemplating the golden sun as he gradually sunk into the west an emblem of that tranquil end toward which themselves were hastening—while the young men and the damsels of the town would take many a moonlight stroll among these favourite haunts, watching the silver beams of chaste Cynthia, tremble along the calm bosom of the bay, or light up the white sail of some gliding bark, and interchanging the honest vows of constant affection. Such was the origin of that renowned walk, *the Battery,* which though ostensibly devoted to the purposes of war, has ever been consecrated to the sweet delights of peace. The favourite walk of declining age—the healthful resort of the feeble invalid—the sunday refreshment of the dusty tradesman—the scene of many a boyish gambol—the rendezvous of many a tender assignation—the comfort of the citizen—the ornament of New York, and the pride of the lovely island of Mannahata.

CHAPTER VI

*How the people of the east country were suddenly afflicted
with a diabolical evil—and their judicious measures
for the extirpation thereof.*

Having thus provided for the temporary security of New Amsterdam, and guarded it against any sudden surprise, the gallant Peter took a hearty pinch of snuff, and snapping his fingers, set the great council of Amphyctions, and their champion, the doughty Alicxsander Partridg at defiance. It is impossible to say, notwithstanding, what might have been the issue of this affair, had not the great council been all at once involved in huge perplexity, and as much horrible dissension sown among its members, as of yore was stirred up in the camp of the brawling warriors of Greece.

The all potent council of the league, as I have shewn in my last chapter, had already announced its hostile determinations, and already was the mighty colony of New Haven and the puissant town of Pyquag, otherwise called Wethersfield—famous for its onions and its witches—and the great trading house of Hartford, and all the other redoubtable little border towns, in a prodigious turmoil, furbishing up their rusty fowling pieces and shouting aloud for war; by which they anticipated easy conquests, and gorgeous spoils, from the little fat dutch villages. But this joyous brawling was soon silenced by the conduct of the colony of Massachusetts. Struck with the gallant spirit of the brave old Peter, and convinced by the chivalric frankness and heroic warmth of his vindication, they refused to believe him guilty of the infamous plot most wrongfully laid at his door. With a generosity for which I would yield them immortal honour, they declared, that no determination of the grand council of the league, should bind the general court of Massachusetts, to join in an offensive war, which should appear to such general court to be unjust.[*]

<hr/>

[*]Haz. Col. S. Pap.

This refusal immediately involved the colony of Massachusetts and the other combined colonies, in very serious difficulties and disputes, and would no doubt have produced a dissolution of the confederacy, but that the great council of Amphyctions, finding that they could not stand alone, if mutilated by the loss of so important a member as Massachusetts, were fain to abandon for the present their hostile machinations against the Manhattoes. Such is the marvellous energy and puissance of those notable confederacies, composed of a number of sturdy, self-will'd, discordant parts, loosely banded together by a puny general government. As it is however, the warlike towns of Connecticut, had no cause to deplore this disappointment of their martial ardour; for by my faith—though the combined powers of the league might have been too potent in the end, for the robustious warriors of the Manhattoes—yet in the interim would the lion hearted Peter and his myrmidons, have choaked the stomachful heroes of Pyquag with their own onions, and have given the other little border towns such a scouring, that I warrant they would have had no stomach to squat on the land, or invade the hen-roost of a New Nederlander for a century to come.

Indeed there was more than one cause to divert the attention of the good people of the east, from their hostile purposes; for just about this time were they horribly beleagured and harassed by the inroads of the prince of darkness, divers of whose liege subjects they detected, lurking within their camp, all of whom they incontinently roasted as so many spies, and dangerous enemies. Not to speak in parables, we are informed, that at this juncture, the unfortunate "east countrie" was exceedingly troubled and confounded by multitudes of losel witches, who wrought strange devices to beguile and distress the multitude; and notwithstanding numerous judicious and bloody laws had been enacted, against all "solem conversing or compacting with the divil, by way of conjuracon or the like,"* yet did the dark crime of witchcraft continue to encrease to an alarming degree, that would almost transcend belief, were not the fact too well authenticated to be even doubted for an instant.

What is particularly worthy of admiration is, that this terrible

*New Plymouth record.

art, which so long has baffled the painful researches, and abstruse studies of philosophers, astrologers, alchymists, theurgists and other sages, was chiefly confined to the most ignorant, decrepid, ugly, abominable old women in the community, who had scarcely more brains than the broomsticks they rode upon. Where they first acquired their infernal education—whether from the works of the ancient Theurgists—the demonology of the Egyptians—the belomancy, or divination by arrows of the Scythians—the spectrology of the Germans—the magic of the Persians—the enchantment of the Laplanders, or from the archives of the dark and mysterious caverns of the Dom Daniel, is a question pregnant with a host of learned and ingenious doubts—particularly as most of them were totally unversed in the occult mysteries of the alphabet.

When once an alarm is sounded, the public, who love dearly to be in a panic, are not long in want of proofs to support it—raise but the cry of yellow fever, and immediately every head-ache, and indigestion, and overflowing of the bile is pronounced the terrible epidemic—In like manner in the present instance, whoever was troubled with a cholic or lumbago, was sure to be bewitched, and woe to any unlucky old woman that lived in his neighbourhood. Such a howling abomination could not be suffered to remain long unnoticed, and it accordingly soon attracted the fiery indignation of the sober and reflective part of the community—more especially of those, who, whilome, had evinced so much active benevolence in the conversion of quakers and anabaptists. The grand council of the amphyctions publicly set their faces against so deadly and dangerous a sin, and a severe scrutiny took place after those nefarious witches, who were easily detected by devil's pinches, black cats, broomsticks, and the circumstance of their only being able to weep three tears, and those out of the left eye.

It is incredible the number of offences that were detected, "for every one of which," says the profound and reverend Cotton Mather, in that excellent work, the history of New England—"we have such a sufficient evidence, that no reasonable man in this whole country ever did question them; *and it will be unreasonable to do it in any other.*"*

*Mather's hist. N. Eng B. 6. ch. 7.

Indeed, that authentic and judicious historian John Josselyn, Gent. furnishes us with unquestionable facts on this subject. "There are none," observes he, "that beg in this country, but there be witches too many—bottle bellied witches and others, that produce many strange apparitions, if you will believe report of a shalop at sea manned with women—and of a ship and great red horse standing by the main mast; the ship being in a small cove to the eastward vanished of a sudden," &c.

The number of delinquents, however, and their magical devices, were not more remarkable than their diabolical obstinacy. Though exhorted in the most solemn, persuasive and affectionate manner, to confess themselves guilty, and be burnt for the good of religion, and the entertainment of the public; yet did they most pertinaciously persist in asserting their innocence. Such incredible obstinacy was in itself deserving of immediate punishment, and was sufficient proof, if proof were necessary, that they were in league with the devil, who is perverseness itself. But their judges were just and merciful, and were determined to punish none that were not convicted on the best of testimony; not that they needed any evidence to satisfy their own minds, for, like true and experienced judges their minds were perfectly made up, and they were thoroughly satisfied of the guilt of the prisoners before they proceeded to try them; but still something was necessary to convince the community at large—to quiet those prying quid nuncs who should come after them—in short, the world must be satisfied. Oh the world—the world!—all the world knows the world of trouble the world is eternally occasioning!— The worthy judges therefore, like myself in this most authentic, minute and satisfactory of all histories, were driven to the necessity of sifting, detecting and making evident as noon day, matters which were at the commencement all clearly understood and firmly decided upon in their own own pericraniums—so that it may truly be said, that the witches were burnt, to gratify the populace of the day—but were tried for the satisfaction of the whole world that should come after them!

Finding therefore that neither exhortation, sound reason, nor friendly entreaty had any avail on these hardened offenders, they resorted to the more urgent arguments of the torture, and having thus absolutely wrung the truth from their stubborn lips—they condemned them to undergo the roasting due unto the heinous crimes they had confessed. Some even carried their perverseness so far, as to expire under the torture, protesting their innocence to the last; but these were looked upon as thoroughly and absolutely possessed, and governed by the devil, and the pious bye-standers, only lamented that they had not lived a little longer, to have perished in the flames.

In the city of Ephesus, we are told, that the plague was expelled by stoning a ragged old beggar to death, whom Appolonius pointed out as being the evil spirit that caused it, and who actually shewed himself to be a demon, by changing into a shagged dog. In like manner, and by measures equally sagacious, a salutary check was given to this growing evil. The witches were all burnt, banished or panic struck, and in a little while there was not an ugly old woman to be found throughout New England—which is doubtless one reason why all their young women are so handsome. Those honest folk who had suffered from their incantations gradually recovered, excepting such as had been afflicted with twitches and aches, which, however assumed the less alarming aspects of rheumatisms, sciatics and lumbagos—and the good people of New England, abandoning the study of the occult sciences, turned their attention to the more profitable hocus pocus of trade, and soon became expert in the legerdemain art of turning a penny. Still however, a tinge of the old leaven is discernable, even unto this day, in their characters—witches occasionally start up among them in different disguises, as physicians, civilians, and divines. The people at large shew a 'cuteness, a cleverness, and a profundity of wisdom, that savours strongly of witchcraft—and it has been remarked, that whenever any stones fall from the moon, the greater part of them are sure to tumble into New England!

CHAPTER VII

*Which records the rise and renown of a valiant commander,
shewing that a man, like a bladder, may be puffed up to
greatness and importance, by mere wind.*

When treating of these tempestuous times, the unknown writer
of the Stuyvesant manuscript, breaks out into a vehement apos-
trophe, in praise of the good St. Nicholas; to whose protecting
care he entirely ascribes the strange dissentions that broke out in
the council of the amphyctions, and the direful witchcraft that
prevailed in the east country—whereby the hostile machinations
against the Nederlanders were for a time frustrated, and his favourite city of New Amsterdam, preserved from imminent peril
and deadly warfare. Darkness and lowering superstition hung
over the fair valleys of the east; the pleasant banks of the Connecticut, no longer echoed with the sounds of rustic gaiety;
direful phantoms and portentous apparitions were seen in the
air—gliding spectrums haunted every wild brook and dreary
glen—strange voices, made by viewless forms, were heard in de-
sart solitudes—and the border towns were so occupied in detecting and punishing the knowing old women, that had produced
these alarming appearances, that for a while the province of New
Nederlandt and its inhabitants were totally forgotten.

The great Peter therefore, finding that nothing was to be immediately apprehended from his eastern neighbours, turned himself about with a praiseworthy vigilance that ever distinguished
him, to put a stop to the insults of the Swedes. These lossel free-
booters my attentive reader will recollect had begun to be very
troublesome towards the latter part of the reign of William the
Testy, having set the proclamations of that doughty little governor at naught, and put the intrepid Jan Jansen Alpendam to a
perfect non plus!

Peter Stuyvesant, however, as has already been shewn, was a
governor of different habits and turn of mind—without more ado

he immediately issued orders for raising a corps of troops to be stationed on the southern frontier, under the command of brigadier general Jacobus Von Poffenburgh. This illustrious warrior had risen to great importance during the reign of Wilhelmus Kieft, and if histories speak true, was second in command to the gallant Van Curlet, when he and his ragged regiment were inhumanly kicked out of Fort Good Hope by the Yankees. In consequence of having been in such a "memorable affair," and of having received more wounds on a certain honourable part that shall be nameless, than any of his comrades, he was ever after considered as a hero, who had "seen some service." Certain it is, he enjoyed the unlimited confidence and friendship of William the Testy; who would sit for hours and listen with wonder to his gunpowder narratives of surprising victories—he had never gained: and dreadful battles—from which he had run away; and the governor was once heard to declare that had he lived in ancient times, he might unquestionably have claimed the armour of Achilles—being not merely like Ajax, a mighty blustering man of battle, but in the cabinet a second Ulysses, that is to say, very valiant of speech and long winded—all which, as nobody in New Amsterdam knew aught of the ancient heroes in question, passed totally uncontradicted.

It was tropically observed by honest old Socrates, of henpecked memory, that heaven had infused into some men at their birth a portion of intellectual gold; into others of intellectual silver; while others were bounteously furnished out with abundance of brass and iron—now of this last class was undoubtedly the great general Von Poffenburgh, and from the great display he continually made, I am inclined to think that dame nature, who will sometimes be partial, had blessed him with enough of those valuable materials to have fitted up a dozen ordinary braziers. But what is most to be admired is, that he contrived to pass off all his brass and copper upon Wilhelmus Kieft, who was no great judge of base coin, as pure and genuine gold. The consequence was, that upon the resignation of Jacobus Van Curlet, who after the loss of fort Goed Hoop retired like a veteran general, to live under the shade of his laurels, the mighty "copper captain" was promoted to his station. This he filled with great importance, always styling himself "commander in chief of the armies of the New Netherlands;" though to tell the truth the armies, or rather army, consisted of a handful of half uniformed, hen stealing, bottle bruizing raggamuffins.

Such was the character of the warrior appointed by Peter Stuyvesant to defend his southern frontier, nor may it be uninteresting to my reader to have a glimpse of his person. He was not very tall, but notwithstanding, a huge, full bodied man, whose size did not so much arise from his being fat, as windy; being so completely inflated with his own importance, that he resembled one of those puffed up bags of wind, which old Eolus, in an incredible fit of generosity, gave to that vagabond warrior Ulysses.

His dress comported with his character, for he had almost as much brass and copper without, as nature had stored away within—His coat was crossed and slashed, and carbonadoed, with stripes of copper lace, and swathed round the body with a crimson sash, of a size and texture of a fishing net, doubtless to keep his valiant heart from bursting through his ribs. His head and whiskers were profusely powdered, from the midst of which his full blooded face glowed like a fiery furnace; and his magnanimous soul seemed ready to bounce out at a pair of large glassy blinking eyes, which projected like those of a lobster.

I swear to thee, worthy reader, if report belie not this great general, I would give half my fortune (which at this moment is not enough to pay the bill of my landlord) to have seen him accoutered cap-a-pie, in martial array—booted to the middle—sashed to the chin—collared to the ears—whiskered to the muzzle—crowned with an overshadowing cocked-hat, and girded with a leathern belt ten inches broad, from which trailed a faulchion of a length that I dare not mention.

Thus equipped, he strutted about, as bitter looking a man of war as the far-famed More of More Hall, when he sallied forth, armed at all points, to slay the Dragon of Wantley—

> "Had you but seen him in this dress
>   How fierce he look'd and how big;
> You would have thought him for to be
>   Some Egyptian Porcupig.
>
> He frighted all, cats, dogs and all,
>   Each cow, each horse, and each hog;

For fear they did flee, for they took him to be
Some strange outlandish hedge hog." *

Notwithstanding all the great endowments and transcendent qualities of this renowned general, I must confess he was not exactly the kind of man that the gallant Peter the Headstrong would have chosen to command his troops—but the truth is, that in those days the province did not abound, as at present, in great military characters; who like so many Cincinnatuses people every little village—marshalling out cabbages, instead of soldiers, and signalizing themselves in the corn field, instead of the field of battle. Who have surrendered the toils of war, for the more useful but inglorious arts of peace, and so blended the laurel with the olive, that you may have a general for a landlord, a colonel for a stage driver, and your horse shod by a valiant "captain of volunteers"—Neither had the great Stuyvesant an opportunity of choosing, like modern rulers, from a loyal band of editors of newspapers—no mention being made in the histories of the times, of any such class of mercenaries, being retained in pay by government, either as trumpeters, champions, or body guards. The redoubtable general Von Poffenburgh, therefore, was appointed to the command of the new levied troops; chiefly because there were no competitors for the station, and partly because it would have been a breach of military etiquette, to have appointed a younger officer over his head—an injustice, which the great Peter would rather have died than have committed.

No sooner did this thrice valiant copper captain receive marching orders, than he conducted his army undauntedly to the southern frontier; through wild lands and savage deserts; over insurmountable mountains, across impassable floods and through impenetrable forests; subduing a vast tract of uninhabited country, and overturning, discomfiting and making incredible slaughter of certain hostile hosts of grass-hoppers, toads and pismires, which had gathered together to oppose his progress—an achievement unequalled in the pages of history, save by the farfamed retreat of old Xenophon and his ten thousand Grecians. All this accomplished, he established on the South (or Delaware) river,

*Ballad of Drag. of Want.

a redoubtable redoubt, named FORT CASIMER, in honour of a favourite pair of brimstone coloured trunk breeches of the governor's. As this fort will be found to give rise to very important and interesting events, it may be worth while to notice that it was afterwards called Nieuw Amstel, and was the original germ of the present flourishing town of NEW CASTLE, an appellation erroneously substituted for *No Castle*, there neither being, nor ever having been a castle, or any thing of the kind upon the premises.

The Swedes did not suffer tamely this menacing movement of the Nederlanders; on the contrary Jan Printz, at that time governor of New Sweden, issued a sturdy protest against what he termed an encroachment upon his jurisdiction.—But the valiant Von Poffenburgh had become too well versed in the nature of proclamations and protests, while he served under William the Testy, to be in any wise daunted by such paper warfare. His fortress being finished, it would have done any man's heart good to behold into what a magnitude he immediately swelled. He would stride in and out a dozen times a day, surveying it in front and in rear; on this side and on that.—Then would he dress himself in full regimentals, and strut backwards and forwards, for hours together, on the top of his little rampart—like a vain glorious cock pidgeon vapouring on the top of his coop. In a word, unless my readers have noticed, with curious eye, the petty commander of a little, snivelling, military post, swelling with all the vanity of new regimentals, and the pomposity derived from commanding a handful of tatterdemalions, I despair of giving them any adequate idea of the prodigious dignity of general Von Poffenburgh.

It is recorded in the delectable romance of Pierce Forest, that a young knight being dubbed by king Alexander, did incontinently gallop into an adjoining forest, and belaboured the trees with such might and main, that the whole court were convinced that he was the most potent and courageous gentleman on the face of the earth. In like manner the great general Von Poffenburgh would ease off that valourous spleen, which like wind is so apt to grow unruly in the stomachs of new made soldiers, impelling them to box-lobby brawls, and broken headed quarrels.—For at such times, when he found his martial spirit waxing hot within him, he would prudently sally forth into the fields, and lugging out his trusty sabre, of full two flemish ells in length, would lay about him most lustily, decapitating cabbages by platoons—hewing down whole phalanxes of sunflowers, which he termed gigantic Swedes; and if peradventure, he espied a colony of honest big bellied pumpkins quietly basking themselves in the sun, "ah caitiff Yankees," would he roar, "have I caught ye at last!"—so saying, with one sweep of his sword, he would cleave the unhappy vegetables from their chins to their waistbands: by which warlike havoc, his choler being in some sort allayed, he would return to his garrison with a full conviction, that he was a very miracle of military prowess.

The next ambition of general Von Poffenburgh was to be thought a strict disciplinarian. Well knowing that discipline is the soul of all military enterprize, he enforced it with the most rigorous precision; obliging every man to turn out his toes, and hold up his head on parade, and prescribing the breadth of their ruffles to all such as had any shirts to their backs.

Having one day, in the course of his devout researches in the bible, (for the pious Eneas himself, could not exceed him in outward religion) encountered the history of Absalom and his melancholy end; the general in an evil hour, issued orders for cropping the hair of both officers and men throughout the garrison. Now it came to pass, that among his officers was one Kildermeester; a sturdy old veteran, who had cherished through the course of a long life, a rugged mop of hair, not a little resembling the shag of a Newfoundland dog; terminating with an immoderate queue, like the handle of a frying pan; and queued so tightly to his head, that his eyes and mouth generally stood ajar, and his eye-brows were drawn up to the top of his forehead. It may naturally be supposed that the possessor of so goodly an appendage would resist with abhorrence, an order condemning it to the shears. Sampson himself could not have held his wig more sacred, and on hearing the general orders, he discharged a tempest of veteran, soldier-like oaths, and dunder and blixums—swore he would break any man's head who attempted to meddle with his tail—queued it stiffer than ever, and whisked it about the garrison, as fiercely as the tail of a crocodile.

The eel-skin queue of old Kildermeester, became instantly an affair of the utmost importance. The commander in chief was too enlightened an officer not to perceive, that the discipline of the garrison, the subordination and good order of the *armies* of the Nieuw Nederlandts, the consequent safety of the whole province, and ultimately the dignity and prosperity of their high mightinesses, the lords states general, but above all, the dignity of the great general Von Poffenburgh, all imperiously demanded the docking of that stubborn queue. He therefore patriotically determined that old Kildermeester should be publicly shorn of his glories in presence of the whole garrison—the old man as resolutely stood on the defensive—whereupon the general, as became a great man, was highly exasperated, and the offender was arrested and tried by a court martial for mutiny, desertion and all the other rigmarole of offences noticed in the articles of war, ending with a "videlicit, in wearing an eel-skin queue, three feet long, contrary to orders"—Then came on arraignments, and trials, and pleadings, and convictings, and the whole country was in a ferment about this unfortunate queue. As it is well known that the commander of a distant frontier post has the power of acting pretty much after his own will, there is little doubt but that the old veteran would have been hanged or shot at least, had he not luckily fallen ill of a fever, through mere chagrin and mortification—and most flagitiously deserted from all earthly command, with his beloved locks unviolated. His obstinacy remained unshaken to the very last moment, when he directed that he should be carried to his grave with his eel-skin queue sticking out of a knot hole in his coffin.

This magnanimous affair obtained the general great credit as an excellent disciplinarian, but it is hinted that he was ever after subject to bad dreams, and fearful visitations in the night—when the grizly spectrum of old Kildermeester would stand centinel by his bed side, erect as a pump, his enormous queue strutting out like the handle.

END OF BOOK V

BOOK VI

Containing the second part of the reign of
Peter the Headstrong—and his gallant
atchievements on the Delaware.

CHAPTER I

*In which is presented a warlike portrait of the Great Peter.—
And how General Von Poffenburgh gave a stout carousal, for
which he got more kicks than coppers.*

Hitherto most venerable and courteous reader, have I shewn thee
the administration of the valourous Stuyvesant, under the mild
moonshine of peace; or rather the grim tranquillity of awful
preparation; but now the war drum rumbles, the brazen trumpet
brays its thrilling note, and the rude clash of hostile arms, speaks
fearful prophecies of coming troubles. The gallant warrior starts
from soft repose, from golden visions and voluptuous ease; where
in the dulcet, "piping time of peace," he sought sweet solace after
all his toils. No more in beauty's syren lap reclined, he weaves
fair garlands for his lady's brows; no more entwines with flowers
his shining sword, nor through the live-long lazy summers day,
chaunts forth his lovesick soul in madrigals. To manhood roused,
he spurns the amorous flute; doffs from his brawny back the robe
of peace, and clothes his pampered limbs in panoply of steel. O'er
his dark brow, where late the myrtle waved; where wanton roses
breathed enervate love, he rears the beaming casque and nodding
plume; grasps the bright shield and shakes the pondrous lance; or
mounts with eager pride his fiery steed; and burns for deeds of
glorious chivalry!

But soft, worthy reader! I would not have you go about to
imagine, that any *preux chevalier* thus hideously begirt with iron
existed in the city of New Amsterdam.—This is but a lofty and
gigantic mode in which we heroic writers always talk of war,
thereby to give it a noble and imposing aspect; equipping our
warriors with bucklers, helms and lances, and a host of other
outlandish and obsolete weapons, the like of which perchance
they had never seen or heard of; in the same manner that a cunning statuary arrays a modern general or an admiral in the accoutrements of a Caesar or an Alexander. The simple truth then

of all this oratorical flourish is this.—That the valiant Peter Stuyvesant all of a sudden found it necessary to scour his trusty blade, which too long had rusted in its scabbard, and prepare himself to undergo those hardy toils of war, in which his mighty soul so much delighted.

Methinks I at this moment behold him in my imagination—or rather I behold his goodly portrait, which still hangs up in the family mansion of the Stuyvesants—arrayed in all the terrors of a true dutch general. His regimental coat of German blue, gorgeously decorated with a goodly shew of large brass buttons, reaching from his waistband to his chin. The voluminous skirts turned up at the corners and separating gallantly behind, so as to display the seat of a sumptuous pair of brimstone coloured trunk breeches—a graceful style still prevalent among the warriors of our day, and which is in conformity to the custom of ancient heroes, who scorned to defend themselves in rear.—His face rendered exceeding terrible and warlike by a pair of black mustachios; his hair strutting out on each side in stiffly pomatumed ear locks and descending in a rat tail queue below his waist; a shining stock of black leather supporting his chin, and a little, but fierce cocked hat stuck with a gallant and fiery air, over his left eye. Such was the chivalric port of Peter the Headstrong; and when he made a sudden halt, planted himself firmly on his solid supporter, with his wooden leg, inlaid with silver, a little in advance, in order to strengthen his position; his right hand stuck a-kimbo, his left resting upon the pummel of his brass hilted sword; his head dressing spiritedly to the right, with a most appalling and hard favoured frown upon his brow—he presented altogether one of the most commanding, bitter looking, and soldierlike figures, that ever strutted upon canvass.—Proceed we now to enquire the cause of this warlike preparation.

The encroaching disposition of the Swedes, on the south, or Delaware river, has been duly recorded in the Chronicles of the reign of William the Testy. These encroachments having been endured with that heroic magnanimity, which is the corner stone, or according to Aristotle, the left hand neighbour of true courage, had been repeated and wickedly aggravated.

The Swedes, who, were of that class of cunning pretenders to Christianity, that read the Bible upside down, whenever it interferes with their interests, inverted the golden maxim, and when their neighbour suffered them to smite him on the one cheek, they generally smote him on the other also, whether it was turned to them or not. Their repeated aggressions had been among the numerous sources of vexation, that conspired to keep the irritable sensibilities of Wilhelmus Kieft, in a constant fever, and it was only owing to the unfortunate circumstance, that he had always a hundred things to do at once, that he did not take such unrelenting vengeance as their offences merited. But they had now a chieftan of a different character to deal with; and they were soon guilty of a piece of treachery, that threw his honest blood in a ferment, and precluded all further sufference.

Printz, the governor of the province of New Sweden, being either deceased or removed, for of this fact some uncertainty exists; he was succeeded by Jan Risingh, a gigantic Swede, and who, had he not been rather in-kneed and splay-footed, might have served for the model of a Sampson, or a Hercules. He was no less rapacious than mighty, and withal as crafty as he was rapacious; so that in fact there is very little doubt, had he lived some four or five centuries before, he would have made one of those wicked giants, who took such a cruel pleasure in pocketing distressed damsels, when gadding about the world, and locking them up in enchanted castles, without a toilet, a change of linen, or any other convenience.—In consequence of which enormities they fell under the high displeasure of chivalry, and all true, loyal and gallant knights, were instructed to attack and slay outright any miscreant they might happen to find above six feet high; which is doubtless one reason that the race of large men is nearly extinct, and the generations of latter ages so exceeding small.

No sooner did governor Risingh enter upon his office, than he immediately cast his eyes upon the important post of Fort Casimer, and formed the righteous resolution of taking it into his possession. The only thing that remained to consider, was the mode of carrying his resolution into effect; and here I must do him the justice to say, that he exhibited a humanity rarely to be met with among leaders; and which I have never seen equalled in modern times, excepting among the English, in their glorious affair at Copenhagen. Willing to spare the effusion of blood, and the miseries of open warfare, he benevolently shunned every thing like avowed hostility or regular siege, and resorted to the less glorious, but more merciful expedient of treachery.

Under pretence therefore, of paying a sociable, neighbourly visit to general Von Poffenburgh, at his new post of Fort Casimer, he made requisite preparation, sailed in great state up the Delaware, displayed his flag with the most ceremonious punctilio, and honoured the fortress with a royal salute, previous to dropping anchor. The unusual noise awakened a veteran dutch centinel, who was napping faithfully on his post, and who after hammering his flint for good ten minutes, and rubbing its edge with the corner of his ragged cocked hat, but all to no purpose, contrived to return the compliment, by discharging his rusty firelock with the spark of a pipe, which he borrowed from one of his comrades. The salute indeed would have been answered by the guns of the fort, had they not unfortunately been out of order, and the magazine deficient in ammunition—accidents to which forts have in all ages been liable, and which were the more excusable in the present instance, as Fort Casimer had only been erected about two years, and general Von Poffenburgh, its mighty commander, had been fully occupied with matters of much greater self importance.

Risingh, highly satisfied with this courteous reply to his salute, treated the fort to a second, for he well knew its puissant and pompous leader, was marvellously delighted with these little ceremonials, which he considered as so many acts of homage paid unto his greatness. He then landed in great state, attended by a suite of thirty men—a prodigious and vain-glorious retinue, for a petty governor of a petty settlement, in those days of primitive simplicity; and to the full as great an army as generally swells the pomp and marches in the rear of our frontier commanders at the present day.

The number in fact might have awakened suspicion, had not the mind of the great Von Poffenburgh been so completely engrossed with an all pervading idea of himself, that he had not room to admit a thought besides. In fact he considered the concourse of Risingh's followers as a compliment to himself—so apt are great men to stand between themselves and the sun, and completely eclipse the truth by their own shadow.

It may readily be imagined how much general Von Poffenburgh was flattered by a visit from so august a personage; his only embarrassment was, how he should receive him in such a manner as to appear to the greatest advantage, and make the most advantageous impression. The main guard was ordered immediately to turn out, and the arms and regimentals (of which the garrison possessed full half a dozen suits) were equally distributed among the soldiers. One tall lank fellow, appeared in a coat intended for a small man, the skirts of which reached a little below his waist, the buttons were between his shoulders and the sleeves half way to his wrists, so that his hands looked like a couple of huge spades—and the coat not being large enough to meet in front, was linked together by loops, made of a pair of red worsted garters. Another had an old cocked hat, stuck on the back of his head and decorated with a bunch of cocks tails—a third had a pair of rusty gaiters hanging about his heels—while a fourth, who was a short duck legged little trojan, was equipped in a huge pair of the general's cast off breeches, which he held up with one hand, while he grasped his firelock with the other. The rest were accoutred in similar style, excepting three graceless raggamuffins, who had no shirts and but a pair and half of breeches between them, wherefore they were sent to the black hole, to keep them out of view. There is nothing in which the talents of a prudent commander are more completely testified, than in thus setting matters off to the greatest advantage; and it is for this reason that our frontier posts at the present day (that of Niagara in particular) display their best suit of regimentals on the back of the centinel who stands in sight of travellers.

His men being thus gallantly arrayed—those who lacked muskets shouldering shovels and pick axes, and every man being ordered to tuck in his shirt tail and pull up his brogues, general Von Poffenburgh first took a sturdy draught of foaming ale, which like the magnanimous More of More-hall* was his invariable practice on all great occasions—which done he put himself at their head, ordered the pine planks, which served as a draw bridge, to be laid down, and issued forth from his castle, like a

---

*"——as soon as he rose,
    To make him strong and mighty,
  He drank by the tale, six pots of ale,
    And a quart of Aqua Vitæ."

mighty giant, just refreshed with wine. But when the two heroes met, then began a scene of warlike parade and chivalric courtesy, that beggars all description. Risingh, who, as I before hinted, was a shrewd, cunning politician, and had grown grey much before his time, in consequence of his craftiness, saw at one glance the ruling passion of the great Von Poffenburgh, and humoured him in all his valorous fantasies.

Their detachments were accordingly drawn up in front of each other; they carried arms and they presented arms; they gave the standing salute and the passing salute—They rolled their drums, they flourished their fifes and they waved their colours—they faced to the left, and they faced to the right, and they faced to the right about—They wheeled forward, and they wheeled backward, and they wheeled into *echellon*—They marched and they countermarched, by grand divisions, by single divisions and by sub-divisions—by platoons, by sections and by files—In quick time, in slow time and in no time at all; for, having gone through all the evolutions of two great armies, including the eighteen manœuvres of Dundas (which, not being yet invented they must have anticipated by intuition or inspiration) having exhausted all that they could recollect or imagine of military tactics, including sundry strange and irregular evolutions, the like of which were never seen before or since, excepting among certain of our newly raised drafts, the two great commanders and their respective troops, came at length to a dead halt, completely exhausted by the toils of war—Never did two valiant train band captains, or two buskin'd theatric heroes, in the renowned tragedies of Pizarro, Tom Thumb, or any other heroical and fighting tragedy, marshal their gallows-looking, duck-legged, heavy-heeled, sheep-stealing myrmidons with more glory and self-admiration.

These military compliments being finished, general Von Poffenburgh escorted his illustrious visitor, with great ceremony into the fort; attended him throughout the fortifications; shewed him the horn works, crown works, half moons, and various other outworks; or rather the places where they ought to be erected, and where they might be erected if he pleased; plainly demonstrating that it was a place of "great capability," and though at present but a little redoubt, yet that it evidently was a formidable fortress, in embryo. This survey over, he next had the whole garrison put under arms, exercised and reviewed, and concluded by ordering the three bridewell birds to be hauled out of the black hole, brought up to the halberts and soundly flogged, for the amusement of his visitor, and to convince him, that he was a great disciplinarian.

There is no error more dangerous than for a commander to make known the strength, or, as in the present case, the weakness of his garrison; this will be exemplified before I have arrived to an end of my present story, which thus carries its moral like a roasted goose his pudding in its very middle. The cunning Rising, while he pretended to be struck dumb outright, with the puissance of the great Von Poffenburgh, took silent note of the incompetency of his garrison, of which he gave a hint to his trusty followers; who tipped each other the wink, and laughed most obstreperously—in their sleeves.

The inspection, review, and flogging being concluded, the party adjourned to the table; for among his other great qualities, the general was remarkably addicted to huge entertainments, or rather carousals, and in one afternoon's campaign would leave more *dead men* on the field, than he ever did in the whole course of his military career. Many bulletins of these bloodless victories do still remain on record; and the whole province was once thrown in amaze, by the return of one of his campaigns; wherein it was stated, that though like captain Bobadel, he had only twenty men to back him, yet in the short space of six months he had conquered and utterly annihilated sixty oxen, ninety hogs, one hundred sheep, ten thousand cabbages, one thousand bushels of potatoes, one hundred and fifty kilderkins of small beer, two thousand seven hundred and thirty five pipes, seventy eight pounds of sugar-plumbs, and forty bars of iron, besides sundry small meats, game, poultry and garden stuff. An atchievement unparalleled since the days of Pantagruel and his all devouring army, and which shewed that it was only necessary to let the great general Von Poffenburgh, and his garrison, loose in an enemies country, and in a little while they would breed a famine, and starve all the inhabitants.

No sooner therefore had the general received the first intimation of the visit of governor Risingh, than he ordered a big dinner to be prepared; and privately sent out a detachment of his most experienced veterans, to rob all the hen-roosts in the neighbourhood, and lay the pig-styes under contribution; a service to which they had been long enured, and which they discharged with such incredible zeal and promptitude, that the garrison table groaned under the weight of their spoils.

I wish with all my heart, my readers could see the valiant Von Poffenburgh, as he presided at the head of the banquet: it was a sight worth beholding—there he sat, in his greatest glory, surrounded by his soldiers, like that famous wine bibber Alexander, whose thirsty virtues he did most ably imitate—telling astounding stories of his hair-breadth adventures and heroic exploits, at which, though all his auditors knew them to be most incontinent and outrageous gasconadoes, yet did they cast up their eyes in admiration and utter many interjections of astonishment. Nor could the general pronounce any thing that bore the remotest semblance to a joke, but the stout Risingh would strike his brawny fist upon the table till every glass rattled again, throwing himself back in his chair, and uttering gigantic peals of laughter, swearing most horribly, it was the best joke he ever heard in his life.— Thus all was rout and revelry and hideous carousal within Fort Casimer, and so lustily did the great Von Poffenburgh ply the bottle, that in less than four short hours he made himself, and his whole garrison, who all sedulously emulated the deeds of their chieftain, dead drunk, in singing songs, quaffing bumpers, and drinking fourth of July toasts, not one of which, but was as long as a Welsh pedigree or a plea in chancery.

No sooner did things come unto this pass, than the crafty Risingh and his Swedes, who had cunningly kept themselves sober, rose on their entertainers, tied them neck and heels, and took formal possession of the fort, and all its dependencies, in the name of queen Christina, of Sweden: administering, at the same time, an oath of allegiance to all the dutch soldiers, who could be made sober enough to swallow it. Risingh then put the fortifications in order, appointed his discreet and vigilant friend Suen Scutz, a tall, wind-dried, water drinking Swede, to the command, and departed bearing with him this truly amiable garrison, and their puissant commander; who when brought to himself by a sound drubbing, bore no little resemblance to a "deboshed fish;" or bloated sea monster, caught upon dry land.

The transportation of the garrison was done to prevent the

transmission of intelligence to New Amsterdam; for much as the cunning Risingh exulted in his stratagem, he dreaded the vengeance of the sturdy Peter Stuyvesant; whose name spread as much terror in the neighbourhood, as did whilome that of the unconquerable Scanderbeg among his scurvy enemies the Turks.

CHAPTER II

*Shewing how profound secrets are strangely brought to light;
with the proceedings of Peter the Headstrong when he heard
of the misfortune of General Von Poffenburgh.*

Whoever first described common fame, or rumour, as belonging
to the sager sex, was a very owl for shrewdness. She has in truth
certain feminine qualities to an astonishing degree; particularly
that benevolent anxiety to take care of the affairs of others,
which keeps her continually hunting after secrets, and gadding
about, proclaiming them. Whatever is done openly and in the
face of the world, she takes but transient notice of, but whenever
a transaction is done in a corner, and attempted to be shrouded
in mystery, then her goddessship is at her wit's end to find it out,
and takes a most mischievous and lady-like pleasure in publishing it to the world. It is this truly feminine propensity that induces her continually to be prying into cabinets of princes;
listening at the key holes of senate chambers, and peering through
chinks and crannies, when our worthy Congress are sitting with
closed doors, deliberating between a dozen excellent modes of
ruining the nation. It is this which makes her so obnoxious to all
wary statesmen and intriguing commanders—such a stumbling
block to private negociations and secret expeditions; which she
often betrays, by means and instruments which never would have
been thought of by any but a female head.

Thus it was in the case of the affair of Fort Casimer. No doubt
the cunning Risingh imagined, that by securing the garrison, he
should for a long time prevent the history of its fate from reaching the ears of the gallant Stuyvesant; but his exploit was blown
to the world when he least expected it, and by one of the last beings he would ever have suspected of enlisting as trumpeter to the
wide mouthed deity.

This was one Dirk Schuiler (or Skulker); a kind of hanger on to
the garrison; who seemed to belong to no body, and in a manner

to be self outlawed. One of those vagabond Cosmopolites, who shirk about the world, as if they had no right or business in it, and who infest the skirts of society, like poachers and interlopers. Every garrison and country village has one or more scape goats of this kind, whose life is a kind of enigma, whose existence is without motive, who comes from the Lord knows where, who lives the Lord knows how, and seems to be made for no other earthly purpose but to keep up the antient and honourable order of idleness—This vagrant philosopher was supposed to have some Indian blood in his veins, which was manifested by a certain Indian complexion and cast of countenance; but more especially by his propensities and habits. He was a tall, lank fellow, swift of foot and long-winded. He was generally equipped in a half Indian dress, with belt, leggings, and moccasons. His hair hung in straight gallows locks, about his ears, and added not a little to his shirking demeanour. It is an old remark, that persons of Indian mixture are half civilized, half savage, and half devil, a third half being expressly provided for their particular convenience. It is for similar reasons, and probably with equal truth, that the back-wood-men of Kentucky are styled half man, half horse and half alligator, by the settlers on the Mississippi, and held accordingly in great respect and abhorrence.

The above character may have presented itself to the garrison as applicable to Dirk Schuiler, whom they familiarly dubbed Galgenbrok, or Gallows Dirk. Certain it is, he appeared to acknowledge allegiance to no one—was an utter enemy to work, holding it in no manner of estimation—but lounged about the fort, depending upon chance for a subsistence; getting drunk whenever he could get liquor, and stealing whatever he could lay his hands on. Every day or two he was sure to get a sound rib-roasting for some of his misdemeanours, which however, as it broke no bones, he made very light of, and scrupled not to repeat the offence, whenever another opportunity presented. Sometimes in consequence of some flagrant villainy, he would abscond from the garrison, and be absent for a month at a time; skulking about the woods and swamps, with a long fowling piece on his shoulder, laying in ambush for game—or squatting himself down on the edge of a pond catching fish for hours together, and bearing no little resemblance to that notable bird ycleped the Mud-poke.

When he thought his crimes had been forgotten or forgiven, he would sneak back to the fort with a bundle of skins, or a bunch of poultry which perchance he had stolen, and exchange them for liquor, with which, having well soaked his carcass, he would lay in the sun and enjoy all the luxurious indolence of that swinish philosopher Diogenes. He was the terror of all the farm yards in the country; into which he made fearful inroads; and sometimes he would make his sudden appearance at the garrison at day break, with the whole neighbourhood at his heels; like a scoundrel thief of a fox, detected in his maraudings and hunted to his hole. Such was this Dirk Schuiler; and from the total indifference he shewed to the world or its concerns, and from his true Indian stoicism and taciturnity, no one would ever have dreamt, that he would have been the publisher of the treachery of Risingh.

When the carousal was going on, which proved so fatal to the brave Von Poffenburgh and his watchful garrison, Dirk skulked about from room to room, being a kind of privileged vagrant, or useless hound, whom nobody noticed. But though a fellow of few words, yet like your taciturn people, his eyes and ears were always open, and in the course of his prowlings he overheard the whole plot of the Swedes. Dirk immediately settled in his own mind, how he should turn the matter to his own advantage. He played the perfect jack-of-both-sides—that is to say, he made a prize of every thing that came in his reach, robbed both parties, stuck the copper bound cocked hat of the puissant Von Poffenburgh, on his head, whipped a huge pair of Risingh's jack boots under his arm, and took to his heels, just before the denouement and confusion at the garrison.

Finding himself completely dislodged from his haunt in this quarter, he directed his flight towards his native place, New Amsterdam, from whence he had formerly been obliged to abscond precipitately, in consequence of misfortune in business—in other words, having been detected in the act of sheep stealing. After wandering many days in the woods, toiling through swamps, fording brooks, swimming various rivers, and encountering a world of hardships that would have killed any other being, but an Indian, a back-wood-man, or the devil, he at length arrived, half famished, and lank as a starved weazle at Communipaw, where he stole a canoe and paddled over to New Amsterdam. Immediately on landing, he repaired to governor Stuyvesant, and in more words than he had ever spoken before, in the whole course of his life, gave an account of the disastrous affair.

On receiving these direful tidings the valiant Peter started from his seat, as did the stout king Arthur when at "merry Carleile," the news was brought him of the uncourteous misdeeds of the "grim barone"—without uttering a word, he dashed the pipe he was smoking against the back of the chimney—thrust a prodigious quid of negro head tobacco into his left cheek—pulled up his galligaskins, and strode up and down the room, humming, as was customary with him, when in a passion a most hideous north-west ditty. But, as I have before shewn, he was not a man to vent his spleen in idle vapouring. His first measure after the paroxysm of wrath had subsided, was to stump up stairs, to a huge wooden chest, which served as his armoury, from whence he drew forth that identical suit of regimentals described in the preceding chapter. In these portentous habiliments he arrayed himself, like Achilles in the armour of Vulcan, maintaining all the while a most appalling silence; knitting his brows and drawing his breath through his clinched teeth. Being hastily equipped, he thundered down into the parlour like a second Magog—jerked down his trusty sword, from over the fire place, where it was usually suspended; but before he girded it on his thigh he drew it from its scabbard, and as his eye coursed along the rusty blade, a grim smile stole over his iron visage—It was the first smile that had visited his countenance for five long weeks; but every one who beheld it, prophesied that there would soon be warm work in the province!

Thus armed at all points, with grizly war depicted in each feature; his very cocked hat assuming an air of uncommon defiance; he instantly put himself on the alert, and dispatched Antony Van Corlear hither and thither, this way and that way, through all the muddy streets and crooked lanes of the city: summoning by sound of trumpet his trusty peers to assemble in instant council.— This done, by way of expediting matters, according to the custom of people in a hurry, he kept in continual bustle, thrusting his bottom into every chair, popping his head out of every window, and stumping up and down stairs with his wooden leg in such brisk and incessant motion, that, as I am informed by an authentic historian of the times, the continual clatter bore no small resemblance to the music of a cooper, hooping a flour barrel.

A summons so peremptory, and from a man of the governor's mettle, was not to be trifled with: the sages forthwith repaired to the council chamber, where the gallant Stuyvesant entered in martial style, and took his chair, like another Charlemagne, among his Paladins. The councillors seated themselves with the utmost tranquillity, and lighting their long pipes, gazed with unruffled composure on his excellency and his regimentals; being, as all councillors should be, not easily flustered, or taken by surprise. The governor, not giving them time to recover from the astonishment they did not feel, addressed them in a short, but soul stirring harangue.

I am extremely sorry, that I have not the advantages of Livy, Thucydides, Plutarch and others of my predecessors, who were furnished as I am told, with the speeches of all their great emperors, generals, and orators, taken down in short hand, by the most accurate stenographers of the time; whereby they were enabled wonderfully to enrich their histories, and delight their readers with sublime strains of eloquence. Not having such important auxiliaries, I cannot possibly pronounce, what was the tenor of governor Stuyvesant's speech. Whether he with maiden coyness hinted to his hearers that "there was a speck of war in the horison;"—that it would be necessary to resort to the "unprofitable trial of which could do each other the most harm,"—or any other delicate construction of language, whereby the odious subject of war, is handled so fastidiously and modestly by modern statesmen; as a gentleman volunteer handles his filthy salt-petre weapons with gloves, lest he should soil his dainty fingers.

I am bold however to say, from the tenor of Peter Stuyvesant's character, that he did not wrap his rugged subject in silks and ermines, and other sickly trickeries of phrase; but spoke forth, like a man of nerve and vigour, who scorned to shrink in words, from those dangers which he stood ready to encounter in very deed. This much is certain, that he concluded by announcing his determination of leading on his troops in person, and routing these costard-monger Swedes, from their usurped quarters at Fort Casimer. To this hardy resolution, such of his council as were awake, gave their usual signal of concurrence, and as to the rest, who had fallen asleep about the middle of the harangue (their "usual custom in the afternoon")—they made not the least objection.

And now was seen in the fair city of New Amsterdam, a prodigious bustle and preparation for iron war. Recruiting parties marched hither and thither, trailing long standards in the mud, with which as at the present day the streets were benevolently covered, for the benefit of those unfortunate wights who are aggrieved with corns. Thus did they lustily call upon and invite all the scrubs, the runagates and the tatterdemalions of the Manhattoes and its vicinity, who had any ambition of six pence a day, and immortal fame into the bargain, to enlist in the cause of glory. For I would have you note that your warlike heroes who trudge in the rear of conquerors, are generally of that illustrious class of gentlemen, who are equal candidates for the army or the bridewell—the halberts or the whipping post—for whom dame fortune has cast an even die whether they shall make their exit by the sword or the halter—and whose deaths shall, at all events, be a lofty example to their countrymen.

But notwithstanding all this martial rout and invitation, the ranks of honour were but scantily supplied; so averse were the peaceful burghers of New Amsterdam to enlist in foreign broils, or stir beyond that home, which rounded all their earthly ideas. Upon beholding this, the great Peter whose noble heart was all on fire with war and sweet revenge, determined to wait no longer for the tardy assistance of these oily citizens, but to muster up his merry men of the Hudson; who, brought up among woods and wilds and savage beasts, like our yeomen of Kentucky, delighted in nothing so much as desperate adventures and perilous expeditions through the wilderness. Thus resolving, he ordered his trusty squire Antony Van Corlear to have his state galley prepared and duly victualled; which being faithfully performed he attended public service at the great church of St. Nicholas, like a true and pious governor, and then leaving peremptory orders with his council to have the chivalry of the Manhattoes marshalled out and appointed against his return, departed upon his recruiting voyage, up the waters of the Hudson.

CHAPTER III

*Containing Peter Stuyvesant's voyage up the Hudson, and
the wonders and delights of that renowned river.*

Now did the soft breezes of the south, steal sweetly over the beauteous face of nature, tempering the panting heats of summer into genial and prolific warmth: when that miracle of hardihood and chivalric virtue, the dauntless Peter Stuyvesant, spread his canvass to the wind, and departed from the fair island of Manna-hata. The galley in which he embarked was sumptuously adorned with pendants and streamers of gorgeous dyes, which fluttered gaily in the wind, or drooped their ends into the bosom of the stream. The bow and poop of this majestic vessel were gallantly bedight, after the rarest dutch fashion, with naked figures of little pursy cupids with periwigs on their heads, and bearing in their hands garlands of flowers, the like of which are not to be found in any book of botany; being the matchless flowers which flourished in the golden age, and exist no longer, unless it be in the imaginations of ingenious carvers of wood and discolourers of canvass.

Thus rarely decorated, in style befitting the state of the puissant potentate of the Manhattoes, did the galley of Peter Stuyvesant launch forth upon the bosom of the lordly Hudson; which as it rolled its broad waves to the ocean, seemed to pause for a while, and swell with pride, as if conscious of the illustrious burthen it sustained.

But trust me gentlefolk, far other was the scene presented to the contemplation of the crew, from that which may be witnessed at this degenerate day. Wildness and savage majesty reigned on the borders of this mighty river—the hand of cultivation had not as yet laid low the dark forests, and tamed the features of the landscape—nor had the frequent sail of commerce yet broken in upon the profound and awful solitude of ages. Here and there might be seen a rude wigwam perched among the cliffs of the mountains, with its curling column of smoke mounting in the transparent atmosphere—but so loftily situated that the whoopings of the savage children, gambolling on the margin of the dizzy heights, fell almost as faintly on the ear, as do the notes of the lark, when lost in the azure vault of heaven. Now and then from the beetling brow of some rocky precipice, the wild deer would look timidly down upon the splendid pageant as it passed below; and then tossing his branching antlers in the air, would bound away into the thickets of the forest.

Through such scenes did the stately vessel of Peter Stuyvesant pass. Now did they skirt the bases of the rocky heights of Jersey, which spring up like everlasting walls, reaching from the waves unto the heavens; and were fashioned, if tradition may be believed, in times long past, by the mighty spirit Manetho, to protect his favourite abodes from the unhallowed eyes of mortals. Now did they career it gaily across the vast expanse of Tappan bay, whose wide extended shores present a vast variety of delectable scenery—here the bold promontory, crowned with embowering trees advancing into the bay—there the long woodland slope, sweeping up from the shore in rich luxuriance, and terminating in the rude upland precipice—while at a distance a long waving line of rocky heights, threw their gigantic shades across the water. Now would they pass where some modest little interval, opening among these stupendous scenes, yet retreating as it were for protection into the embraces of the neighbouring mountains, displayed a rural paradise, fraught with sweet and pastoral beauties; the velvet tufted lawn—the bushy copse—the tinkling rivulet, stealing through the fresh and vivid verdure—on whose banks was situated some little Indian village, or peradventure, the rude cabin of some solitary hunter.

The different periods of the revolving day seemed each with cunning magic, to diffuse a different charm over the scene. Now would the jovial sun break gloriously from the east, blazing from the summits of the eastern hills and sparkling the landscape with a thousand dewy gems; while along the borders of the river were seen heavy masses of mist, which like midnight caitiffs, disturbed at his approach, made a sluggish retreat, rolling in sullen reluctance up the mountains. At such times all was brightness and life and gaiety—the atmosphere seemed of an indescribable pureness and transparency—the birds broke forth in wanton madrigals, and the freshening breezes wafted the vessel merrily on her course. But when the sun sunk amid a flood of glory in the west, mantling the heavens and the earth with a thousand gorgeous dyes—then all was calm and silent and magnificent. The late swelling sail hung lifelessly against the mast—the simple seaman with folded arms leaned against the shrouds, lost in that involuntary musing which the sober grandeur of nature commands in the rudest of her children. The vast bosom of the Hudson was like an unruffled mirror, reflecting the golden splendour of the heavens, excepting that now and then a bark canoe would steal across its surface, filled with painted savages, whose gay feathers glared brightly, as perchance a lingering ray of the setting sun, gleamed upon them from the western mountains.

But when the fairy hour of twilight spread its magic mists around, then did the face of nature assume a thousand fugitive charms, which to the worthy heart that seeks enjoyment in the glorious works of its maker, are inexpressibly captivating. The mellow dubious light that prevailed, just served to tinge with illusive colours, the softened features of the scenery. The deceived but delighted eye sought vainly to discern in the broad masses of shade, the separating line between the land and water; or to distinguish the fading objects that seemed sinking into chaos. Now did the busy fancy supply the feebleness of vision, producing with industrious craft a fairy creation of her own. Under her plastic wand the barren rocks frowned upon the watery waste, in the semblance of lofty towers and high embattled castles—trees assumed the direful forms of mighty giants, and the inaccessible summits of the mountains seemed peopled with a thousand shadowy beings.

Now broke forth from the shores the notes of an innumerable variety of insects, who filled the air with a strange but not inharmonious concert—while ever and anon was heard the melancholy plaint of the Whip-poor-will, who, perched on some lone tree, wearied the ear of night with his incessant moanings. The mind, soothed into a hallowed melancholy by the solemn mystery of the scene, listened with pensive stillness to catch and distinguish each sound, that vaguely echoed from the shore—now and then startled perchance by the whoop of some straggling savage, or the dreary howl of some caitiff wolf, stealing forth upon his nightly prowlings.

Thus happily did they pursue their course, until they entered upon those awful defiles denominated THE HIGHLANDS, where it would seem that the gigantic Titans had erst waged their impious war with heaven, piling up cliffs on cliffs, and hurling vast masses of rock in wild confusion. But in sooth very different is the history of these cloud-capt mountains.—These in ancient days, before the Hudson poured his waters from the lakes, formed one vast prison, within whose rocky bosom the omnipotent Manetho confined the rebellious spirits who repined at his controul. Here, bound in adamantine chains, or jammed in rifted pines, or crushed by ponderous rocks, they groaned for many an age.—At length the lordly Hudson, in his irresistible career towards the ocean, burst open their prison house, rolling his tide triumphantly through its stupendous ruins.

Still however do many of them lurk about their old abodes; and these it is, according to venerable legends, that cause the echoes which resound throughout these awful solitudes; which are nothing but their angry clamours when any noise disturbs the profoundness of their repose.—But when the elements are agitated by tempest, when the winds are up and the thunder rolls, then horrible is the yelling and howling of these troubled spirits—making the mountains to rebellow with their hideous uproar; for at such times it is said, they think the great Manetho is returning once more to plunge them in gloomy caverns and renew their intolerable captivity.

But all these fair and glorious scenes were lost upon the gallant Stuyvesant; naught occupied his active mind but thoughts of iron war, and proud anticipations of hardy deeds of arms. Neither did his honest crew trouble their vacant minds with any romantic speculations of the kind. The pilot at the helm quietly smoked his pipe, thinking of nothing either past present or to come—those of his comrades who were not industriously snoring under the hatches, were listening with open mouths to Antony Van Corlear; who, seated on the windlass, was relating to them the marvellous history of those myriads of fire flies, that sparkled like gems and spangles upon the dusky robe of night. These, according

to tradition, were originally a race of pestilent sempiternous bel-
dames, who peopled these parts long before the memory of man;
being of that abominated race emphatically called *brimstones;*
and who for their innumerable sins against the children of men,
and to furnish an awful warning to the beauteous sex, were
doomed to infest the earth in the shape of these threatening and
terrible little bugs; enduring the internal torments of that fire,
which they formerly carried in their hearts and breathed forth in
their words; but now are sentenced to bear about forever—in
their tails!

And now am I going to tell a fact, which I doubt me much my
readers will hesitate to believe; but if they do, they are welcome
not to believe a word in this whole history, for nothing which it
contains is more true. It must be known then that the nose of
Antony the trumpeter was of a very lusty size, strutting boldly
from his countenance like a mountain of Golconda; being sumptuously bedecked with rubies and other precious stones—the true
regalia of a king of good fellows, which jolly Bacchus grants to
all who bouse it heartily at the flaggon. Now thus it happened,
that bright and early in the morning, the good Antony having
washed his burley visage, was leaning over the quarter railing of
the galley, contemplating it in the glassy wave below—Just at this
moment the illustrious sun, breaking in all his splendour from
behind one of the high bluffs of the Highlands, did dart one of
his most potent beams full upon the refulgent nose of the sounder
of brass—the reflection of which shot straightway down, hissing
hot, into the water, and killed a mighty sturgeon that was sporting beside the vessel! This huge monster being with infinite labour hoisted on board, furnished a luxurious repast to all the
crew, being accounted of excellent flavour, excepting about the
wound, where it smacked a little of brimstone—and this, on my
veracity, was the first time that ever sturgeon was eaten in these
parts, by christian people.*

When this astonishing miracle came to be made known to

*Domine Hans Megapolensis, treating of the country about Albany in a letter
which was written some time after the settlement thereof, says, "There is in the
river, great plenty of Sturgeon, which we christians do not make use of; but the
Indians eate them greedilie."

Peter Stuyvesant, and that he tasted of the unknown fish, he, as may well be supposed, marvelled exceedingly; and as a monument thereof, he gave the name of *Anthony's Nose* to a stout promontory in the neighbourhood—and it has continued to be called Anthony's nose ever since that time.

But hold—Whether am I wandering?—By the mass, if I attempt to accompany the good Peter Stuyvesant on this voyage, I shall never make an end, for never was there a voyage so fraught with marvellous incidents, nor a river so abounding with transcendent beauties, worthy of being severally recorded. Even now I have it on the point of my pen to relate, how his crew were most horribly frightened, on going on shore above the highlands, by a gang of merry roystering devils, frisking and curvetting on a huge flat rock, which projected into the river—and which is called the *Duyvel's Dans-Kamer* to this very day—But no! Diedrich Knickerbocker—it becomes thee not to idle thus in thy historic wayfaring.

Recollect that while dwelling with the fond garrullity of age, over these fairy scenes, endeared to thee, by the recollections of thy youth, and the charms of a thousand legendary tales which beguiled the simple ear of thy childhood; recollect that thou art trifling with those fleeting moments which should be devoted to loftier themes.—Is not time—relentless time!—shaking with palsied hand, his almost exhausted hour glass before thee?—hasten then to pursue thy weary task, lest the last sands be run, ere thou hast finished thy renowned history of the Manhattoes.

Let us then commit the dauntless Peter, his brave galley and his loyal crew, to the protection of the blessed St. Nicholas; who I have no doubt will prosper him in his voyage, while we await his return at the great city of New Amsterdam.

CHAPTER IV

Describing the powerful army that assembled at the city of New Amsterdam—together with the interview between Peter the Headstrong, and general Von Poffenburgh, and Peter's sentiments touching unfortunate great men.

While thus the enterprizing Peter was coasting, with flowing sail up the shores of the lordly Hudson, and arousing all the phlegmatic little dutch settlements upon its borders, a great and puissant concourse of warriors was assembling at the city of New Amsterdam. And here that most invaluable fragment of antiquity, the Stuyvesant manuscript, is more than commonly particular; by which means I am enabled to record the illustrious host that encamped themselves in the public square, in front of the fort, at present denominated the Bowling Green.

In the centre then, was pitched the tent of the men of battle of the Manhattoes, who being the inmates of the metropolis, composed the life guards of the governor. These were commanded by the valiant Stoffel Brinkerhoff, who whilome had acquired such immortal fame at Oyster Bay—they displayed as a standard, a mighty beaver *rampant* on a field of orange; being the arms of the province, and denoting the persevering industry, and the amphibious origin of the valiant Nederlanders.*

Then might be seen on their right hand, the vassals of that renowned Mynheer, Michael Paw,† who lorded it over the fair

---

*This was likewise the great seal of the New Netherlands, as may still be seen in ancient records.

†Besides what is mentioned by the Stuyvesant MS. I have found mention made of this illustrious Patroon in another manuscript, which says: "De Heer (or the Squire) Michael Paw, a dutch subject, about 10th Aug. 1630, by deed purchased Staten Island. N. B. The same Michael Paw had what the dutch call a colonie at Pavonia, on the Jersey shore opposite New York, and his overseer in 1636, was named Corns. Van Vorst—a person of same name in 1769, owned Pawles Hook, and a large farm at Pavonia, and is a lineal descendant from Van Vorst."

regions of ancient Pavonia, and the lands away south, even unto the Navesink mountains,* and was moreover patroon of Gibbet Island. His standard was borne by his trusty squire, Cornelius Van Vorst; consisting of a huge oyster *recumbent* upon a sea-green field; being the armorial bearings of his favourite metropolis, Communipaw. He brought to the camp a stout force of warriors, heavily armed, being each clad in ten pair of linsey woolsey breeches, and overshadowed by broad brimmed beavers, with short pipes twisted in their hatbands. These were the men who vegetated in the mud along the shores of Pavonia; being of the race of genuine copperheads, and were fabled to have sprung from oysters.

At a little distance was encamped the tribe of warriors who came from the neighbourhood of Hell-gate. These were commanded by the Suy Dams, and the Van Dams, most incontinent hard swearers, as their names betoken—they were terrible looking fellows, clad in broad skirted gaberdines, of that curious coloured cloth, called thunder and lightning—and bore as a standard three Devil's-darning-needles, *volant*, in a flame coloured field.

Hard by was the tent of the men of battle from the marshy borders of the Wael-bogtig,† and the country thereabouts—these were of a sour aspect, by reason that they lived on crabs which abound in these parts. They were the first institutors of that honourable order of knighthood, called *Fly market shirks*, and if tradition speak true, did likewise introduce the far-famed step in dancing, called "double trouble." They were commanded by the fearless Jacobus Varra Vanger, and had moreover a jolly band of Brooklyn ferry-men, who performed a brave concerto on conch shells.

But I refrain from pursuing this minute description, which goes on to describe the warriors of Bloemen dael, and Weehawk, and Hoboken, and sundry other places, well known in history

---

*So called from the Navesink tribe of Indians that inhabited these parts—at present they are erroneously denominated the Neversink, or Neversunk mountains.

†I. E. The *Winding Bay*, named from the winding of its shores. This has since been corrupted by the vulgar into the *Wallabout*, and is the basin which shelters our infant navy.

and song—for now does the sound of martial music alarm the people of New Amsterdam, sounding afar from beyond the walls of the city. But this alarm was in a little while relieved, for lo, from the midst of a vast cloud of dust, they recognized the brimstone coloured breeches, and splendid silver leg of Peter Stuyvesant, glaring in the sun beams; and beheld him approaching at the head of a formidable army, which he had mustered along the banks of the Hudson. And here the excellent, but anonymous writer of the Stuyvesant manuscript breaks out into a brave and glorious description of the forces, as they defiled through the principal gate of the city, that stood by the head of wall street.

First of all came the Van Bummels who inhabit the pleasant borders of the Bronx—These were short fat men, wearing exceeding large trunk breeches, and are renowned for feats of the trencher—they were the first inventors of Suppawn or Mush and milk—Close in their rear marched the Van Vlotens of Kaats kill, most horrible quaffers of new cyder, and arrant braggarts in their liquor—After them came the famous Van Pelts of Esopus, dextrous horsemen, mounted upon goodly switch tailed steeds of the Esopus breed—these were mighty hunters of minks and musk rats, whence came the word *Peltry*—Then the Van Nests of Kinderhook, valiant robbers of birds nests, as their name denotes; to these if report may be believed, are we indebted for the invention of slap jacks, or buck-wheat cakes.—Then the Van Grolls of Anthony's Nose, who carried their liquor in fair round little pottles, by reason they could not bouse it out of their canteens, having such rare long noses.—Then the Gardeniers of Hudson and thereabouts, distinguished by many triumphant feats, such as robbing water melon patches, smoking rabbits out of their holes and the like; and by being great lovers of roasted pigs tails; these were the ancestors of the renowned congress man of that name.—Then the Van Hoesens of Sing-Sing, great choristers and players upon the jews harp; these marched two and two, singing the great song of St. Nicholas.—Then the Counhovens, of Sleepy Hollow, these gave birth to a jolly race of publicans, who first discovered the magic artifice of conjuring a quart of wine into a pint bottle.— Then the Van Courtlandts who lived on the wild banks of the Croton, and were great killers of wild ducks, being much spoken of for their skill in shooting with the long bow.—Then the Bun-

schotens of Nyack and Kakiat who were the first that did ever kick
with the left foot; they were gallant bush-whackers and hunters of
racoons by moon-light.—Then the Van Winkles of Haerlem, potent suckers of eggs, and noted for running of horses and running
up of scores at taverns; they were the first that ever winked with
both eyes at once.—Lastly came the KNICKERBOCKERS of the
great town of Scaghtikoke, where the folk lay stones upon the
houses in windy weather, lest they should be blown away. These
derive their name, as some say, from *Knicker* to shake, and *Beker*
a goblet, indicating thereby that they were sturdy toss pots of
yore; but in truth it was derived from *Knicker* to nod, and *Boeken*
books; plainly meaning that they were great nodders or dozers
over books—from them did descend the writer of this History.

Such was the legion of sturdy bush beaters that poured into the
grand gate of New Amsterdam; the Stuyvesant manuscript indeed speaks of many more, whose names I omit to mention, seeing that it behoves me to hasten to matters of greater moment.
Nothing could surpass the joy and martial pride of the lion
hearted Peter as he reviewed this mighty host of warriors, and he
determined no longer to defer the gratification of his much wished
for revenge, upon the scoundrel Swedes at Fort Casimer.

But before I hasten on to record those unmatchable events,
which will be found in the sequel of this renowned history, let me
pause to notice the fate of Jacobus Von Poffenburgh, the discomfited commander in chief of the armies of the New Netherlands.
Such is the inherent uncharitableness of human nature, that
scarcely did the news become public of his deplorable discomfi-
ture at Fort Casimer; than a thousand scurvy rumours were set
afloat in New Amsterdam, wherein it was insinuated, that he had
in reality a treacherous understanding with the Swedish commander; that he had long been in the practice of privately com-
municating with the Swedes, together with divers hints about
"secret service money"—To all which deadly charges I do not
give a jot more credit—than I think they deserve.

Certain it is, that the general vindicated his character by the
most vehement oaths and protestations, and put every man out of
the ranks of honour who dared to doubt his integrity. Moreover
on returning to New Amsterdam, he paraded up and down the
streets with a crew of hard swearers at his heels—sturdy bottle

companions, whom he gorged and fattened, and who were ready to bolster him through all the courts of justice—Heroes of his own kidney, fierce whiskered, broad shouldered, colbrand looking swaggerers—not one of whom but looked as if he could eat up an ox, and pick his teeth with the horns. These life guard men quarreled all his quarrels, were ready to fight all his battles, and scowled at every man that turned up his nose at the general, as though they would devour him alive. Their conversation was interspersed with oaths like minute guns, and every bombastic rodomontade was rounded off by a thundering execration, like a patriotic toast honoured with a discharge of artillery.

All these valorous vapourings had a considerable effect in convincing certain profound sages, many of whom began to think the general a hero of most unutterable loftiness and magnanimity of soul, particularly as he was continually protesting *on the honour of a soldier*—a marvelously high sounding asseveration. Nay one of the members of the council went so far as to propose they should immortalize him by an imperishable statue of plaster of Paris!

But the vigilant Peter the Headstrong was not thus to be deceived—Sending privately for the commander in chief of all the armies, and having heard all his story, garnished with the customary pious oaths, protestations and ejaculations—"Harkee, *Metgelsel*," cried he, "though by your own account you are the most brave, upright and honourable man in the whole province, yet do you lie under the misfortune of being most damnably traduced, and immeasureably despised. Now though it is certainly hard to punish a man for his misfortunes, and though it is very possible you are totally innocent of the crimes laid to your charge, yet as heaven, at present, doubtless for some wise purpose, sees fit to withhold all proofs of your innocence, far be it from me to counteract its sovereign will. Beside, I cannot consent to venture my armies with a commander whom they despise, or to trust the welfare of my people to a champion whom they distrust. Retire therefore, my friend, from the irksome toils and cares of public life, with this comforting reflection—that if you are guilty, you are but enjoying your just reward—and if you are innocent, that you are not the first great and good man, who has most wrong-

fully been slandered and maltreated in this wicked world—
doubtless to be better treated in a better world, where there shall
be neither error, calumny nor persecution.—In the mean time let
me never see your face again, for I have a horrible antipathy to
the countenances of unfortunate great men like yourself."

CHAPTER V

In which the Author discourses very ingenuously of himself.—
After which is to be found much interesting history about
Peter the Headstrong and his followers.

As my readers and myself, are about entering on as many perils
and difficulties, as ever a confederacy of meddlesome knights-
errant wilfully ran their heads into; it is meet that like those hardy
adventurers, we should join hands, bury all differences, and swear
to stand by one another, in weal or woe, to the end of the enterprize. My readers must doubtless perceive, how completely I have
altered my tone and deportment, since we first set out together. I
warrant they then thought me a crabbed, cynical, impertinent little son of a Dutchman; for I never gave them a civil word, nor so
much as touched my beaver, when I had occasion to address them.
But as we jogged along together, in the high-road of my history, I
gradually began to relax, to grow more courteous, and occasionally to enter into familiar discourse, until at length I came to conceive a most social, companionable kind of regard for them. This
is just my way—I am always a little cold and reserved at first, particularly to people about whom I neither know nor care the value
of a brass farthing or a Vermont bank note, and am only to be
completely won by long intimacy.

Besides, why should I have been sociable to the host of how-
d'ye-do acquaintances, who flocked around me at my first appearance? They were merely attracted by a new face; many of them
only stared me full in the title page, and then walked off without saying a word; while others lingered yawningly through the
preface, and having gratified their short-lived curiosity, soon
dropped off one by one.—But more especially to try their mettle, I had recourse to an expedient, similar to one which we are
told was used, by that peerless flower of chivalry, king Arthur;
who before he admitted any knight to his intimacy, first required
that he should shew himself superior to danger or hardships, by

encountering unheard of mishaps, slaying some dozen giants, vanquishing wicked enchanters, not to say a word of dwarfs, hyppogriffs and fiery dragons. On a similar principle I cunningly led my readers, at the first sally, into two or three knotty chapters, where they were most woefully belaboured and buffetted, by a host of pagan philosophers and infidel writers. It did my midriff good, by reason of the excessive laughter into which I was thrown, at seeing the utter confusion and dismay of my valiant cavaliers—some dropped down dead (*asleep*) on the field; others threw down my book in the middle of the first chapter, took to their heels, and never ceased scampering until they had fairly run it out of sight; when they stopped to take breath, to tell their friends what troubles they had undergone, and to warn all others from venturing on so thankless an expedition. Every page thinned my ranks more and more; and of the mighty host that first set out, but a comparatively few made shift to survive, in exceedingly battered condition, through the five introductory chapters.

What then! would you have had me take such sun shine, faint hearted recreants to my bosom, at our first acquaintance? No—no. I reserved my friendship for those who deserved it; for those who undauntedly bore me company, in despite of difficulties, dangers and fatigues. And now as to those who adhere to me at present, I take them affectionately by the hand.—Worthy and thrice beloved readers! brave and well tried comrades! who have faithfully followed my footsteps through all my wanderings—I salute you from my heart—I pledge myself to stand by you to the last; and to conduct you, (so heaven speed this trusty weapon which I now hold between my fingers,) triumphantly to the end of this our stupenduous undertaking.

But hark! while we are thus talking, the city of New Amsterdam is in a constant bustle. The gallant host of warriors encamped in the bowling green are striking their tents; the brazen trumpet of Antony Van Corlear makes the welkin to resound with portentous clangour—the drums beat—the standards of the Manhattoes, of Hell-gate and of Michael Paw wave proudly in the air. And now behold where the mariners are busily prepared, hoisting the sails of yon top sail schooner, and those two clump built Albany sloops, which are to waft the army of the Nederlanders to gather immortal laurels on the Delaware!

The entire population of the city, man woman and child, turned out to behold the chivalry of New Amsterdam, as it paraded the streets previous to embarkation. Many a dirty pocket handkerchief was waved out of the windows; many a fair nose was blown in melodious sorrow, on the mournful occasion. The grief of the fair dames and beauteous damsels of Grenada, could not have been more vociferous on the banishment of the gallant tribe of Abencerrages, than was that of the kind hearted *Yfrouws* of New Amsterdam, on the departure of their intrepid warriors. Every love sick maiden fondly crammed the pockets of her hero with gingerbread and dough-nuts—many a copper ring was exchanged and crooked sixpence broken, in pledge of eternal constancy—and there remain extant to this day, some love verses written on that occasion, sufficiently crabbed and incomprehensible to confound the whole universe.

But it was a moving sight to see the buxom lasses, how they hung about the doughty Antony Van Corlear—for he was a jolly, rosy faced, lusty bachelor, and withal a great royster, fond of his joke and a desperate rogue among the women. Fain would they have kept him to comfort them while the army was away; for besides what I have said of him, it is no more than justice to add, that he was a kind hearted soul, noted for his benevolent attentions in comforting disconsolate wives during the absence of their husbands—and this made him to be very much regarded by the honest burghers of the city. But nothing could keep the valiant Antony from following the heels of the old governor, whom he loved as he did his very soul—so embracing all the young vrouws and giving every one of them that had good teeth and a clean mouth, a dozen hearty smacks—he departed loaded with their kind wishes.

Nor was the departure of the gallant Peter among the least causes of public distress. Though the old governor was by no means indulgent to the follies and waywardness of his subjects; and had turned over a complete "new leaf," from that which was presented in the days of William the Testy, yet some how or another he had become strangely popular among the people. There is something so captivating in personal bravery, that, with the common mass of mankind, it takes the lead of most other merits. The simple folk of New Amsterdam looked upon Peter Stuyvesant, as a prodigy of valour. His wooden leg, that trophy of his martial encounters, was regarded with reverence and admiration. Every old burgher had a budget of miraculous stories to tell about the exploits of Hard-koppig Piet, wherewith he regaled his children, of a long winter night, and on which he dwelt with as much delight and exaggeration, as do our honest country yeomen on the hardy adventures of old general Putnam (or as he is familiarly termed *Old Put*,) during our glorious revolution—Not an individual but verily believed the old governor was a match for Belzebub himself; and there was even a story told with great mystery, and under the rose, of his having shot the devil with a silver bullet one dark stormy night, as he was sailing in a canoe through Hell-gate—But this I do not record as being an absolute fact—perish the man, who would let fall a drop that should discolour the pure stream of history!

Certain it is, not an old woman in New Amsterdam, but considered Peter Stuyvesant as a tower of strength, and rested satisfied, that the public welfare was secure as long as he was in the city. It is not surprising then that they looked upon his departure as a sore affliction. With heavy hearts they draggled at the heels of his troop, as they marched down to the river side to embark. The governor from the stern of his schooner, gave a short, but truly patriarchal address to his citizens; wherein he recommended them to comport like loyal and peaceful subjects—to go to church regularly on sundays, and to mind their business all the week besides—That the women should be dutiful and affectionate to their husbands—looking after no bodies concerns but their own: eschewing all gossipings, and morning gaddings—and carrying short tongues and long petticoats. That the men should abstain from ward meetings and porter houses, entrusting the cares of government to the officers appointed to support them—staying home, like good citizens, making money for themselves, and getting children for the benefit of their country. That the burgomasters should look well to the public interest—not oppressing the poor, nor indulging the rich—not tasking their sagacity to devise new laws, but faithfully enforcing those which were already made—rather bending their attention to prevent evil than to punish it; ever recollecting that civil magistrates should consider themselves more as guardians of public morals, than rat catchers employed to entrap public delinquents. Finally, he exhorted them, one and all, high and low, rich and poor, to conduct themselves *as well as they could*; assuring them that if they faithfully and conscientiously complied with this golden rule there was no danger but that they would all conduct themselves well enough.—This done he gave them a paternal benediction; the sturdy Antony sounded a most loving farewell with his trumpet, the jolly crews put up a lusty shout of triumph, and the invincible armada swept off proudly down the bay.

The good people of New Amsterdam crowded down to the Battery—that blest resort, from whence so many a tender prayer has been wafted, so many a fair hand waved, so many a tearful look been cast by lovesick damsel, after the lessening bark, which bore her adventurous swain to distant climes!—Here the populace watched with straining eyes the gallant squadron, as it slowly floated down the bay, and when the intervening land at the Narrows shut it from their sight, gradually dispersed with silent tongues and downcast countenances.

A heavy gloom hung over the late bustling city—The honest burghers smoked their pipes in profound thoughtfulness, casting many a wistful look to the weather cock, on the church of St. Nicholas, and all the old women, having no longer the presence of Hard-koppig Piet to hearten them, gathered their children home, and barricadoed the doors and windows every evening at sun down.

In the mean while the armada of the sturdy Peter proceeded prosperously on its voyage, and after encountering about as many storms and water spouts and whales and other horrors and phenomena, as generally befall adventurous landsmen, in perilous voyages of the kind; after undergoing a severe scouring from that deplorable and unpitied malady called sea sickness; and suffering from a little touch of constipation or dispepsy, which was cured by a box of Anderson's pills, the whole squadron arrived safely in the Delaware.

Without so much as dropping anchor and giving his wearied ships time to breathe after labouring so long in the ocean, the intrepid Peter pursued his course up the Delaware, and made a sudden appearance before Fort Casimer. Having summoned the astonished garrison by a terrific blast from the trumpet of the long winded Van Corlear, he demanded, in a tone of thunder, an instant surrender of the fort. To this demand Suen Scutz, the wind dried commandant, replied in a shrill, whiffling voice, which by reason of his extreme spareness, sounded like the wind whistling through a broken bellows—"that he had no very strong reasons for refusing, except that the demand was particularly disagreeable, as he had been ordered to maintain his post to the last extremity." He requested time therefore, to consult with governor Risingh, and proposed a truce for that purpose.

The choleric Peter, indignant at having his rightful fort so treacherously taken from him, and thus pertinaceously withheld; refused the proposed armistice, and swore by the pipe of St. Nicholas, which like the sacred fire was never extinguished, that unless the fort was surrendered in ten minutes, he would incontinently storm the works, make all the garrison run the gauntlet, and split their scoundrel of a commander, like a pickled shad. To give this menace the greater effect, he drew forth his trusty sword, and shook it at them with such a fierce and vigorous motion, that doubtless, if it had not been exceedingly rusty, it would have lightened terror into the eyes and hearts of the enemy. He then ordered his men to bring a broadside to bear upon the fort, consisting of two swivels, three muskets, a long duck fowling piece and two brace of horse pistols.

In the mean time the sturdy Van Corlear marshalled all his forces, and commenced his warlike operations.—Distending his cheeks like a very Boreas, he kept up a most horrific twanging of his trumpet—the lusty choristers of Sing-Sing broke forth into a hideous song of battle—the warriors of Brooklyn and the Wael bogtig blew a potent and astounding blast on their conch shells, all together forming as outrageous a concerto, as though five thousand French orchestras were displaying their skill in a modern overture—at the hearing of which I warrant me not a Swede in the fortress but felt himself literally distilling away, with pure affright and bad music.

Whether the formidable front of war thus suddenly presented, smote the garrison with sore dismay—or whether the concluding terms of the summons, which mentioned that he should surrender *at discretion*, were mistaken by Suen Scutz, who though a Swede, was a very considerate easy tempered man—as a compliment to his discretion, I will not take upon me to say; certain it is, he found it impossible to resist so courteous a demand. Accordingly, in the very nick of time, just as the cabin boy had gone after a coal of fire, to discharge the swivels, a chamade was beat on the rampart, by the only drum in the garrison, to the no small satisfaction of both parties; who, notwithstanding their great stomach for fighting, had full as good an inclination, to eat a quiet dinner, as to exchange black eyes and bloody noses.

Thus did this impregnable fortress, once more return to the domination of their high mightinesses; Scutz, and his garrison of twenty men, were allowed to march out with the honours of war, and the victorious Peter, who was as generous as brave, permitted them to keep possession of all their arms and ammunition—the same on inspection being found totally unfit for service, having long rusted in the magazine of the fortress, even before it was wrested by the Swedes from the magnanimous, but windy Von Poffenburgh. But I must not omit to mention, that the governor was so well pleased with the services of his faithful squire Van Corlear, in the reduction of this great fortress, that he made him on the spot, lord of a goodly domain in the vicinity of New Amsterdam—which goes by the name of Corlear's Hook, unto this very day.*

The unexampled liberality of the valiant Stuyvesant, towards the Swedes, who certainly had used his government very scurvily—occasioned great surprize in the city of New Amsterdam—nay, certain of those factious individuals, who had been enlightened by the political meetings, that prevailed during the days of William the Testy—but who had not dared to indulge their meddlesome habits, under the eye of their present ruler; now emboldened by his absence, dared even to give vent to their censures in the streets—Murmurs, equally loud with those uttered by that nation of genuine grumblers, the British, in consequence of the convention of Portugal; were heard in the very council chamber of New Amsterdam; and there is no knowing whether they would

---

*De Vriez, makes mention in one of his voyages of *Corlears Hoek*, and *Corlears Plantagie,* or *Bouwery;* and that too, at an earlier date than the one given by Mr. Knickerbocker—De Vriez, is no doubt a little incorrect in this particular. EDITOR.

not have broken out into downright speeches and invectives, had not the sturdy Peter, privately sent home his walking staff, to be laid as a mace, on the table of the council chamber, in the midst of his councillors; who, like wise men took the hint, and forever after held their peace.

CHAPTER VI

*In which is shewn the great advantage the Author
has over his reader in time of battle—together with divers
portentous movements—which betoken that something
terrible is about to happen.*

"Strike while the Iron is hot," was a favourite saying of Peter the
Great, while an apprentice in a blacksmith's shop, at Amsterdam.
It is one of those proverbial sayings, which speak a word to the
ear, but a volume to the understanding—and contain a world of
wisdom, condensed within a narrow compass—Thus every art
and profession has thrown a gem of the kind, into the public
stock, enriching society by some sage maxim and pithy apothegm
drawn from its own experience; in which is conveyed, not only
the arcana of that individual art or profession, but also the important secret of a prosperous and happy life. "Cut your coat according to your cloth," says the taylor—"Stick to your last," cries the
cobler—"Make hay while the sun shines," says the farmer—
"Prevention is better than cure," hints the physician—Surely a
man has but to travel through the world, with open ears, and
by the time he is grey, he will have all the wisdom of Solomon—and
then he has nothing to do but to grow young again, and turn it to
the best advantage.

"Strike while the Iron is hot," was not more invariably the saying of Peter the great, than it was the practice of Peter the Headstrong. Like as a mighty alderman, when at a corporation feast
the first spoonful of turtle soup salutes his palate, feels his impatient appetite but ten fold quickened, and redoubles his vigorous
attacks upon the tureen, while his voracious eyes, projecting
from his head, roll greedily round devouring every thing at
table—so did the mettlesome Peter Stuyvesant, feel that intolerable hunger for martial glory, which raged within his very bowels, inflamed by the capture of Fort Casimer, and nothing could
allay it, but the conquest of all New Sweden. No sooner therefore

had he secured his conquest, than he stumped resolutely on, flushed with success, to gather fresh laurels at Fort Christina.*

This was the grand Swedish post, established on a small river (or as it is termed, creek,) of the same name, which empties into the Delaware: and here that crafty governor Jan Risingh, like another Charles the twelfth, commanded his subjects in person.

Thus have I fairly pitted two of the most potent chieftans that ever this country beheld, against each other, and what will be the result of their contest, I am equally anxious with my readers to ascertain. This will doubtless appear a paradox to such of them, as do not know the way in which I write. The fact is, that as I am not engaged in a work of imagination, but a faithful and veritable history, it is not necessary, that I should trouble my head, by anticipating its incidents and catastrophe. On the contrary, I generally make it a rule, not to examine the annals of the times whereof I treat, further than exactly a page in advance of my own work; hence I am equally interested in the progress of my history, with him who reads it, and equally unconscious, what occurrence is next to happen. Darkness and doubt hang over each coming chapter—with trembling pen and anxious mind I conduct my beloved native city through the dangers and difficulties, with which it is continually surrounded; and in treating of my favourite hero, the gallant Peter Stuyvesant, I often shrink back with dismay, as I turn another page, lest I should find his undaunted spirit hurrying him into some dolorous misadventure.

Thus am I situated at present. I have just conducted him into the very teeth of peril—nor can I tell, any more than my reader, what will be the issue of this horrid din of arms, with which our ears are mutually assailed. It is true, I possess one advantage over my reader, which tends marvelously to soothe my apprehensions—which is, that though I cannot save the life of my favourite hero, nor absolutely contradict the event of a battle, (both of which misrepresentations, though much practised by the French writers, of the present reign, I hold to be utterly unworthy of a scrupulous historian) yet I can now and then make him

---

*The formidable fortress and metropolis to which Mr. Knickerbocker alludes, is at present a flourishing little town called Christiana, about thirty seven miles from Philadelphia, on your route to Baltimore.—EDITOR.

bestow on his enemy a sturdy back stroke, sufficient to fell a giant; though in honest truth he may never have done any thing of the kind—or I can drive his antagonist clear round and round the field, as did Dan Homer most falsely make that fine fellow Hector scamper like a poltroon around the walls of Troy; for which in my humble opinion the prince of Poets, deserved to have his head broken—as no doubt he would, had those terrible fellows the Edinburgh reviewers, existed in those days—or if my hero should be pushed too hard by his opponent, I can just step in, and with one dash of my pen, give him a hearty thwack over the sconce, that would have cracked the scull of Hercules himself—like a faithful second in boxing, who when he sees his principal down, and likely to be worsted, puts in a sly blow, that knocks the wind out of his adversary, and changes the whole state of the contest.

I am aware that many conscientious readers will be ready to cry out "foul play!" whenever I render such assistance—but I insist that it is one of those little privileges, strenuously asserted and exercised by historiographers of all ages—and one which has never been disputed. An historian, in fact, is in some measure bound in honour to stand by his hero—the fame of the latter is entrusted to his hands, and it is his duty to do the best by it he can. Never was there a general, an admiral or any other commander, who in giving an account of any battle he had fought, did not sorely belabour the enemy; and I have no doubt that, had my heroes written the history of their own atchievements, they would have hit much harder blows, than any I shall recount. Standing forth therefore, as the guardian of their fame, it behoves me to do them the same justice, they would have done themselves; and if I happen to be a little hard upon the Swedes, I give free leave to any of their descendants, who may write a history of the state of Delaware, to take fair retaliation, and thump Peter Stuyvesant as hard as they please.

Therefore stand by for broken heads and bloody noses! my pen has long itched for a battle—siege after siege have I carried on, without blows or bloodshed; but now I have at length got a chance, and I vow to heaven and St. Nicholas, that, let the chronicles of the times say what they please, neither Sallust, Livy, Tacitus, Polybius, or any other battle monger of them all, did ever record a fiercer fight, than that in which my valiant chieftans are now about to engage.

And thou, most excellent reader, who, for thy faithful adherence to my heels, I could lodge in the best parlour of my heart—be not uneasy—trust the fate of our favourite Stuyvesant to me—for by the rood, come what will, I'll stick by Hard-koppig Piet to the last; I'll make him drive about these lossels vile as did the renowned Launcelot of the lake, a herd of recreant cornish Knights—and if he does fall, let me never draw my pen to fight another battle, in behalf of a brave man, if I don't make these lubberly Swedes pay for it!

No sooner had Peter Stuyvesant arrived before fort Christina than he proceeded without delay to entrench himself, and immediately on running his first parallel, dispatched Antony Van Corlear, that incomparable trumpeter, to summon the fortress to surrender. Van Corlear was received with all due formality, hoodwinked at the portal, and conducted through a pestiferous smell of salt fish and onions, to the citadel, a substantial hut built of pine logs. His eyes were here uncovered, and he found himself in the august presence of governor Risingh, who, having been accidentally likened to Charles XII, the intelligent reader will instantly perceive, must have been a tall, robustious, able bodied, mean looking man, clad in a coarse blue coat with brass buttons, a shirt which for a week, had longed in vain for the wash-tub, a pair of foxey coloured jack boots—and engaged in the act of shaving his grizly beard, at a bit of broken looking glass, with a villainous patent Brummagem razor. Antony Van Corlear delivered in a few words, being a kind of short hand speaker, a long message from his excellency, recounting the whole history of the province, with a recapitulation of grievances, enumeration of claims, &c.&c. and concluding with a peremptory demand of instant surrender: which done, he turned aside, took his nose between his thumb and finger, and blew a tremendous blast, not unlike the flourish of a trumpet of defiance—which it had doubtless learned from a long and intimate neighbourhood with that melodious instrument.

Governor Risingh heard him through, trumpet and all, but with infinite impatience; leaning at times, as was his usual custom, on the pommel of his sword, and at times twirling a huge steel watch chain or snapping his fingers. Van Corlear having finished he bluntly replied, that Peter Stuyvesant and his summons might go to the D——l, whither he hoped to send him and his crew of raggamuffins before supper time. Then unsheathing his brass hilted sword, and throwing away the scabbard—"Fore gad," quod he, "but I will not sheathe thee again, until I make a scabbard of the smoke dried leathern hide, of this runegate Dutchman." Then having flung a fierce defiance in the teeth of his adversary, by the lips of his messenger, the latter was reconducted to the portal, with all the ceremonious civility due to the trumpeter, squire and ambassador of so great a commander, and being again unblinded, was courteously dismissed with a tweak of the nose, to assist him in recollecting his message.

No sooner did the gallant Peter receive this insolent reply, than he let fly a tremendous volley of red hot, four and forty pounder execrations, that would infallibly have battered down the fortifications and blown up the powder magazines, about the ears of the fiery Swede, had not the ramparts been remarkably strong, and the magazine bomb proof. Perceiving that the works withstood this terrific blast, and that it was utterly impossible (as it really was in those unphilosophic days) to carry on a war with words, he ordered his merry men all, to prepare for immediate assault. But here a strange murmur broke out among his troops, beginning with the tribe of the Van Bummels, those valiant trencher men of the Bronx, and spreading from man to man, accompanied with certain mutinous looks and discontented murmurs. For once in his life, and only for once, did the great Peter turn pale, for he verily thought his warriors were going to faulter in this hour of perilous trial, and thus tarnish forever the fame of the province of New Nederlands.

But soon did he discover to his great joy, that in this suspicion he deeply wronged this most undaunted army; for the cause of this agitation and uneasiness simply was, that the hour of dinner was at hand, and it would have almost broken the hearts of these regular dutch warriors, to have broken in upon the invariable routine of their habits. Beside it was an established rule among our valiant ancestors, always to fight upon a full stomach, and to this may be doubtless attributed the circumstance that they came to be so renowned in arms.

And now are the hearty men of the Manhattoes, and their no less hearty comrades, all lustily engaged under the trees, buffeting stoutly with the contents of their wallets, and taking such affectionate embraces of their canteens and pottles, as though they verily believed they were to be the last. And as I foresee we shall have hot work in a page or two, I advise my readers to do the same, for which purpose I will bring this chapter to a close; giving them my word of honour that no advantage shall be taken of this armistice, to surprise, or in any wise molest, the honest Nederlanders, while at their vigorous repast.

Before we part however, I have one small favour to ask of them; which is, that when I have set both armies by the ears in the next chapter, and am hurrying about, like a very devil, in the midst—they will just stand a little on one side, out of harms way—and on no account attempt to interrupt me by a single question or remonstrance. As the whole spirit, hurry and sublimity of the battle will depend on my exertions, the moment I should stop to speak, the whole business would stand still—wherefore I shall not be able to say a word to my readers, throughout the whole of the next chapter, but I promise them in the one after, I'll listen to all they have to say, and answer any questions they may ask.

CHAPTER VII

Containing the most horrible battle ever recorded in poetry or prose; with the admirable exploits of Peter the Headstrong.

"Now had the Dutchmen snatch'd a huge repast," and finding themselves wonderfully encouraged and animated thereby, prepared to take the field. Expectation, says a faithful matter of fact dutch poet, whose works were unfortunately destroyed in the conflagration of the Alexandrian library—Expectation now stood on stilts. The world forgot to turn round, or rather stood still, that it might witness the affray; like a fat round bellied alderman, watching the combat of two chivalric flies upon his jerkin. The eyes of all mankind, as usual in such cases, were turned upon Fort Christina. The sun, like a little man in a crowd, at a puppet shew, scampered about the heavens, popping his head here and there, and endeavouring to get a peep between the unmannerly clouds, that obtruded themselves in his way. The historians filled their ink-horns—the poets went without their dinners, either that they might buy paper and goose-quills, or because they could not get any thing to eat—antiquity scowled sulkily out of its grave, to see itself outdone—while even posterity stood mute, gazing in gaping extacy of retrospection, on the eventful field!

The immortal deities, who whilome had seen service at the "affair" of Troy—now mounted their feather-bed clouds, and sailed over the plain, or mingled among the combatants in different disguises, all itching to have a finger in the pie. Jupiter sent off his thunderbolt to a noted coppersmiths, to have it furbished up for the direful occasion. Venus, swore by her chastity she'd patronize the Swedes, and in semblance of a blear eyed trull, paraded the battlements of Fort Christina, accompanied by Diana, as a serjeant's widow, of cracked reputation—The noted bully Mars, stuck two horse pistols into his belt, shouldered a rusty firelock, and gallantly swaggered at their elbow, as a drunken corporal—while Apollo trudged in their rear, as a bandy-legged fifer, playing most villainously out of tune.

On the other side, the ox-eyed Juno, who had won a pair of black eyes over night, in one of her curtain lectures with old Jupiter, displayed her haughty beauties on a baggage waggon—Minerva, as a brawny gin suttler, tucked up her skirts, brandished her fists, and swore most heroically, in exceeding bad dutch, (having but lately studied the language) by way of keeping up the spirits of the soldiers; while Vulcan halted as a club-footed blacksmith, lately promoted to be a captain of militia. All was silent horror, or bustling preparation; war reared his horrid front, gnashed loud his iron fangs, and shook his direful crest of bristling bayonets.

And now the mighty chieftans marshalled out their hosts. Here stood stout Risingh, firm as a thousand rocks—encrusted with stockades, and entrenched to the chin in mud batteries—His artillery consisting of two swivels and a carronade, loaded to the muzzle, the touch holes primed, and a whiskered bombardier stationed at each, with lighted match in hand, waiting the word. His valiant infantry, that had never turned back upon an enemy (having never seen any before)—lined the breast work in grim array, each having his mustachios fiercely greased, and his hair pomatomed back, and queued so stiffly, that he grinned above the ramparts like a grizly death's head.

There came on the intrepid Hard-koppig Piet,—a second Bayard, without fear or reproach—his brows knit, his teeth clenched, his breath held hard, rushing on like ten thousand bellowing bulls of Bashan. His faithful squire Van Corlear, trudging valiantly at his heels, with his trumpet gorgeously bedecked with red and yellow ribbands, the remembrances of his fair mistresses at the Manhattoes. Then came waddling on his sturdy comrades, swarming like the myrmidons of Achilles. There were the Van Wycks and the Van Dycks and the Ten Eycks—the Van Nesses, the Van Tassels, the Van Grolls; the Van Hœsens, the Van Giesons, and the Van Blarcoms—The Van Warts, the Van Winkles, the Van Dams; the Van Pelts, the Van Rippers, and the Van Brunts.—There were the Van Horns, the Van Borsums, the Van Bunschotens; the Van Gelders, the Van Arsdales, and the Van Bummels—The

Vander Belts, the Vander Hoofs, the Vander Voorts, the Vander Lyns, the Vander Pools and the Vander Spiegels.—There came the Hoffmans, the Hooglands, the Hoppers, the Cloppers, the Oothouts, the Quackenbosses, the Roerbacks, the Garrebrantzs, the Onderdonks, the Varra Vangers, the Schermerhorns, the Brinkerhoffs, the Bontecous, the Knickerbockers, the Hockstrassers, the Ten Breecheses and the Tough Breecheses, with a host more of valiant worthies, whose names are too crabbed to be written, or if they could be written, it would be impossible for man to utter—all fortified with a mighty dinner, and to use the words of a great Dutch poet

—"Brimful of wrath and cabbage!"

For an instant the mighty Peter paused in the midst of his career, and mounting on a rotten stump addressed his troops in eloquent low dutch, exhorting them to fight like *duyvels*, and assuring them that if they conquered, they should get plenty of booty—if they fell they should be allowed the unparalleled satisfaction, while dying, of reflecting that it was in the service of their country—and after they were dead, of seeing their names inscribed in the temple of renown and handed down, in company with all the other great men of the year, for the admiration of posterity.—Finally he swore to them, on the word of a governor (and they knew him too well to doubt it for a moment) that if he caught any mother's son of them looking pale, or playing craven, he'd curry his hide till he made him run out of it like a snake in spring time.—Then lugging out his direful snickersnee, he brandished it three times over his head, ordered Van Corlear to sound a tremendous charge, and shouting the word "St. Nicholas and the Manhattoes!" courageously dashed forwards. His warlike followers, who had employed the interval in lighting their pipes, instantly stuck them in their mouths, gave a furious puff, and charged gallantly, under cover of the smoke.

The Swedish garrison, ordered by the cunning Risingh not to fire until they could distinguish the whites of their assailants' eyes, stood in horrid silence on the covert-way; until the eager dutchmen had half ascended the glacis. Then did they pour into them such a tremendous volley, that the very hills quaked around, and were terrified even unto an incontinence of water, insomuch that certain springs burst forth from their sides, which continue to run unto the present day. Not a dutchman but would have bit the dust, beneath that dreadful fire, had not the protecting Minerva kindly taken care, that the Swedes should one and all, observe their usual custom of shutting their eyes and turning away their heads, at the moment of discharge.

But were not the muskets levelled in vain, for the balls, winged with unerring fate, went point blank into a flock of wild geese, which, like geese as they were, happened at that moment to be flying past—and brought down seventy dozen of them—which furnished a luxurious supper to the conquerors, being well seasoned and stuffed with onions.

Neither was the volley useless to the musqueteers, for the hostile wind, commissioned by the implacable Juno, carried the smoke and dust full in the faces of the dutchmen, and would inevitably have blinded them, had their eyes been open. The Swedes followed up their fire, by leaping the counterscarp, and falling tooth and nail upon the foe, with furious outcries. And now might be seen prodigies of valour, of which neither history nor song have ever recorded a parallel. Here was beheld the sturdy Stoffel Brinkerhoff brandishing his lusty quarter staff, like the terrible giant Blanderon his oak tree (for he scorned to carry any other weapon,) and drumming a horrific tune upon the heads of whole squadrons of Swedes. There were the crafty Van Courtlandts, posted at a distance, like the little Locrian archers of yore, and plying it most potently with the long bow, for which they were so justly renowned. At another place were collected on a rising knoll the valiant men of Sing-Sing, who assisted marvellously in the fight, by chaunting forth the great song of St. Nicholas. In a different part of the field might be seen the Van Grolls of Anthony's nose; but they were horribly perplexed in a defile between two little hills, by reason of the length of their noses. There were the Van Bunschotens of Nyack and Kakiat, so renowned for kicking with the left foot, but their skill availed them little at present, being short of wind in consequence of the hearty dinner they had eaten—and they would irretrievably have been put to rout, had they not been reinforced by a gallant corps of *Voltigeurs* composed of the Hoppers, who advanced to their assistance nimbly on one foot. At another place might you see the Van Arsdales, and the Van Bummels, who ever went together, gallantly pressing forward to bombard the fortress—but as to the Gardeniers of Hudson, they were absent from the battle, having been sent on a marauding party, to lay waste the neighbouring water-melon patches. Nor must I omit to mention the incomparable atchievement of Antony Van Corlear, who, for a good quarter of an hour waged horrid fight with a little pursy Swedish drummer, whose hide he drummed most magnificently; and had he not come into the battle with no other weapon but his trumpet, would infallibly have put him to an untimely end.

But now the combat thickened—on came the mighty Jacobus Varra Vanger and the fighting men of the Wael Bogtig; after them thundered the Van Pelts of Esopus, together with the Van Rippers and the Van Brunts, bearing down all before them—then the Suy Dams and the Van Dams, pressing forward with many a blustering oath, at the head of the warriors of Hell-gate, clad in their thunder and lighting gaberdines; and lastly the standard bearers and body guards of Peter Stuyvesant, bearing the great beaver of the Manhattoes.

And now commenced the horrid din, the desperate struggle, the maddening ferocity, the frantic desperation, the confusion and self abandonment of war. Dutchman and Swede commingled, tugged, panted and blowed. The heavens were darkened with a tempest of missives. Carcasses, fire balls, smoke balls, stink balls and hand grenades, jostling each other, in the air. Bang! went the guns—whack! struck the broad swords—thump! went the cudgels—crash! went the musket stocks—blows—kicks—cuffs—scratches—black eyes and bloody noses swelling the horrors of the scene! Thick-thwack, cut and hack, helter-skelter, higgledy-piggledy, hurley-burley, head over heels, klip-klap, slag op slag, bob over bol, rough and tumble!——Dunder and blixum! swore the dutchmen, splitter and splutter! cried the Swedes—Storm the works! shouted Hard-koppig Piet—fire the mine! roared stout Risingh—Tantara-ra-ra! twang'd the trumpet of Antony Van Corlear—until all voice and sound became unintelligible—grunts of pain, yells of fury, and shouts of triumph commingling in one hideous clamour. The earth shook as if struck with a paralytic stroke—The trees shrunk aghast, and wilted at the sight—The rocks burrowed in the ground like rabbits, and even Christina creek turned from its course, and ran up a mountain in breathless terror!

Nothing, save the dullness of their weapons, the damaged condition of their powder, and the singular accident of one and all striking with the flat instead of the edge of their swords, could have prevented a most horrible carnage—As it was, the sweat prodigiously streaming, ran in rivers on the field, fortunately without drowning a soul, the combatants being to a man, expert swimmers, and furnished with cork jackets for the occasion—but many a valiant head was broken, many a stubborn rib belaboured, and many a broken winded hero drew short breath that day!

Long hung the contest doubtful, for though a heavy shower of rain, sent by the "cloud compelling Jove," in some measure cooled their ardour, as doth a bucket of water thrown on a group of fighting mastiffs, yet did they but pause for a moment, to return with tenfold fury to the charge, belabouring each other with black and bloody bruises. Just at this juncture was seen a vast and dense column of smoke, slowly rolling towards the scene of battle, which for a while made even the furious combatants to stay their arms in mute astonishment—but the wind for a moment dispersing the murky cloud, from the midst thereof emerged the flaunting banner of the immortal Michael Paw. This noble chieftain came fearlessly on, leading a solid phalanx of oyster-fed Pavonians, who had remained behind, partly as a *corps de reserve,* and partly to digest the enormous dinner they had eaten. These sturdy yeomen, nothing daunted, did trudge manfully forward, smoking their pipes with outrageous vigour, so as to raise the awful cloud that has been mentioned; but marching exceedingly slow, being short of leg and of great rotundity in the belt.

And now the protecting deities of the army of New Amsterdam, having unthinkingly left the field and stept into a neighbouring tavern to refresh themselves with a pot of beer, a direful catastrophe had well nigh chanced to befall the Nederlanders. Scarcely had the myrmidons of the puissant Paw attained the front of battle, before the Swedes, instructed by the cunning Rising, levelled a shower of blows, full at their tobacco pipes. Astounded at this unexpected assault, and totally discomfited at seeing their pipes broken by this "d—d nonsense," the valiant dutchmen fall in vast confusion—already they begin to fly—like a frightened drove of unwieldy Elephants they throw their own army in an uproar—bearing down a whole legion of little Hoppers—the sacred banner on which is blazoned the gigantic oyster of Communipaw is trampled in the dirt—The Swedes pluck up new spirits and pressing on their rear, apply their feet *a parte poste* with a vigour that prodigiously accelerates their motions—nor doth the renowned Paw himself, fail to receive divers grievous and intolerable visitations of shoe leather!

But what, Oh muse! was the rage of the gallant Peter, when from afar he saw his army yield? With a voice of thunder did he roar after his recreant warriors, putting up such a war whoop, as did the stern Achilles, when the Trojan troops were on the point of burning all his gunboats. The dreadful shout rung in long echoes through the woods—trees toppled at the noise; bears, wolves and panthers jumped out of their skins, in pure affright; several wild looking hills bounced clear over the Delaware; and all the small beer in Fort Christina, turned sour at the sound!

The men of the Manhattoes plucked up new courage when they heard their leader—or rather they dreaded his fierce displeasure, of which they stood in more awe than of all the Swedes in Christendom—but the daring Peter, not waiting for their aid, plunged sword in hand, into the thickest of the foe. Then did he display some such incredible atchievements, as have never been known since the miraculous days of the giants. Wherever he went the enemy shrunk before him—with fierce impetuosity he pushed forward, driving the Swedes, like dogs, into their own ditch—but as he fearlessly advanced, the foe, like rushing waves which close upon the scudding bark, thronged in his rear, and hung upon his flank with fearful peril. One desperate Swede, who had a mighty heart, almost as large as a pepper corn, drove his dastard sword full at the hero's heart. But the protecting power that watches over the safety of all great and good men turned aside the hostile blade, and directed it to a large side pocket, where reposed an enormous Iron Tobacco Box, endowed like the shield of Achilles with supernatural powers—no doubt in consequence of its being piously decorated with a portrait of the blessed St. Nicholas. Thus was the dreadful blow repelled, but not without occasioning to the great Peter a fearful loss of wind.

Like as a furious bear, when gored by worrying curs, turns fiercely round, shews his dread teeth, and springs upon the foe, so did our hero turn upon the treacherous Swede. The miserable varlet sought in flight, for safety—but the active Peter, seizing him by an immeasurable queue, that dangled from his head—"Ah Whoreson Caterpillar!" roared he, "here is what shall make dog's meat of thee!" So saying he whirled his trusty sword, and made a blow, that would have decapitated him, had he, like Briarcus, half a hundred heads, but that the pitying steel struck short and shaved the queue forever from his crown. At this very moment a cunning arquebusier, perched on the summit of a neighbouring mound, levelled his deadly instrument, and would have sent the gallant Stuyvesant, a wailing ghost to haunt the Stygian shore—had not the watchful Minerva, who had just stopped to tie up her garter, saw the great peril of her favourite chief, and dispatched old Boreas with his bellows; who in the very nick of time, just as the direful match descended to the pan, gave such a lucky blast, as blew all the priming from the touch hole!

Thus waged the horrid fight—when the stout Risingh, surveying the battle from the top of a little ravelin, perceived his faithful troops, banged, beaten and kicked by the invincible Peter. Language cannot describe the choler with which he was seized at the sight—he only stopped for a moment to disburthen himself of five thousand anathemas; and then drawing his immeasurable cheese toaster, straddled down to the field of combat, with some such thundering strides, as Jupiter is said by old Hesiod to have taken, when he strode down the spheres, to play off his sky rockets at the Titans.

No sooner did these two rival heroes come face to face, than they each made a prodigious start of fifty feet, (flemish measure) such as is made by your most experienced stage champions. Then did they regard each other for a moment, with bitter aspect, like two furious ram cats, on the very point of a clapper clawing. Then did they throw themselves in one attitude, then in another, striking their swords on the ground, first on the right side, then on the left, at last at it they went, like five hundred houses on fire! Words cannot tell the prodigies of strength and valour, displayed in this direful encounter—an encounter, compared to which the far famed battles of Ajax with Hector, of Eneas with Turnus,

Orlando with Rodomont, Guy of Warwick with Colbrand the Dane, or of that renowned Welsh Knight Sir Owen of the mountains with the giant Guylon, were all gentle sports and holliday recreations. At length the valiant Peter watching his opportunity, aimed a fearful blow with the full intention of cleaving his adversary to the very chine; but Risingh nimbly raising his sword, warded it off so narrowly, that glancing on one side, it shaved away a huge canteen full of fourth proof brandy, that he always carried swung on one side; thence pursuing its tranchant course, it severed off a deep coat pocket, stored with bread and cheese—all which dainties rolling among the armies, occasioned a fearful scrambling between the Swedes and Dutchmen, and made the general battle to wax ten times more furious than ever.

Enraged to see his military stores thus woefully laid waste, the stout Risingh collecting all his forces, aimed a mighty blow, full at the hero's crest. In vain did his fierce little cocked hat oppose its course; the biting steel clove through the stubborn ram beaver, and would infallibly have cracked his gallant crown, but that the scull was of such adamantine hardness that the brittle weapon shivered into five and twenty pieces, shedding a thousand sparks, like beams of glory, round his grizzly visage.

Stunned with the blow the valiant Peter reeled, turned up his eyes and beheld fifty thousand suns, besides moons and stars, dancing Scotch reels about the firmament—at length, missing his footing, by reason of his wooden leg, down he came, on his seat of honour, with a crash that shook the surrounding hills, and would infallibly have wracked his anatomical system, had he not been received into a cushion softer than velvet, which providence, or Minerva, or St. Nicholas, or some kindly cow, had benevolently prepared for his reception.

The furious Risingh, in despight of that noble maxim, cherished by all true knights, that "fair play is a jewel," hastened to take advantage of the hero's fall; but just as he was stooping to give the fatal blow, the ever vigilant Peter bestowed him a sturdy thwack over the sconce, with his wooden leg, that set some dozen chimes of bells ringing triple bob-majors in his cerebellum. The bewildered Swede staggered with the blow, and in the mean time the wary Peter, espying a pocket pistol lying hard by (which had dropped from the wallet of his faithful squire and trumpeter Van

Corlear during his furious encounter with the drummer) discharged it full at the head of the reeling Risingh—Let not my reader mistake—it was not a murderous weapon loaded with powder and ball, but a little sturdy stone pottle, charged to the muzzle with a double dram of true dutch courage, which the knowing Van Corlear always carried about him by way of replenishing his valour. The hideous missive sung through the air, and true to its course, as was the mighty fragment of a rock, discharged at Hector by bully Ajax, encountered the huge head of the gigantic Swede with matchless violence.

This heaven directed blow decided the eventful battle. The ponderous pericranium of general Jan Risingh sunk upon his breast; his knees tottered under him; a deathlike torpor seized upon his Titan frame, and he tumbled to the earth with such tremendous violence, that old Pluto started with affright, lest he should have broken through the roof of his infernal palace.

His fall, like that of Goliah, was the signal for defeat and victory—The Swedes gave way—the Dutch pressed forward; the former took to their heels, the latter hotly pursued—Some entered with them, pell mell, through the sally port—others stormed the bastion, and others scrambled over the curtain. Thus in a little while the impregnable fortress of Fort Christina, which like another Troy had stood a siege of full ten *hours,* was finally carried by assault, without the loss of a single man on either side. Victory in the likeness of a gigantic ox fly, sat perched upon the little cocked hat of the gallant Stuyvesant, and it was universally declared, by all the writers, whom he hired to write the history of his expedition, that on this memorable day he gained a sufficient quantity of glory to immortalize a dozen of the greatest heroes in Christendom!

CHAPTER VIII

In which the author and reader, while reposing after the battle,
fall into a very grave and instructive discourse—
after which is recorded the conduct of Peter Stuyvesant
in respect to his victory.

Thanks to St. Nicholas! I have fairly got through this tremendous battle: let us sit down, my worthy reader, and cool ourselves, for truly I am in a prodigious sweat and agitation—Body o'me, but this fighting of battles is hot work! And if your great commanders, did but know what trouble they give their historians, they would not have the conscience to atchieve so many horrible victories. I already hear my reader complaining, that throughout all this boasted battle, there is not the least slaughter, nor a single individual maimed, if we except the unhappy Swede, who was shorn of his queue by the tranchant blade of Peter Stuyvesant—all which is a manifest outrage on probability, and highly injurious to the interest of the narrative.

For once I candidly confess my captious reader has some grounds for his murmuring—But though I could give a variety of substantial reasons for not having deluged my whole page with blood, and swelled the cadence of every sentence with dying groans, yet I will content myself with barely mentioning one; which if it be not sufficient to satisfy every reasonable man on the face of the earth, I will consent that my book shall be cast into the flames—The simple truth then is this, that on consulting every history, manuscript and tradition, which relates to this memorable, though long forgotten battle, I cannot find that a single man was killed, or even wounded, throughout the whole affair!

My readers, if they have any bowels, must easily feel the distressing situation in which I was placed. I had already promised to furnish them with a hideous and unparalleled battle—I had made incredible preparations for the same—and had moreover worked myself up into a most warlike and blood-thirsty state of mind—my honour, as a historian, and my feelings, as a man of spirit, were both too deeply engaged in the business, to back out. Beside, I had transported a great and powerful force of warriors from the Nederlandts, at vast trouble and expense, and I could not reconcile it to my own conscience, or to that reverence which I entertain for them, and their illustrious descendants, to have suffered them to return home, like a renowned British expedition—with a flea in their ears.

How to extract myself from this dilemma was truly perplexing. Had the inexorable fates only allowed me half a dozen dead men, I should have been contented, for I would have made them such heroes as abounded in the olden time, but whose race is now unfortunately extinct. Men, who, if we may believe those authentic writers, the poets, could drive great armies like sheep before them, and conquer and desolate whole cities by their single arm. I'd have given every mother's son of them as many lives as a cat, and made them die hard, I warrant you.

But seeing that I had not a single carcass at my disposal, all that was left for me, was to make the most I could of my battle, by means of kicks and cuffs, and bruises—black eyes, and bloody noses, and such like ignoble wounds. My greatest difficulty however, was, when I had once put my warriors in a passion, and let them loose into the midst of the enemy; to keep them from doing mischief. Many a time had I to restrain the sturdy Peter, from cleaving a gigantic Swede, to the very waist-band, or spitting half a dozen little fellows on his sword, like so many sparrows—And when I had set some hundreds of missives flying in the air, I did not dare to suffer one of them to reach the ground, lest it should have put an end to some unlucky Dutchman.

The reader cannot conceive how much I suffered from thus in a manner having my hands tied, and how many tempting opportunities I had to wink at, where I might have made as fine a death blow, as any recorded in history or song.

From my own experience, I begin to doubt most potently of the authenticity of many of Dan Homer's stories. I verily believe, that when he had once launched one of his hearty blades among a crowd of the enemy, he cut down many an honest fellow, without any authority for so doing, excepting that he presented a fair mark—and that often a poor devil was sent to grim Pluto's domains, merely because he had a name that would give a sounding turn to a period. But I disclaim all such unprincipled liberties—let me but have truth and the law on my side, and no man would fight harder than myself—but since the various records I consulted did not warrant it, I had too much conscience to kill a single soldier.—By St. Nicholas, but it would have been a pretty piece of business! My enemies the critics, who I foresee will be ready enough to lay any crime they can discover, at my door, might have charged me with murder outright—and I should have esteemed myself lucky to escape, with no harsher verdict than manslaughter!

And now gentle reader that we are tranquilly sitting down here, smoking our pipes, permit me to indulge in a melancholy reflection which at this moment passes across my mind.—How vain, how fleeting, how uncertain are all those gaudy bubbles after which we are panting and toiling in this world of fair delusions. The wealthy store which the hoary miser has painfully amassed with so many weary days, so many sleepless nights, a spendthrift heir shall squander away in joyless prodigality—The noblest monuments which pride has ever reared to perpetuate a name, the hand of time shall shortly tumble into promiscuous ruins—and even the brightest laurels, gained by hardiest feats of arms, may wither and be forever blighted by the chilling neglect of mankind.—"How many illustrious heroes," says the good Boëtius, "who were once the pride and glory of the age, hath the silence of historians buried in eternal oblivion!" And this it was, that made the Spartans when they went to battle, solemnly to sacrifice to the muses, supplicating that their atchievements should be worthily recorded. Had not Homer tuned his lofty lyre, observes the elegant Cicero, the valour of Achilles had remained unsung.—And such too, after all the toils and perils he had braved, after all the gallant actions he had atchieved, such too had nearly been the fate of the chivalric Peter Stuyvesant, but that I fortunately stepped in and engraved his name on the indelible tablet of history, just as the caitiff Time was silently brushing it away forever!

The more I reflect, the more am I astonished to think, what important beings are we historians! We are the sovereign censors who decide upon the renown or infamy of our fellow mortals—We are the public almoners of fame, dealing out her favours according to our judgment or caprice—we are the benefactors of kings—we are the guardians of truth—we are the scourgers of guilt—we are the instructors of the world—we are—in short, what are we not!—And yet how often does the lofty patrician or lordly Burgomaster stalk contemptuously by the little, plodding, dusty historian like myself, little thinking that this humble mortal is the arbiter of his fate, on whom it shall depend whether he shall live in future ages, or be forgotten in the dirt, as were his ancestors before him. "Insult not the dervise" said a wise caliph to his son, "lest thou offend thine historian;" and many a mighty man of the olden time, had he observed so obvious a maxim, would have escaped divers cruel wipes of the pen, which have been drawn across his character.

But let not my readers think I am indulging in vain glorious boasting, from the consciousness of my own power and importance. On the contrary I shudder to think what direful commotions, what heart rending calamities we historians occasion in the world—I swear to thee, honest reader, as I am a man, I weep at the very idea!—Why, let me ask, are so many illustrious men daily tearing themselves away from the embraces of their distracted families—slighting the smiles of beauty—despising the allurements of fortune, and exposing themselves to all the miseries of war?—Why are renowned generals cutting the throats of thousands who never injured them in their lives?—Why are kings desolating empires and depopulating whole countries? in short, what induces all great men, of all ages and countries to commit so many horrible victories and misdeeds, and inflict so many miseries upon mankind and on themselves; but the mere hope that we historians will kindly take them into notice, and admit them into a corner of our volumes. So that the mighty object of all their toils, their hardships and privations is nothing but *immortal fame*—and what is immortal fame?——why, half a page of dirty paper!——alas! alas! how humiliating the idea— that the renown of so great a man as Peter Stuyvesant, should depend upon the pen of so little a man, as Diedrich Knickerbocker!

And now, having refreshed ourselves after the fatigues and

perils of the field, it behoves us to return once more to the scene of conflict, and inquire what were the results of this renowned conquest. The Fortress of Christina being the fair metropolis and in a manner the Key to New Sweden, its capture was speedily followed by the entire subjugation of the province. This was not a little promoted by the gallant and courteous deportment of the chivalric Peter. Though a man terrible in battle, yet in the hour of victory was he endued with a spirit generous, merciful and humane—He vaunted not over his enemies, nor did he make defeat more galling by unmanly insults; for like that mirror of Knightly virtue, the renowned Paladin Orlando, he was more anxious to do great actions, than to talk of them after they were done. He put no man to death; ordered no houses to be burnt down; permitted no ravages to be perpetrated on the property of the vanquished, and even gave one of his bravest staff officers a severe rib-roasting, who was detected in the act of sacking a hen roost.

He moreover issued a proclamation inviting the inhabitants to submit to the authority of their high mightinesses; but declaring, with unexampled clemency, that whoever refused, should be lodged at the public expense, in a goodly castle provided for the purpose, and have an armed retinue to wait on them in the bargain. In consequence of these beneficent terms, about thirty Swedes stepped manfully forward and took the oath of allegiance; in reward for which they were graciously permitted to remain on the banks of the Delaware, where their descendants reside at this very day. But I am told by sundry observant travellers, that they have never been able to get over the chap-fallen looks of their ancestors, and do still unaccountably transmit from father to son, manifest marks of the sound drubbing given them by the sturdy Amsterdammers.

The whole country of New Sweden, having thus yielded to the arms of the triumphant Peter, was reduced to a colony called South River, and placed under the superintendance of a lieutenant governor; subject to the controul of the supreme government at New Amsterdam. This great dignitary, was called Mynheer William Beekman, or rather *Beck*man, who derived his surname, as did Ovidius Naso of yore, from the lordly dimensions of his nose, which projected from the centre of his countenance, like the beak of a parrot. Indeed, it is furthermore insinuated by various ancient records, that this was not only the origin of his name, but likewise the foundation of his fortune, for, as the city was as yet unprovided with a clock, the public made use of Mynheer Beckman's face, as a sun dial. Thus did this romantic, and truly picturesque feature, first thrust itself into public notice, dragging its possessor along with it, who in his turn dragged after him the whole Beckman family—These, as the story further adds, were for a long time among the most ancient and honourable families of the province, and gratefully commemorated the origin of their dignity, not as your noble families in England would do, by having a glowing proboscis emblazoned in their escutcheon, but by one and all, wearing a right goodly nose, stuck in the very middle of their faces.

Thus was this perilous enterprize gloriously terminated, with the loss of only two men; Wolfert Van Horne, a tall spare man, who was knocked overboard by the boom of a sloop, in a flaw of wind: and fat Brom Van Bummel, who was suddenly carried off by a villainous indigestion; both, however, were immortalized, as having bravely fallen, in the service of their country. True it is, Peter Stuyvesant had one of his limbs terribly fractured, being shattered to pieces in the act of storming the fortress; but as it was fortunately his wooden leg, the wound was promptly and effectually healed.

And now nothing remains to this branch of my history, but to mention, that this immaculate hero, and his victorious army, returned joyously to the Manhattoes, marching under the shade of their laurels, as did the followers of young Malcolm, under the moving forest of Dunsinane. Thus did they make a solemn and triumphant entry into New Amsterdam, bearing with them the conquered Risingh, and the remnant of his battered crew, who had refused allegiance. For it appears that the gigantic Swede, had only fallen into a swound, at the end of the battle, from whence he was speedily restored by a wholesome tweak of the nose.

These captive heroes were lodged, according to the promise of the governor, at the public expense, in a fair and spacious castle;

being the prison of state, of which Stoffel Brinkerhoff, the immortal conqueror of Oyster Bay, was appointed Lord Lieutenant; and which has ever since remained in the possession of his descendants.*

It was a pleasant and goodly sight to witness the joy of the people of New Amsterdam, at beholding their warriors once more returned, from this war in the wilderness. The old women thronged round Antony Van Corlear, who gave the whole history of the campaign with matchless accuracy; saving that he took the credit of fighting the whole battle himself, and especially of vanquishing the stout Risingh, which he considered himself as clearly entitled to, seeing that it was effected by his own stone pottle. The schoolmasters throughout the town gave holliday to their little urchins, who followed in droves after the drums, with paper caps on their heads and sticks in their breeches, thus taking the first lesson in vagabondizing. As to the sturdy rabble they thronged at the heels of Peter Stuyvesant wherever he went, waving their greasy hats in the air, and shouting "Hard-koppig Piet forever!"

It was indeed a day of roaring rout and jubilee. A huge dinner was prepared at the Stadt-house in honour of the conquerors, where were assembled in one glorious constellation, the great and the little luminaries of New Amsterdam. There were the lordly Schout and his obsequious deputy—the Burgomasters with their officious Schepens at their elbows—the subaltern officers at the elbows of the Schepens, and so on to the lowest grade of illustrious hangers-on of police; every Tag having his Rag at his side, to finish his pipe, drink off his heel-taps, and laugh at his flights of immortal dullness. In short—for a city feast is a city feast all the world over, and has been a city feast ever since the creation—the dinner went off much the same as do our great corporation junkettings and fourth of July banquets. Loads of fish, flesh and fowl were devoured, oceans of liquor drank, thousands of pipes smoked, and many a dull joke honoured with much obstreperous fat sided laughter.

I must not omit to mention that to this far-famed victory Peter

*This castle though very much altered and modernized is still in being. And stands at the corner of Pearl Street, facing Coentie's slip.

Stuyvesant was indebted for another of his many titles—for so hugely delighted were the honest burghers with his atchievements, that they unanimously honoured him with the name of *Pieter de Groodt,* that is to say Peter the Great, or as it was translated by the people of New Amsterdam, *Piet de Pig*—an appellation which he maintained even unto the day of his death.

END OF BOOK VI

BOOK VII

Containing the third part of the reign of
Peter the Headstrong—his troubles with the
British nation, and the decline and fall
of the Dutch dynasty.

CHAPTER I

How Peter Stuyvesant relieved the sovereign people from the burthen of taking care of the nation—with sundry particulars of his conduct in time of peace.

The history of the reign of Peter Stuyvesant, furnishes a melancholy picture of the incessant cares and vexations inseparable from government; and may serve as a solemn warning, to all who are ambitious of attaining the seat of power. Though crowned with victory, enriched by conquest, and returning in triumph to his splendid metropolis, his exultation was checked by beholding the sad abuses that had taken place during the short interval of his absence.

The populace, unfortunately for their own comfort, had taken a deep draught of the intoxicating cup of power, during the reign of William the Testy; and though, upon the accession of Peter Stuyvesant they felt, with a certain instinctive perception, which mobs as well as cattle possess, that the reins of government had passed into stronger hands, yet could they not help fretting and chafing and champing upon the bit, in restive silence. No sooner, therefore, was the great Peter's back turned, than the quid nuncs and pot-house politicians of the city immediately broke loose, and indulged in the most ungovernable freaks and gambols.

It seems by some strange and inscrutable fatality, to be the destiny of most countries, and (more especially of your enlightened republics,) always to be governed by the most incompetent man in the nation, so that you will scarcely find an individual throughout the whole community, but who shall detect to you innumerable errors in administration, and shall convince you in the end, that had he been at the head of affairs, matters would have gone on a thousand times more prosperously. Strange! that government, which seems to be so generally understood should invariably be so erroneously administered—strange, that the talent of legislation so prodigally bestowed, should be denied to the only man in the nation, to whose station it is requisite!

Thus it was in the present instance, not a man of all the herd of pseudo politicians in New Amsterdam, but was an oracle on topics of state, and could have directed public affairs incomparably better than Peter Stuyvesant. But so perverse was the old governor in his disposition, that he would never suffer one of the multitude of able counsellors by whom he was surrounded, to intrude his advice and save the country from destruction.

Scarcely therefore had he departed on his expedition against the Swedes, than the old factions of William Kieft's reign began to thrust their heads above water, and to gather together in political meetings, to discuss "the state of the nation." At these assemblages the busy burgomasters and their officious schepens made a very considerable figure. These worthy dignitaries were no longer the fat, well fed, tranquil magistrates that presided in the peaceful days of Wouter Van Twiller—On the contrary, being elected by the people, they formed in a manner, a sturdy bulwark, between the mob and the administration. They were great candidates for popularity, and strenuous advocates for the rights of the rabble; resembling in disinterested zeal the wide mouthed tribunes of ancient Rome, or those virtuous patriots of modern days, emphatically denominated "the friends of the people."

Under the tuition of these profound politicians, it is astonishing how suddenly enlightened the swinish multitude became, in matters above their comprehensions. Coblers, Tinkers and Taylors all at once felt themselves inspired, like those religious ideots, in the glorious times of monkish illumination; and without any previous study or experience, became instantly capable of directing all the movements of government. Nor must I neglect to mention a number of superannuated, wrong headed old burghers, who had come over when boys, in the crew of the *Goede Vrouw,* and were held up as infallible oracles by the enlightened mob. To suppose a man who had helped to discover a country, did not know how it ought to be governed was preposterous in the extreme. It would have been deemed as much a heresy, as at the present day to question the political talents, and universal infallibility of our old "heroes of '76"—and to doubt that he who had fought for a government, however stupid he might naturally be, was not competent to fill any station under it.

But as Peter Stuyvesant had a singular inclination to govern his province without the assistance of his subjects, he felt highly incensed on his return to find the factious appearance they had assumed during his absence. His first measure therefore was to restore perfect order, by prostrating the dignity of the sovereign people in the dirt.

He accordingly watched his opportunity, and one evening when the enlightened mob was gathered together in full caucus, listening to a patriotic speech from an inspired cobbler, the intrepid Peter, like his great namesake of all the Russias, all at once appeared among them with a countenance, sufficient to petrify a mill stone. The whole meeting was thrown in consternation—the orator seemed to have received a paralytic stroke in the very middle of a sublime sentence, he stood aghast with open mouth and trembling knees, while the words horror! tyranny! liberty! rights! taxes! death! destruction! and a deluge of other patriotic phrases, came roaring from his throat, before he had power to close his lips. The shrewd Peter took no notice of the skulking throng around him, but advancing to the brawling bully-ruffian, and drawing out a huge silver watch, which might have served in times of yore as a town clock, and which is still retained by his decendants as a family curiosity, requested the orator to mend it, and set it going. The orator humbly confessed it was utterly out of his power, as he was unacquainted with the nature of its construction. "Nay, but," said Peter "try your ingenuity man, you see all the springs and wheels, and how easily the clumsiest hand may stop it and pull it to pieces; and why should it not be equally easy to regulate as to stop it." The orator declared that his trade was wholly different, he was a poor cobbler, and had never meddled with a watch in his life. There were men skilled in the art, whose business it was to attend to those matters, but for his part, he should only mar the workmanship, and put the whole in confusion——"Why harkee master of mine," cried Peter, turning suddenly upon him, with a countenance that almost petrified the patcher of shoes into a perfect lapstone—"dost thou pretend to meddle with the movements of government—to regulate and correct and patch and cobble a complicated machine, the principles of which are above thy comprehension, and its simplest operations too subtle for thy understanding; when thou canst not correct a trifling error in a common piece of mechanism, the whole mystery of which is open to thy inspection?—Hence with thee to the leather and stone, which are emblems of thy head; cobble thy shoes and confine thyself to the vocation for which heaven has fitted thee—But," elevating his voice until it made the welkin ring, "if ever I catch thee, or any of thy tribe, whether square-head, or platter breech, meddling with affairs of government; by St. Nicholas but I'll have every mother's bastard of ye flea'd alive, and your hides stretched for drum heads, that ye may henceforth make a noise to some purpose!"

This threat and the tremendous voice in which it was uttered, caused the whole multitude to quake with fear. The hair of the orator rose on his head like his own swine's bristles, and not a knight of the thimble present, but his mighty heart died within him, and he felt as though he could have verily escaped through the eye of a needle.

But though this measure produced the desired effect, in reducing the community to order, yet it tended to injure the popularity of the great Peter, among the enlightened vulgar. Many accused him of entertaining highly aristocratic sentiments, and of leaning too much in favour of the patricians. Indeed there was some appearance of ground for such a suspicion, for in his time did first arise that pride of family and ostentation of wealth, that has since grown to such a height in this city.* Those who drove their own waggons, kept their own cows, and possessed the fee simple of a cabbage garden, looked down, with the most gracious, though mortifying condescension, on their less wealthy neighbours; while those whose parents had been cabin passengers in the Goede Vrouw, were continually railing out, about the dignity of ancestry—Luxury began to make its appearance under divers forms, and even Peter Stuyvesant himself (though in truth his sta-

---

*In a work published many years after the time of which Mr. Knickerbocker treats (in 1701. By C. W. A. M.) it is mentioned "Frederick Philips was counted the richest Mynheer in New York, and was said to have *whole hogsheads of Indian money or wampum;* and had a son and daughter, who according to the Dutch custom should divide it equally."   EDITOR.

tion required a little state and dignity) appeared with great pomp of equipage on public occasions, and always rode to church in a yellow waggon with flaming red wheels!

From this picture my readers will perceive, how very faithfully many of the peculiarities of our ancestors have been retained by their descendants. The pride of purse still prevails among our wealthy citizens. And many a laborious tradesman, after plodding in dust and obscurity in the morning of his life, sits down out of breath in his latter days to enact the gentleman, and enjoy the dignity honestly earned by the sweat of his brow. In this he resembles a notable, but ambitious housewife, who after drudging and stewing all day in the kitchen to prepare an entertainment; flounces into the parlour of an evening, and swelters in all the magnificence of a maudlin fine lady.

It is astonishing, moreover, to behold how many great families have sprung up of late years, who pride themselves excessively on the score of ancestry. Thus he who can look up to his father without humiliation assumes not a little importance—he who can safely talk of his grandfather, is still more vain-glorious, but he who can look back to his great grandfather, without stumbling over a cobler's stall, or running his head against a whipping post, is absolutely intolerable in his pretensions to family—bless us! what a piece of work is here, between these mushrooms of an hour, and these mushrooms of a day!

For my part I look upon our old dutch families as the only local nobility, and the real lords of the soil—nor can I ever see an honest old burgher quietly smoking his pipe, but I look upon him with reverence as a dignified descendant from the Van Rensellaers, the Van Zandts, the Knickerbockers, and the Van Tuyls.

But from what I have recounted in the former part of this chapter, I would not have my reader imagine, that the great Peter was a tyrannical governor, ruling his subjects with a rod of iron—on the contrary, where the dignity of authority was not implicated, he abounded with generosity and courteous condescension. In fact he really believed, though I fear my more enlightened republican readers will consider it a proof of his ignorance and illiberality, that in preventing the cup of social life from being dashed with the intoxicating ingredient of politics, he promoted the tranquility and happiness of the people—and by detaching their minds from subjects which they could not understand, and which only tended to inflame their passions, he enabled them to attend more faithfully and industriously to their proper callings; becoming more useful citizens and more attentive to their families and fortunes.

So far from having any unreasonable austerity, he delighted to see the poor and the labouring man rejoice, and for this purpose was a great promoter of holidays and public amusements. Under his reign was first introduced the custom of cracking eggs at Paas or Easter. New year's day was also observed with extravagant festivity—and ushered in by the ringing of bells and firing of guns. Every house was a temple to the jolly god—Oceans of cherry brandy, true Hollands and mulled cyder were set afloat on the occasion; and not a poor man in town, but made it a point to get drunk, out of a principle of pure economy—taking in liquor enough to serve him for half a year afterwards.

It would have done one's heart good also to have seen the valiant Peter, seated among the old burghers and their wives of a saturday afternoon, under the great trees that spread their shade over the Battery, watching the young men and women, as they danced on the green. Here he would smoke his pipe, crack his joke, and forget the rugged toils of war, in the sweet oblivious festivities of peace. He would occasionally give a nod of approbation to those of the young men who shuffled and kicked most vigorously, and now and then give a hearty smack, in all honesty of soul, to the buxom lass that held out longest, and tired down all her competitors—infallible proofs of her being the best dancer. Once it is true the harmony of the meeting was rather interrupted. A young vrouw, of great figure in the gay world, and who, having lately come from Holland, of course led the fashions in the city, made her appearance in not more than half a dozen petticoats, and these too of most alarming shortness.—An universal whisper ran through the assembly, the old ladies all felt shocked in the extreme, the young ladies blushed, and felt excessively for the "poor thing," and even the governor himself was observed to be a little troubled in mind. To complete the astonishment of the good folks, she undertook in the course of a jig, to describe some astonishing figures in algebra, which she had learned from a dancing master at Rotterdam.—Whether she was too animated in flourishing her feet, or whether some vagabond Zephyr took the liberty of obtruding his services, certain it is that in the course of a grand evolution, that would not have disgraced a modern ball room, she made a most unexpected display—Whereat the whole assembly were thrown into great admiration, several grave country members were not a little moved, and the good Peter himself, who was a man of unparalleled modesty, felt himself grievously scandalized.

The shortness of the female dresses, which had continued in fashion, ever since the days of William Kieft, had long offended his eye, and though extremely averse to meddling with the petticoats of the ladies, yet he immediately recommended, that every one should be furnished with a flounce to the bottom. He likewise ordered that the ladies, and indeed the gentlemen, should use no other step in dancing, than shuffle and turn, and double trouble; and forbade, under pain of his high displeasure, any young lady thenceforth to attempt what was termed "exhibiting the graces."

These were the only restrictions he ever imposed upon the sex, and these were considered by them, as tyrannical oppressions, and resisted with that becoming spirit, always manifested by the gentle sex, whenever their privileges are invaded—In fact, Peter Stuyvesant plainly perceived, that if he attempted to push the matter any further, there was danger of their leaving off petticoats altogether; so like a wise man, experienced in the ways of women, he held his peace, and suffered them ever after to wear their petticoats and cut their capers, as high as they pleased.

CHAPTER II

How Peter Stuyvesant was much molested by the moss troopers
of the East, and the Giants of Merry-land—and how a dark
and horrid conspiracy was carried on in the British Cabinet,
against the prosperity of the Manhattoes.

We are now approaching towards what may be termed the very pith and marrow of our work, and if I am not mistaken in my forebodings, we shall have a world of business to dispatch, in the ensuing chapters. Thus far have I come on prosperously, and even beyond my expectations; for to let the reader into a secret (and truly we have become so extremely intimate, that I believe I shall tell him all my secrets before we part) when I first set out upon this marvellous, but faithful little history, I felt horribly perplexed to think how I should ever get through with it—and though I put a bold face on the matter, and vapoured exceedingly, yet was it naught but the blustering of a braggadocio at the commencement of a quarrel, which he feels sure he shall have to sneak out of in the end.

When I reflected, that this illustrious province, though of prodigious importance in the eyes of its inhabitants and its historian, had in sober sadness, but little wealth or other spoils to reward the trouble of assailing it, and that it had little to expect from running wantonly into war, save a sound drubbing—When I pondered all these things in my mind, I began utterly to despair, that I should find either battles, or bloodshed, or any other of those calamities, which give importance to a nation, to enliven my history withal.—I regarded this most amiable of provinces, in the light of an unhappy maiden, to whom Heaven had not granted sufficient charms, to excite the diabolical attempts of wicked man; who had no cruel father to persecute and oppress her, no abominable ravisher to run away with her, and who had not strength nor courage enough, of her own accord, to act the heroine, and go in "quest of adventures"—in short, who was doomed to vegetate, in a tranquil, unmolested, hopeless, howling state of virginity, and finally to die in peace, without bequeathing a single misery, or outrage, to those warehouses of sentimental woe, the circulating libraries.

But thanks to my better stars, they have decreed otherwise. It is with some communities, as it is with certain meddlesome individuals, they have a wonderful facility at getting into scrapes, and I have always remarked, that those are most liable to get in, who have the least talent at getting out again. This is doubtless occasioned by the excessive *valour* of those little states; for I have likewise noticed, that this rampant and ungovernable virtue, is always most unruly where most confined; which accounts for its raging and vapouring so amazingly in little states, little men, and ugly little women more especially. Thus this little province of Nieuw Nederlandts has already drawn upon itself a host of enemies; has had as many hard knocks, as would gratify the ambition of the most warlike nation; and is in sober sadness, a very forlorn, distressed, and woe begone little province!—all which was no doubt kindly ordered by providence, to give interest and sublimity, to this most pathetic of histories.

But I forbear to enter into a detail of the pitiful maraudings and harrassments, that for a long while after the victory on the Delaware, continued to insult the dignity and disturb the repose of the Nederlanders. Never shall the pen which has been gloriously wielded in the tremendous battle of Fort Christina, be drawn in scurvy border broils and frontier skirmishings—nor the historian who put to flight stout Risingh and his host, and conquered all New Sweden, be doomed to battle it in defence of a pig stye or a hen roost, and wage ignoble strife with squatters and moss troopers! Forbid it all ye muses, that a Knickerbocker should ever so far forget what is due to his family and himself!

Suffice it then in brevity to say, that the implacable hostility of the people of the east, which had so miraculously been prevented from breaking out, as my readers must remember, by the sudden prevalence of witchcraft, and the dissensions in the council of Amphyctions, now again displayed itself in a thousand grievous and bitter scourings upon the borders.

Scarcely a month passed but what the little dutch settlements on the frontiers were alarmed by the sudden appearance of an invading army from Connecticut. This would advance resolutely through the country, like a puissant caravan of the deserts, the women and children mounted in carts loaded with pots and kettles, as though they meant to boil the honest dutchmen alive, and devour them like so many lobsters. At the tail of these carts would stalk a crew of long limbed, lank sided varlets, with axes on their shoulders and packs on their backs, resolutely bent upon *improving* the country in despite of its proprietors. These settling themselves down, would in a little while completely dislodge the unfortunate Nederlanders; elbowing them out of those rich little bottoms and fertile valleys, in which your dutch yeomanry are so famous for nestling themselves—For it is notorious that wherever these shrewd men of the east get a footing, the honest dutchmen do gradually disappear, retiring slowly like the Indians before the whites; being totally discomfited by the talking, chaffering, swapping, bargaining disposition of their new neighbours.

All these audacious infringements on the territories of their high mightinesses were accompanied, as has before been hinted, by a world of rascally brawls, ribroastings and bundlings, which would doubtlessly have incensed the valiant Peter to wreak immediate chastisement, had he not at the very same time been perplexed by distressing accounts, from Mynheer Beckman, who commanded the territories at South river.

The rebellious Swedes who had so graciously been suffered to remain about the Delaware, already began to shew signs of mutiny and disaffection. But what was worse, a peremptory claim was laid to the whole territory, as the rightful property of lord Baltimore, by Fendal, a chieftain who ruled over the colony of Maryland, or Merry-land as it was anciently called, because that the inhabitants not having the fear of the Lord before their eyes, were notoriously prone to get fuddled and make *merry* with mint julep and apple toddy. Nay, so hostile was this bully Fendal, that he threatened, unless his claim was instantly complied with, to march incontinently at the head of a potent force of the roaring boys of Merryland, together with a great and mighty train of giants who infested the banks of the Susquehanna*—and to lay waste and depopulate the whole country of South river.

---

*We find very curious and wonderful accounts of these strange people (who were doubtless the ancestors of the present Marylanders) made by master Hariot, in

By this it is manifest that this boasted colony, like all great acquisitions of territory, soon became a greater evil to the conqueror, than the loss of it was to the conquered; and caused greater uneasiness and trouble, than all the territory of the New Netherlands besides. Thus providence wisely orders, that one evil shall balance another. The conqueror who wrests the property of his neighbour, who wrongs a nation and desolates a country, though he may acquire increase of empire, and immortal fame, yet ensures his own inevitable punishment. He takes to himself a cause of endless anxiety—he incorporates with his late sound domain, a loose part—a rotten disaffected member; which is an exhaustless source of internal treason and disunion, and external altercation and hostility—Happy is that nation, which compact, united, loyal in all its parts, and concentrated in its strength, seeks no idle acquisition of unprofitable and ungovernable territory—which, content to be prosperous and happy, has no ambition to be great. It is like a man well organized in all his system, sound in health, and full of vigour; unincumbered by useless trappings, and fixed in an unshaken attitude. But the nation, insatiable of territory, whose domains are scattered, feebly united, and weakly organized, is like a senseless miser sprawling among golden stores, open to every attack, and unable to defend the riches he vainly endeavours to overshadow.

At the time of receiving the alarming dispatches from South river, the great Peter was busily employed in quelling certain Indian troubles that had broken out about Esopus, and was moreover meditating how to relieve his eastern borders, on the Connecticut. He however sent word to Mynheer Beckman to be of good heart, to maintain incessant vigilance, and to let him know if matters wore a more threatening appearance; in which

---

his interesting history. "The Susquesahanocks"—observes he, "are a giantly people, strange in proportion, behaviour and attire—their voice sounding from them as if out a cave. Their tobacco pipes were three quarters of a yard long, carved at the great end with a bird, beare, or other device, sufficient to beat out the braines of a horse, (and how many asses braines are beaten out, or rather men's braines smoked out and asses brains haled in, by our lesser pipes at home.) The calfe of one of their legges was measured three quarters of a yard about, the rest of his limbs proportionable."

Master Hariot's Journ . . . Purch. Pil.

case he would incontinently repair with his warriors of the Hudson, to spoil the merriment of these Merry landers; for he coveted exceedingly to have a bout, hand to hand, with some half a score of these giants—having never encountered a giant in his whole life, unless we may so call the stout Risingh, and he was but a little one.

Nothing however appeared further to molest the tranquillity of Mynheer Beckman and his colony. Fendal and his Myrmidons remained at home, carousing it soundly upon hoe cakes, bacon, and mint julep, and running horses, and fighting cocks, for which they were greatly renowned. At hearing of this Peter Stuyvesant was highly rejoiced, for notwithstanding his inclination to measure weapons with these monstrous men of the Susquehanna, yet he had already as much employment nearer home, as he could turn his hands to. Little did he think, worthy soul, that this southern calm, was but the deceitful prelude to a most terrible and fatal storm, then brewing, which was soon to burst forth and overwhelm the unsuspecting city of New Amsterdam!

Now so it was, that while this excellent governor was, like a second Cato, giving his little senate laws, and not only giving them, but enforcing them too—while he was incessantly travelling the rounds of his beloved province—posting from place to place to redress grievances, and while busy at one corner of his dominions all the rest getting into an uproar—At this very time, I say, a dark and direful plot was hatching against him, in that nursery of monstrous projects, the British Cabinet. The news of his atchievements on the Delaware, according to a sage old historian of New Amsterdam, had occasioned not a little talk and marvel in the courts of Europe. And the same profound writer assures us that the cabinet of England began to entertain great jealousy and uneasiness at the encreasing power of the Manhattoes, and the valour of its sturdy yeomanry.

Agents we are told, were at work from the Amphyctionic council of the East, earnestly urging the cabinet to assist them in subjugating this fierce and terrible little province, and that sagacious cabinet, which ever likes to be dabbling in dirty water, had already began to lend an ear to their importunities. Just at this time Lord Baltimore, whose bullying agent, as has before been mentioned, had so alarmed Mynheer Beckman, laid his claim before the cabinet to the lands of South river, which he complained were unjustly and forcibly detained from him, by these daring usurpers of the New Nederlandts.

At this it is said his majesty Charles II, who though Defender of the Faith, was an arrant, lounging, rake-helly roystering wag of a Prince, settled the whole matter by a dash of the pen, by which he made a present of a large tract of North America, including the province of New Netherlands, to his brother the duke of York—a donation truly loyal, since none but great monarchs have a right to give away, what does not belong to them.

That this munificent gift might not be merely nominal, his majesty on the 12th of March 1664, ordered that a gallant armament should be forthwith prepared, to invade the city of New Amsterdam by land and water, and put his brother in complete possession of the premises.

Thus critically are situated the affairs of the New Netherlanders. The honest burghers, so far from thinking of the jeopardy in which their interests are placed, are soberly smoking their pipes and thinking of nothing at all—the privy councillors of the province, are at this moment snoring in full quorum, like the drones of five hundred bagpipes, while the active Peter, who takes all the labour of thinking and acting upon himself, is busily devising some method of bringing the grand council of Amphyctions to terms. In the mean while an angry cloud is darkly scowling on the horizon—soon shall it rattle about the ears of these dozing Nederlanders and put the mettle of their stout hearted governor completely to the trial.

But come what may, I here pledge my veracity, that in all warlike conflicts and subtle perplexities, he shall still acquit himself with the gallant bearing and spotless honour of a noble minded obstinate old cavalier—Forward then to the charge!—shine out propitious stars on the renowned city of the Manhattoes; and may the blessing of St. Nicholas go with thee—honest Peter Stuyvesant!

CHAPTER III

Of Peter Stuyvesant's expedition into the east Country,
shewing that though an old bird, he did not understand trap.

Great nations resemble great men in this particular, that their greatness is seldom known, until they get in trouble; adversity has therefore, been wisely denominated the ordeal of true greatness, which like gold, can never receive its real estimation until it has passed through the furnace. In proportion therefore as a nation, a community or an individual (possessing the inherent quality of greatness) is involved in perils and misfortunes, in proportion does it rise in grandeur—and even when sinking under calamity, like a house on fire, makes a more glorious display, than ever it did, in the fairest period of its prosperity.

The vast empire of China, though teeming with population and imbibing and concentrating the wealth of nations, has vegetated through a succession of drowsy ages; and were it not for its internal revolution, and the subversion of its ancient government by the Tartars, might have presented nothing but an uninteresting detail of dull, monotonous prosperity. Pompeia and Herculaneum might have passed into oblivion, with a herd of their contemporaries, had they not been fortunately overwhelmed by a volcano. The renowned city of Troy has acquired celebrity only from its ten years distress, and final conflagration—Paris rises in importance, by the plots and massacres, which have ended in the exaltation of the illustrious Napoleon—and even the mighty London itself, has skulked through the records of time, celebrated for nothing of moment, excepting the Plague, the great fire and Guy Faux's gunpowder plot! Thus cities and empires seem to creep along, enlarging in silent obscurity under the pen of the historian, until at length they burst forth in some tremendous calamity—and snatch as it were, immortality from the explosion!

The above principle being plainly advanced, strikingly illustrated, and readily admitted, my reader will need but little discernment to perceive, that the city of New Amsterdam and its dependent province, are on the high road to greatness. Dangers and hostilities threaten them from every side, and it is really a matter of astonishment to me, how so small a state, has been able in so short a time, to entangle itself in so many difficulties. Ever since the province was first taken by the nose, at the fort of Good Hope, in the tranquil days of Wouter Van Twiller, has it been gradually encreasing in historic importance; and never could it have had a more appropriate chieftain to conduct it to the pinnacle of grandeur, than Peter Stuyvesant.

He was an iron headed old veteran, in whose fiery heart sat enthroned all those five kinds of courage described by Aristotle, and had the philosopher mentioned five hundred more to the back of them, I verily believe, he would have been found master of them all—The only misfortune was, that he was deficient in the better part of valour called discretion, a cold blooded virtue which could not exist in the tropical climate of his mighty soul. Hence it was he was continually hurrying into those unheard of enterprises that gave an air of chivalric romance to all his history, and hence it was that he now conceived a project, the very thought of which makes me to tremble while I write.

This was no other than to repair in person to the mighty council of the Amphyctions, bearing the sword in one hand and the olive branch in the other—to require immediate reparation for the innumerable violations of that treaty which in an evil hour he had formed—to put a stop to those repeated maraudings on the eastern borders—or else to throw his gauntlet and appeal to arms for satisfaction.

On declaring this resolution in his privy council, the venerable members were seized with vast astonishment, for once in their lives they ventured to remonstrate, setting forth the rashness of exposing his sacred person, in the midst of a strange and barbarous people, with sundry other weighty remonstrances—all which had about as much influence upon the determination of the headstrong Peter, as though you were to endeavour to turn a rusty weather cock, with a broken winded bellows.

Summoning therefore to his presence, his trusty follower Antony Van Corlear, he commanded him to hold himself in readiness to accompany him the following morning, on this his hazardous enterprise. Now Antony the trumpeter was a little stricken in years, yet by dint of keeping up a good heart, and having never known care or sorrow (having never been married) he was still a hearty, jocund rubicond, gamesome wag, and of great capacity in the doublet. This last was ascribed to his living a jolly life on those domains at the Hook, which Peter Stuyvesant had granted to him, for his gallantry at Fort Casimer.

Be this as it may, there was nothing that more delighted Antony, than this command of the great Peter, for he could have followed the stout hearted old governor to the world's end, with love and loyalty—and he moreover still remembered the frolicking and dancing and bundling, and other disports of the east country, and entertained dainty recollection of numerous kind and buxom lasses, whom he longed exceedingly again to encounter.

Thus then did this mirror of hardihood set forth, with no other attendant but his trumpeter, upon one of the most perilous enterprises ever recorded in the annals of Knight errantry.—For a single warrior to venture openly among a whole nation of foes; but above all, for a plain downright dutchman to think of negociating with the whole council of New England—never was there known a more desperate undertaking!—Ever since I have entered upon the chronicles of this peerless but hitherto uncelebrated chieftain, has he kept me in a state of incessant action and anxiety with the toils and dangers he is constantly encountering—Oh! for a chapter of the tranquil reign of Wouter Van Twiller, that I might repose on it as on a feather bed!

Is it not enough Peter Stuyvesant, that I have once already rescued thee from the machinations of these terrible Amphyctions, by bringing the whole powers of witchcraft to thine aid?—Is it not enough, that I have followed thee undaunted, like a guardian spirit, into the midst of the horrid battle of Fort Christina?—That I have been put incessantly to my trumps to keep thee safe and sound—now warding off with my single pen the shower of dastard blows that fell upon thy rear—now narrowly shielding thee from a deadly thrust, by a mere tobacco box—now casing thy dauntless scull with adamant, when even thy stubborn ram beaver failed to resist the sword of the stout Risingh—and now, not merely bringing thee off alive, but triumphant, from the clutches of the gigantic Swede, by the desperate means of a paltry stone pottle?—Is not all this enough, but must thou still be plunging into new difficulties and jeopardizing in headlong enterprises, thyself, thy trumpeter, and thy historian!

But all this is empty talk. What influence can I expect to have, when even his councillors, who never before attempted to advise him in their lives, have spoken to no effect. All that remains is quietly to take up my pen, as did Antony his trumpet, and faithfully follow at his heels—and I swear that, like the latter, so truly do I love the hairbrained valour of this fierce old Cavalier, that I feel as if I could follow him through the world, even though (which Heaven forefend) he should lead me through another volume of adventures.

And now the ruddy faced Aurora, like a buxom chambermaid, draws aside the sable curtains of the night, and out bounces from his bed the jolly red haired Phœbus, startled at being caught so late in the embraces of Dame Thetis. With many a stable oath, he harnesses his brazen footed steeds, and whips and lashes, and splashes up the firmament, like a loitering post boy, half an hour behind his time. And now behold that imp of fame and prowess the headstrong Peter, bestriding a raw boned, switch tailed charger, gallantly arrayed in full regimentals, and bracing on his thigh that trusty brass hilted sword, which had wrought such fearful deeds on the banks of the Delaware.

Behold hard after him his doughty trumpeter Van Corlear, mounted on a broken winded, wall eyed, calico mare; his sturdy stone pottle which had laid low the mighty Risingh, slung under his arm, and his trumpet displayed vauntingly in his right hand, decorated with a gorgeous banner, on which is emblazoned the great beaver of the Manhattoes. See them proudly issuing out of the city gate, like an iron clad hero of yore, with his faithful squire at his heels, the populace following them with their eyes, and shouting many a parting wish, and hearty cheering.— Farewel, Hardkoppig-Piet! Farewel honest Antony!—Pleasant be your wayfaring—prosperous your return! The stoutest hero that ever drew a sword, and the worthiest trumpeter that ever trod shoe leather!

Legends are lamentably silent about the events that befel our adventurers, in this their adventurous travel, excepting the

Stuyvesant Manuscript, which gives the substance of a pleasant little heroic poem, written on the occasion by Domine Ægidius Luyck,* who appears to have been the poet-laureat of New Amsterdam. This inestimable manuscript assures us, that it was a rare spectacle to behold the great Peter and his loyal follower, hailing the morning sun, and rejoicing in the clear countenance of nature, as they pranced it through the pastoral scenes of Bloemen Dael;† which in those days was a sweet and rural valley, beautified with many a bright wild flower, refreshed by many a pure streamlet, and enlivened here and there by a delectable little dutch cottage, sheltered under some gently swelling hill, and almost buried in embowering trees.

Now did they enter upon the confines of Connecticut, where they encountered many grievous difficulties and perils. At one place they were assailed by some half a score of country squires and militia colonels, who, mounted on goodly steeds, hung upon their rear for several miles, harassing them exceedingly with guesses and questions, more especially the worthy Peter, whose silver chas'd leg excited not a little marvel. At another place hard by the renowned town of Stamford, they were set upon by a great and mighty legion of church deacons, who imperiously demanded of them five shillings, for travelling on Sunday, and threatened to carry them captive to a neighbouring church whose steeple peer'd above the trees; but these the valiant Peter put to rout with little difficulty, insomuch that they bestrode their canes and gallopped off in horrible confusion, leaving their cocked hats behind in the hurry of their flight. But not so easily did he escape from the hands of a crafty man of Pyquag; who with undaunted perseverance, and repeated onsets, fairly bargained him out of his goodly switch-tailed charger, leaving in place thereof a villainous, spavined, foundered Narraganset pacer.

But maugre all these hardships, they pursued their journey cheerily, along the course of the soft flowing Connecticut, whose gentle waves, says the song, roll through many a fertile vale, and

---

*This Luyck, was moreover, rector of the Latin school in Nieuw Nederlandt, 1663. There are two pieces of verses to Ægidius Luyck in D. Selyn's MSS. of poesies, upon his marriage with Judith Van Isendoorn. Old MS.
†Now called Blooming Dale, about four miles from New York.

sunny plain; now reflecting the lofty spires of the bustling city, and now the rural beauties of the humble hamlet; now echoing with the busy hum of commerce, and now with the cheerful song of the peasant.

At every town would Peter Stuyvesant, who was noted for war-like punctilio, order the sturdy Antony to sound a courteous salutation; though the manuscript observes, that the inhabitants were thrown into great dismay, when they heard of his approach. For the fame of his incomparable atchievements on the Delaware, had spread throughout the East country, and they dreaded lest he had come to take vengeance on their manifold transgressions.

But the good Peter rode through these towns with a smiling aspect; waving his hand with inexpressible majesty and conde-scension; for he verily believed that the old clothes which these ingenious people had thrust into their broken windows, and the festoons of dried apples and peaches which ornamented the fronts of their houses, were so many decorations in honour of his ap-proach; as it was the custom in days of chivalry, to compliment renowned heroes, by sumptuous displays of tapestry and gor-geous furniture. The women crowded to the doors to gaze upon him as he passed, so much does prowess in arms, delight the gentle sex. The little children too ran after him in troops, staring with wonder at his regimentals, his brimstone breeches, and the silver garniture of his wooden leg. Nor must I omit to mention the joy which many strapping wenches betrayed, at beholding the jovial Van Corlear, who had whilome delighted them so much with his trumpet, when he bore the great Peter's challenge to the Amphyctions. The kind-hearted Antony alighted from his calico mare, and kissed them all with infinite loving kindness—and was right pleased to see a crew of little trumpeters crowding around him for his blessing; each of whom he patted on the head, bade him be a good boy, and gave him a penny to buy mo-lasses candy.

The Stuyvesant manuscript makes but little further mention of the governor's adventures upon this expedition, excepting that he was received with extravagant courtesy and respect by the great council of the Amphyctions, who almost talked him to death with complimentary and congratulatory harangues. Of his nego-ciations with the grand council I shall say nothing, as there are more important matters which call for the attention of myself, my readers, and Peter Stuyvesant. Suffice it to mention, it was like all other negociations—a great deal was said, and very little done: one conversation led to another—one conference begat misunderstandings which it took a dozen conferences to explain; at the end of which the parties found themselves just where they were at first; excepting that they had entangled themselves in a host of questions of etiquette, and conceived a cordial distrust of each other that rendered their future negociations ten times more difficult than ever.*

In the midst of all these perplexities, which bewildered the brain and incensed the ire of the sturdy Peter, who was of all men in the world, perhaps, the least fitted for diplomatic wiles, he privately received the first intimation of the dark conspiracy which had been matured in the Cabinet of England. To this was added the astounding intelligence that a hostile squadron had already sailed from England, destined to reduce the province of New Netherlands, and that the grand council of Amphyctions had engaged to co-operate, by sending a great army to invade New Amsterdam by land.

Unfortunate Peter! did I not enter with sad forebodings upon this ill starred expedition! did I not tremble when I saw thee, with no other councillor but thine own head, with no other armour but an honest tongue, a spotless conscience and a rusty sword! with no other protector but St. Nicholas—and no other attendant but a brokenwinded trumpeter—Did I not tremble when I beheld thee thus sally forth, to contend with all the knowing powers of New England.

Oh how did the sturdy old warrior rage and roar, when he found himself thus entrapped, like a lion in the hunter's toil. Now did he determine to draw his trusty sword, and manfully to fight his way through all the countries of the east. Now did he resolve to break in upon the council of the Amphyctions and put every mother's son of them to death.—At length, as his

---

*For certain of the particulars of this ancient negociation see Haz. Col. State Pap. It is singular that Smith is entirely silent with respect to the memorable expedition of Peter Stuyvesant above treated of by Mr. Knickerbocker. EDITOR.

direful wrath subsided, he resorted to safer though less glorious expedients.

Concealing from the council his knowledge of their machinations, he privately dispatched a trusty messenger, with missives to his councillors at New Amsterdam, apprizing them of the impending danger, commanding them immediately to put the city in a posture of defence, while in the mean time he endeavoured to elude his enemies and come to their assistance. This done he felt himself marvellously relieved, rose slowly, shook himself like a rhinoceros, and issued forth from his den, in much the same manner as giant Despair is described to have issued from Doubting castle, in the chivalric history of the Pilgrim's Progress.

And now much does it grieve me that I must leave the gallant Peter in this perilous jeopardy: but it behoves us to hurry back and see what is going on at New Amsterdam, for greatly do I fear that city is already in a turmoil. Such was ever the fate of Peter Stuyvesant, while doing one thing with heart and soul, he was too apt to leave every thing else at sixes and sevens. While, like a potentate of yore, he was absent attending to those things in person, which in modern days are trusted to generals and ambassadors, his little territory at home was sure to get in an uproar—All which was owing to that uncommon strength of intellect, which induced him to trust to nobody but himself, and which had acquired him the renowned appellation of Peter the Headstrong.

CHAPTER IV

How the people of New Amsterdam, were thrown into a great panic, by the news of a threatened invasion, and how they fortified themselves very strongly—with resolutions.

There is no sight more truly interesting to a philosopher, than to contemplate a community, where every individual has a voice in public affairs, where every individual thinks himself the atlas of the nation, and where every individual thinks it his duty to bestir himself for the good of his country—I say, there is nothing more interesting to a philosopher, than to see such a community in a sudden bustle of war. Such a clamour of tongues—such a bawling of patriotism—such running hither and thither—every body in a hurry—every body up to the ears in trouble—every body in the way, and every body interrupting his industrious neighbour—who is busily employed in doing nothing! It is like witnessing a great fire, where every man is at work like a hero—some dragging about empty engines—others scampering with full buckets, and spilling the contents into the boots of their neighbours—and others ringing the church bells all night, by way of putting out the fire. Little firemen—like sturdy little knights storming a breach, clambering up and down scaling ladders, and bawling through tin trumpets, by way of directing the attack.—Here one busy fellow, in his great zeal to save the property of the unfortunate, catches up an anonymous chamber utensil, and gallants it off with an air of as much self-importance, as if he had rescued a pot of money—another throws looking glasses and china, out of the window, by way of saving them from the flames, while those who can do nothing else, to assist in the great calamity run up and down the streets with open throats, keeping up an incessant cry of *Fire! Fire! Fire!*

"When the news arrived at Corinth," says the grave and profound Lucian—though I own the story is rather trite, "that Philip was about to attack them, the inhabitants were thrown into violent alarm. Some ran to furbish up their arms; others rolled stones to build up the walls—every body in short, was employed, and every body was in the way of his neighbour. Diogenes alone, was the only man who could find nothing to do—whereupon determining not to be idle when the welfare of his country was at stake, he tucked up his robe, and fell to rolling his tub with might and main, up and down the Gymnasium." In like manner did every mother's son, in the patriotic community of New Amsterdam, on receiving the missives of Peter Stuyvesant, busy himself most mightily in putting things in confusion, and assisting the general uproar. "Every man"—saith the Stuyvesant Manuscript—"flew to arms!"—by which is meant, that not one of our honest dutch citizens would venture to church or to market, without an old fashioned spit of a sword, dangling at his side, and a long dutch fowling piece on his shoulder—nor would he go out of a night without a lanthorn; nor turn a corner, without first peeping cautiously round, lest he should come unawares upon a British army—And we are informed, that Stoffel Brinkerhoff, who was considered by the old women, almost as brave a man as the governor himself—actually had two one pound swivels mounted in his entry, one pointing out at the front door, and the other at the back.

But the most strenuous measure resorted to on this aweful occasion, and one which has since been found of wonderful efficacy, was to assemble popular meetings. These brawling convocations, I have already shewn, were extremely obnoxious to Peter Stuyvesant, but as this was a moment of unusual agitation, and as the old governor was not present to repress them, they broke out with intolerable violence. Hither therefore, the orators and politicians repaired, and there seemed to be a competition among them, who should bawl the loudest, and exceed the other in hyperbolical bursts of patriotism, and in resolutions to uphold and defend the government. In these sage and all powerful meetings it was determined *nem. con.* that they were the most enlightened, the most dignified, the most formidable and the most ancient community upon the face of the earth—and finding that this resolution was so universally and readily carried, another was immediately proposed—whether it was not possible and politic to exterminate Great Britain? upon which sixty nine members spoke most eloquently in the affirmative, and only one arose to suggest some doubts—who as a punishment for his treasonable presumption, was immediately seized by the mob and tarred and feathered—which punishment being equivalent to the Tarpeian Rock, he was afterwards considered as an outcast from society and his opinion went for nothing—The question therefore, being unanimously carried in the affirmative, it was recommended to the grand council to pass it into a law; which was accordingly done—By this measure the hearts of the people at large were wonderfully encouraged, and they waxed exceeding choleric and valourous—Indeed the first paroxysm of alarm having in some measure subsided; the old women having buried all the money they could lay their hands on; and their husbands daily getting fuddled with what was left—the community began even to stand on the offensive. Songs were manufactured in low dutch and sung about the streets, wherein the English were most woefully beaten, and shewn no quarter, and popular addresses were made, wherein it was proved to a certainty, that the fate of old England depended upon the will of the New Amsterdammers.

Finally, to strike a violent blow at the very vitals of Great Britain, a grand caucus of the wiser inhabitants assembled; and having purchased all the British manufactures they could find, they made thereof a huge bonfire—and in the patriotic glow of the moment, every man present, who had a hat or breeches of English workmanship, pulled it off and threw it most undauntedly into the flames—to the irreparable detriment, loss and ruin of the English manufacturers. In commemoration of this great exploit, they erected a pole on the spot, with a device on the top intended to represent the province of Nieuw Nederlandts destroying Great Britain, under the similitude of an Eagle picking the little Island of Old England out of the globe; but either through the unskillfulness of the sculptor, or his ill timed waggery, it bore a striking resemblance to a goose, vainly striving to get hold of a dumpling.

CHAPTER V

*Shewing how the grand Council of the New Netherlands
came to be miraculously gifted with long tongues.—
Together with a great triumph of Economy.*

It will need but very little witchcraft on the part of my enlightened reader—particularly if he is in any wise acquainted with the ways and habits of that most potent and blustering monarch, the sovereign people—to discover, that notwithstanding all the incredible bustle and talk of war that stunned him in the last chapter, the renowned city of New Amsterdam is in sad reality, not a whit better prepared for defence than before. Now, though the people, having got over the first alarm, and finding no enemy immediately at hand, had with that valour of tongue, for which your illustrious rabble is so famous, run into the opposite extreme, and by dint of gallant vapouring and rodomontado had actually talked themselves into the opinion that they were the bravest and most powerful people under the sun, yet were the privy councillors of Peter Stuyvesant somewhat dubious on that point. They dreaded moreover lest that stern hero should return and find, that instead of obeying his peremptory orders, they had wasted their time in listening to the valiant hectorings of the mob, than which they well knew there was nothing he held in more exalted contempt.

To make up therefore as speedily as possible for lost time, a grand divan of the councillors and robustious Burgomasters was convened, to talk over the critical state of the province and devise measures for its safety. Two things were unanimously agreed upon in this venerable assembly: first, that the city required to be put in a state of defence—and secondly, that as the danger was imminent, there should no time be lost—which points being settled, they immediately fell to making long speeches and belabouring one another in endless and intemperate disputes. For about this time was this unhappy city first visited by that talking endemic so universally prevalent in this country, and which so invariably evinces itself, wherever a number of wise men assemble together; breaking out in long, windy speeches, caused, as physicians suppose, by the foul air which is ever generated in a crowd. Now it was, moreover, that they first introduced the ingenious method of measuring the merits of an harangue by the hour-glass; he being considered the ablest orator who spoke longest on a question—For which excellent invention it is recorded, we are indebted to the same profound dutch critic who judged of books by their bulk, and gave a prize medal to a stupendous volume of flummery—because it was "as tick as a cheese."

The reporters of the day, therefore, in publishing the debates of the grand council, seem merely to have noticed the length of time each member was on the floor—and the only record I can find of the proceedings in the important business of which we are treating, mentions, that "Mynheer —— made a very animated speech of six hours and a half, in favour of fortification—He was followed by Mynheer —— on the other side, who spoke with great clearness and precision for about eight hours—Mynheer —— suggested an amendment of the bill by substituting in the eighth line, the words *'four and twenty,'* instead of 'twenty four,' in support of which he offered a few remarks, which only took up three hours and a quarter—and was followed by Mynheer Windroer in a most pithy, nervous, concise, elegant, ironical, argumentative strain of eloquence, superior to any thing which ever issued from the lips of a Cicero, a Demosthenes, or any orator, either of antient or modern times—he occupied the floor the whole of yesterday; this morning he arose in continuation, and is in the middle of the second branch of his discourse, at this present writing; having already carried the council through their second nap—We regret," concludes this worthy reporter, "that the irresistable propensity of our Stenographer to nod, will prevent us from giving the substance of this truly luminous and *lengthy* speech."

This sudden passion for endless harangues, so little consonant with the customary gravity and taciturnity of our sage forefathers, is supposed by certain learned philosophers of the time, to have been imbibed, together with divers other barbarous propensities, from their savage neighbours; who were peculiarly noted for their *long talks* and *council fires;* and who would never undertake any affair of the least importance, without previous debates and harangues among their chiefs and *old men*. But let its origin be what it may, it is without doubt a cruel and distressing disease, which has never been eradicated from the body politic to this day; but is continually breaking out, on all occasions of great agitation, in alarming and obnoxious flatulencies, whereby the said body politic is grievously afflicted, as with a wind cholic.

Thus then did Madam Wisdom, (who for some unaccountable, but doubtlessly whimsical reason, the wits of antiquity have represented under the form of a woman) seem to take a mischievous pleasure in jilting the grave and venerable councillors of New Amsterdam. The old factions of Square heads and Platter Breeches, which had been almost strangled by the herculean grasp of Peter Stuyvesant, now sprung up with tenfold violence—To complete the public confusion and bewilderment, the fatal word *Economy*, which one would have thought was dead and buried with William the Testy, was once more set afloat, like the apple of discord, in the grand council of the New Nederlandts—according to which sound principle of policy, it was deemed more expedient to throw away twenty thousand guilders upon an inefficient plan of defence, than thirty thousand on a good and substantial one—the province thus making a clear saving of ten thousand guilders.

But when they came to discuss the mode of defence, then began a war of words that baffles all description. The members being, as I observed, drawn out into opposite parties, were enabled to proceed with amazing system and regularity in the discussion of the questions before them. Whatever was proposed by a Square head, was opposed by the whole tribe of Platter breeches, who like true politicians, considered it their first duty to effect the downfall of the Square heads—their second, to elevate themselves, and their third, to consult the welfare of the country. This at least was the creed of the most upright among the party, for as to the great mass, they left the third consideration out of the question altogether.

In this great collision of hard heads, it is astonishing the number of projects for defence, that were struck out, not one of which had ever been heard of before, nor has been heard of since, unless it be in very modern days—projects that threw the windmill system of the ingenious Kieft completely in the back ground—Still, however, nothing could be decided on, for as fast as a formidable host of air castles were reared by one party, they were demolished by the other—the simple populace stood gazing in anxious expectation of the mighty egg, that was to be hatched, with all this cackling, but they gazed in vain, for it appeared that the grand council was determined to protect the province as did the noble and gigantic Pantagruel his army—by covering it with his tongue.

Indeed there was a magnanimous portion of the members, fat, self important old burghers, who smoked their pipes and said nothing, excepting to negative every plan of defence that was offered. These were of that class of wealthy old citizens who having amassed a fortune, button up their pockets, shut their mouths, look rich and are good for nothing all the rest of their lives. Like some phlegmetic oyster, which having swallowed a pearl, closes its shell, settles down in the mud and parts with its life sooner than its treasure. Every plan of defence seemed to these worthy old gentlemen pregnant with ruin. An armed force was a legion of locusts, preying upon the public property—to fit out a naval armament was to throw their money into the sea—to build fortifications was to bury it in the dirt. In short they settled it as a sovereign maxim, so long as their pockets were full, no matter how much they were drubbed—A kick left no scar—a broken head cured itself—but an empty purse was of all maladies the slowest to heal, and one in which nature did nothing for the patient.

Thus did this venerable assembly of *sages,* lavish away that time which the urgency of affairs rendered invaluable, in empty brawls and long winded arguments, without even agreeing, except on the point with which they started, namely, that there was no time to be lost, and delay was ruinous. At length St. Nicholas, taking compassion on their distracted situation, and anxious to preserve them from total anarchy, so ordered, that in the midst of one of their most noisy and patriotic debates, when they had nearly fallen to loggerheads in consequence of not being able to convince each other, the question was happily settled by a messenger, who bounced into the chamber and informed them, that the hostile fleet had arrived, and was actually advancing up the bay!

Thus was all further necessity of either fortifying or disputing completely obviated, and thus was the grand council saved a world of words, and the province a world of expense—a most absolute and glorious triumph of economy!

CHAPTER VI

In which the troubles of New Amsterdam appear to thicken— Shewing the bravery in time of peril, of a people who defend themselves by resolutions.

Like a ward committee of politic cats, who, when engaged in clamorous gibberings, and catterwaulings, eyeing one another with hideous grimaces, spitting in each other's faces, and on the point of breaking forth into a general clapper-clawing, are suddenly put to scampering rout and confusion by the startling appearance of a house-dog—So was the no less vociferous council of New Amsterdam, amazed, astounded, and totally dispersed, by the sudden arrival of the enemy. Every member made the best of his way home, waddling along as fast as his short legs could fag under their heavy burthen, and wheezing as he went with corpulency and terror. When he arrived at his castle, he barricadoed the street door, and buried himself in the cider cellar, without daring to peep out, lest he should have his head carried off by a cannon ball.

The sovereign people all crowded into the market place, herding together with the instinct of sheep who seek for safety in each others company, when the shepherd and his dog are absent and the wolf is prowling round the fold. Far from finding relief however, they only encreased each others terrors. Each man looked ruefully in his neighbour's face, in search of encouragement, but only found in its woe begone lineaments, a confirmation of his own dismay. Not a word now was to be heard of conquering Great Britain, not a whisper about the sovereign virtues of economy— while the old women heightened the general gloom by clamorously bewailing their fate, and incessantly calling for protection on St. Nicholas and Peter Stuyvesant.

Oh how did they bewail the absence of the lion hearted Peter!—and how did they long for the comforting presence of Antony Van Corlear! Indeed a gloomy uncertainty hung over the fate of these adventurous heroes. Day after day had elapsed since the alarming message from the governor, without bringing any further tidings of his safety. Many a fearful conjecture was hazarded as to what had befallen him and his loyal squire. Had they not been devoured alive by the Cannibals of Piscataway and Cape Cod?—were they not put to the question by the great council of Amphyctions?—were they not smothered in onions by the terrible men of Pyquag?—In the midst of this consternation and perplexity, when horror like a mighty night-mare sat brooding upon the little, fat, plethoric city of New Amsterdam, the ears of the multitude were suddenly startled by a strange and distant sound—it approached—it grew louder and louder—and now it resounded at the city gate. The public could not be mistaken in the well known sound—A shout of joy burst from their lips as the gallant Peter, covered with dust, and followed by his faithful trumpeter, came gallopping into the market place.

The first transports of the populace having subsided, they gathered round the honest Antony, as he dismounted from his horse, overwhelming him with greetings and congratulations. In breathless accents he related to them the marvellous adventures through which the old governor and himself had gone, in making their escape from the clutches of the terrible Amphyctions. But though the Stuyvesant Manuscript, with its customary minuteness where any thing touching the great Peter is concerned, is very particular, as to the incidents of this masterly retreat, yet the critical state of the public affairs, will not allow me to indulge in a full recital thereof. Let it suffice to say, that while Peter Stuyvesant was anxiously revolving in his mind, how he could make good his escape with honour and dignity, certain of the ships sent out for the conquest of the Manhattoes touched at the Eastern ports, to obtain needful supplies, and to call on the grand council of the league, for its promised co-operation. Upon hearing of this, the vigilant Peter, perceiving that a moment's delay was fatal, made a secret and precipitate decampment, though much did it grieve his lofty soul, to be obliged to turn his back even upon a nation of foes. Many hair-breadth scapes and divers perilous mishaps, did they sustain, as they scoured, without sound of trumpet, through the fair regions of the east. Already was the country in an uproar with hostile preparation—and they were obligated to take a large circuit in their flight, lurking along, through the woody mountains of the Devil's back bone; from whence the valiant Peter sallied forth one day, like a lion, and put to route a whole legion of squatters, consisting of three generations of a prolific family, who were already on their way to take possession of some corner of the New Netherlands. Nay, the faithful Antony had great difficulty at sundry times, to prevent him in the excess of his wrath, from descending down from the mountains, and falling sword in hand, upon certain of the border towns, who were marshalling forth their draggle-tailed militia.

The first movements of the governor on reaching his dwelling, was to mount the roof, from whence he contemplated with rueful aspect the hostile squadron. This had already come to anchor in the bay, and consisted of two stout frigates, having on board, as John Josselyn, gent. informs us, three hundred valiant red coats. Having taken this survey, he sat himself down, and wrote an epistle to the commander, demanding the reason of his anchoring in the harbour without obtaining previous permission so to do. This letter was couched in the most dignified and courteous terms, though I have it from undoubted authority, that his teeth were clinched, and he had a bitter sardonic grin upon his visage, all the while he wrote. Having dispatched his letter, the grim Peter stumped to and fro about the town, with a most war-betokening countenance, his hands thrust into his breeches pockets, and whistling a low dutch psalm tune, which bore no small resemblance to the music of a north east wind, when a storm is brewing—the very dogs as they eyed him skulked away in dismay—while all the old and ugly women of New Amsterdam, ran howling at his heels, imploring him to save them from murder, robbery, and piteous ravishment!

The reply of Col. Nichols, who commanded the invaders, was couched in terms of equal courtesy with the letter of the governor—declaring the right and title of his British Majesty to the province; where he affirmed the dutch to be mere interlopers; and demanding that the town, forts, &c. should be forthwith rendered into his majesty's obedience and protection—promising at the same time, life, liberty, estate and free trade, to every dutch denizen, who should readily submit to his majesty's government.

Peter Stuyvesant read over this friendly epistle with some such harmony of aspect as we may suppose a crusty farmer, who has long been fattening upon his neighbour's soil, reads the loving letter of John Stiles, that warns him of an action of ejectment. The old governor however, was not to be taken by surprize, but thrusting, according to custom, a huge quid of tobacco into his cheek, and cramming the summons into his breeches pocket, promised to answer it the next morning. In the mean time he called a general council of war of his privy councillors and Burgomasters, not for the purpose of asking their advice, for that, as has been already shewn, he valued not a rush; but to make known unto them his sovereign determination, and require their prompt adherence.

Before, however, he convened his council he resolved upon three important points; *first,* never to give up the city without a little hard fighting, for he deemed it highly derogatory to the dignity of so renowned a city, to suffer itself to be captured and stripped, without receiving a few kicks into the bargain. *Secondly,* that the majority of his grand council were a crew of arrant platter breeches, utterly destitute of true bottom—and *thirdly*—that he would not therefore suffer them to see the summons of Col. Nichols, lest the easy terms it held out, might induce them to clamour for a surrender.

His orders being duly promulgated, it was a piteous sight to behold the late valiant Burgomasters, who had demolished the whole British empire in their harangues; peeping ruefully out of their nests, and then crawling cautiously forth, dodging through narrow lanes and alleys; starting at every little dog that barked, as if it had been a discharge of artillery—mistaking lamp posts for British grenadiers, and in the excess of their panic, metamorphosing pumps into formidable soldiers, levelling blunderbusses at their bosoms! Having however, in despite of numerous perils and difficulties of the kind, arrived safe, without the loss of a single man, at the hall of assembly, they took their seats and awaited in fearful silence the arrival of the governor. In a few moments the wooden leg of the intrepid Peter, was heard in regular and stout-hearted thumps upon the stair case—He entered the chamber, arrayed in full suit of regimentals, a more than ordinary quantity of flour shook into his ear locks, and carrying his trusty toledo, not girded on his thigh, but tucked under his arm. As the governor never equipped himself in this portentous manner, unless something of martial nature was working within his fearless pericranium, his council regarded him ruefully as a very Janus bearing fire and sword in his iron countenance—and forgot to light their pipes in breathless suspence.

The great Peter was as eloquent as he was valorous—indeed these two rare qualities seemed to go hand in hand in his composition; and, unlike most great statesmen, whose victories are only confined to the bloodless field of argument, he was always ready to enforce his hardy words, by no less hardy deeds. Like another Gustavus addressing his Dalecarlians, he touched upon the perils and hardships he had sustained in escaping from his inexorable foes—He next reproached the council for wasting in idle debate and impertinent personalities that time which should have been devoted to their country—he then recalled the golden days of former prosperity, which were only to be regained by manfully withstanding their enemies—endeavoured to rouse their martial fire, by reminding them of the time, when, before the frowning walls of fort Christina, he led them on to victory—when they had subdued a whole army of fifty Swedes—and subjugated an immense extent of uninhabited territory.—He strove likewise to awaken their confidence, by assuring them of the protection of St. Nicholas; who had hitherto maintained them in safety; amid all the savages of the wilderness, the witches and squatters of the east, and the giants of Merry land. Finally he informed them of the insolent summons he had received, to surrender, but concluded by swearing to defend the province as long as heaven was on his side, and he had a wooden leg to stand upon. Which noble sentence he emphasized by a tremendous thwack with the broad side of his sword upon the table, that totally electrified his auditors.

The privy councillors, who had long been accustomed to the governor's way, and in fact had been brought into as perfect discipline, as were ever the soldiers of the great Frederick; saw that there was no use in saying a word—so lighted their pipes and smoked away in silence, like fat and discreet councillors. But the Burgomasters being less under the governor's controul—considering themselves as representatives of the sovereign people, and being moreover inflated with considerable importance and self-sufficiency, which they had acquired at those notable schools of wisdom and morality, the popular meetings; (whereof in fact I am told certain of them had been chairmen) these I say, were not so easily satisfied. Mustering up fresh spirit, when they found there was some chance of escaping from their present perilous jeopardy, without the disagreeable alternative of fighting, they arrogantly requested a copy of the summons to surrender, that they might shew it to a general meeting of the people.

So insolent and mutinous a request would have been enough to have roused the gorge of the tranquil Van Twiller himself—what then must have been its effect upon the great Stuyvesant, who was not only a Dutchman, a Governor, and a valiant wooden legged soldier to boot, but withal a man of the most stomachful and gunpowder disposition. He burst forth into a blaze of heroical indignation, to which the famous rage of Achilles was a mere pouting fit—swore not a mother's son of them should see a syllable of it—that they deserved, every one of them, to be hung, drawn and quartered, for traitorously daring to question the infallibility of government—that as to their advice or concurrence, he did not care a whiff of tobacco for either—that he had long been harrassed and thwarted by their cowardly councils; but that they might henceforth go home, and go to bed like old women; for he was determined to defend the colony himself, without the assistance of them or their adherents! So saying he tucked his sword under his arm, cocked his hat upon his head, and girding up his loins, stumped indignantly out of the council chamber— every body making room for him as he passed.

No sooner had he gone than the sturdy Burgomasters called a public meeting in front of the Stadt-house, where they appointed as chairman one Dofue Roerback, a mighty gingerbread baker in the land, and formerly of the cabinet of William the Testy. He was looked up to, with great reverence by the populace, who considered him a man of dark knowledge, seeing he was the first that imprinted new year cakes with the mysterious hieroglyphics of the Cock and Breeches, and such like magical devices.

This great Burgomaster, who still chewed the cud of ill will against the valiant Stuyvesant, in consequence of having been ignominiously kicked out of his cabinet—addressed the greasy multitude in an exceeding long-winded speech, in which he informed them of the courteous summons to surrender—of the governor's refusal to comply therewith—of his denying the pub-

lic a sight of the summons, which he had no doubt, from the well
known liberality, humanity, and forbearance, of the British nation, contained conditions highly to the honour and advantage of
the province.

He then proceeded to speak of his excellency in high sounding
terms, suitable to the dignity and grandeur of his station, com-
paring him to Nero, Caligula, and other great men of yore, of
whom he had often heard William the Testy discourse in his
learned moods—Assuring the people, that the history of the
world did not contain a despotic outrage to equal the present, for
atrocity, cruelty, tyranny, blood-thirstiness, battle, murder, and
sudden death—that it would be recorded in letters of fire, on the
blood-stained tablet of history! that ages would roll back with
sudden horror, when they came to view it! That the womb of
time—(by the way your orators and writers take strange liberties
with the womb of time, though some would fain have us believe
that time is an old gentleman) that the womb of time, pregnant
as it was with direful horrors, would never produce a parallel
enormity!—that posterity would be struck dumb with petrifying
astonishment, and howl in unavailing indignation, over the records
of irremediable barbarity!—With a variety of other heart-rending,
soul stirring tropes and figures, which I cannot enumerate—
Neither indeed need I, for they were exactly the same that are used
in all popular harangues and fourth of July orations at the present
day, and may be classed in rhetoric under the general title of Rigmarole.

The patriotic address of Burgomaster Roerback had a wonderful effect upon the populace, who, though a race of sober phlegmatic Dutchmen, were amazing quick at discerning insults; for
your ragged rabble, though it may bear injuries without a murmur, yet is always marvellously jealous of its sovereign dignity.
They immediately fell into the pangs of tumultuous labour, and
brought forth, not only a string of right wise and valiant resolutions, but likewise a most resolute memorial, addressed to the
governor, remonstrating at his conduct—which he no sooner received than he handed it into the fire; and thus deprived posterity
of an invaluable document, that might have served as a precedent
to the enlightened coblers and taylors, of the present day, in their
sage intermeddlings with politics.

CHAPTER VII

Containing a doleful disaster of Antony the Trumpeter—
And how Peter Stuyvesant, like a second Cromwell suddenly
dissolved a rump Parliament.

Now did the high minded Pieter *de Groodt,* shower down a pan-
nier load of benedictions upon his Burgomasters, for a set of
self-willed, obstinate, headstrong varlets, who would neither be
convinced nor persuaded; and determined henceforth to have
nothing more to do with them, but to consult merely the opinion
of his privy councillors, which he knew from experience to be the
best in the world—inasmuch as it never differed from his own.
Nor did he omit, now that his hand was in, to bestow some thousand left-handed compliments upon the sovereign people; whom
he railed at for a herd of arrant poltroons, who had no relish for
the glorious hardships and illustrious misadventures of battle—but
would rather stay at home, and eat and sleep in ignoble ease,
than gain immortality and a broken head, by valiantly fighting in
a ditch!

Resolutely bent however upon defending his beloved city, in
despite even of itself, he called unto him his trusty Van Corlear,
who was his right hand man in all times of emergency. Him
did he adjure to take his war denouncing trumpet, and mounting his horse, to beat up the country, night and day—Sounding
the alarm along the pastoral borders of the Bronx—startling
the wild solitudes of Croton, arousing the rugged yeomanry
of Weehawk and Hoboken—the mighty men of battle of Tappan Bay*—and the brave boys of Tarry town and Sleepy hollow—
together with all the other warriors of the country round about;
charging them one and all, to sling their powder horns, shoulder

---

*A corruption of Top-paun; so called from a tribe of Indians which boasted 150
fighting men. See Ogilvie. EDITOR.

their fowling pieces, and march merrily down to the Manhattoes.

Now there was nothing in all the world, the divine sex excepted, that Antony Van Corlear loved better than errands of this kind. So just stopping to take a lusty dinner, and bracing to his side his junk bottle, well charged with heart inspiring Hollands, he issued jollily from the city gate, that looked out upon what is at present called Broadway; sounding as usual a farewell strain, that rung in sprightly echoes through the winding streets of New Amsterdam—Alas! never more were they to be gladdened by the melody of their favourite trumpeter!

It was a dark and stormy night when the good Antony arrived at the famous creek (sagely denominated Hærlem *river*) which separates the island of Manna-hata from the main land. The wind was high, the elements were in an uproar, and no Charon could be found to ferry the adventurous sounder of brass across the water. For a short time he vapoured like an impatient ghost upon the brink, and then, bethinking himself of the urgency of his errand, took a hearty embrace of his stone bottle, swore most valourously that he would swim across, *en spijt den Duyvel* (in spite of the devil!) and daringly plunged into the stream.—Luckless Antony! scarce had he buffetted half way over, when he was observed to struggle most violently as if battling with the spirit of the waters—instinctively he put his trumpet to his mouth and giving a vehement blast—sunk forever to the bottom!

The potent clangour of his trumpet, like the ivory horn of the renowned Paladin Orlando, when expiring in the glorious field of Roncesvalles, rung far and wide through the country, alarming the neighbours round, who hurried in amazement to the spot—Here an old Dutch burgher, famed for his veracity, and who had been a witness of the fact, related to them the melancholy affair; with the fearful addition (to which I am slow of giving belief) that he saw the duyvel, in the shape of a huge Moss-bonker with an invisible fiery tail, and vomiting boiling water, seize the sturdy Antony by the leg, and drag him beneath the waves. Certain it is, the place, with the adjoining promontory, which projects into the Hudson, has been called *Spijt den duyvel* or *Spiking devil,* ever since—the restless ghost of the unfortunate Antony still haunts the surrounding solitudes, and his trumpet has often been heard by the neighbours, of a stormy night, mingling with the howling of the blast. No body ever attempts to swim over the creek after dark; on the contrary, a bridge has been built to guard against such melancholy accidents in future—and as to Moss-bonkers, they are held in such abhorrence, that no true Dutch-man will admit them to his table, who loves good fish, and hates the devil.

Such was the end of Antony Van Corlear—a man deserving of a better fate. He lived roundly and soundly, like a true and jolly batchelor, until the day of his death; but though he was never married, yet did he leave behind some two or three dozen chil-dren, in different parts of the country—fine, chubby, brawling, flatulent little urchins, from whom, if legends speak true, (and they are not apt to lie) did descend the innumerable race of edi-tors, who people and defend this country, and who are bounti-fully paid by the people for keeping up a constant alarm—and making them miserable. Would that they inherited the worth, as they do the wind, of their renowned progenitor!

The tidings of this lamentable catastrophe imparted a severer pang to the bosom of Peter Stuyvesant, than did even the inva-sion of his beloved Amsterdam. It came ruthlessly home to those sweet affections that grow close around the heart, and are nourished by its warmest current. As some lorn pilgrim wan-dering in trackless wastes, while the rude tempest whistles through his hoary locks, and dreary night is gathering around, sees stretched cold and lifeless, his faithful dog—the sole com-panion of his lonely journeying, who had shared his solitary meal, who had so often licked his hand in humble gratitude, who had lain in his bosom, and been unto him as a child—So did the generous hearted hero of the Manhattoes contemplate the untimely end of his faithful Antony. He had been the hum-ble attendant of his footsteps—he had cheered him in many a heavy hour, by his honest gaiety, and had followed him in loy-alty and affection, through many a scene of direful peril and mishap—he was gone forever—and that too, at a moment when every mongrel cur seemed skulking from his side—This—Peter Stuyvesant—this was the moment to try thy magnanimity; and this was the moment, when thou didst indeed shine forth—Peter *the Headstrong!*

The glare of day had long dispelled the horrors of the last stormy night; still all was dull and gloomy. The late jovial Apollo hid his face behind lugubrious clouds, peeping out now and then, for an instant, as if anxious, yet fearful, to see what was going on, in his favourite city. This was the eventful morning, when the great Peter was to give his reply, to the audacious summons of the invaders. Already was he closetted with his privy council, sitting in grim state, brooding over the fate of his favourite trumpeter, and anon boiling with indignation as the insolence of his recreant Burgomasters flashed upon his mind. While in this state of irritation, a courier arrived in all haste from Winthrop, the subtle governor of Connecticut, councilling him in the most affectionate and disinterested manner to surrender the province, and magnifying the dangers and calamities to which a refusal would subject him.—What a moment was this to intrude officious advice upon a man, who never took advice in his whole life!—The fiery old governor strode up and down the chamber, with a vehemence, that made the bosoms of his councillors to quake with awe—railing at his unlucky fate, that thus made him the constant butt of factious subjects, and jesuitical advisers.

Just at this ill chosen juncture, the officious Burgomasters, who were now completely on the watch, and had got wind of the arrival of mysterious dispatches, came marching in a resolute body, into the room, with a legion of Schepens and toad-eaters at their heels, and abruptly demanded a perusal of the letter. Thus to be broken in upon by what he esteemed a "rascal rabble," and that too at the very moment he was grinding under an irritation from abroad, was too much for the spleen of the choleric Peter. He tore the letter in a thousand pieces*—threw it in the face of the nearest Burgomaster—broke his pipe over the head of the next—hurled his spitting box at an unlucky Schepen, who was just making a masterly retreat out at the door, and finally dissolved the whole meeting *sine die,* by kicking them down stairs with his wooden leg!

As soon as the Burgomasters could recover from the confusion into which their sudden exit had thrown them, and had taken a little time to breathe, they protested against the conduct of the

*Smith's History of N. Y.

governor, which they did not hesitate to pronounce tyrannical, un-constitutional, highly indecent, and somewhat disrespectful. They then called a public meeting, where they read the protest, and addressing the assembly in a set speech related at full length, and with appropriate colouring and exaggeration, the despotic and vindictive deportment of the governor; declaring that, for their own parts, they did not value a straw the being kicked, cuffed, and mauled by the timber toe of his excellency, but they felt for the dignity of the sovereign people, thus rudely insulted by the outrage committed on the seats of honour of their representatives. The latter part of the harangue had a violent effect upon the sensibility of the people, as it came home at once, to that delicacy of feeling and jealous pride of character, vested in all true mobs: and there is no knowing to what act of resentment they might have been provoked, against the redoubtable Hard-koppig Piet—had not the greasy rogues been somewhat more afraid of their sturdy old governor, than they were of St. Nicholas, the English—or the D——l himself.

CHAPTER VIII

Shewing how Peter Stuyvesant defended the city of New Amsterdam for several days, by dint of the strength of his head.

Pause, oh most considerate reader! and contemplate for a moment the sublime and melancholy scene, which the present crisis of our history presents! An illustrious and venerable little town—the metropolis of an immense extent of flourishing but unenlightened, because uninhabited country—Garrisoned by a doughty host of orators, chairmen committee-men, Burgomasters, Schepens and old women—governed by a determined and strong headed warrior, and fortified by mud batteries, pallisadoes and resolutions—blockaded by sea, beleaguered by land, and threatened with direful desolation from without; while its very vitals are torn, and griped, and becholiced with internal faction and commotion! Never did the historic pen record a page of more complicated distress, unless it be the strife that distracted the Israelites during the siege of Jerusalem—where discordant parties were cutting each others throats, at the moment when the victorious legions of Titus had toppled down their bulwarks, and were carrying fire and sword, into the very sanctum sanctorum of the temple.

Governor Stuyvesant having triumphantly, as has been recorded, put his grand council to the rout, and thus delivered himself from a multitude of impertinent advisers, dispatched a categorical reply to the commanders of the invading squadron; wherein he asserted the right and title of their High Mightinesses the lords States general to the province of New Netherlands, and trusting in the righteousness of his cause, set the whole British nation at defiance! My anxiety to extricate my readers, and myself, from these disastrous scenes, prevents me from giving the whole of this most courteous and gallant letter, which concluded in these manly and affectionate terms.

"As touching the threats in your conclusion, we have nothing to answer, only that we fear nothing but what God, (who is as just as merciful) shall lay upon us; all things being in his gracious disposal, and we may as well be preserved by him with small forces, as by a great army; which makes us to wish you all happiness and prosperity, and recommend you to his protection—My lords your thrice humble and affectionate servant and friend

P. Stuyvesant."

Thus having resolutely thrown his gauntlet, the brave Hard-koppig Piet stuck a huge pair of horse pistols in his belt, girded an immense powder horn on his side—thrust his sound leg into a Hessian boot, and clapping his fierce little war hat on top of his head—paraded up and down in front of his house, determined to defend his beloved city to the last.

While all these woeful struggles and dissensions were prevailing in the unhappy little city of New Amsterdam, and while its worthy but ill starred governor was framing the above quoted letter, the English commanders did not remain idle. They had agents secretly employed to foment the fears and clamours of the populace, and moreover circulated far and wide through the adjacent country a proclamation, repeating the terms they had already held out in their summons to surrender, and beguiling the simple Nederlanders with the most crafty and conciliating professions. They promised every man who voluntarily submitted to the authority of his British majesty, that he should retain peaceable possession of his house, his vrouw and his cabbage garden. That he should be suffered to smoke his pipe, speak dutch, wear as many breeches as he pleased, and import bricks, tiles and stone jugs from Holland, instead of manufacturing them on the spot—That he should on no account be compelled to learn the English language, or keep accounts in any other way than by casting them up upon his fingers, and chalking them down upon the crown of his hat; as is still observed among the dutch yeomanry at the present day. That every man should be allowed quietly to inherit his father's hat, coat, shoe-buckles, pipe, and every other personal appendage, and that no man should be obliged to conform to any improvements, inventions, or any other modern innovations, but on the contrary should be permitted to build his house, follow his trade, manage his farm, rear his hogs, and educate his children, precisely as his ancestors did before him since time immemorial—Finally, that he should have all the benefits of free trade; and should not be required to acknowledge any other saint in the calendar than saint Nicholas, who should thenceforward, as before, be considered the tutelar saint of the city.

These terms, as may be supposed, appeared very satisfactory to the people; who had a great disposition to enjoy their property unmolested, and a most singular aversion to engage in a contest, where they could gain little more than honour and broken heads—the first of which they held in philosophic indifference, the latter in utter detestation. By these insidious means, therefore, did the English succeed in alienating the confidence and affections of the populace from their gallant old governor, whom they considered as obstinately bent upon running them into hideous misadventures, and did not hesitate to speak their minds freely, and abuse him most heartily—behind his back.

Like as a mighty grampus, who though assailed and buffeted by roaring waves and brawling surges, still keeps on an undeviating course; and though overwhelmed by boisterous billows, still emerges from the troubled deep, spouting and blowing with tenfold violence—so did the inflexible Peter pursue, unwavering, his determined career, and rise contemptuous, above the clamours of the rabble.

But when the British warriors found by the tenor of his reply that he set their power at defiance, they forthwith dispatched recruiting officers to Jamaica, and Jericho, and Nineveh, and Quag, and Patchog, and all those redoubtable towns which had been subdued of yore by the immortal Stoffel Brinkerhoff, stirring up the valiant progeny of Preserved Fish, and Determined Cock, and those other illustrious squatters, to assail the city of New Amsterdam by land. In the mean while the hostile ships made awful preparation to commence a vehement assault by water.

The streets of New Amsterdam now presented a scene of wild dismay and consternation. In vain did the gallant Stuyvesant order the citizens to arm and assemble in the public square or market place. The whole party of Platter breeches in the course of a single night had changed into arrant old women—a metamorphosis only to be paralleled by the prodigies recorded by Livy as having happened at Rome at the approach of Hannibal, when statues sweated in pure affright, goats were converted into sheep, and cocks turning into hens ran cackling about the streets.

The harrassed Peter, thus menaced from without and tormented from within—baited by the burgomasters and hooted at by the rabble, chafed and growled and raged like a furious bear tied to a stake and worried by a legion of scoundrel curs. Finding however that all further attempt to defend the city was in vain, and hearing that an irruption of borderers and moss troopers was ready to deluge him from the east, he was at length compelled, in spite of his mighty heart, which swelled in his throat until it had nearly choked him, to consent to a treaty of surrender.

Words cannot express the transports of the people, on receiving this agreeable intelligence; had they obtained a conquest over their enemies, they could not have indulged greater delight—The streets resounded with their congratulations—they extolled their governor as the father and deliverer of his country—they crowded to his house to testify their gratitude, and were ten times more noisy in their plaudits, than when he returned, with victory perched upon his beaver, from the glorious capture of Fort Christina—But the indignant Peter shut up his doors and windows and took refuge in the innermost recesses of his mansion, that he might not hear the ignoble rejoicings of the rabble.

In consequence of this consent of the governor, a parley was demanded of the besieging forces to treat of the terms of surrender. Accordingly a deputation of six commissioners was appointed on both sides, and on the 27th August, 1664, a capitulation highly favourable to the province, and honourable to Peter Stuyvesant, was agreed to by the enemy, who had conceived a high opinion of the valour of the men of the Manhattoes, and the magnanimity and unbounded discretion of their governor.

One thing alone remained, which was, that the articles of surrender should be ratified, and signed by the chivalric Peter—When the commissioners respectfully waited upon him for this purpose, they were received by the hardy old warrior, with the most grim and bitter courtesy. His warlike accoutrements were laid aside—an old India night gown was wrapped around his rugged limbs, a red woollen night cap overshadowed his frowning brow, and an iron grey beard, of three days growth, heightened the grizly terrors of his visage. Thrice did he seize a little worn out stump of a pen, and essay to sign the loathesome paper—thrice did he clinch his teeth, and make a most horrible countenance, as though a pestiferous dose of rhubarb, senna, and ipecacuanha, had been offered to his lips, at length dashing it from him, he seized his brass hilted sword, and jerking it from the scabbard, swore by St. Nicholas, he'd sooner die than yield to any power under heaven.

In vain was every attempt to shake this sturdy resolution—menaces, remonstrances, revilings were exhausted to no purpose—for two whole days was the house of the valiant Peter besieged by the clamourous rabble, and for two whole days did he betake himself to his arms, and persist in a magnanimous refusal to ratify the capitulation—thus, like a second Horatius Cocles, bearing the hole brunt of war, and defending this modern Rome, with the prowess of his single arm!

At length the populace finding that boisterous measures, did but incense more determined opposition, bethought themselves of a humble expedient, by which haply, the governor's lofty ire might be soothed, and his resolution undermined. And now a solemn and mournful procession, headed by the Burgomasters, and Schepens, and followed by the enlightened vulgar, moves slowly to the governor's dwelling—bearing the unfortunate capitulation. Here they found the stout old hero, drawn up like a giant into his castle—the doors strongly barricadoed, and himself in full regimentals, with his cocked hat on his head, firmly posted with a blunderbuss at the garret window.

There was something in this formidable position that struck even the ignoble vulgar, with awe and admiration. The brawling multitude could not but reflect with self abasement, upon their own degenerate conduct, when they beheld their hardy but deserted old governor, thus faithful to his post, like a forlorn hope, and fully prepared to defend his ungrateful city to the last. These compunctions however, were soon overwhelmed, by the recurring tide of public apprehension. The populace arranged themselves before the house, taking off their hats, with most respectful humility—One of the Burgomasters, of that popular class of orators, who, as old Sallust observes, are "talkative rather than eloquent" stepped forth and addressed the governor in a speech of three hours length; detailing in the most pathetic terms the calamitous situation of the province, and urging him in a constant repetition of the same arguments and words, to sign the capitulation.

The mighty Peter eyed him from his little garret window in grim silence—now and then his eye would glance over the surrounding rabble, and an indignant grin, like that of an angry mastiff, would mark his iron visage—But though he was a man of most undaunted mettle—though he had a heart as big as an ox, and a head that would have set adamant to scorn—yet after all he was a mere mortal:—wearied out by these repeated oppositions and this eternal haranguing, and perceiving that unless he complied, the inhabitants would follow their inclinations, or rather their fears, without waiting for his consent, he testily ordered them to hand him up the paper. It was accordingly hoisted to him on the end of a pole, and having scrawled his name at the bottom of it, he excommunicated them all for a set of cowardly, mutinous, degenerate platter-breeches—threw the capitulation at their heads, slammed down the window, and was heard stumping down the stairs with the most vehement indignation. The rabble incontinently took to their heels; even the Burgomasters were not slow in evacuating the premises, fearing lest the sturdy Peter might issue from his den, and greet them with some unwelcome testimonial of his displeasure.

CHAPTER IX

Containing reflections on the decline and fall of empires, with the final extinction of the Dutch Dynasty.

Among the numerous events, which are each in their turn the most direful and melancholy of all possible occurrences, in your interesting and authentic history; there is none that occasions such heart rending grief to your historian of sensibility, as the decline and fall of your renowned and mighty empires! Like your well disciplined funeral orator, whose feelings are properly tutored to ebb and flow, to blaze in enthusiastic eulogy, or gush in overwhelming sorrow—who has reduced his impetuous grief to a kind of manual—has prepared to slap his breast at a comma, strike his forehead at a semicolon; start with horror at a dash—and burst into an ungovernable paroxysm of despair at a note of admiration! Like unto him your woe begone historian ascends the rostrum; bends in dumb pathos over the ruins of departed greatness; casts an upbraiding eye to heaven, a glance of indignant misery on the surrounding world; settles his features into an expression of unutterable agony, and having by this eloquent preparation, invoked the whole animate and inanimate creation to unite with him in sorrow, draws slowly his white handkerchief from his pocket, and as he applies it to his face, seems to sob to his readers, in the words of a most tear shedding dutch author, "You who have noses, prepare to blow them now!"—or rather, to quote more literally "let every man blow his own nose!"

Where is the reader who can contemplate without emotion, the disastrous events by which the great dynasties of the world have been extinguished? When wandering, with mental eye amid the awful and gigantic ruins of kingdoms, states and empires—marking the tremendous convulsions that shook their foundations and wrought their lamentable downfall—the bosom of the melancholy enquirer swells with sympathy, commensurate to the sublimity of the surrounding horrors—each petty feeling—each private misery, is overpowered and forgotten; like a helpless mortal struggling under the night mare; so the unhappy reader pants and groans, and labours, under one stupendous grief—one vast immoveable idea—one immense, one mountainous—one overwhelming mass of woe!

Behold the great Assyrian Empire, founded by Nimrod, that mighty hunter, extending its domains over the fairest portion of the globe—encreasing in splendour through a long lapse of fifteen centuries, and terminating ingloriously in the reign of the effeminate Sardinapalus, consumed in the conflagration of his capital by the Median Arbaces.

Behold its successor, the Median Empire, augmented by the warlike power of Persia, under the sceptre of the immortal Cyrus, and the Egyptian conquests of the desert-braving Cambyses—accumulating strength and glory during seven centuries—but shook to its centre, and finally overthrown, in the memorable battles of the Granicus, the Issus, and the plains of Arbela, by the all conquering arm of Alexander.

Behold next the Grecian Empire; brilliant, but brief, as the warlike meteor with which it rose and descended—existing but seven years, in a blaze of glory—and perishing, with its hero, in a scene of ignominious debauchery.

Behold next the Roman Eagle, fledged in her Ausonean aerie, but wheeling her victorious flight over the fertile plains of Asia—the burning desarts of Africa, and at length spreading wide her triumphant wings, the mistress of the world! But mark her fate—view the imperial Rome, the emporium of taste and science—the paragon of cities—the metropolis of the universe—ravaged, sacked and overturned by successive hordes of fierce barbarians—and the unwieldy empire, like a huge but over ripe pumpkin, splitting into the western empire of the renowned Charlemagne, and the eastern or Greek Empire of Leo the Great—which latter, after enduring through six long centuries, is dismembered by the unhallowed hands of the Saracens.

Behold the Saracenic empire, swayed by the puissant Gengis Khan, lording it over these conquered domains, and, under the reign of Tamerlane subduing the whole Eastern region. Then cast an eye towards the Persian mountains. Mark how the fiery shepherd Othman, with his fierce compeers, descend like a whirlwind on the Nicomedian plains. Lo! the late fearless Saracen succumbs—he flies! he falls! His dynasty is destroyed, and the Ottoman crescent is reared triumphant on its ruins!

Behold——but why should we behold any more? Why should we rake among the ashes of extinguished greatness?—Kingdoms, Principalities, and Powers, have each had their rise, their progress, and their fall—each in its turn has swayed a mighty sceptre—each has returned to its primeval nothingness. And thus did it fare with the empire of their High Mightinesses, at the illustrious metropolis of the Manhattoes, under the peaceful reign of Walter the Doubter—the fractious reign of William the Testy, and the chivalric reign of Peter Stuyvesant—alias, Pieter de Groodt—alias, Hard-koppig-Piet—which meaneth Peter the Headstrong!

The patron of refinement, hospitality, and the elegant arts, it shone resplendent, like a jewel in a dunghill, deriving additional lustre from the barbarism of the savage tribes, and European hordes, by which it was surrounded. But alas! neither virtue, nor talents, eloquence, nor economy, can avert the inavertable stroke of fate. The Dutch Dynasty, pressed, and assailed on every side, approached to its destined end. It had been puffed, and blown up from small beginnings, to a most corpulent rotundity—it had resisted the constant incroachments of its neighbouring foes, with phlegmatic magnanimity—but the sudden shock of invasion was too much for its strength.

Thus have I seen a crew of truant urchins, beating and belabouring a distended bladder, which maintained its size, uninjured by their assaults—At length an unlucky brat, more knowing than the rest, collecting all his might, bounces down with his bottom upon the inflated globe—The contact of contending spheres is aweful and destructive—the bloated membrane yields—it bursts, it explodes with a noise strange and equivocal, wonderfully resembling thunder—and is no more.

And now nought remains but sadly and reluctantly to deliver up this excellent little city into the hands of its invaders. Willingly would I, like the impetuous Peter, draw my trusty weapon and defend it through another volume; but truth, unalterable truth forbids the rash attempt, and what is more imperious still, a phantom, hideous, huge and black, forever haunts my mind, the direful spectrum of my landlord's bill—which like a carrion crow hovers around my slow expiring history, impatient of its death, to gorge upon its carcass.

Suffice it then in brevity to say, that within three hours after the surrender, a legion of British beef fed warriors poured into New Amsterdam, taking possession of the fort and batteries. And now might be heard the busy sound of hammers made by the old Dutch burghers, who industriously nailed up their doors and windows to protect their vrouws from these fierce barbarians; whom they contemplated in silent sullenness from the attic story, as they paraded through the streets.

Thus did Col. Richard Nichols, the commander of the British force enter into quiet possession of the conquered realm as *locum tenant* for the duke of York. The victory was attended with no other outrage than that of changing the name of the province and its metropolis, which thenceforth were denominated NEW YORK, and so have continued to be called unto the present day. The inhabitants according to treaty were allowed to maintain quiet possession of their property, but so inveterately did they retain their abhorrence to the British nation, that in a private meeting of the leading citizens, it was unanimously determined never to ask any of their conquerors to dinner.

Such was the fate of the renowned province of New Netherlands, and it formed but one link in a subtle chain of events, originating at the capture of Fort Casimer, which has produced the present convulsions of the globe!—Let not this assertion excite a smile of incredulity, for extravagant as it may seem, there is nothing admits of more conclusive proof—Attend then gentle reader to this plain deduction, which if thou are a king, an emperor, or other powerful potentate, I advise thee to treasure up in thy heart—though little expectation have I that my work will fall into such hands, for well I know the care of crafty ministers, to keep all grave and edifying books of the kind out of the way of unhappy monarchs—lest peradventure they should read them and learn wisdom.

By the treacherous surprisal of Fort Casimer, then, did the crafty Swedes enjoy a transient triumph; but drew upon their heads the vengeance of Peter Stuyvesant, who wrested all New Sweden from their hands—By the conquest of New Sweden Peter Stuyvesant aroused the claims of Lord Baltimore, who appealed to the cabinet of Great Britain, who subdued the whole province of New Netherlands—By this great atchievement the whole extent of North America from Nova Scotia to the Floridas, was rendered one entire dependency upon the British crown—but mark the consequence—The hitherto scattered colonies being thus consolidated, and having no rival colonies to check or keep them in awe, waxed great and powerful, and finally becoming too strong for the mother country, were enabled to shake off its bonds, and by a glorious revolution became an independent empire——But the chain of effects stopped not here; the successful revolution in America produced the sanguinary revolution in France, which produced the puissant Buonaparte who produced the French Despotism, which has thrown the whole world in confusion!—Thus have these great powers been successively punished for their ill-starred conquests—and thus, as I asserted, have all the present convulsions, revolutions and disasters that overwhelm mankind, originated in the capture of little Fort Casimer, as recorded in this eventful history.

Let then the potentates of Europe, beware how they meddle with our beloved country. If the surprisal of a comparatively insignificant fort has overturned the economy of empires, what (reasoning from analogy) would be the effect of conquering a vast republic?—It would set all the stars and planets by the ears—the moon would go to loggerheads with the sun—the whole system of nature would be hurled into chaos—unless it was providentially rescued by the Millenium!

CHAPTER X

Containing the dignified retirement, and mortal surrender of Peter the Headstrong.

Thus then have I concluded this renowned historical enterprize; but before I lay aside my weary pen, there yet remains to be performed one pious duty. If among the incredible host of readers that shall peruse this book, there should haply be found any of those souls of true nobility, which glow with celestial fire, at the history of the generous and the brave, they will doubtless be anxious to know the fate of the gallant Peter Stuyvesant. To gratify one such sterling heart of gold I would go more lengths, than to instruct the cold blooded curiosity of a whole fraternity of philosophers.

No sooner had that high mettled cavalier signed the articles of capitulation than, determined not to witness the humiliation of his favourite city, he turned his back upon its walls and made a growling retreat to his *Bouwery*, or country seat, which was situated about two miles off, where he passed the remainder of his days in patriarchal retirement. There he enjoyed that tranquillity of mind, which he had never known amid the distracting cares of government, and tasted the sweets of absolute and uncontrouled authority, which his factious subjects had so often dashed with the bitterness of opposition.

No persuasions could ever induce him to revisit the city—on the contrary he would always have his great arm chair placed with its back to the windows, which looked in that direction; until a thick grove of trees planted by his own hand grew up and formed a screen, that effectually excluded it from the prospect. He railed continually at the degenerate innovations and improvements introduced by the conquerors—forbade a word of their detested language to be spoken in his family, a prohibition readily obeyed, since none of the household could speak any thing but dutch—and even ordered a fine avenue to be cut down in front of his house, because it consisted of English cherry trees.

The same incessant vigilance, that blazed forth when he had a vast province under his care, now shewed itself with equal vigour, though in narrower limits. He patrolled with unceasing watchfulness around the boundaries of his little territory; repelled every encroachment with intrepid promptness; punished every vagrant depredation upon his orchard or his farm yard with inflexible severity—and conducted every stray hog or cow in triumph to the pound. But to the indigent neighbour, the friendless stranger, or the weary wanderer, his spacious door was ever open, and his capacious fire place, that emblem of his own warm and generous heart, had always a corner to receive and cherish them. There was an exception to this, I must confess, in case the ill starred applicant was an Englishman or a Yankee, to whom, though he might extend the hand of assistance, he could never be brought to yield the rites of hospitality. Nay, if peradventure some straggling merchant of the east, should stop at his door with his cart load of tin ware or wooden bowls, the fiery Peter would issue forth like a giant from his castle, and make such a furious clattering among his pots and kettles, that the vender of *"notions"* was fain to betake himself to instant flight.

His ancient suit of regimentals, worn threadbare by the brush, were carefully hung up in the state bed chamber, and regularly aired the first fair day of every month—and his cocked hat and trusty sword, were suspended in grim repose, over the parlour mantle-piece, forming supporters to a full length portrait of the renowned admiral Von Tromp. In his domestic empire he maintained strict discipline, and a well organized, despotic government; but though his own will was the supreme law, yet the good of his subjects was his constant object. He watched over, not merely, their immediate comforts, but their morals, and their ultimate welfare; for he gave them abundance of excellent admonition, nor could any of them complain, that when occasion required, he was by any means niggardly in bestowing wholesome correction.

The good old Dutch festivals, those periodical demonstrations of an overflowing heart and a thankful spirit, which are falling into sad disuse among my fellow citizens, were faithfully observed in the mansion of governor Stuyvesant. New year was truly a day of open handed liberality, of jocund revelry, and warm hearted congratulation—when the bosom seemed to swell with genial good-fellowship—and the plenteous table, was attended with an unceremonious freedom, and honest broad mouthed merriment, unknown in these days of degeneracy and refinement. Paas and Pinxter were scrupulously observed throughout his dominions; nor was the day of St. Nicholas suffered to pass by, without making presents, hanging the stocking in the chimney, and complying with all its other ceremonies.

Once a year, on the first day of April, he used to array himself in full regimentals, being the anniversary of his triumphal entry into New Amsterdam, after the conquest of New Sweden. This was always a kind of saturnalia among the domestics, when they considered themselves at liberty in some measure, to say and do what they pleased; for on this day their master was always observed to unbend, and become exceeding pleasant and jocose, sending the old greyheaded negroes on April fools errands for pigeons milk; not one of whom but allowed himself to be taken in, and humoured his old master's jokes; as became a faithful and well disciplined dependant. Thus did he reign, happily and peacefully on his own land—injuring no man—envying no man—molested by no outward strifes; perplexed by no internal commotions—and the mighty monarchs of the earth, who were vainly seeking to maintain peace, and promote the welfare of mankind, by war and desolation, would have done well to have made a voyage to the little island of Manna-hata, and learned a lesson in government, from the domestic economy of Peter Stuyvesant.

In process of time, however, the old governor, like all other children of mortality, began to exhibit evident tokens of decay. Like an aged oak, which though it long has braved the fury of the elements, and still retains its gigantic proportions, yet begins to shake and groan with every blast—so the gallant Peter, though he still bore the port and semblance of what he was, in the days of his hardihood and chivalry, yet did age and infirmity begin to sap the vigour of his frame—but his heart, that most unconquerable citadel, still triumphed unsubdued. With matchless avidity, would he listen to every article of intelligence, concerning the battles between the English and Dutch—Still would his pulse beat high, whenever he heard of the victories of De Ruyter—and his countenance lower, and his eye brows knit, when fortune turned in favour of the English. At length, as on a certain day, he had just smoked his fifth pipe, and was napping after dinner, in his arm chair, conquering the whole British nation in his dreams, he was suddenly aroused by a most fearful ringing of bells, rattling of drums, and roaring of cannon, that put all his blood in a ferment. But when he learnt, that these rejoicings were in honour of a great victory obtained by the combined English and French fleets, over the brave De Ruyter, and the younger Von Tromp, it went so much to his heart, that he took to his bed, and in less than three days, was brought to death's door, by a violent cholera morbus! But even in this extremity, he still displayed the unconquerable spirit of Peter *the Headstrong;* holding out, to the last gasp, with most inflexible obstinacy, against a whole army of old women, who were bent upon driving the enemy out of his bowels, after a true Dutch mode of defence, by inundating the seat of war, with catnip and penny royal.

While he thus lay, lingering on the verge of dissolution; news was brought him, that the brave De Ruyter, had suffered but little loss—had made good his retreat—and meant once more to meet the enemy in battle. The closing eye of the old warrior kindled at the words—he partly raised himself in bed—a flash of martial fire beamed across his visage—he clinched his withered hand, as if he felt within his gripe that sword which waved in triumph before the walls of Fort Christina, and giving a grim smile of exultation, sunk back upon his pillow, and expired.

Thus died Peter Stuyvesant, a valiant soldier—a loyal subject—an upright governor, and an honest Dutchman—who wanted only a few empires to desolate, to have been immortalized as a hero!

His funeral obsequies were celebrated with the utmost grandeur and solemnity. The town was perfectly emptied of its inhabitants, who crowded in throngs to pay the last sad honours to their good old governor. All his sterling qualities rushed in full tide upon their recollections, while the memory of his foibles, and his faults, had expired with him. The ancient burghers contended who should have the privilege of bearing the pall; the populace strove who should walk nearest to the bier—and the melancholy procession was closed by a number of grey headed negroes, who had wintered and summered in the household of their departed master, for the greater part of a century.

With sad and gloomy countenances the multitude gathered round the grave. They dwelt with mournful hearts, on the sturdy virtues, the signal services and the gallant exploits of the brave old veteran. They recalled with secret upbraidings, their own factious oppositions to his government—and many an ancient burgher, whose phlegmatic features had never been known to relax, nor his eyes to moisten—was now observed to puff a pensive pipe, and the big drop to steal down his cheek—while he muttered with affectionate accent and melancholy shake of the head—"Well den—Hard-koppig Piet ben gone at last!"

His remains were deposited in the family vault, under a chapel, which he had piously erected on his estate and dedicated to St. Nicholas—and which stood on the identical spot at present occupied by St. Mark's church, where his tomb stone is still to be seen. His estate, or *Bouwery,* as it was called, has ever continued in the possession of his descendants, who by the uniform integrity of their conduct, and their strict adherence to the customs and manners that prevailed in the *good old times,* have proved themselves worthy of their illustrious ancestor. Many a time and oft, has the farm been haunted at night by enterprizing money-diggers, in quest of pots of gold, said to have been buried by the old governor—though I cannot learn that any of them have ever been enriched by their researches—and who is there, among my native born fellow citizens, that does not remember, when in the mischievous days of his boyhood, he conceived it a great exploit, to rob "Stuyvesant's orchard" on a holliday afternoon.

At this strong hold of the family may still be seen certain memorials of the immortal Peter. His full length portrait frowns in martial terrors from the parlour wall—his cocked hat and sword still hang up in the best bed room—His brimstone coloured breeches were for a long while suspended in the hall, until some years since they occasioned a dispute between a new married couple—and his silver mounted wooden leg is still treasured up in the store room as an invaluable relique.

————

And now worthy reader, ere I take a sad farewell—which alas! must be forever—willingly would I part in cordial fellowship, and bespeak thy kind hearted remembrance. That I have not written a better history of the days of the patriarchs is not my fault—had any other person written one, as good I should not have attempted it at all.—That many will hereafter spring up and surpass me in excellence, I have very little doubt, and still less care; well knowing, that when the great Christovallo Colon (who is vulgarly called Columbus) had once stood his egg upon its end, every one at table could stand his up a thousand times more dexterously.—Should any reader find matter of offence in this history, I should heartily grieve, though I would on no account question his penetration by telling him he is mistaken—his good nature by telling him he is captious—or his pure conscience by telling him he is startled at a shadow.—Surely if he is so ingenious in finding offence where none is intended, it were a thousand pities he should not be suffered to enjoy the benefit of his discovery.

I have too high an opinion of the understanding of my fellow citizens, to think of yielding them any instruction, and I covet too much their good will, to forfeit it by giving them good advice. I am none of those cynics who despise the world, because it despises them—on the contrary, though but low in its regard I look up to it with the most perfect good nature, and my only sorrow is, that it does not prove itself worthy of the unbounded love I bear it.

If however in this my historic production—the scanty fruit of a long and laborious life—I have failed to gratify the dainty palate of the age, I can only lament my misfortune—for it is too late in the season for me even to hope to repair it. Already has withering age showered his sterile snows upon my brow; in a little while, and this genial warmth which still lingers around my heart, and throbs—worthy reader—throbs kindly towards thyself, shall be chilled forever. Haply this frail compound of dust, which while alive may have given birth to naught but unprofitable weeds, may form a humble sod of the valley, from whence shall spring many a sweet wild flower, to adorn my beloved island of Manna-hata!

FINIS

The Author's Apology

*The following preface
first appeared in the revised
edition of 1848.*

The following work, in which at the outset nothing more was contemplated than a temporary jeu d'esprit, was commenced in company with my brother, the late Peter Irving, Esq. Our idea was to parody a small handbook which had recently appeared, entitled "A Picture of New York." Like that, our work was to begin with an historical sketch; to be followed by notices of the customs, manners, and institutions of the city; written in a serio-comic vein, and treating local errors, follies, and abuses with good-humored satire.

To burlesque the pedantic lore displayed in certain American works, our historical sketch was to commence with the creation of the world; and we laid all kinds of works under contribution for trite citations, relevant or irrelevant, to give it the proper air of learned research. Before this crude mass of mock erudition could be digested into form, my brother departed for Europe, and I was left to prosecute the enterprise alone.

I now altered the plan of the work. Discarding all idea of a parody on the "Picture of New York," I determined that what had been originally intended as an introductory sketch should comprise the whole work, and form a comic history of the city. I accordingly moulded the mass of citations and disquisitions into introductory chapters forming the first book; but it soon became evident to me that, like Robinson Crusoe with his boat, I had begun on too large a scale, and that to launch my history successfully I must reduce its proportions. I accordingly resolved to confine it to the period of the Dutch domination, which in its rise, progress, and decline presented that unity of subject required by classic rule. It was a period, also, at that time almost a terra incognita in history. In fact, I was surprised to find how few of my fellow-citizens were aware that New York had ever been called New Amsterdam, or had heard of the names of its early Dutch governors, or cared a straw about their ancient Dutch progenitors.

This, then, broke upon me as the poetic age of our city; poetic from its very obscurity; and open, like the early and obscure days of ancient

Rome, to all the embellishments of heroic fiction. I hailed my native city as fortunate above all other American cities in having an antiquity thus extending back into the regions of doubt and fable; neither did I conceive I was committing any grievous historical sin in helping out the few facts I could collect in this remote and forgotten region with figments of my own brain, or in giving characteristic attributes to the few names connected with it which I might dig up from oblivion.

In this, doubtless, I reasoned like a young and inexperienced writer besotted with his own fancies; and my presumptuous trespasses into this sacred, though neglected, region of history have met with deserved rebuke from men of soberer minds. It is too late, however, to recall the shaft thus rashly launched. To any one whose sense of fitness it may wound, I can only say with Hamlet,

> Let my disclaiming from a purposed evil
> Free me so far in your most generous thoughts,
> That I have shot my arrow o'er the house,
> And hurt my brother.

I will say this in further apology for my work: that if it has taken an unwarrantable liberty with our early provincial history, it has at least turned attention to that history and provoked research. It is only since this work appeared that the forgotten archives of the province have been rummaged, and the facts and personages of the olden time rescued from the dust of oblivion and elevated into whatever importance they may actually possess.

The main object of my work, in fact, had a bearing wide from the sober aim of history, but one which I trust will meet with some indulgence from poetic minds. It was to embody the traditions of our city in an amusing form; to illustrate its local humors, customs, and peculiarities; to clothe home scenes and places and familiar names with those imaginative and whimsical associations so seldom met with in our new country, but which live like charms and spells about the cities of the old world, binding the heart of the native inhabitant to his home.

In this I have reason to believe I have in some measure succeeded. Before the appearance of my work the popular traditions of our city were unrecorded; the peculiar and racy customs and usages derived from our Dutch progenitors were unnoticed or regarded with indifference or adverted to with a sneer. Now they form a convivial currency and are brought forward on all occasions; they link our whole community together in good humor and good fellowship; they are the rallying points of home feeling; the seasoning of our civic festivities; the staple of local tales and local pleasantries; and are so harped upon by our writers of popular fiction that I find myself almost crowded off the legendary ground which I was the first to explore, by the host who have followed in my footsteps.

I dwell on this head because, at the first appearance of my work, its aim and drift were misapprehended by some of the descendants of the Dutch worthies; and because I understand that now and then one may still be found to regard it with a captious eye. The far greater part, however, I have reason to flatter myself, receive my good humored picturings in the same temper with which they were executed; and when I find, after a lapse of nearly forty years, this haphazard production of my youth still cherished among them; when I find its very name become a "household word," and used to give the home stamp to everything recommended for popular acceptation, such as Knickerbocker societies, Knickerbocker insurance companies, Knickerbocker steamboats, Knickerbocker omnibuses, Knickerbocker bread, and Knickerbocker ice; and when I find New Yorkers of Dutch descent priding themselves upon being "genuine Knickerbockers," I please myself with the persuasion that I have struck the right chord; that my dealings with the good old Dutch times, and the customs and usages derived from them, are in harmony with the feelings and humors of my townsmen; that I have opened a vein of pleasant associations and quaint characteristics peculiar to my native place, and which its inhabitants will not willingly suffer to pass away; and that, though other histories of New York may appear of higher claims to learned acceptation, and may take their dignified and appropriate rank in the family library, Knickerbocker's history will still be received with good-humored indulgence and be thumbed and chuckled over by the family fireside.

W. I.

Sunnyside, 1848.

Notes

p. xxxi *Dedication:* The New-York Historical Society had been founded in 1804 with a mission to collect and preserve "whatever may relate to the natural, civic, or ecclesiastical History of the United States in general, and of this State in particular." As the introduction notes, the Society was famously unsuccessful in its early years at recovering documents and artifacts related to New Amsterdam, a lacuna the group tried to remedy by issuing an "Address to the Public" in 1807 that contained a minutely detailed request for information "respecting the first settlement of new-York by the Dutch," including "the number of the settlers;

> the time of their arrival, their general character; their condition with respect to property; the authority and encouragements under which they came; or any other circumstances attending the first attempt at colonization? . . . Can you give any information which will throw light on the state of *morals* in our country, at different periods, such as the comparative frequency of *drunkenness, gambling, duelling, suicide, conjugal infidelity, prostitution,* &c. &c.? . . .

Taken all together, Knickerbocker's "eyewitness" accounts of Dutch battles and Dutch lawmaking, his detailed cultural litanies, geographical reasoning and etymological explanations, confident historiography and erudite-sounding footnotes offer a thorough (and thoroughly satirical) reproach to the Society's utter failure to provide any of the above, as well as a tantalizingly complete response to its many questions.

p. 1 *Account of the Author:* The "Account of the Author" builds on the *New York Evening Post* advertisements for a missing "Knickerbocker" that are discussed in the introduction to this volume. In addition to giving further biographical information about Diedrich Knickerbocker, the "Account" also provides a brief physical description of the historian, and mentions his "few grey hairs plaited and clubbed behind," "olive velvet breeches and . . . small cocked hat," and "bright pair of silver shoe-buckles[.]" Significantly, it is the only time in the *History* that a picture of Knickerbocker is rendered for the reader, and the details of his dress and person as described in the "Account" became the springboard for more than a century's worth of artistic and commercial representations of the narrator. These would include serving as "Father Knickerbocker," the literal embodiment of the consolidation of the five boroughs of New York City in 1898; as the spokesman for Knickerbocker Beer; and as the first mascot of the New York Knickerbockers basketball team.

p. 9 Gibbon's Rome: The works to which Knickerbocker here ambitiously compares his *History* are indeed "voluminous." *The Decline and Fall of Rome* was published by the English historian Edward Gibbon in six volumes (1776–88), as was the eminent Scottish philosopher David Hume's *History of England* (1754–62). Tobias Smollett, better known for satirical novels such as *Humphrey Clinker,* wrote a rival *Compleat History of England* in 1757, which was subsequently revised, updated, and marketed "as a Continuation of Mr. Hume's History." By the early nineteenth century a combination *History of England* (sometimes abridged and sometimes as many as thirteen volumes) was being sold by British booksellers with both authors' names on the title page, a development that would not have pleased Hume. Irving does not mention the English writer Oliver Goldsmith's *History of England* (1771), despite his affinity for Goldsmith, with whom he would later be compared, and whose biography he would publish in 1849. Perhaps this is because Goldsmith prefaced his own history by noting that the goal of his book was not to "add to our historical knowledge, but to contract it," a plan not in keeping with Knickerbocker's "swelling" plans for a "noble superstructure" of New York history.

p. 26 *seeks for it in its proper place:* This is the first of several jibes at the expense of explorers such as Henry Hudson, Giovanni da Verrazzano, and others, who mistook the East Coast of North America and New York in particular for a shortcut to the Pacific Ocean.

p. 26 *our theatre:* The reference by Knickerbocker to "our theatre" is a puzzling one. It may be understood as a "tell," signaling to those in the know that this mysterious "Diedrich Knickerbocker" is related to

"Jonathan Oldstyle," Irving's early nom de plume as theater critic and social commentator for his brother Peter Irving's paper, the *Morning Chronicle,* in 1802 and 1803. But New York City's Park Theatre, where Irving saw the plays he described (and which was the city's preeminent theater from its construction in the 1790s through the 1820s), did not have the cupola on which the historian so strenuously insists. Illustrations show the original theater to have had a simple, Federal-style exterior (in his first letter, Oldstyle criticized the "*heavyishness*" of the architecture), although by the time of Irving's *History,* the interior had been remodeled: the three tiers of boxes of the original theater were now lit with gas lamps and the domed ceiling, whose "little perriwig'd cupids, tumbling head over heel," had attracted Oldstyle's notice in 1802, had been completely repainted.

p. 31 *Christovallo Colon . . . clumsily nick-named Columbus:* Irving would return to the adventures of Christopher Columbus during his first visit to Spain in 1826, an appointment to the American Legation in Madrid. He would publish *Life and Voyages of Columbus* in 1828 and *Voyages and Discoveries of the Companions of Columbus* in 1831.

p. 32 *Think you . . . savages to exterminate:* Throughout the *History,* Irving describes Manhattan before its discovery in prelapsarian terms. His surprisingly contemporary sensitivity to the original state of the island and his grave comments on the subsequent treatment by the Dutch of both its aboriginal inhabitants and its natural resources (see: "the RIGHT BY EXTERMINATION, or, in other words, the RIGHT BY GUNPOWDER," p. 47) provide a valuable and instructive counterpoint to the book's broad satire that is often overlooked by contemporary readers.

p. 37 *jolter heads. . . . appellations:* As the reader may have guessed, all of these "appellations" loosely translate as "stupid head."

p. 48 *sailing in the air:* Irving may have had hot-air balloons in mind: the first flight carrying humans was made in 1783, the year he was born. George Washington witnessed the first hot-air balloon flight (by the Frenchman Jean Pierre Blanchard) in North America on January 7, 1793.

p. 56 *New York Gazette edited by Solomon Lang:* John "Solomon" Lang was the editor of the *New York Gazette* newspaper at the time of Irving's writing; the newspaper was indeed famous for its devotion to shipping news, and little else. Lang would later be spoofed again in

"Fanny," Fitzgreene Halleck's 1819 satirical ode to New York society, as "the sapient Mr. Lang. The world of him / Knows much, yet not one-half so much as he / Knows of the world . . ."

p. 63 *cat-heads . . . prodigious poop:* Irving uses sailors' slang to create an extended bawdy pun on the female form. Catheads are commonly defined as horizontal beams that extend from each side of a ship's bow (or front) to raise and carry the ship's anchor, while the "poop" is a term for the highest deck to be found at the stern (or back) of a vessel.

p. 63 *Gibbet Island:* By the time of Irving's writing, this island in New York Harbor had been rechristened Ellis Island after Samuel Ellis, who purchased it in 1785. It was not the first time the island had endured a name change, either: it had been called Gull Island by the Mohegan tribe, and Oyster Island by the Dutch settlers who harvested the bivalves there (once extremely plentiful—and safely edible—around New York City). The nickname "Gibbet Island" was given after a pirate named Anderson was hanged there in 1765. Irving returned to the subject of the pleasant little island with the gruesome history in October 1839, when he published a ghost story entitled "The Guests from Gibbet Island" in *Knickerbocker* magazine. The story was collected in the *Book of the Hudson: Collected from the Various Works of Diedrich Knickerbocker, edited by Geoffrey Crayon,* which G. P. Putnam published in 1849 in order to capitalize on Irving's (and Knickerbocker's) fame.

p. 64 *tremendous and uncouth sound . . . miserably perished to a man:* Irving once again addresses the "right by extermination" with Knickerbocker's wry suggestion that the deaths of the Native American population of Communipaw is due only to the fatal cacophony of "low dutch." Knickerbocker's mention of the "Tammany Society of the day" refers to the St. Tammany Society or Columbian Order, a popular patriotic and charitable organization that originated in Philadelphia but was adopted by New Yorkers in 1786. The group, which held to republican and anti-elitist principles, made a fetish of Native American symbols and terminology, calling the chairman of the board of directors the "Grand Sachem" and his members "braves," and parading through the city streets in Indian regalia on patriotic holidays. At the time of the *History*'s publication, the Tammany Society had already become a powerful political force in New York, but it had not lost its incongruous Native American associations.

p. 64 *carried the village of* Communipaw *by storm:* Communipaw and Pavonia are now part of the city of Jersey City, New Jersey, population 240,000 in 2000.

p. 69 *great men and great families of doubtful origin . . . descended from a god:* This is not the first time Irving has lampooned the pretensions of New York's nouveaux riches: in the pages of *Salmagundi* he often spoofed the pretensions of "modern upstarts and mushroom cockneys" who "violated" his contemporary city with their flashy clothes and carriages and their ignorance of the "venerable" social traditions observed by "true Hollanders . . . and their unsophisticated descendants."

p. 72 *Printer's Devil:* This is the first time that Irving includes a note from an ostensible "Printer's Devil," a nickname usually given to a printer's apprentice. While Knickerbocker has supplied his own citations, and an unnamed "editor" contributes footnotes, the Printer's Devil appears to have been requisitioned to provide supporting details or corrections specifically related to the geography or municipal history of New York City. The distribution of labor between Knickerbocker, his "Editor," and his "Printer's Devil" is left purposefully vague; the layering of these sporadic, sometimes nonsensical notes one upon the next ends by subverting (if not positively derailing) the confident, forward propulsion of Knickerbocker's tale. Rather than clarifying and reassuring the reader, the *History*'s footnotes only render the text more opaque. Later nineteenth-century American writers, particularly Herman Melville, Nathaniel Hawthorne, and Edgar Allan Poe would adopt and improve Irving's destabilizing technique in their fiction.

p. 73 *MANNA-HATTA:* Irving's use of "Manna-hatta" prefigures Walt Whitman's euphoric cry at the end of "Crossing Brooklyn Ferry," published in *Leaves of Grass* in 1855:

> Stand up, tall masts of Mannahatta!—stand up, beautiful hills of Brooklyn!
> Throb, baffled and curious brain! throw out questions and answers!

p. 81 *ST. NICHOLAS:* Irving's treatment of the characteristics of St. Nicholas and the Dutch traditions surrounding his saint's day (December 6) would inform "A Visit to Saint Nicholas," the poem attributed to Clement Clarke Moore. First published anonymously in 1823, the titular "jolly old elf" keeps a "stump of a pipe . . . held tight in his teeth."

p. 83 Peach War: The Peach War was an actual skirmish between Dutch settlers and Native Americans in 1655 that began with the killing of a young Native American girl who had stolen a peach from the orchard of colonist Henry Van Dyck. The Native American retaliation lasted three days, and was indeed as "bloody" as Knickerbocker here suggests. This battle took place during the governorship of Peter Stuyvesant, but Knickerbocker seems uncharacteristically unspecific as to the chronology, placing this last major hostility between the Dutch and the Native Americans in a vague and distant past.

p. 99 *Old MS:* The note on the Fly Market may be interpreted as Knickerbocker's answer to Samuel Mitchill's treatment of the same in the *Picture of New York:*

> This part of the city . . . was originally a salt meadow . . . forming such a disposition of land and water as was called by the Dutch *Vlaie,* a valley or wet piece of ground; when a market was first held there, it was called the *Fly,* or *Vlaie Market,* the Valley or Meadow Market; from which has come the corruption of "Fly market" [sic]. This name certainly ought to be rejected and a better one adopted.

In another instance of historiographical one-upmanship, Knickerbocker points out Mitchill's mistake: that this "corrupted" name was originally *Smits Vleye,* or Smith Fly, not just "Vlaie Market," and that it was once an Edenic field, home only to "flocks of vociferous geese."

p. 102 *the cows, in a laudable fit of patriotism:* Knickerbocker's suggestion that the cows of New Amsterdam were the first urban planners is topical as well as comic. In 1807 the Common Council of New York voted to authorize the entire island above present-day Houston Street to be surveyed and laid out in "streets, roads, and public squares, of such width, extent, and direction, as to them shall seem most conducive to public good, and to shut up, or direct to be shut up, any streets or parts thereof which have been heretofore laid out . . . [but] not accepted by the Common Council." At the time of Irving's writing, an engineer named John Randel Jr. and a team of "Commissioners of Streets and Roads" were in the process of designing and implementing the New York City street "grid" as it exists today, although the ancient and crooked streets of lower Manhattan (including those ostensibly laid out by the cows of the Kieft regime) would be allowed to keep their tipsy trajectories.

p. 103 *very efficacious in producing the yellow fever:* Yellow fever was by no means an historical footnote for Irving's New York–based readers, but an ongoing crisis in urban public health. As recently as 1805 an epidemic of the disease had necessitated a large-scale, enforced evacuation of Manhattan's lower wards to the pastoral reaches of Greenwich Village, where the air and water were considered more healthful than in the congested neighborhoods south of Chambers Street.

p. 103 *yellow dutch bricks . . . weather cock:* Irving's own Hudson Valley home, Sunnyside, would later be constructed along these exact lines.

p. 106 *called dough nuts, or oly koeks—a delicious kind of cake:* While culinary historians and doughnut aficionados quibble over Irving's interchangeable usage of "dough nut" and "oly koek," his reference to the favorite fried confection is generally accepted to be the first in American literature, and a vote for the Dutch origins of the doughnut in general.

p. 112 *when the shad in the Hudson were all salmon:* This refers to Samuel Mitchill's attempt to publicly debunk the Reverend Samuel Miller's claim (made on the basis of Robert Juet's journal from the *Half Moon*) that salmon were once native to the Hudson River. Miller made this claim in a "Discourse" on Henry Hudson that he delivered to the New-York Historical Society in 1809, which Mitchill contested the same year in an open letter to the Society. "Salmon love clear and limpid water," he argued, "and I should question much whether the ooze and mud of [the Hudson] was so agreeable to them." Instead, the "Herring, the Shad, and the Sturgeon [are] the annual visitants to this stream," Mitchill declared, referring Miller to "the Dutch word 'salm' or 'salmpie,' commonly in use to signify *salmon,* [but which] means also, in ordinary and loose conversation and composition, *trout.*" Irving's mischievous, casual reference to this debate is particularly intriguing because it suggests that the writer was following the frustrations of the Society with exceptional interest and care. Mitchill's anti-salmon letter was published as an appendix to Miller's lecture in the Historical Society's *Collections . . . For the Year 1809,* but that volume was not published until 1810, months after Irving's satire appeared. Irving embroidered his *History* with a host of such pointed details and references, whose seeming scholarly and scientific plausibility had the effect of calling the work of actual (nonmock) historians into question.

p. 123 *rambling propensity:* This description of the "Yankey farmer" prefigures one of Irving's next "Knickerbocker" creations, the Connecticut schoolmaster Ichabod Crane, who "tarries" in the Dutch village of Sleepy Hollow while courting the "country heiress" Katrina Van Tassel, dreaming all along of that very same journey into the wilderness with wife and worldly possessions in tow:

> Nay, his busy fancy already realized his hopes, and presented to him the blooming Katrina, with a whole family of children, mounted on the top of a wagon loaded with household trumpery, with pots and kettles dangling beneath, and he beheld himself bestriding a pacing mare, with a colt at her heels, setting out for Kentucky, Tennessee, or the Lord knows where!

p. 129 *Struldbruggs:* In *Gulliver's Travels,* Jonathan Swift's 1726 satire, the "Struldbruggs" are referred to as the "Immortals," those who are "born exempt from that universal Calamity of human Nature, have their Minds free and disengaged, without the Weight and Depression of Spirits caused by the continual Apprehension of Death."

p. 145 *Ever Duckings:* The real Evert Duyckinck was a friend of Irving's who would later edit a volume of tributes to the author, published after his death, entitled *Irvingiana* (1860).

p. 148 *"dunder and blixum!":* These are variants on the Dutch words for "thunder" and "lightning." The words would later appear as the names of a pair of St. Nicholas's flying reindeer in the original 1823 publication of "A Visit from Saint Nicholas." These two reindeer have more recently been referred to as "Donder and Blixen."

p. 152 *Preserved Fish:* While Knickerbocker, a Dutch partisan, is spoofing the New England custom of giving children tongue-twisting Old Testament or Quaker first names (which, when combined with English last names, could have unintentionally humorous results), there was a real New Yorker named Preserved Fish (1766–1846), a well-to-do shipping magnate whose name would have been familiar to Irving (and to his merchant brothers) in 1809.

p. 170 Quid: A topical aside for Irving. "Quids" (also "Tertium Quids") was a nickname given to various third-party factions who leveraged their influence in local, state, and national elections in the first decade of the nineteenth century. In New York City they are generally understood to have been the Republican faction that did not support the 1808 bid for the governorship of Dewitt Clinton, even after the Republican majority had endorsed him.

p. 188 *Tom Paine:* It would have been impossible for Stuyvesant to read the work of Thomas Paine, who was born in 1737 and published his most famous pamphlet, *Common Sense,* in 1776. Paine died in New York in June 1809, just six months before the *History* was published, so it is possible that Irving includes him in this litany of political philosophers as a kind of memorial homage.

p. 202 *long sided Connecticut schoolmaster:* This is another prefigurement of Ichabod Crane, the lanky, Connecticut-born schoolmaster of "The Legend of Sleepy Hollow."

p. 240 *Dirk Schuiler:* In an 1851 letter to his friend Jesse Merwin, the model for schoolmaster Ichabod Crane in "The Legend of Sleepy Hollow," Irving told him that the "character of Dirk Schuyler [sic]" came from Merwin's tales of "John Moore, the vagabond admiral of the lake" at Kinderhook, and the pranks that Irving and Merwin pulled on Moore in 1808. The idea of an earlier Knickerbocker character being inspired by stories told by the living inspiration for a later Knickerbocker character has a kind of backward symmetry that the Dutch historian would applaud.

p. 244 *But trust me gentlefolk:* Irving's rhapsodic depictions of the "wildness and savage majesty" of the Hudson River inspired the poet William Cullen Bryant and the artists Thomas Cole, Asher Durand, and William Guy Wall, who would come to be known as the foremost members of the Hudson River School of painting. Irving's Hudson River writings would also help drive tourism to the region, and prompt the construction of several resorts, such as the Catskill Mountain House. Some of these vacation spots would later advertise their proximity to "Rip's cabin" or other landmarks of Irving's stories.

p. 253 *Van Winkles:* In the story "Rip Van Winkle," Knickerbocker will compare his hero unflatteringly to his martial ancestors, who "figured so gallantly in the chivalrous days of Peter Stuyvesant, and accompanied him to the siege of Fort Christina." This is also an opportunity for Knickerbocker to corroborate Seth Handaside's remarks about his own Scaghtikoke ancestry.

p. 267 *Brummagem:* An expression meaning "cheap and showy" as well as "counterfeit," from a dialect form of Birmingham, the English city that was known in the seventeenth century as a center for the manufacture of counterfeit coins.

p. 272 *"Brimful of wrath and cabbage!":* The great Dutch poet here is Knickerbocker (Irving) himself: there is no previous usage to be found.

p. 295 *mushrooms of a day:* Another reference to the New York nouveaux riches Irving lampooned as "mushroom upstarts" in *Salmagundi.*

p. 296 *true Hollands:* Also known as Holland gin, a liquor distilled from rye and barley and flavored with juniper berries, that was originally manufactured in Holland.

p. 302 *hoe cakes, bacon, and mint julep:* Like the poet Joel Barlow before him, who hymned "Hoe-Cake, fair Virginia's pride!" in his poem "The Hasty Pudding," Irving takes an interest in the foods of other American regions. Hoe cakes, which are made from cornmeal and fried in oil, are not unlike the Dutch "dough nut" whose praises he prefers to sing.

p. 332 *compelled to learn the English language:* Like Stuyvesant, some of Irving's Dutch American contemporaries were still refusing to adopt the English language in their communities. Mitchill's *Picture of New York* particularly notices the neighborhood of Flatbush, Brooklyn, for its poignant adherence to the Dutch language in the face of certain dissipation:

> The principal inhabitants of this county are descendants of the Dutch settlers, who first encroached upon the natives, in these parts. They have Dutch preaching in some of the religious meeting-houses, and many families learn no other language, until they are old enough to go abroad. But there are no Dutch schools, and, consequently, the language is on the decline.

The Dutch language was also still in active use in upstate New York, where Dutch was spoken by the descendants of the original settlers into the early nineteenth century, and used as the language of record by town courts and Dutch Reformed churches until the Revolutionary War.

p. 343 *English cherry trees:* Regardless of whether or not Stuyvesant decimated his cherry orchard in a Washingtonian manner, one fruit tree from Stuyvesant's "bouwerie" survived to outlive Irving himself: a pear tree, which had reportedly been planted on the Dutch governor's farm in 1647. The tree, revered by New Yorkers as a last tangible connection to New Amsterdam, finally succumbed in 1867. A plaque at the north-east corner of Third Avenue and Thirteenth Street commemorates the spot where it stood.

p. 344 *stocking in the chimney:* Another St. Nicholas innovation that would reappear in Moore's poem "A Visit from St. Nicholas": "the stockings were hung by the chimney with care / In hopes that Saint Nicholas soon would be there."

THE STORY OF PENGUIN CLASSICS

Before 1946 . . . "Classics" are mainly the domain of academics and students; readable editions for everyone else are almost unheard of. This all changes when a little-known classicist, E. V. Rieu, presents Penguin founder Allen Lane with the translation of Homer's *Odyssey* that he has been working on in his spare time.

1946 Penguin Classics debuts with *The Odyssey,* which promptly sells three million copies. Suddenly, classics are no longer for the privileged few.

1950s Rieu, now series editor, turns to professional writers for the best modern, readable translations, including Dorothy L. Sayers's *Inferno* and Robert Grave's unexpurgated *Twelve Caesars*.

1960s The Classics are given the distinctive black covers that have remained a constant throughout the life of the series. Rieu retires in 1964, hailing the Penguin Classics list as "the greatest educative force of the twentieth century."

1970s A new generation of translators swells the Penguin Classics ranks, introducing readers of English to classics of world literature from more than twenty languages. The list grows to encompass more history, philosophy, science, religion, and politics.

1980s The Penguin American Library launches with titles such as *Uncle Tom's Cabin* and joins forces with Penguin Classics to provide the most comprehensive library of world literature available from any paperback publisher.

1990s The launch of Penguin Audiobooks brings the classics to a listening audience for the first time, and in 1999 the worldwide launch of the Penguin Classics Web site extends their reach to the global online community.

The 21st Century Penguin Classics are completely redesigned for the first time in nearly twenty years. This world-famous series now consists of more than 1,300 titles, making the widest range of the best books ever written available to millions—and constantly redefining what makes a "classic."

The Odyssey continues . . .

The best books ever written

PENGUIN ⏺ CLASSICS

SINCE 1946

Find out more at www.penguinclassics.com

Visit www.vpbookclub.com

CLICK ON A CLASSIC
www.penguinclassics.com

The world's greatest literature at your fingertips

Constantly updated information on more than a thousand titles,
from Icelandic sagas to ancient Indian epics, Russian drama to
Italian romance, American greats to African masterpieces

•

The latest news on recent additions to the list, updated
editions, and specially commissioned translations

•

Original essays by leading writers

•

A wealth of background material, including biographies
of every classic author from Aristotle to Zamyatin, plot
synopses, readers' and teachers' guides, useful web links

•

Online desk and examination copy assistance for academics

•

Trivia quizzes, competitions, giveaways, news on
forthcoming screen adaptations